FERAL

MONSTERS & ARTIFACTS BOOK ONE

TRISH HEINRICH

BEAUTIFUL FIRE

CONTENTS

GLOSSARY OF SCOTTISH TERMS

Note on using Dublin: there is a Dublin, Scotland as well as a Dublin Ireland, and upon advice from a Scottish friend, I chose to set the book in Dublin rather than Edinburgh because I wanted something a bit more pastoral. Thank you.

Glossary of Scottish Words
Eejit-Idiot
Numpty-stupid
Blether-chatter box
Ken-know
Lass-girl
Hen-girl
Bonny-pretty
Aye-yes
Nae bother-not a problem
Naw-no
Nick-steal
Steamin-drunk

Bawbag-scrotum (can be both derogatory or in an affectionate way used.)

Cunt-both the woman's vulva, etc and a catch all (not even kidding)

Peely-wally-someone who is pale or looking sickly

Pissed-drunk

Haver-talk nonesense

Bairn-child

Welcome Letter from the Secret Archive

*H*ello there and welcome to the Secret Archive!

As an an agent-in-training there are a few things you need to know before starting your first day. One of the most important is that some of your new co-workers are not human.

Yes, it's true! Supernaturals or Monsters are real. Although some of them actually prefer the term 'Monster' we caution against using this term as it is offensive to some of the supernaturals you will be working closely with. Don't worry if you suddenly feel overwhelmed, we have extensive sensitivity training for new agents!

But in preparation for that class and your first day, we ask that you please peruse this helpful glossary. In it you will find the exact terminology for the supernaturals you'll encounter, along with helpful descriptions, general powers and abilities and a few faux pas to avoid if at all possible.

You may not know that someone is a supernatural if they are wearing the glamour that gives them the ability to pass as human. This spell is known only to the supernatural community and attempting to find out the particulars of the spell will result in immediate termination and memory wipe.

Thank you for joining the fight to protect humanity from the mystical artifacts that constantly threaten our existence. The job is dangerous, the hours are long but the rewards are worth it.
Sincerely,
Director Angelica Dearborne

Glossary of common supernaturals–Part One

Ephemeral: You will not encounter many Ephemeral's in your time here though you may out on missions. Ephemerals are, much like Moth-people, very secretive and not much is known about them, including their origins or even what their true form is. They can mask their appearance as human without the use of the traditional glamour that the rest of the supernatural community uses, and can shift into smoky shadows and slip through solid surfaces. Their most preferred form looks very much like a leather winged humanoid demon hybrid with a tail and horns of various shapes. Many have red or purple skin in this form with black or gray eyes and pointed canines. You will generally not know if you are working with an Ephemeral as they prefer not to disclose that except to our hiring department. For additional questions regarding your Ephemeral co workers, please call Sarah M. Summers.

Fae: This is a term that actually encompasses a wide range of supernaturals that all have their origins within the same ancient supernatural group. The web of ancestry is so tangled among the Fae that most you meet will swear to having one of the Tuatha de Danaan as a direct ancestor, and most aren't exaggerating. Fae fall into four main groups with many sub groups under them that include beings such as Goblins, Leprechauns and the occasional Satyr, none of which you will likely encounter during your time here. You may encounter one of the other four however, they include: Earth Fae, Water Fae, Wind Fae and the far more elusive, High Fae. Fae look mostly humanoid in appearance with skin colors ranging from snow white to indigo. Their hair and eye color run the gamut depending on the group they hail from. All Fae have tell tale pointed ears and canines. For additional questions regarding your Fae co workers please call Morgan Bell.

Gargoyles: It has only been in the last century that Gargoyles have joined our ranks. With their ability to sense other supernatural creatures with varying degrees of accuracy, they are some of our most powerful agents when tracking artifacts that are in the possession of other supernaturals. Although they are extremely strong, they are vulnerable to harm as any of us are unless they raise up their stone skin, a natural magic that makes them invulnerable to harm for upwards of two minutes. In appearance they range from six feet tall to over eight. Their skin has a range of colors from very light green that's almost white to a dark purple. Eyes range in shade from dark green to purple, to red, yellow and orange. They have tails of various lengths and prehensile strength that they use in battle. Their wings are their most vulnerable part and often times these are hidden beneath a secondary glamour for their protection. Never, ever touch a Gargoyle's wings! Not only is it against our code of conduct to touch another agent without permission, but you will immediately activate their defensive instincts and end up with a few broken bones if you're lucky. Most Gargoyles have horns of various sizes and lengths. These will light up when they are tracking other supernaturals. Gargoyles have family units but they are not as tight knit as other supernatural groups and female Gargoyles appear human though they have many of the same magical gifts as their male counterparts, such as heightened tracking and stone skin. For additional questions regarding your Gargoyle co workers, please call Salli Richards.

Harpy: Like the Ephemerals, there are not many Harpies in our employ. This is not for lack of trying, this is simply because they do not tend to work well with others. Their skill at theft and subterfuge is unparalleled. Some of the best con women and thieves in history were Harpies. To the best of our knowledge, all Harpies are women. They are generally between five and six and half feet tall, with vibrant plumage on their legs, lower torso, back and wings. Their arms and chests are covered in very fine hair or fur that matches their plumage. Their feet are like that of an Eagle with razor sharp talons, and their hands often sport very sharp claws. They appear very much like a human woman in the face except for their razor sharp teeth and unusually bright eyes. Most Harpies must wear sunglasses outside because their eyes are extremely sensitive to light. Their abilities can include illusions, hypnosis and the ability to see infrared light. In extremely rare instances, they've been known to influence the weather. For additional questions regarding your Harpy co workers please call AelloTalon

Mothman/woman: One of the most elusive and secretive of all the supernaturals you will encounter, the Mothpeople have a rich history dating back to the golden age of Queen Elizabeth herself. Once the prized companions of her court, these sensitive and mysterious supernaturals were the inspiration for the fairies of Shakespeare's Midsummer Night's Dream, and were valued councilors and warriors for the English crown. When James first took the throne, however, his religious zealotry was unleashed on this community and they were driven underground. Hunted as demons and witches, Mothpeople were thought extinct until fifty years ago when they sent envoys to the Orc and Gargoyle leaders seeking inclusion into the world at large. Mothpeople have the most variation in their appearances depending on their hive, climate and general sensibilities. Most are slender, between five and seven feet in height with gorgeous wings that boast intricate patterns of various colors. They have three sets of arms, with the middle and bottom sporting pincer-like hands, and the top pair ending in hands very much like a human's in appearance, though they are covered in fine hair that feels velvety soft to the touch. Their faces are generally oval shaped with two very large eyes that are either dark brown or black. The color of a Mothpersons body and wings are dependent on their hive and there is therefore no common color scheme. Mothpeople are highly secretive about their hives and will not answer your questions about their coloring so please do not ask. Each are graced with antennae that act as a sort of radar helping them take in their environment. They have various gifts including teleportation, spectral sight and foresight. In rare instances, their eyes may take on a red tinge. If you ever see a Mothperson with red tinged eyes, back away slowly and get your supervisor as this indicates that they are about to experience or are in the throes of their battle blood, a heightened state that gives them enhanced speed and strength. Even a Mothperson who is your friend may harm you in this state. Do not try to calm them down on your own! For additional questions regarding your Mothperson co workers, please call West Pleasant.

Orc: The first supernatural beings to align themselves with the Secret Archive, some of our most decorated agents have been Orcs. Fiercely loyal to their family groups, Orcs have a heightened sense of taste and smell that gives them the most refined palates on the planet. They have the ability to know down to the season and year in some cases where a food has been sourced. They also pass on generational memories of taste so that the foods of their ancestors are preserved in the palates of every generation. Appearances vary from light green to very dark green, with eye colors ranging from dark red, various shades of blue and purple. Their height can vary depending on if they are also human or other supernatural species. Most Orcs range from six feet tall to just over seven, with a few even topping out around eight if their heritage is unimpeded by human parentage. Most male Orcs have tusks of various lengths. Rings around the tusks indicate leadership and status in the family group. Most are incredibly proud of their rings so it is a good conversation starter if you're struggling to get to know a male Orc. Female Orcs are rarely seen outside of family groups without their glamours up in order to protect them from harm. Female orcs are actually very rare, as most Orc babies are male. Thus most Orcs have human or Gargoyle parentage in their backgrounds. Orcs do not believe in monogamous couplings between members of their species, with one Orc female sometimes having up to six male mates in her family group. If you see an Orc female do not approach her as she will likely have male Orcs in attendance as bodyguards or mates and they can be very territorial. For additional questions regarding your Orc co workers, please call K. Nanjiani.

Werewolf: Hunted to near extinction, Werewolves are one of the oldest groups of supernaturals you will encounter, second only to Fae. They guard the truth of their origins very closely but we believe it is connected with Druid nature magics. After the battle of Culloden, they went underground until glamours were perfected to hide their true natures more effectively. Standing anywhere from six feet to seven and half, most have fur covering the majority of their bodies in a range of colors. Eye color is also a wide range, falling within the spectrum of human colors. Though originating in Scotland, Werewolves (and to a lesser degree Werebears) can be found in most every country, though you would never know it. Though their numbers have increased in the last fifty years, they remain suspicious of outsiders and do not trust humans easily. During the three days of the full moon Werewolves must retreat to the countryside to let their more primal side out. If you ever find yourself in the company of a Werewolf during this period, please retreat slowly and do not provoke them. For additional questions regarding your Werewolf co workers, please call Viktor Sheen

This concludes part one of your glossary. Please report to HR Director Millicent O'Meara for further instruction and sensitivity training.

PROLOGUE

ANGELICA

I looked out at the London skyline from my obscenely expensive penthouse apartment. It has a lovely view from the expansive windows in the living room. A delicious burn from the whiskey in my hand traveled down my throat and I sighed. If only everything were as simple as a glass of good liquor to sooth the nerves. But nothing about my job as Director of the Secret Archive was simple. Not cleaning up the messes left by the previous one. Not protecting my few remaining agents. Not safeguarding the dangerous artifacts so the world didn't go up in a fiery ball.

The Secret Archive, the organization that had stood in the breach between the world and the dangerous artifacts for hundreds of years, was in shambles, not that most people knew that, of course.

No, only myself and the council truly knew how damn dire the situation was.

My predecessor, a power hungry psychopath by the name of Francesca, had corrupted the Archive's original purpose by using artifacts as weapons, bargaining chips, and means of human experimentation.

She'd created an atmosphere of terror within the organization to the point where half our agents had splintered off to form a rogue group that was currently waging a war against us.

The other half that was left had either fled upon her death, or tried to stick around on the promise that I would be a different kind of leader. And of those half, many had decided to leave anyway once they realized just how much damage Francesca had done to their mental health.

Which left me, the new director, with a rather big problem.

We were severely under staffed and artifacts were being stolen left and right by the rogue group calling themselves the Protectors.

I snorted into my whiskey at the ridiculously self-righteous name.

"Protectors my ass," I murmured.

"What about your ass?"

I jumped at Trey's voice, fighting the blush that was threatening to rise to my cheeks.

The staggeringly handsome Korean man leaned against my doorway, arms crossed and a smirk on his face, showing off his dimples. Trey was my liaison with the council, who, understandably, didn't trust me with the powers of the Director's role yet. He was to observe and report back to the council, but he was supposed to be neutral.

Yeah, right.

"Do you ever knock?" I asked, setting the drink down on my glass coffee table.

"I love what you've done here," he remarked. "When Francesca owned it, the place had a heavy feel to it."

I hadn't really wanted the apartment that went with the title, not at first. But when I found out that it once belonged to Francesca, I couldn't resist coming in and seizing everything she'd owned.

The precious artwork she'd stolen had been donated to a museum, while every scrap of her other belongings, down to the last crystal champagne flute, had been sold at auction and the proceeds given to the families of her victims. Francesca would have absolutely hated that.

Poetic justice if you ask me.

The penthouse was huge, far bigger than I would ever need on my own. Still, I had redecorated it with special care in case any of my children came to visit.

My grown children. I'm old enough for grown children. Which means I definitely should not be allowing this man to flirt with me, or give in to the temptation to flirt back.

It didn't matter that Trey was several hundred years old, and a Dragon. It didn't matter that my husband had been dead for almost nine months. Or that I sometimes woke from dreams of Trey's hands all over my body, his tail wrapped around my ankle while he…

No, none of that mattered.

Trey looked at least twenty years younger than me, and he was my colleague.

I was a widow and a grandmother, albeit relatively young for both. And I was here to do a very dangerous, very important job.

I was not here to take a lover.

No matter how much he smoldered at me from the across the room.

"What do you want, Trey?" I asked, pushing as much ice into my voice as possible.

"The council is concerned about your solution to our staffing problem."

"Oh? And do they have alternative, because I am all ears."

"Sadly, no. And so they've given you permission to proceed with caution."

"How generous," I muttered into my glass.

"But I have some questions for you about this, off the record."

"Really, off the record?"

His smile faded to a serious frown, the color of his scales on his hands, which looked like tattoos to the unsuspecting, glowed. His glamour made him appear human, but in all reality Trey had four different Dragon forms, each powerful in their own way. I had never seen any of them, but I'd seen moments of emotional agitation when his glamour would let through some of his latent power. Now was one such moment, and it made me wary.

"What's wrong?" I asked.

"The supernatural community was brutalized under Francesca's time," he began, a rolling growl under his words.

"I know, that's why I intend to approach them with respect and caution. To prove to them that we are different, on their side."

"How?"

I let out a long breath.

"I'm not sure. Each group has different rules, different opinions and experiences with the Archive. Some worse than others. I confess that I am unsure how to proceed."

Trey swaggered toward me a grin on his face.

"I humbly volunteer as tribute."

I snorted.

"You've been watching too many movies."

"I admit, I have a soft spot for the teen dystopian dramas. To think they actually made a franchise out of a ritual Dragon youths once performed. Though, not to the death of course."

I rubbed my temple in tight circles to try and relieve the pain behind my eyes.

"Trey, I have a headache. Does this conversation have an end?"

He moved closer and plucked the drink from my fingers.

"What do you think—?"

"A scalp massage while I tell you."

He'd never asked to touch me before, nor had he ever done more than flirt from a distance. Now, however, his sweet scented breath was brushing against my face and I could see the flecks of cobalt in his dark eyes, the whisper of blue in his thick black hair. He was beautiful, in a way only something cloaked in mystery and danger could be.

"Fine," I sighed, and turned around.

One hand went to my shoulder, his touch warmer than a Mundane, like me. With his other hand, he plunged his long, nimble fingers into my hair and began to work my scalp in firm motions.

I closed my eyes in spite of myself; god, did it feel good to be touched, to be cared for even if it was vastly inappropriate to let a council member do this.

He's the one that asked. I just…oh my goodness! He has magic fingers.

"Now," he whispered as his other hand began to work on the knots in my shoulder, "I propose that I work beside you as *consultant*, of sorts, to the supernatural community. I could help you navigate their customs, their painful history with the former director, and act as a liaison between you and them."

Heat from his body was melting into mine, and I wanted so much to lean against him, to feel the hardness of his muscles against me. I held onto my focus by the slimmest margin and remembered my personal rules.

No more romance.

No one else added to the list of people who could get hurt if I screw all this up.

Professional, simple relationships only.

"Why would you do that?" I asked, desperately trying to keep my voice even.

"Because I think this could work. In fact, I think you've short changed how brilliant this actually is in giving us an edge against the Protectors. You get in good with the supernatural community again, and perhaps they will start to fill our field agent ranks."

"And since the Protectors seem hell bent on keeping the ranks of supernaturals they have to a small number…yes, that makes sense."

"You see," his lips came dangerously close to the shell of my ear, "we make a good team, Director."

"Don't call me that," I turned my head before I could think better of it.

His eyes bore into mine and for a second his fingers stilled on my body. Trey's mouth was close, his breath ghosting across my face. I'd be lying if I said he didn't do things to my body that a woman in my position could not afford to indulge in. Not when I'd learned the hard way what it was like for a Mundane to fall for someone with supernatural powers.

Slow, agonizing torture punctuated by fleeting moments of happiness. Never again.

I extricated myself from his grip and snatched my whiskey from the coffee table.

"My apologies," his voice was just a touch breathy.

I couldn't help smiling at the fact that I'd actually gotten to *him* for a change.

"Call me Angelica when we are alone and Director Dearborne when we're with others. But never just *Director*. That was Francesca, not me."

"I understand."

Those words held far more than just an agreement about what to call me. Trey really did understand why I hated that woman, why the memory of her brought a bitter fury to my blood. She'd used and tormented my family for thirty years, threatening my children and imprisoning my husband before finally killing him. And I had been the one to end her life with a swipe of a sword, like some kind of hero in a book.

It had been necessary.

It had been justice.

So why does the memory still make me sick?

I finished off my whiskey and turned to face Trey, who had been waiting patiently this whole time.

"Find me a meeting with someone, anyone," I instructed. "I want to begin immediately. We need more agents."

"Still no word on the missing shipment?"

"No, and now I have two dead field agents."

Trey grimaced.

"I'm sorry."

"Don't be sorry, help me beat them."

Trey's lips curled up and damn him! He looked like he was about to say something down right smutty or devious.

Or both. And isn't that just my type?

At the thought of David, I tightened my jaw and shut down any attraction to Trey. It wasn't that David would want me to remain a widow forever. He wouldn't. But the thought of anyone in my life after what had happened to him…

I just can't.

"Angelica?" Trey whispered. "What's wrong?"

"Nothing. I'm tired."

He gave me a slow nod.

"You know, if we are going to be working together like this, we should get to know one another. Become friends."

"Why?"

"Because friends work together better. And I think you could use one."

The last part was devoid of any flirtation, anything coy. He was being sincere and it shot straight through my defenses because he was right. I was bone achingly lonely, and I needed someone I could talk to about all the fears and complications of my new life. I wouldn't burden my two oldest children with it, even though they'd been a part of the Archive not that long ago. Their experiences were the stuff of nightmares, my oldest in particular. Having someone I could unload on at the end of a hard day, or have by my side in the case of a difficult decision, could make all the difference.

"Alright," I said, extending my hand to him. "Friends."

His shake was firm, warm. My fingers grazed the scales on the back of his hands and a tiny zing of power rolled up my fingers, like I'd gotten a little shock.

"Sorry," he grimaced, pulling back, "it can be challenging holding my glamour for long periods of time. Sometimes, things leak out."

"It's alright. I suppose you can drop it around me, if you're comfortable with that."

He cocked an eyebrow.

"Would *you* be comfortable with that?"

I seriously thought about that. I'd had limited contact with most supernaturals since taking over this position. We did have some on staff, though most were relegated to non-agent roles, like security and artifact storage. I wasn't unfamiliar with them. But I knew enough to know that a *Dragon* was an entirely different thing than an Orc or Mothman.

"I believe I would. And if we are to be working together more, I would think I need to become more comfortable with at least one of your true forms."

He nodded.

"That makes sense. But not tonight. I'll meet you at your office tomorrow morning. You like two sugars in your coffee, right?"

"Yes. Why?"

"Impress your new friend 101, feed their caffeine addiction."

He smirked and showed himself out of my penthouse.

I hated to admit that I missed him already.

And that I was looking forward to seeing him tomorrow.

I'm just lonely for a friend, that's all.

I nodded at myself.

"Yes, that's all it is."

(Curious about Angelica and her family? Read more about Angelica's history with Francesca and the Archive in The Silver City Celestials series.)

CHAPTER ONE

FRASER

I didn't want to be here.

I mean, I wanted to be here drinking beer, but I would have rather it was with one of my brothers, or another member of my clan. I would have rather it have been purely fun and social, instead of the dire situation that now faced me.

Sunlight streamed in through the large windows, illuminating the spotless floors and tables polished to a shine. The belief that all pubs were grimy establishments may have been true for Mundane pubs, but the supernatural ones didn't smell or look like a stables. We took pride in our places of refuge, especially since throughout history, our kind has been hunted so brutally. Werewolves perhaps especially.

The booths at the Ace and Gryphon were nice and roomy to accommodate the usually large stature of the magical creatures that frequented the pub. Like most of our pubs in Scotland, this one was the site of a former bank. Unlike most of them, this one had a protective glamour and boundary spell around it to both disguise the clientele and keep Mundanes the hell away.

I shifted in the booth, the old leather groaning under my massive, furry body, and took a long pull from my pint. I wasn't the only

Werewolf. There were four at the table near mine, and one incredibly large Werebear that just barely fit in the chair he was perched atop. A couple of Harpies were giving a Mothman a hard time but he seemed to like it, the eejit.

Two Gargoyles were shooting darts, the pints clenched in their fists looked like a child's sippy cup. I was a little surprised to see a few Mundane lasses sitting with the Ephemerals in the corner so I tried to see into the gloom the creatures projected. If the Mundanes were being hypnotized into sitting with those creepy bastards, I'd have to step in. But after some not at all subtle staring, I was able to determine that they were fine.

Mundanes were what we called the unmagical crowd. The ones in the corner didn't know they were in a pub that catered to beings that they might see as monsters. They saw exactly what the glamour made them see: regular men and women in for a pint or two in the middle of the day.

The only Mundanes that could darken the door of the Ace and Gryphon had to be with one of our kind, and even then, most of them weren't given permission to see beyond the glamour that protected us and the bar. If they weren't with one of us, the Mundanes gave this place a wide berth, good whiskey or not.

The glamours had evolved over the years, from spelled charms that wore off in a few hours to specialized magical tattoos that were created specifically for each supernatural. We all received our permanent glamours when we reached whatever age was maturity to our species. For most supernaturals, it was eighteen. And if there was any growing left to be done, our glamours would change with us. Not only that, but whenever our glamours were in place, it felt real to anyone touching us. The clothes we wore in the disguise, our hair, muscles, skin, all of it. No one, not even another supernatural, would be able to tell the difference. We could alter any part of our bodies, making aspects of our true form disappear if we wanted to. Or, if someone wanted to be very strange, we could manipulate our bodies into any kind of hybrid combinations. If

I wanted, I could have yellow eyes all the time, or longer fingers. But I wasn't stupid. Mundanes feared what they didn't understand. And throughout our long history living alongside them, the one thing we all could agree on was that Mundanes never would, or could, rightly understand us.

Oh sure, there were a few exceptions. But they were just that. Exceptions. The rule was to be hunted and killed, and in my kind's case, to be destroyed damn near from existence. We still didn't have many numbers, not compared to the days of the Druids. And even less compared to the days of the ancient Scottish clans.

But the glamours, originally created by the Druids, had helped keep us through the dark times. And when witches had discovered how to do it for all the supernaturals, it had enabled us to come out of hiding, to create relationships with others outside our species. It didn't mean we always got along. There had been wars to be sure. But given how precarious our existence was in some ways, getting along was a matter of survival.

I checked my watch and growled, causing the Harpies to stare at me. Werewolves weren't exactly known for their patience, and right now mine was stretched thin. I'd asked the damn Gargoyle to be here half an hour ago and yet here I was, sitting alone and nursing my pint like a lass, stood up on a date.

I was the liaison between the MacDonald Werewolf clan and the Secret Archive, a job that had been forced upon me by the previous director to protect my clan. I had no idea how she'd met her demise, but I didn't shed a tear for that cow. She'd cost my clan good men and women with her scheming and threats, including my grand-dad. He'd sacrificed himself so we'd have safety, thrusting my brother, Angus, into the Alpha role. Angus wasn't the trusting sort before all that blew up, and after, he'd become less so. The fact that I had agreed to take on a role as go between with the organization that had killed the man that had raised us had caused a rift between Angus and me, one that still made my heart ache. I loved my brother, respected him. We'd been close as bairns, but time, and the burden of responsibility, had made Angus hard, withdrawn. There were many days that I wondered if I knew my brother at all.

James says this new director isn't like the other, she's firm but fair. We'll see, won't we? If the arse ever shows up.

My claws scraped against the glass of the pint and I decided to just drain the damn thing. The amber liquid ran down my throat and I closed my eyes on a huff of breath. The Earth Fae that ran the brewery for most of the magical pubs in Scotland knew their shit. I didn't care much for beer anywhere else, but this brew reminded me somehow of running out under a moonlit, cloudless sky; the wind in my fur, the scent of wood smoke in the air.

That's some powerful magic they've infused in there. No wonder it was so pricey.

I hadn't been out to the country for more than the three full-moon nights every month in ages. It would be nice to just walk the hills at my leisure without the frenzy that over took us during the full moon. But in the past few years, I'd been too busy making sure my clan was protected to enjoy a break out in the countryside. And I wasn't just protecting them from the Secret Archive, but from the other clans.

Campbell in particular.

I huffed out a frustrated breath through my nose, startling the Harpy walking by.

"What's the matter wolf?" she asked, her serrated teeth gleaming in the light from the window. "You lonely?"

The Harpy wasn't bad looking, as her species went. Her breasts were high and firm under the shirt she wore for decency among us all, and her feathers shone red and blue with golden accents that matched her eyes. And the claws on her feet were clean, something that couldn't be said for some of her ilk. I knew by the flush on her face that she wanted me to take her into the bathroom and fuck her quick and dirty.

Well, maybe I didn't know it that specifically, but I was pretty sure she wouldn't say no if I suggested it.

She ran her long talon through the black fur along my shoulder, grazing the bare skin on my chest. I didn't wear a shirt, just a kilt and a sporran, for personals.

"You waiting on someone?" she whispered. "Me maybe?"

It had been an embarrassingly long time since I'd rutted with anyone. And while my cock might stir at the thought of rough, anonymous fucking, it also left a hollow ache in my chest. Unbidden, *her* face came to mind. The way she'd stared at me, cowered and spat out her disgust at the blood on my hands, matted in my fur. Silvia had been the only Mundane I'd ever fallen in love with. I was going to reveal myself to her, ask her to be my mate, when someone from a rival clan had attacked us. I'd gone into a rage, let the glamour that made me look human slip, and ripped the assailant apart with my bare claws.

Understandably, Silvia had been shocked, frightened.

I had expected that.

But not the sheer and utter disgust, horror even in those lovely eyes. She'd run from me, called the police when I showed up at her door, and moved back to London within the week. That was over a year ago, and I hadn't been able to stomach being with a female since.

I winced unwillingly and took the Harpy's hand off my body.

"Not today, lass," I whispered, letting a growl into the syllables.

Her bottom lip stuck out in a pout.

"Well, if you change your mind—"

"I won't. Now unless ya want to get me another pint, ya can get yer feathered arse away from me."

She turned with a glare, muttering something about grumpy Werewolves and how I needed to get laid.

I was about to growl at the Mothman behind the bar for another pint when the door opened and everyone went completely still. Fear and trepidation thickened the air in a second, and that was usually enough to at least get the Werewolves growling. But the scent underneath all that was what silenced them, and me. It was what had the Ephemerals disappearing into their shadows, the Gargoyles putting on their stone skin. It had the Harpies hissing, a posture more than anything.

It was the smell of magic. Very old, and very powerful magic.

Like brimstone, and the beginning of the world. That's not James, it's…

I turned slowly, knowing better than to move too quickly when something this old and powerful was in the room.

The click of long claws on the stone floor was the only sound as the being drew closer. When I'd finally managed to turn around, I realized that our reactions were actually very well deserved. In fact, if we were smart, we would be running out the door.

The two Mundanes stared with wide eyes at the complete change in the pub.

"Lassies," the Mothman said, gliding out from behind the bar, "I think it's time for ya to leave."

The Mundanes nodded and scampered out of the pub through the back door. I was ashamed to admit that I envied them for a moment.

A very tall, very broad blue scaled Dragon stepped to the middle of the pub, his scales flowing over his skin like water tinged with sunlight. His blue-gold eyes surveyed the room, and each creature that gaze fell upon bowed their head in reverence. Spikes ran from the top of his head, down the middle of his back and followed the slope of a serpentine tail that twitched, feeling out the parts of the room the Dragon couldn't currently see. His hand could easily cover my entire head, and I was sure he had at least six inches on me. Considering that I was one of the largest werewolves of my clan, that was saying something.

However, if he was in his full form, we'd all be ants on the ground for him to stomp as he burned the world down. Dragons were more powerful than most anything on Earth, and that made them the most terrifying. This was likely his most simple true form, which resembled a very large, upright lizard, though I would never, in a million years, tell him that to his face.

Lucky for us, Dragons didn't seem too intent on destruction these days. They also didn't tend to leave their palatial estates either.

So why is this one strolling into the pub as if it's the most normal of occurrences?

When his gaze snapped to mine, I began to bow and the damn thing chuckled. The sound rumbled through my body to my very bones. It took everything I had to not let my legs give out.

"Fraser MacDonald?" he asked.

"Aye," I answered, trying to look him square in the eye.

"James sends his regrets, but he was unavoidably detained."

My eyes narrowed. This Dragon could've squashed me into jelly without much effort, but that didn't mean I would just roll over and accept his words. James had a dangerous role at the Secret Archive, one that could have easily put him in this Dragon's cross hairs. Just because he was a nearly one hundred year old Gargoyle didn't mean that he couldn't be killed.

And for a Dragon, it wouldn't be difficult.

"Detained, ya say?"

"Yes."

"How?"

"Well, I didn't kill him and eat him if that's what you're worried about."

"I didn't say ya did. But then, I don't ken ya, do I?"

The Dragon's eyes narrowed. Even though my stomach flipped, I didn't look away. If I was going to die, it wouldn't be as a coward.

My fellow Werewolves apparently didn't feel the same because their chairs scrapped back and they fled the pub, followed quickly by the Gargoyles, the Werebear and the Harpies.

With the exception of a very pissed Mothman patron who was asleep in a booth, and the very nervous Mothman who owned the pub and was currently twittering behind the bar, the Dragon and I were alone.

"James said you were a stubborn, suspicious one," the Dragon growled.

"Don't recall him talkin' about workin' with a Dragon."

"I didn't kill James. I'm from the London office, Director Dearborne sent me."

Relief surged through me, but I bit back on it and my head bowed before I could stop myself. I was one of the strongest of my clan, second only to my older brother. But the animal in me couldn't help but recognize the stronger one in this being.

I glared up at him, the bastard still smiling in a way that had me wishing I could take a swing at him without risking my life.

The Dragon sat across from me, barely fitting into the oversized booth. I had the feeling that I looked like a bairn next to this being and that didn't help my need to get back a little bit of control in the situation.

The Mothman that owned the pub scurried over, nervously wringing his hands.

"Honored to have one of the ancient ones at the Ace and Gryphon," he stammered. "What can I get ya? On the house, of course."

"That's generous but unnecessary," the Dragon replied, never looking away from me. "I'll have whatever Fraser is having."

"Another pint," I said, holding the Dragon's gaze.

"Sure, sure."

The Mothman was back so fast that he must've transported, and then was gone just as fast. The only sound now was the pissed Mothman's snoring in the corner as the Dragon and I drank our pints.

"Didn't catch yer name."

"Trey Park."

"Well *Trey*, why isn't James here?"

"You don't trust very easily do you?"

"That's rich comin' from a Dragon."

Trey chuckled.

"Touché," he took another pull and closed his eyes. "That's incredible."

"The Earth Fae in Scotland know how to brew good beer."

"And whiskey."

I tipped my head to that because I couldn't argue.

"To answer your question," Trey said, "James is trying to track down a missing shipment of artifacts. But your request caught the director's eye and she asked me to check in."

"The director," I said slowly.

Trey's expression became serious and he nodded.

"She's different than Francesca."

"Really? How?"

"Well, for one she's not crazy."

I snorted.

"And for another," he continued, "she wants to bring the organization back to its roots."

"Its roots?"

"Helping to keep the world safe from these artifacts. To be neutral and not allow the artifacts to be used in any way that would impact humanity. Negatively or positively. Complete neutrality."

"That's a bonny dream."

"I won't argue that she's carved out a damn near impossible task for herself. But her sincerity and determination are real."

I studied the Dragon, my claws tapping against the glass of the pint.

"The last director killed many a good clansman of mine," my voice was low, the faces of the departed floating past my memory. "If not for my grand-dad, we might've been destroyed."

"I know. She did a lot of damage. Director Dearborne is trying to make amends and fix our reputation with the supernatural communities."

"And that's why you're here? Because I'll be honest, sendin' a Dragon is either a very large threat, or a bit of overkill in the customer service department."

Trey laughed at that and took another drink of beer.

"You're not wrong."

"About which?"

"Both."

"So, yer threatenin' me?"

"No, sending a Dragon to investigate is a clear sign of how important the clans are to us."

I nodded and took a pull from my glass. There was a lot he wasn't saying, and it was the unknown that had me more nervous than before. My clan had come through a lot in the last few years between the previous director and the conflicts with the other clans, the Campbells in particular. Now, just when I thought we'd come through all of it to a new day, the rug had been pulled from under us.

"Why don't you tell me the situation, as you see it," Trey said.

I studied this Dragon, trying to see behind the power and beauty of his species to discern if he was being completely honest with me. Dragons were shrewd, secretive to a fault and greedy arses. But the one thing they generally weren't was eejits. They'd been scarce during the previous director's time, and she'd not been foolish enough to threaten them. The fact that this Dragon trusted the new director said something.

I just hope it says that I can trust him with our clan's safety.

"How much do ya know about clan politics?" I asked.

"Enough to know that the MacDonalds and the Campbells have been at each other's throats for hundreds of years."

I nodded.

"Aye, that we have. But in recent years, the leaders of both clans have tried to put all of that behind them. It's been shaky, to say the least. And to shore it up, make it a bit more stable, my older brother Angus has agreed to marry the clan leader's granddaughter, Imogen. Everything was on track for a Beltane matin' ceremony, until two weeks ago when Angus nearly ruined it all by sleepin' with his ex, Lizzie."

Trey frowned.

"That sounds unfortunate, but why do you think it's supernatural in nature?"

"Because Angus is the steadiest man I've ever met. He didn't want to break it off with Lizzie, that was true. They'd been off and on since high school. But Angus knew it was the best thing for the clan. Hell, he was the one that suggested it. This turnabout isn't normal for him. But it's not the only thing. The day after, two of my clansman went into Campbell territory and started shite on purpose. They'd been under their Alpha's orders not to go anywhere near the Campbells until things settled down. But they did it anyway. Now, if you're unfamiliar with an Alpha's command, let me tell you, most of us can't break that hold. Me? Maybe. But these two were barely out of school, they shouldn't have been able to disobey."

"Unless they were aided by something powerful."

"Aye, such as an artifact. Now, you tell me that there's some missin', enough that James couldn't come personally. I may not understand what goes on in that secret place of yers, but I know when somethin' isn't right with my clan."

"I think your instincts are definitely something to listen to. And that's why I'm asking you to come to the London office, and present this to the director. She can take a closer look at things and assign you an agent to investigate."

I gave him growling chuckle.

"I can't just up and leave in the middle of this kind of thing! The clan needs me."

"I agree that they need you, but what good are you going to do by staying here? You're the liaison, you need to present this to the director."

I swore under my breath and finished off the pint.

"Fine," I ground out. "But she better deliver me someone who can fix this."

Trey's smile was tight.

"I'm sure she'll find you the very best."

CHAPTER TWO

DAPHNE

The soft fabric of my black jumper suspender skirt swished around my legs as I walked along the sidewalk on a beautifully brisk London morning. It may have been June but that didn't seem to matter to the weather, which had been cool and wet most of the week. I tilted my face up and closed my eyes on a sigh. Even so, the sun was a deliciously warm contrast to the cool air and I wished I could sit outside all morning reading. But, alas, both my jobs required my attention and neither were the outdoors type.

I adjusted the strap of my tote, which was heavy with my latest research project about the sexual practices of Basilisks. It was extremely difficult to parse fact from fiction in this area, but I desperately needed to know if the artifact that had come in last week was indeed a Basilisk fertility pillow or just some odd cushion with lizards embroidered all over it.

Normally, this kind of mystery would dominate my mind fully. I'd go without sleep or meals as I tried to find the facts. But not today. Because today, at last, I would be offered a permanent position at Eden college. I was sure that was why the dean of the anthropology department wanted to speak with me. After all, I'd taken their lowest enrolled class and turned it into the most sought after course for two years running. Even though academia was not my passion, I had decided a long time ago that the only way I'd ever stop my family from lobbing verbal missiles of sneering judgment at me was to prove my worth as a professor. Or at the very least, get a research grant from a respectable university.

I would have much preferred to hunker down into my job with the Secret Archive, and expand the department, even organize artifact finding expeditions. Just the thought sent a thrill through my body. But I could never tell my family about my real passions, much less my job with the Archive. The most I could divulge was my cover story, which got more than a few sneers, snorts and eye rolls. I was the family joke, the one that everyone hoped no one asked about at faculty fundraisers. And if they did, I was talked about in hushed whispers as if I were some cautionary tale.

At least they've stopped commenting on my weight and how it's keeping me from finding a husband.

I forced such thoughts away. No use going down that mine field in my psyche. Even if I'd worked hard to diffuse much of their comments and judgements about my weight over the years, there was always a few that liked to stick around and cause me pain. But not today! Today was going to be a good day! The best day!

"Professor Daphne Reynolds," I dared to speak it out loud.

It had a delightful ring to it.

I practically skipped the last half block to the headquarters of the Secret Archive, which was hidden within a very old building that appeared to be merely a branch of the restoration department of the museum. Most of the offices were above ground, but the warehouse was below. There were five sub basements, each divided into different departments depending on the types of artifacts housed there.

"Good morning, Nigel," I said to the security guard.

He was glamoured so that he looked like any other rather dumpy security guard when, in reality, he was a seven and half foot tall Orc with green skin stretched over muscles that were as big as my head in some places. Like a lot of Orcs, Nigel was quite the foodie, having the extremely sensitive and refined palette of his species. The few times he's invited me out for wine tasting or the opening of a new restaurant, it has been quite the experience. I don't think I'll ever drink a merlot again without wondering if Nigel would be able to pick out whether or not there had been basil growing nearby or if there had been a light frost that year.

"Morning, Daphne," he grinned at me, revealing dazzling white teeth. "You seem happy."

"I am. It stopped raining."

Nigel chuckled.

"That it did. Oh, your assistant, what's his name…Reggie?"

My smile faltered.

"Yes?"

"He's waiting for you in the receiving room, something about a new shipment."

"Oh, bollocks!"

Nigel snorted at me, with my American accent, using distinctly British slang, but let's be honest, they have the best terms.

"I've got to get to him before he does something stupid," I said, running inside.

The last time I'd left Reggie alone with a crate of new artifacts he'd held a bauble from a Dionysian temple up to the light and everyone within a twelve-foot radius almost ended up in an orgy.

The initial lobby that was open to the public was filled with my coworkers manning the front desks, meeting contacts or ordering from the cart. It was still somewhat strange to see the abundance of smiles and happy conversation. It wasn't that long ago that everyone was too afraid of being killed or experimented on to do much more than keep their heads down and work. Though their glamours were firmly in place, I recognized more than a few supernaturals, which was also new. Everything about it lightened my spirits. Perhaps the promises of

Director Dearborne were true, and this really was a new day for the Archive.

The previous director, Francesca, had been lacking in both conscience and any regard whatsoever for her agents. Her only aim was power, at any cost. She'd killed or tortured those that stepped out of line and did horrifying experiments on others. I'd heard the rumors, of course. That was half the point. Step out of line and you'll be sent to the Lab.

But that was then. Now, things are different and I hope to god they stay that way.

I scanned my key card and took the elevator up to the third floor where new shipments waited for me. When the elevator doors opened, I stepped into the short line behind my coworkers to await decontamination. Beyond us was the receiving room; a huge, open space split into different sections in the hopes of keeping artifacts separated enough to not interact with one another. Most thought the process of neutralizing and initially examining the artifacts was a bit dull, but I was always thrilled to discover what might lie within the crates. What new truth might I uncover?

As the cool air of the decontamination chamber blasted over me, I realized that today was the fifth month anniversary of my promotion to head of the department. Running the neglected Sexual Artifacts division wasn't all I'd thought it would be when I took the job. The offer of running my very own department had felt like a sure sign of wonderful things to come, that all of my hard work had paid off and I was finally being recognized.

And then I was shown the division.

A run down set of shelves and crates in the bowels of the London office, the place looked like it used to be a medieval dungeon.

Turns out, it had been, which explained the ghost that currently resided there.

That reminds me, I need to see if the Hauntings department has any advice for communicating with spirits. Peter the poltergeist is going to move the wrong artifact one of these days and then I'll be cleaning Minotaur cum out of the vents. Again.

Once I was given leave to exit the decontamination chamber, I took a quick look at my outfit to make sure it was alright and nodded my thanks to the technician, who wasn't looking at all. I'd chosen this outfit, with its three quarter length crimson turtleneck, shin length flared skirt and high waist because it both flattered my curves and looked as fun as it did professional. I wanted to walk into that meeting with the dean as my most confident self, and this was one the outfits that always made me feel just that. I smoothed back my unruly black curls and tied them back. The chamber was really hell on my hair, and I wondered if there was anyone I could reasonably talk to about that. But the moment I stepped into the busy receiving room and spied Reggie about to open a crate, all worries about my appearance fled.

"Reggie, don't you dare!" I shouted across the cavernous space.

Half a dozen heads turned and stared but I ignored them. I really did not need to see my coworkers sans pants and grinding on one another right now. Reggie, a young Mothman with unusual yellow and crimson coloring in his wings, jumped back. I cringed a little at how scared he looked, and made a mental note to check in with him after I'd reminded him of the rules pertaining to new artifacts.

Reggie had been stolen from his hive as an egg many years ago. Poor thing had no knowledge of any of his family and no one had been able to track them down. He'd lived his entire existence in one of the sub basements as a sort of research assistant at the Lab. He wouldn't talk about what he'd seen there, and honestly, I preferred not to know.

While Reggie had been excited to work with me and be out of the small sub basement that had been his only home, he was still too frightened to venture outside the building, even with the offer of a glamour to hide his true nature from the humans. I kept trying though, and maybe one day he'd take me up on a trip to the bookstore. The young Mothman was absolutely obsessed with Regency romance novels.

"Sorry," he said, his voice surprisingly deep for such a thin being.

"Thank you. I really do need you to follow the protocols."

He nodded.

"Although, I do understand the curiosity," I said with a smile. "It's always exciting, isn't it?"

He gave me a bright grin.

"Yes!"

I handed Reggie a pair of gloves that would fit the hands on his first set of arms, hoping he remembered not to use his lower ones to handle anything. He had three arms on each side; the middle and lower arms had hands that looked more like pincers and could extend to various lengths, which was very handy for reaching the taller shelves in the department.

During this part of his job, Reggie was in charge of cataloguing the artifact on the secure tablets we all used, but sometimes I had to hand him something, and the last I wanted was for him to activate it. I slipped on my own pair of gloves and opened the first crate, an old school wooden box with sawdust and hay inside. It covered a medium sized copper box with a hieroglyph and the name of Cleopatra the seventh on it. I sprayed it with the neutralizing solution, a thin, somewhat goopy pink liquid that would temporarily put the artifact into a neutral state.

Ever so carefully, I opened it and gasped.

Inside was a gorgeous necklace of gold and topaz, with golden serpents twining themselves around each jewel. I turned it over and saw a faint inscription. Reggie brought the magnifying lamp to me and I examined the writing.

"It's Latin…To my beloved queen, my Aphrodite," I read out loud.

I searched through the packing to find the slip that was supposed to accompany the item. It was buried at the bottom and I nearly fell over into the crate as I searched.

"Cleopatra's topaz necklace grants the wearer the ability to seduce a powerful man or woman. Over time, mutual obsession can set in, wearer and the one seduced will do anything to keep the other."

I'd never gotten an artifact that didn't have some kind of horrible draw back to its use. And while I knew that someday I might tire of constantly handling dangerous mystical objects, I wasn't there yet.

Not even close.

For the next hour we looked through all the crates tagged for my department, sending a few to the other departments because they really didn't belong with us. The last crate was small, buried behind all the others. It looked a bit worse for wear, the metal scratched and dented. The shipping label was faint but the date was clear.

"This came in a year ago," I said, looking around. "Why am I just now getting this?"

"Maybe it was just overlooked?"

"Hmm…perhaps."

Goose flesh rose on my arms, my instincts telling me that this was something a bit more dangerous than the other things we'd looked at this morning.

"Have the tank of solution ready," I said to him, not taking my eyes off the metal box.

Reggie scrambled to get the small tank of neutralizing solution we kept handy and rolled it over. I pried the top of the metal box off with slow precision. It didn't look like an artifact itself, but I'd been doing this long enough to know that looks can be quite deceiving.

When the lid slipped off, that feeling of danger increased, causing my stomach to lurch. Inside, the packing material was old and smelled faintly of mold. Nestled within was a small disk made out of quartz, perfectly round.

Even with my gloves on I could feel the vibration of power emanating from it. Heat suffused my core and I had to bite back a moan.

"Hand me the spray," I said, wincing at how breathy my voice had become.

Reggie fumbled with it and stepped away. I assumed he was as affected as I was and I didn't want to embarrass the poor man, so I purposely did not look his way. With great care, I sprayed the neutralizer on the disc, coating it thoroughly.

The arousal left me, though I still trembled from the force of it.

"What is that?" Reggie asked after a moment.

Now that I could think clearly, I carefully lifted the disk out and brought it under the magnifying lamp.

Through the pinkish solution I saw carefully inscribed symbols; bull horns with what could've been the sun behind them at the top. At the bottom, the head of what could've been a cow with a crescent moon behind it.

"This might be Druid iconography," I murmured. "...possibly from a fertility ritual...maybe the great union..."

"There's more in the box," Reggie said.

I carefully set the disk down and went back to the box. Sure enough, there were two talismans hanging from beautiful silver chains.

One of the talismans had the horns and sun, the other the cow and crescent moon. On the back were more symbols that I didn't recognize. I had come across a few artifacts from the Druid faith but none from their sex magic. My heart picked up and a flush of excitement rose to my cheeks. It wasn't arousal of the body. No this time, it was my mind that was excited.

Here before me was a mystery, a chance to discover something no one in the archive had.

"I need to go to my office," I said, more to myself. "I should have some resources to decipher this."

"Should I bring the artifacts?"

My eyes took in the delicate art work along the edge of the disk, wishing I could run my bare finger along it. Would it be raised, or depressed like a carving?

"Daphne?"

"What would they have used to carve this?" I said to myself.

One of Reggie's hands clasped my shoulder and I realized that he'd been talking.

"Hmm?"

"The artifacts?"

"Oh! Oh yes, well the ones we've neutralized you can bring down our warehouse. I'll meet you there."

I carefully packed the artifacts back into the box and tucked it under my arm.

"Are you sure about that thing?" Reggie asked as I walked into the passenger elevator.

"Of course, it's been neutralized."

He raised an eyebrow and handed me the spray bottle.

"Just in case."

I gave him a sheepish grin. Usually I was the one to make him stop and think. The fact that he was doing it to me was strange, and yet also, nice. He didn't judge my tendency to lose myself in my work. He just simply tried to help.

"See you downstairs," I said just before the doors closed.

CHAPTER THREE

DAPHNE

My office was just off the storage area Reggie and I humorously called the warehouse. There were garages bigger than the space we'd been given, but "warehouse" sounded better than storage closet.

And honestly, the storage closet was my office.

I'd managed to squeeze in a few plants that were struggling to thrive under grow lights just to give the gray stone walls a little bit of color, along with one accent wall of soft green. My desk was an antique roll top that was flanked by two bookshelves overflowing with texts. I wanted a third bookcase but had no idea where I'd actually put it. Shelves that had been here when the space housed mops and cleaning supplies now contained a few changes of clothes, some toiletries and my notebooks. Those closest to my desk were reserved for whatever artifact I was studying so the disk and talismans were now spread out on special cloth just above me.

I leaned over to snag one of my copies of ancient runic alphabet, over extended however, and began to topple over when invisible hands grasped my arms and pulled me back.

"Oh, thank you, Peter."

The air to my right shimmered and I took that as "You're welcome".

"I feel the need to apologize for yelling at you last week. I know you were just trying to help, but certain artifacts cannot be shelved near others without terrible consequences. If you want to be of use, I can of course train you. Another set of hands around here would be nice."

The air shimmered again.

"I wish I could hear you," I sighed.

"He says that would be nice," Reggie said from behind me.

I spun around and stared at him.

His pale skin flushed and his wings fluttered, a motion I've come to realize means that Reggie is nervous or embarrassed.

"You can hear him?" I asked incredulously.

"Every Moth hive has certain gifts. Some like me, can communicate with spirits."

His eyes sparkled as he stared just above my head and I had to hide a smile.

I think Reggie has a little crush.

"If you know that, perhaps you can find your family," I said instead.

He shook his head.

"I wouldn't know how to act in a hive family. For now, it's enough to have a purpose with you here. And to be making friends."

My chest ached for the pain this poor being had withstood all his life. I wished I could take it away, set him free to go out and find a life.

But maybe he's being truthful. Maybe, for now, this really is all he needs.

"Well," I said, forcing cheerfulness, "you can begin training Peter in how to shelve artifacts if you have some time."

Reggie's flush deepened and his wings fluttered again.

"I-I can do that. Yeah…absolutely."

The air shimmered and he chuckled.

"Should I ask?"

"Uh…it's kind of a joke between us," Peter answered.

"Oh, I see. Well in that case, continue."

I turned back to my notebook when I realized that the hands on my desk clock were at the same locations as the last time I looked. Upon closer inspection, it was apparent that the clock had stopped. My stomach dropped as I dug my phone out of my purse. We didn't get the best reception down here and when I was working on an artifact I tended to turn it on silent anyway. Nothing worse than being at the cusp of a breakthrough and someone's post on Facebook interrupting the train of thought.

"Oh no!" I dropped my phone on my desk and jumped up.

"What's wrong?" Reggie asked.

"I missed my meeting with the dean! Where are my shoes?"

One of them floated in the air, held aloft by Peter, and the other was on one of my book shelves for some reason.

"Thank you," I said to the poltergeist. "Reggie, store these three in a box with a shallow layer of solution. I'm not sure the best place for them yet."

He nodded and got to work on the container as I tore my hair free from the now messy pony tail and attempted to get the tangles out with my fingers. Maybe the dean would understand if I told him that my job with the museum had run late.

Of course, it's supposed to be a part time position in the archival departm ent...

When I got to the main floor, I ignored the stares of the other agents as I ran past the offices and conference room. It was a half hour walk to the Office of the Dean, and I was already an hour late so I'd have to take a cab if I didn't want it to be even worse than it already was. The cab was mercifully quick and the traffic not as clogged as usual around the university. I'm sure I tipped him far too much when I shoved some money at the cabbie and barreled out. But instead of darting up the stairs, I collided with my uncle George as he descended the steps.

"Daphne, there you are," he huffed.

Uncle George taught in a different department than I, but he was great friends with the dean. Even though he'd put in a word for me, and that's why the dean had relented and given me a chance, I'd more than proven that I deserved that position.

I gave him a shaky smile.

"I know I'm late, I was researching a new artifact that came in."

"That's no excuse for blowing off your meeting."

"I just told you I didn't blow it off, I got caught up. But I was heading there now. Would you like to join me?"

Uncle George shook his head.

"Daphne, you really do live up to your nickname."

My mouth pressed into a thin line as a sharp pang shot through me at his words.

Daft-ne was the nickname he was referring to, courtesy of his oldest son when we were children. It had caught on quickly among the cousins and even a few of the aunts and uncles. The few times I'd tried to tell them it wasn't a kind nickname the reaction was always the same.

"Really Daft-ne, it's just all in good fun. You need to lighten up."

I'd finally just decided to grit my teeth and try to ignore it. But Uncle George throwing it out there now, when I'd worked so hard the last two years to prove myself the opposite, hurt more than I could say.

"I don't know what you mean," I snapped, "but I don't want to keep the dean waiting so if you'll excuse me…"

"He won't be there."

His words stopped me mid step.

"He, Professor Elliot and I already had the meeting."

"I don't understand, how could that be? It was regarding *my* class."

"*Your* class?" he asked with a raised eyebrow. "Is that…oh now, you didn't think that you were going to keep it, did you?"

Heat rushed to my pale cheeks and I fought back the impulse to panic. A terrible thought was starting to blossom in my mind but I didn't want to face it. There was no way that all my hard work was for nothing, that I could've been overlooked *again* because of my age and gender. Right?

When I couldn't get any words past the lump in my throat my uncle walked up to me, his expression more amused than sympathetic.

"You did good work on that class, really. The dean was happy with the way you rewrote the curriculum and how you increased enrollment. You did the department proud."

"But?" I whispered.

"But, you don't have the experience that Elliot does. And you tend to be…well, a little difficult when it comes to working with others."

The flush deepened because I knew exactly what he was talking about.

"You mean," I said, trying to keep my voice even, "that I don't allow my male colleagues to take advantage of me."

Uncle George sighed.

"Your need to see what isn't there is part of the problem, yes."

My eyes widened.

"Wasn't there? Professor Morten groped my ass at the department mixer!"

"And he apologized for being in his cups. It was an honest mistake."

"That he's made many times before. And then there's the fact that Professor Elliot is only still there because his family is rich and donates money to the college. Otherwise I'm sure his laziness and complete lack of proper boundaries with his students would warrant his dismissal."

"For someone who is so anxious to make a name in academia you are very quick to burn bridges, my dear."

"And for someone who claims to be a feminist, you are very quick to dismiss a woman when she says something about one of your friends that you don't like."

Uncle George's face had gone from pasty to deep red, and he was glaring at me in a way that brought back more than a few memories of when he'd railed at me as a child. But, unlike then, I would not shrink or try to disappear under that gaze. He was wrong. They all were, and damned if I let him make me feel bad about standing up for myself.

"I'm disappointed, Daphne," he said, his voice harsh. "I got you the job with the Archive hoping it would give you discipline. I stuck my neck out for you with the dean and gave you that class to teach. You've been granted so many chances, and every time your inability to control your tongue has destroyed them. I had hoped that this time you'd at last learn to leash your less than desirable character traits. But perhaps you are simply a lost cause."

While it was true that I wouldn't have even known about the Secret Archive without my uncle George bringing me in, I had already been on the path to exploring the paranormal in our world. I firmly believed I would've found me way here without his help. And as for the class…

If I say this, he'll be angry with me for months. But, in for a penny, as they say.

"If you remember, Uncle, I had already overhauled the curriculum and had been meeting with the dean for a month before you intervened. I was doing the work myself to get that job."

His grin turned cruel and I braced myself.

"And without my intervention, you would've still been begging at his door for the scrap work of other departments. I had at least secured you an intern position with Lowell today."

"Intern position? For the class that I essentially rebuilt?"

"Lower your damn voice," he hissed as people began to stare as they walked by.

"I will not," my chest heaved and tears burned my eyes. "You have the gall, the utter temerity, to believe that I didn't earn that position? That all I deserved was to be an intern after two years of hard work?"

"Humility would be a good thing for you to develop, my dear."

"Fuck humility."

His eyes grew huge and now his face was turning purple.

Coarse language was the tool of the uneducated, according to my family. And while four letter words weren't my usual mode of communication, sometimes nothing else would do.

"If you'll excuse me, I have to get back to an important research assignment."

I turned on my heel, feeling my uncle's hot stare at my back the entire time as I tried to get a cab. I held it together as I waited but the moment I closed the door, tears raced from my eyes.

Oh, teaching wasn't my passion, that was true, but I was good at it. I knew that much from my students' reactions. I much more preferred the solitude of my books and the space to let my mind breath and explore new ideas. I loved sipping tea in the wee hours of the night as the answer to a question was suddenly discovered.

But even with all of that, I had wanted that job, had wanted to see the looks on my family's face as 'Daft-ne', the butt of their jokes, suddenly had what they all did.

Would it have made a difference though, with Uncle George claiming to have gotten it all for me? Poor Daft-ne, couldn't get it on her own so she had to have Uncle George do it for her.

The truth of that didn't take the pain away and by the time I'd arrived back at the Archive and made it down to my department at the Secret Archive, I was barely holding back sobs.

"I'll never earn their respect, will I?"

That realization just made me cry harder, so when the doors opened and I stepped out to find Reggie standing there with a party hat and balloons that said "Congrats on your new job!", I started to wail uncontrollably.

One of the balloons popped and I jumped.

"No, Peter, I don't think it's the balloons," Reggie said, slipping the hat off. "I think she didn't get it."

Reggie put all three of his surprisingly strong arms around me and I sobbed into his collar bone as he rubbed my back. Soon, a tissue box came floating my way and I plucked several from it.

"I'm sorry," Reggie said.

"Thank you," I hiccupped.

"I don't know," Reggie said to the air before turning to me. "Do you still want cake?"

"Cake?"

"Um…well, I looked online about what people do at parties even though it's just the three of us, and all of the articles said that there's usually cake. So I got one."

It was so wonderfully sweet and innocent and it made me burst into fresh tears.

Reggie continued to hug me until this wave passed and then cleared his throat.

"Peter says to tell you that it's chocolate. Does that matter?"

I let out a soft chuckle in spite of how my head was starting to ache.

"Sometimes, but it doesn't really matter at the moment. Anything would be nice."

I blew my nose and dried my eyes as my Mothman assistant and the poltergeist that was apparently now a full-fledged member of our department cut pieces from the small round cake. I didn't have much of an appetite to be honest, but Reggie smiled at me with such sympathy and hope, as if this slice of cake could heal the gaping wound my uncle had left me with. I was just about to shove the first bite into my mouth when the door opened and a beautiful Korean man stepped into my sad little warehouse.

Reggie trilled next to me, his wings shuddering violently before he stepped a little in front of me. I'd never seen him upset like this before and I was shocked to realize it was a protective kind of reaction.

The man in front of me grinned down at Reggie.

"I'm not here to immolate her," his deep voice was amused. "Director Dearborne needs to see Ms. Reynolds."

"Me?" I squeaked.

"Yes. There's a case that's come up that requires your particular knowledge."

A sound like a tin can being dropped made me jump and I looked over to see one of the empty neutralizer containers had been tipped over. The air shimmered around it and I realized that Peter must've done it.

"Don't worry, little poltergeist," the man said. "I'll be sure to return her in one piece."

Reggie turned to me, his long eyebrows that acted as sort of antennae were standing straight up and there was an odd red gleam to his dark brown eyes.

"I don't understand, why are the two of you so upset?" I asked.

"Because," Reggie whispered, "he's a Dragon."

I nearly dropped my cake at the revelation. Partly from terror and partly from some of the most acute curiosity I'd ever experienced. Dragons were the most elusive of all the supernaturals, I'd honestly began to think they were more legend than fact, but here was one standing in front of me.

"Really?" I asked, doing my best to bite back the thousands of questions careening through my mind.

"Yes, really," the Dragon-man answered, crossing his arms and grinning at me. "But I generally don't advertise the fact. How did you know, Mothman?"

"I can see it," Reggie said, his voice going deeper.

The Dragon man's eyes narrowed and he stepped closer to Reggie.

"You're the Mothman that used to be Dr. Raylin's assistant, is that correct?"

Reggie went absolutely still at the mention of that monster's name.

"Yes," he finally answered, "and if it's all the same to you, I'd rather forget that man ever existed."

The Dragon-man's eyes softened.

"Yes, of course, forgive me for my lack of care. I was just fascinated by the fact that you can see through my glamour. That's an unusual gift."

"So I've been told," Reggie replied, and then turned to me. "I can go with you, make sure…make sure you're okay."

I glanced at the Dragon-man, who was watching us with an expression that was equal parts annoyance and sadness. I had been here long enough to know that sometimes people like me would be summoned to the director's office and never return. Or if they did, they were never the same. Reggie, with where he'd been forced to work, had likely seen exactly what had happened to those poor people.

But this director is different. Right?

"I'll be alright," I said, forcing a smile on my face and patting him on the shoulder. "Why don't you enjoy the cake and I'll be right back."

Reggie gave the Dragon a look, his eyes definitely turned red this time, and that same trilling sound rolled up from his throat. The Dragon nodded, as if understanding what that sound meant. I started to take a step forward when the air in front of me shimmered and I waved Peter away.

"Now, really you two, I'll be fine!"

"She will be," the Dragon said, "and time is of the essence, so if you two are done being mother hens, we need to go."

"They're simply concerned for me. It wasn't that long ago that a summons to *that* office was never a good thing."

The Dragon had the decency to look a teensy bit chagrined before turning toward the elevator.

I gave Peter and Reggie a shaky smile and followed, hoping that this meeting wasn't to tell me I'd been replaced.

Wouldn't that be the perfect ending to this day?

When the doors closed, an awkward silence descended upon us. I glanced down at the Dragon-man's hands, which were clasped in front of him. It looked like he had intricate blue tattoos on the backs of his hands that disappeared under the cuffs of his immaculate suit jacket. But as I stared at them, I realized that they were scales.

"Fascinating…" I murmured.

"What was that?"

"Nothing," I said, straightening up because I'd begun to bend down and examine the man's hands.

"I am used to the curiosity of Mundanes," his voice was wry.

I tried to school my features into something professional as I took that statement as a go-ahead to ask a few questions.

"Is it true that you have multiple true forms? Not just the one very large one?"

His jaw set and he drew a long breath, debating on if he should answer me. After a beat, he replied matter-of-factly, "Yes. Including my glamour, I have four of various sizes and appearances."

"Do you lay eggs?"

His lips twisted into a little grin.

"How impertinent."

I sucked in a breath.

"Oh my gosh, I'm so sorry—"

He chuckled.

"Yes. The females lay them and the males sit on them."

"What do the different colors of your scales mean, if anything?"

"They indicate family groups generally."

With that answer, his carefree expression darkened and I could guess why.

"There aren't many of you left, are there?" I asked, sadness gripping my heart.

"No. There are not."

The elevator stopped and I glanced at the man next to me. There was indeed a sense of power about him, ancient and complex. But beyond that was a creature who lived extraordinarily long and was nearing extinction.

"I'm sorry," I said, for lack of anything to say.

He gave me a sad smile and ushered me out of the elevator.

"You have nothing to apologize for Ms. Reynolds. My name is Trey Park by the way. Forgive me not telling you sooner, but your coworkers were quite protective."

"Yes, they can be. I'm sorry about that."

"Don't be. It's nice to see that Francesca couldn't kill the kindness in some of the people here. It speaks well that they are loyal to you."

I flushed with the compliment. After what had transpired with my uncle, it was like a balm to hear Trey indicate that I was valuable.

When we stopped outside of the simple office door I could hear a low, snarling voice from inside and stopped. Who was that? Surely not the director? And why was I here? Trey hadn't said a word on the way up. Was it a bad thing and that's why he distracted me by answering my questions?

I swallowed and waited for him to open the door, collecting myself. Whatever the reason I'd been summoned here, I would face it head on and without fear.

CHAPTER FOUR

FRASER

I crossed my arms as I stared at the attractive blond white woman behind the simple desk. Even though she was supposed to be very different than her predecessor, I kept my glamour firmly in place, not willing to allow my true form to be exposed to a person with so much power who I didn't ken.

She seemed unperturbed by the act, which surprised me.

Francesca would've lobbed several threats my way by now. Interesting.

"I do think you have an artifact problem," Director Dearborne said with a sigh. "Have there been any mysterious packages arrive or have there been any new people that have inserted themselves into your clan?"

"Naw."

She nodded and made a note on a tablet.

"Well, we are rather short staffed, but I believe have someone who may be able to at the very least shed some light on what we could be looking for."

Director Dearborne gave me a reassuring smile to which I only nodded.

"You know," she said, "I read your file."

"Aye?"

"You were treated abominably by Francesca. Your entire clan was. It took courage to stand up to her as long as you did. I know it doesn't bring back your dead clansmen and women but I am truly sorry for what transpired."

I dipped my head in acknowledgement. It was a decent beginning, but she was right, it didn't bring them back.

And if I don't get back soon, goddess only knows what trouble some of those eejits will get up to. Angus was having a hard enough time controlling the young ones.

I started to pace, which really meant I managed three or four steps until my long stride caused me to have to turn around. Her office wasn't huge but neither was it tiny. Still, even in my glamoured form, I was big and took up much of the space.

"Would you like something to drink while you wait?" she asked.

"Naw."

"It shouldn't be long."

"I makin' ya nervous, madam Director?"

Her lips quirked up.

"Would you believe that you're not nearly the most intimidating man I've ever met?"

That stopped me in my tracks, and I wondered if the rumors were true about this woman. That she'd been married to a celestial-human male and had four celestial children. That she'd lost her husband because of the archive and her children had almost been taken by Francesca. That she'd fought and resisted the machinations of this place against her family for decades, only to lose her husband in the end.

And now, here she sat, in the same position as the woman that had made her life hell.

Looking into her deceptively beautiful gaze, I could believe all of those things. There was a strength lurking there, under the smiles and designer clothes that I would not want to tangle with.

"Aye, I would, lass."

She chuckled.

"I've not been called a lass in quite some time."

"It didn't indicate age."

"I know it's just..." a glimpse of bone deep grief flashed across her face and was gone almost before I could notice.

"So, where is this expert of yers?" I asked, not wanting to dredge anything up for her.

"Trey was fetching them. I can't imagine what's taking so long."

"The Dragon?"

"Yes."

"He works for you?"

Her lips pressed together, a flush creeping up her throat.

"Not exactly."

Interesting.

The door finally opened and in stepped the Dragon I'd met three days ago, but this time in his glamour, which was an extremely posh Korean man. He nodded at me and turned his attention the director.

"Sorry, it took a little bit," he said.

"You frightened her," Director Dearborne said, her voice chiding.

"No. This office did."

"Ah, I see," she looked around the Dragon and smiled. "It's alright, dear. I need your expertise. Please come in."

I expected a weary eyed agent that looked like they'd been traveling. Or even another creature like myself. Instead, when Trey finally moved into the room, there stood a short, bonny lass with the greenest eyes I'd ever seen. She stared at the director, bow shaped lips open just a little and her pale cheeks flushed. I told myself it was the surprise of finding such a young hen standing there that had me staring, speechless. But the animal in me knew differently. Especially when she stepped up to the desk, a mere three feet away from me and her scent hit me full.

I couldn't help it, I breathed her in deep. Most people think that Werewolves only smell the physical; your sweat, your arousal, your fear. And that's true for almost every being, whether we want to or no. But there are times, after we've formed strong bonds with another, or mated with them, when we can smell the soul, the deep shadows and hidden parts. It's rare, and very personal. We usually don't do it unless given permission.

Which was why, when her scent filled my nostrils, I was almost knocked back on my heels.

She smelled of the highlands under a full moon, of heather in the spring and the brine of the ocean. There was the yearning to know things there, the curiosity of a child and the strength of spirit that spoke of a stubborn nature. It stirred deep things in me, and I found myself inching closer. Who was this creature? What was she that she could illicit such an instant response? Was she a Were? Perhaps a Fae or something else? Her soul had touches of something ancient, or what others referred to as 'an old soul', so perhaps in her past she'd been a witch, maybe a Druid?

I couldn't explain why I suddenly *knew* in this way. It was far too intimate for strangers, and I felt like a creeper as I stared at her. How had she done this? Why did it happen? And how could I get the scent of her out of my mind?

All of my confusion must've shown on my face because the Dragon eyed me and moved the woman away.

How dare he!

Before common sense could ground me, before I could stop the instincts of my animal side, I growled a him, low and long in the back of my throat.

She jumped, her eyes becoming even larger as she took me in.

"Oh, I…uh…I am sorry. Did I do something?"

Aye, she'd done something alright. But what exactly, I couldn't say. I had to get a hold of my primal side or I'd lose control, and that was a very, very bad idea.

I stepped back and leaned against the wall, far enough away that her scent didn't intoxicate me as it had before. Whatever this creature was, she was only here to give information. Once she'd given it, she would leave and I would settle once again.

The thought brought a pain to my chest and a deep frown creased my forehead as I tried to find the reason for it.

Maybe it's just nerves or…I didn't know. Best to ignore it, get what I need and leave. The clan needs me.

She glanced at me out of the corner of her eye, pale cheeks flushing.

"Mr. Fraser MacDonald, this is Ms. Daphne Reynolds," Director Dearborne said, "our expert in artifacts that could cause this sort of problem."

She gave me nervous smile and I simply nodded at her.

"What sort of problem is it?" she asked timidly.

"The kind that makes us think an artifact from your department might be involved," Trey answered with more than a little humor in his voice.

"Oh," she whispered, biting her lip.

The flush deepened, once again her gaze slid over to me.

It was a simple thing, a normal thing considering.

And yet, it sent heat coursing through me, and I grit my teeth to keep back a whimper.

What the hell is wrong with me? I haven't been this unsettled by a woman…well, ever. Maybe Lowell is right, maybe I do need to get my cock seen to.

My younger brother could be a libidinous twat but sometimes he hit the nail on the head.

"If you're uncomfortable with Mr. MacDonald's presence, we can have him wait outside," the director offered, glancing in my direction with more than a little judgment.

I braced myself for the woman to agree. It wouldn't be the first time I'd made someone uncomfortable, but for some reason the thought of her sending me out was especially awful.

Instead of a meek nod of her head, Daphne's shoulders straightened, her chin lifted in a clear act of defiance. To my further surprise she looked square in my eyes, holding me in her vibrant green pools as she shook her head.

"That won't be necessary," she said, not looking away. "If he's uncomfortable, he may of course leave, but it needn't be on my account."

Strong willed and beautiful.

My lips curled up into a smile in spite of myself and I nodded.

She nodded back, smoothing her hands down the front of her black skirt as she turned back to the director, who had a smirk on her lips that I didn't want to know the meaning behind.

The director laid out the problem while I simply watched in fascination as the woman's face went from flustered to thoughtful. The skin above her nose developed a tiny wrinkle and she sifted through the notes Director Dearborne had taken during our conversation.

"Fascinating," she murmured. "Not all artifacts can affect supernatural creatures. Especially not Werewolves. So, we're looking for something very potent, likely with ties to passion turned sour…or perhaps ancient cults of Inanna…or even Kali. When did this start?"

"Two weeks ago," I answered.

She nodded and tapped the end of a pen against her full lips. It made not looking at them damn near impossible and it was only with the most strenuous tug on my will that I stopped myself from imagining what they would feel like on my body.

"And has anyone else exhibited any desire to go back to prior lovers, or has any other unusual behavior of a sexual nature occurred?"

She asked the question without a trace of shame or shyness, something I hadn't seen very often from humans, if that was what she was.

"Not that I know of," I said after a moment.

"And has the violence been escalating, spreading?"

"To some degree, aye."

She nodded again.

"Do you have any idea what could cause this kind of disturbance?" Director Dearborne asked.

"Well, desire and upheaval aren't really mutually exclusive. Most ancient cultures equated sexual passion with acts of aggression and war. It could be any number of things. A statue of Astarte, or perhaps one of the jewels from Mata Hari's head dress, we only have half of those. Of course, some of these artifacts are only able to be used by women so…hmmmm…"

Her voice drifted off as she scribbled somethings down in a notebook the director had given her.

"Any other insights?" Director Dearborne asked.

But the lass kept murmuring to herself, which would've been adorable if it wasn't also doing strange things to me. Her mouth was hypnotic, I wanted to find out if those pink pillows were as soft as they looked, what she tasted like, if she'd return my kisses in my true form, or be horrified by it.

I need to get a grip. Or maybe visit the boxing ring tonight, get some of this frustration out.

"Ms. Reynolds?" the director said, snapping both myself and the woman back to the present.

"Hm? Oh sorry, got lost in my thoughts."

"Can you narrow down what we might be looking for?"

"I don't know honestly. What you're describing could be attributed to about half a dozen possible artifacts, none of which we currently have in my department. In order to say with any certainty, I'd have to know more, observe the people affected perhaps. I can make you a list of the possible items, if that would help."

"You say that you need to see the effects, is that correct?" the director clarified.

"Well…I mean it would help but—"

"And you passed your field fitness test, correct?"

Daphne swallowed.

"Just barely."

"Well then, that settles it."

"What does?" I asked.

"Ms. Reynolds will go with you to investigate the situation," Director Dearborn turned to the lass. "Given his clan's history with us, it might be better for you to go undercover, perhaps as a friend or girlfriend?"

"What?" I growled, stalking over to the woman. "Are ya insane?"

Daphne took a step back and looked at Director Dearborne, and then at me.

"You wanted our help," the director said, "and Ms. Reynolds is the expert on artifacts of this nature. I trust her opinion. If she feels that further investigation is needed, then she is the single best person to handle it."

"My clan doesn't care for outsiders," I said through gritted teeth. "And Angus would never allow anyone from your organization to have access to the clan. He nearly throttled me for comin' here to begin with."

"That's why I suggested that she be undercover."

I glanced over at Daphne, who was still wide eyed and obviously as shocked as I was to hear the suggestion.

She's green, I bet she's never been in the field before. I can use that, though it'll make me a right twat.

"I asked for someone who knew what they were doin'," I said, the words bitter on my tongue. "I asked for a good agent, and yer sendin' me someone who has no field experience."

Daphne gasped and I didn't have the courage to meet her eye, not when I knew I'd see such hurt there.

I'm sorry lass, but I really am doing you a favor. Someone like you is too far out of their depth when it comes to a Werewolf clan.

"Mr. MacDonald," Director Dearborne began.

"If I may, Director," Daphne said.

Now I had no choice but to face her. But when I did, my breath stilled in my chest. Her eyes were lit up with a fire that spoke of grit and a refusal to be stepped on. Her back was straight and her head was tilted up to meet my gaze, exposing a long, beautiful neck that I had a very hard time tearing my eyes from.

"I may not have experience in the field," she began, the slightest tremble in her otherwise firm voice, "but I have more than enough experience in research and in recognizing artifacts of this kind. No other agent will have the ability to see the nuances of the many different artifacts this could be. The director wasn't lying when she said you'd get the best. But if you're too squeamish—"

"Squeamish?" I scoffed.

"— to trust us, then I suggest you continue to try and solve this yourself. Though, I will warn you, these kinds of artifacts tend to escalate situations very quickly and violently. Good day, Mr. MacDonald."

She turned on her heel, causing her skirt to swish and allowing me a glimpse of a gorgeous leg. I was dumb founded by the guts on this lass! Even if she was a Mundane, which I was starting to believe she was, the hen had the heart of a Were; strong and fearless. It was the shock and, frankly, the arousal that this realization on which I blamed my next reckless action.

"Och, stop lass!" I shouted just before she walked out.

She turned and crossed her arms under her breasts, pushing them up like she was presenting them to me. I had a hell of a time not staring.

"Yes, Mr. MacDonald?"

I cleared my throat and tried to keep my expression firm.

"I didn't think of it the way ya just presented it to me."

She waited, the barest hint of a smile at the corners of her mouth.

"I expected a soldier, not a professor," I continued. "So…I do appreciate yer willingness to investigate."

She nodded and began to step back inside the office.

"But," I said, causing her to pause mid step, "my clan won't trust just a friend. Not even a girlfriend who isn't a Were. I'm sorry, that's just the truth of it."

"What will they accept, Mr. MacDonald?" Director Dearborne asked.

"One of their own. Ya haven't got any Weres on staff, have ya?"

"Not anymore I'm afraid."

"One of their own you said?" Daphne asked.

Something told me I'd regret answering her, but I did it anyway.

"Aye."

"Would a mate do?"

The air in the room thickened around me, and all I could see was this woman with her eyes as green as the hills. Her expression was so open, so innocent. She had no idea what she'd just proposed to me, what it could cost her.

But if she's right, and the artifact is going to make things a lot worse, do I have a choice?

"Aye," I said, my mouth dry. "But you need to slow down, lass. This isn't just a matter of sayin' it and it's so. This would require somethin' more."

"What is that something more?" she asked, brows furrowing.

She was approaching this professionally, clinically even, and I could admire that. But just the thought of putting my mark on this woman had my insides burning. Mating bites were sacred, part of our culture dating back to when the Druids first created us. It was also dangerous between a Mundane and Werewolf. Sometimes, accidents happened. If a Werewolf was too rough, and allowed the rutting frenzy that usually followed to take over, the woman could be harmed.

I didn't worry about the frenzy; that only happened between mates that had a true connection and I didn't ken this lass. But the way she was affecting me could cause me to slip up, to let my primal side out a little too much. I could scare the shit out of her at the very least. Or worse.

Either I do this and she comes with to solve the problem, or I'm on my own. Och, this is a right mucked up situation. Damned either way.

I ran a hand through my hair and let out a long sigh.

"I would have to bite ya," I said, not meeting her eye. "I can't tell ya much about the bite, it's a sacred thing to Werewolves. But I can say that my saliva would make ya smell like me, signalin' to the other males that yer not free. It is seen as a sign of devotion, of belongin'. In days of old, only this was needed to be mated for life."

"Oh," she breathed. "That is…quite serious."

"So you see, it's not somethin' to be entered into lightly."

"Is it reversible?" she asked.

"Aye. Our witches have a way to remove the mark, though from what I understand, it's not pleasant."

"Ms. Reynolds, you don't have to do anything you're not comfortable with," Director Dearborne said.

"Do you have anyone else that can do this?" she asked.

"No."

"Well then," Daphne took a deep breath, walked toward me and…

Bloody hell, she's baring her throat to me.

A growl rolled out of me in spite of all my attempts to hold it back, and my body stirred in ways I hadn't felt in a very long time. My hand went to her jaw, my calloused finger tips grazing her soft skin, dragging a gasp of surprise from her mouth. I wanted to seize her, haul her full body to mine and taste her. It would have been easy; after all, she was offering it to me without any hesitation. But it wasn't right to do it here, in front of these people as if she meant nothing, as if she were just a tool to scratch a confusing itch.

"Naw, lass," I ground out, gently putting my hand on her shoulder and pushing her away from me. "This isn't some nip and we're done. It's not for public consumption."

"Wait a minute, Mr. MacDonald," Director Dearborn said. "You said a bite, not a fuck."

"Don't be crass," I spat at her. "I would never take advantage. And even though we would be mated in the eyes of my clan, and I am fully within my rights to take the lass, I would never, ever do it. That's not part of the deal, I swear to that."

"But this is a sacred thing, correct?" Daphne asked.

"Aye."

"I understand, and I apologize for assuming as I did. How would you like to proceed? Even though this is a ruse, I want you to be as comfortable as possible."

I couldn't help a chuckle.

"I'm not getting' nipped, lass. Where would *you* be comfortable?"

"Well…if it needs to be private then I suppose my apartment?"

"Alright then, tonight at seven," I replied and began to walk toward the door.

I had to get out of here before I became an even bigger eejit.

She took a deep breath and gave me a smile that was attempting confidence.

"Wonderful. I shall do some research into possible artifacts in the meantime. When are we to leave for your clan?"

"Tomorrow. But I'll have to get another train ticket."

I took a step when her voice stopped me.

"I've never been to Scotland. Where are we going?"

"Dublin. And before you ask, there is a Dublin in Scotland, it's a hamlet outside of Ardross."

I tried to leave again.

"Oh, i know. There are some wonderful old estates around Dublin," her voice was animated, filled with excitement. "Some of them are from before Culloden. But, I suppose we aren't going sightseeing. Though it's possible one of your clan picked up something from the surrounding hills…hmmm…that would be something to look into. Perhaps I will see the historical places after all!"

My feet froze to the ground as images of her at our clan's country estate rose up in my mind, so clear I could almost feel it. Her face illuminated by the moon, her back against the garden wall as I tore her thin night dress with a single claw right down the middle…

Och, I can't be thinking such things about the lass. She's there to do a job, not wet my cock.

"Can I go now?" I snapped.

Daphne's eyes widened as she stared at me.

"Oh, I'm sorry, I'm blathering on. Yes, of course. I'll see you at seven. Do you need the address?"

I was already stabbing the elevator button with my finger.

"Text it to me."

I didn't even turn around. I had to get away from her, get some fresh air and try to ignore all the ways she was affecting me.

CHAPTER FIVE

DAPHNE

I watched Fraser MacDonald flee the office like the hounds of hell were chasing him. He'd been gruff to the point of rude and angry throughout the meeting and it was only at the end that I saw any softening from him at all. But even that had been strange and confusing.

I could still feel the warm brush of his fingers against my jaw. It had sent tingles down my body and I wondered if he could sense the way my core heated, the rush of adrenaline stimulating my mind with lurid pictures of us.

He'd been wearing his human glamour the entire meeting, so I had no idea what he actually looked like but I imagined he was probably quite tall and broad considering how his glamour had appeared. Over slightly tanned skin, six feet tall, built like a tank and with a trimmed beard that made him look positively wild. Then there was the chest hair peeking out from under his button down and the generous sprinkling of it over his forearms, which had been on full display from his rolled up sleeves. His thick thighs had strained the fabric of his dark jeans and the ass that I'd spied as he walked away…Dear god!

Beautiful as he was with his glamour on, I couldn't help picturing his true form.

I wonder what his actual hair would feel like. Is it coarse or soft? Is his snout long or short? And is he really that warm all the time or did it have something to do with the thermostat in here because honestly, I'm a bit overheated myself. Good lord, I need to think of something else.

I hoped that I looked more at ease than I felt because at that moment, my stomach was home to about a thousand butterflies and I was sure that my face was flushed as if I'd been running. I kept running my hand down the front of my skirt and trying to think of anything except how horrified he'd been at the thought of giving me the mating bite.

Well, I can't really blame him can I? We're complete strangers and while he may not be a romantic, it sounds as if this is something sacred to his clan. And here I am, practically bullying him into doing it. Oh lord, I should probably apologize...or maybe I was too hasty insisting on—

"Ms. Reynolds?" Director Dearborne said, and from her tone I could tell that this wasn't the first time she'd said my name.

"Oh, yes, I apologize, Director. I was digesting the meeting."

Her lips quirked up.

"I'm sure. Now that Mr. MacDonald is gone, I want to make it clear that you do not have to do anything you are uncomfortable with. We don't know a lot about the mating bite of Werewolves and how it affects us."

I tried to picture what the bite would it be like, while also doing my best not to become aroused at the thought of his teeth sinking into me. Even if he hadn't been a supernatural creature, I was stupidly attracted to men like him; closed off and mysterious with a body that even under his clothes was outrageously muscular.

Honestly, men like that are not supposed to exist outside of novels. Though I suppose he's not a man he's a Werewolf...a feral, sexy Werewolf that I'd very much like to see in his true form...maybe as he bends me over some furniture...

I swallowed, now positive that the room was too hot.

"Are you alright?" Director Dearborne asked.

My head snapped up and I tried to reign in my libido, which had always been healthy, but this was the first time it was like a runaway train.

Come now, Daphne! This is a chance at a real promotion, to do something more. You must lock this away and approach it like any other research project.

"I'm fine," I said, giving her a shaky smile.

"Alright then, I need to make this clear. I am not willing to sacrifice your comfort or safety for a mission. So if at any time you want to be extricated, you must let us know, do you understand?"

"Of course."

"Is there anything I should know about your department before you leave tomorrow?"

"I don't believe so. Reggie is new but capable of holding things down. And I think Peter understands not to move things around anymore."

"Who's Peter?" Director Dearborne questioned.

"Oh, the poltergeist that lives in my department. Quite harmless really."

"I…I see."

I was used to people having an unsettled reaction to Peter but I had thought that the director knew about this already.

"I'll send the Outfitters to your home in the morning with your approved gear. Do you have any questions?"

I blew out my lips, my mind spinning too fast for me to catch hold of anything other than a faint sense of panic mixed with excitement.

"No, not at the moment. But I may later."

"Well," the director said with a lopsided grin, "you're dismissed, I suppose."

"Oh…Oh yes, of course. Thank you."

I scurried out and down the hall, my legs shaking and my heart thumping wildly in my chest. Of all the things the director could've called me into her office for, this was never an option in my wildest dreams. In one day, I'd been denied a job I had wanted but not been especially passionate about, only to be semi promoted in my top secret job that I was passionate about.

What a strange turn of events to be sure.

By the time I found my way back to my tiny office, my mind was crowded with the research options. I should look into possible artifacts, but my mind kept straying to questions about the Highland Werewolves, which inevitably led to lurid images that I definitely should not be thinking about at work.

I was so focused on this that when Reggie grabbed me in a hug, I screamed in shock.

"Did they hurt you?" he demanded. "Oh my gosh, did I hurt you?'

"No, no, nothing like that," I said, pushing against him until he let me go. "They wanted my help with a situation in Dublin. I'm actually going undercover on my first field mission. Isn't that exciting?!"

I bounced on my toes and clapped my hands together, as the fear took a momentary backseat.

Reggie's huge brown eyes stared at me, his wings fluttering, and then he smiled.

"I knew that someday, someone would recognize how wonderful you are. Congratulations."

"Thank you, Reggie, truly that is so very kind of you. Now, I have a mountain of work to do before meeting my contact and leaving tomorrow. You can have the rest of the day off, spend some time with Peter if you'd like, I'm sure he could use the company. And while I'm gone, you're in charge."

"Wait, what?" he gulped.

"You can do it. I know you can. Just put any shipments you're unsure of to the side and I'll take a look when I get back. It shouldn't be longer than a few days at most. I'm going to finish up a few things before leaving."

The air shimmered to my left and Reggie flushed.

"Thanks, Peter," he whispered before turning back to me. "I won't let you down."

"Of course you won't."

I gave him one last hug before going to my office and finishing up the work from this morning. The Druid artifacts still needed some attention, but no matter how much I tried to focus on the fascinating pieces, my mind kept wandering to what I might expect from tonight.

Despite the glamour, there had been the barest hint of something primal underneath Fraser's rugged good looks. A touch of a beast, leashed but wanting to come out. Would I get to see that side tonight, in my apartment? Now that I was alone in my office, my mind seemed to think it was alright to shed the academic questions and latch onto the more basic ones. Would the bite be an arousing act? Would it hurt a lot? Or would the pain be erotic? Would he want sex with me after? Would I want that? Would we both be overwhelmed with the desire enough to throw caution to the wind?

Will I, at last, experience being with a creature?

The question sent a rush of heat through me and my cheeks flushed.

In college, my studies about sex and culture had led me to the intersection of the macabre and sexual fantasy. I'd told myself it was just for study, that it wasn't anything more. And then I'd begun to have sex dreams about monsters dragging me out of my bed and doing darkly erotic acts with me in their lairs.Or chasing me through the night, ignoring my cries for help and taking me rough on the soft floor of a forest. It had been embarrassing at first, but the more I studied the more I realized that this was nothing to be ashamed of. It was a kink, one that might be different than others, but that didn't make it bad.

Fast forward to me attempting to write on that very subject for an end of year project and I suddenly had to face just how much shame there really was in academic circles when it came to sex, of any kind, but especially a kink like dub con monster boinking. And then there was the way my colleagues, and boyfriend, at the time had treated me when they found out about my interest. I'd never been able to forget the looks of disgust that had been shot my way. Or the whispers about the kind of woman that would want *that* kind of sex.

After that experience, I'd kept it my desires strictly in the realm of masturbatory fantasy, never telling another person about it for fear of their reaction.

Now here I was, about to receive a mating bite from a very sexy Werewolf. To say that I was aroused was a severe understatement.

But I have to remember that all this is for a cover story. It's not real! I cannot confuse fiction with fact. I can't run away with any of my fantasies tonight.

The thought sent my erotic hopes crashing and I was back down to earth, faced with the realities of the mission before me. I straightened my shoulders and tried to put a lid on my libido.

Best to face this rationally.

But the moment I pictured Fraser's huge, muscled frame morphing into an equally large, fur covered Werewolf, my best intentions disintegrated and I was carried away on whimsy.

I wonder if he'll hold me during the bite…he'd have to wouldn't he?

My breath picked up at the thought of being pressed against that huge body, of having his teeth sink into my flesh, marking me as his.

His…I'm going to be…No, best not to think about it like that. This is necessary for my cover, that's all. Nothing more.

But the damage to my focus had been thoroughly done and now I was flushed, my heart racing. I could almost feel his huge hands on my body. Would I be chest to chest with him, or would he pull my back to his front?

Would he be gentle or primal?

Would his eyes still be that rich brown from his glamour, or would they be yellow?

Wonderfully lurid thoughts unspooled in my mind, and I tried desperately to bring it all back to an academic focus.

Tried, and failed miserably.

So I put the Druid artifacts in a temporary holding unit and decided to search the Archive database for everything I could find on Werewolves and their mating rituals.

For professional purposes. After all, I'm going to need to know what I'm getting myself into…right?

CHAPTER SIX

FRASER

I paced outside in front of the building of Daphne's flat, looking at my watch for the third time and no less frustrated to discover that it was only two minutes since the last time I looked at it.

She was late, and my mind wandered to every single possible way someone might have harmed her on the way from Archive headquarters to her flat. It was ridiculous and strange. I wasn't even this protective of my brothers, and half the time they needed to be reined in. But this was just part of the odd way my mind and body had reacted to Daphne. Since leaving her in that office, I'd been unsettled. I thought maybe some food would help, maybe some whiskey. Maybe a brisk walk all over London and back.

Nothing worked.

So I'd decided to come to the flat at little early, hoping to suss out what this woman was. If I could do that, then I could possibly buy a charm from someone to help manage these impulses better.

That had been half an hour ago.

Now I was worse than ever and ready to tear apart this bloody city to find out what had happened to the lass. I was growling, my glamour slipping just a little in my eyes and sometimes my hands. It was scaring anyone that came near me and I knew that I had to get a hold of myself before I exposed what I was. That would cause more trouble that I didn't need right now.

Breathe. Just breathe. She's comin', she's just late, detained by work or maybe someone needed to talk to her…and then decided to lure her into a dark alley and mug her.

I pulled at my hair as frustration became anger.

Not only was I losing it over a woman that I didn't even know, I was about to tear off and try to find her like some kind of love sick, mated fool. And I hadn't even bitten her yet. What the hell was going to happen when I did?

It was madness, utter madness, to do this when I had no idea why my primal side was reacting to her in this way. I could hurt her, scare her and then I'd have to see that look in her beautiful green eyes.

The thought of making her terrified of me, of seeing the same disgust and horror that Silvia had worn on that day now on Daphne's face…

But why? Why should that matter to me? This woman is no one, just a means to an end. She'll find the artifact in a few days and be gone. What do I care if she thinks I'm a monster or not?

"It doesn't matter, Fraser, so get yer head out of yer arse and get a hold of yerself," I muttered.

I nodded, repeating this as I forced myself to stand still and stop acting like a pup with no self-control.

I'd managed to stop the racing of my mind and find a place approaching calm indifference when her scent came to me on the night air. It was tinged with the musty smell of books and leather, making me sneeze.

A minute later she appeared across the street, carrying an overstuffed tote that matched her shoes and scribbling something in a notebook as she walked. When I spied her, I had to stop myself from running up to her and demanding to know why she was late. It afforded me a few seconds to observe her, unaware. I took in the way she walked, and held herself. The way her lips moved as she scribbled, talking to herself about what? A spell, an answer to what was happening to my clan perhaps? If that was the case, then maybe she wouldn't have to go with me.

The thought brought a sigh of relief mixed with disappointment, which I ignored. Living with this constant storm inside of me was already exhausting and it had only been a few hours. I was about to simply call out and encourage her to walk a little faster when she crossed the street with her nose still buried in her stupid notebook.

What is she doing?

I peeled away from the building just as a car came straight for her. My heart lurched when she didn't even look up from what she was doing. She was about to be smashed to pieces and I panicked, leapt over the bench in front of me and sprinted across the street. Just as my arms went around her, the cab careened around us.

The cabbie screamed obscenities but I heard them from a distance. This woman was pressed tight against me, my hands around her upper arms. She stared up at me, eyes wide with shock and those kissable lips open as she gasped.

"Mr. MacDonald," she breathed, "where did you come from?"

"Where did I…?" I pulled her after me the rest of the way across the street. "Do ya have a death wish, lass? Ya cross the street without lookin' often, do ya?"

She looked back at the street, at me, then the street and back at me. Her skin was flushed and she gave me a lopsided smile.

"I'm sorry, I was lost in my notes," she said, tucking the notebook in her bag. "It's why I'm late actually. I was doing some research for the case."

"Did you find anythin'?"

"Not much I'm afraid," she looked down at where I still held her arms.

I let her go like she was a hot iron and stepped back. I'd have to be careful how close I allowed myself to get around her. She was trouble, and the last thing I needed was more of that.

"Sorry," I said, clearing my throat, "it's not every day I almost see a lass mowed down by a car."

"Yes, I'm sorry about that. I can sometimes get very distracted, but I assure you, I will be focused and aware on this job."

"That's good."

I waited as she stared up at me and shifted from foot to foot. Her scent was teasing my nose, like a hook in a fish's mouth, reeling me in and making it difficult not to lean toward her.

"Great, yeah, okay. Do you want to…"

A gurgling rumble rolled up from her stomach. She clapped her hands over her belly and gave me a wide eyed look of pure embarrassment.

"Sorry," she said. "I haven't had much to eat today between the fascinating artifacts we got in and the research I was doing about your mating rituals, which didn't really lead to anything because there aren't any records on the subject. Well, no reliable records I should say, it's honestly one of the most frustrating parts of my job, trying to sift truth from fiction. I mean you would not believe how many authors insist that Lycans and Werewolves are the same creatures when so clearly they…aren't…um…"

Her voice faded, lips moving in little pulses as if she were trying to find more words to add to the virtual fire hose she'd lobbed at me. In spite of the fact that I was tensing every muscle to resist whatever power she was unknowingly using, her voice had reeled me in and now I was close once again, my eyes intent on hers. I had to grudgingly admit that I wanted to know what else was in that mind, how was it so full that it overflowed and rushed out of those infinitely kissable lips? I took a step back and crossed my arms, schooling my features into a glare that usually had grown men scurrying away. I hated the thought of intimidating her, but maybe it was one way to get whatever magic she was using on me to dissipate and not come back.

"Sorry," she cleared her throat again and also took a small step back. "I can get a little verbose."

"I see that."

Her stomach growled again and she squeezed her eyes shut. I sighed, and swore under my breath. She was hungry and I couldn't just demand that she wait to get something for supper.

"There's a pub up on the corner," I gestured toward it, "would ya like to get a bite before…uh…"

"The *bite*?" she asked, grinning up at me.

And damn it, in spite of how hard I tried not to, my lips ticked up a little.

"Exactly."

"Sure, that would be nice."

I made sure to keep my strides small so that Daphne wouldn't have to run to keep up with me, even though I really did want this done as soon as possible.

"I wonder," she said, "if I might ask you a few questions about your clan, for our cover story?"

"I don't ken if that's necessary, yer only going to be there a few days."

"Oh…yes, I suppose…but if I'm to be your mate—"

"Ya only need to appear to be," I snapped, "and that doesn't need twenty questions. Just a bite."

"Oh. Alright," her voice, so bright and confident a moment ago, became small and her smile wobbly.

The point was to get her to back off, but I didn't want to take away the wonderful way she carried herself, or the spark of curiosity in her eye.

Can't have both. Och, this going to be a long meal.

We walked the rest of the short distance in silence. I hadn't known Daphne more than a few hours, but even I knew that her silence meant something was wrong. And, considering my behavior, it was probably my fault.

We found a table in the back and I squeezed into the booth. I missed the supernatural pubs in Scotland, of which there were many.

"What can I get you?" asked the waiter.

"Beer," I said. "Meat pie."

"Gin and tonic please, and a fish and chips."

The waiter nodded, leaving us in tense silence once more. I looked anywhere except at Daphne, which was hard when that was all I wanted to do. Our drinks arrived quickly, giving me something to do with my hands, and Daphne let out a little sigh of relief. She took a pull from her glass before getting her notebook out and starting to scribble in there.

My eyes wandered down to her bowed head, the curls falling against one flushed cheek. I wanted to wind those dark tendrils around my finger, to feel it's silkiness for myself. But instead, I took a long pull from my beer and ended up finishing it.

Daphne glanced up, and chuckled.

"Done already?"

"Aye."

She waited, and my mind cast about for something else to add, but I couldn't think of anything. So I waved down the waiter, ordered another and cringed internally at my behavior. There was being stand offish and there was being rude. I didn't want to be the latter.

"What are ya writin'?" I asked.

"What I read before I forget it."

"You can remember what ya read, word for word?"

"Sometimes. This is more general ideas, bits of information."

I nodded and silence once again took hold of us, more uncomfortable than before.

In the background, a Proclaimers song started and Daphne's head whipped up.

"Oh! I love this song. It's so romantic."

I snorted.

"You don't agree?"

"'I'm gonna be'? It's the whipped man's national anthem."

She opened and closed her mouth, her smile fading a bit and went back to her notebook.

Bloody hell, I keep sticking my foot in my mouth with this lass. And I shouldn't care but I do!

My mind scrambled for a safe topic to break the uncomfortable silence while we waited for our food.

"So," I said, forcing a smile into my voice, "Daphne, tell me how ya became the head of the…um…."

"Sexual Artifacts department?"

"Aye, that."

Her head tipped to the side as she took me in and I didn't care for feeling like I was a mystery to be solved.

"Well?"

"Sorry," she said, and took a sip of her drink. "It's just…well, I often find that supernaturals aren't as prudish about sex as Mundanes so I was surprised that you stumbled over it."

I fidgeted with the handle of my pint and shrugged.

"I didn't ken how comfortable ya were talkin' about it."

"Well, I'm actually quite comfortable. My job doesn't leave room for much else."

Now it was my turn to frown at her and try to see the hidden nooks and crannies of her mind. She came across like an adorable librarian, yet she had no shame when speaking of her profession.

"How did ya come to study this, if ya didn't mind me askin'?"

"I have always been curious about connections between people, about the politics of gender and how we got here. But it wasn't until I got to high school that I realized how much of a role sex has had in creating culture, in particular women's sexuality and the freedom we're are or aren't given to express it and how that can affect cultural norms in a broader context."

"Ya do all that with those artifacts?"

"Well not exactly, but I do apply my studies on sex and culture there."

Our food arrived and I knew that the waiter had heard her; his face was as red as a beet and he nearly dropped my meat pie in my lap in his hurry to leave.

"See?" Daphne said, chuckling. "Sex is shameful and mysterious when really it should be something we commonly, openly discuss so that it's demystified. It should be just as acceptable in stories as the violence we see so often. More so, in fact, since sex is far more of a natural act than violence. And while yes, not everyone is interested in it, it is still a more universally experienced act than, say, blowing up a building or taking out a giant shark. Not to mention, the health benefits of partaking in some kind of stimulation regularly. Did you know that some ancient cultures not only encouraged regular visitation to their fertility temples for sexual rites, but they also taught self-pleasure? I actually have several ancient cultures' version of sex toys from various fertility temples in my department. It's fascinating really, the things we could learn just from not being so prudish about something so natural."

The lass was telling me about her passions, her job, but my body wasn't getting the message that this was just a discussion. And while her enthusiasm was purely of an informational nature, I was frustrated to discover that my cock was as hard as a rock under the table. Images of how Daphne liked to be pleasured, and just where I could do that pleasuring, were filling my head faster than I could toss them out. I shifted in my seat, trying to adjust or just get my body to behave.

"Ya sound like a professor. Why are ya not teachin' this stuff?" I asked, hoping for ground that was less 'stimulating'.

Her face fell a little and she didn't answer me right away. Instead, she dug into her food with earnest and now my horny mind had a new thing to latch onto: the sight of her mouth opening around her fork, the way she chewed like she was savoring every bloody bite.

Fuck, lass! Do ya have to eat like yer having an orgasm?

I highly doubted she actually was intending to torture me, or be so damn alluring, but the fact remained; Daphne Reynolds was currently wreaking havoc with my self-control.

"I, uh, actually used to be a…well, sort of a professor," she finally said.

Her voice had gone flat, her smile more apologetic than enthusiastic. The animal in me wanted to know what had happened to change her mood. Had I said something and if so, how could I make it up to her?

Had someone else? In which case, who, and where, were they so I could beat them to a pulp?

"How do ya 'used to be' a professor?"

"It's a long story. But no, I have never been able to teach any of this. Most universities already have a similar curriculum or they're not interested, as I learned the hard way today."

She looked so forlorn, like this situation had sucked all the sunshine from her. And I could not stand it. I may be deeply annoyed by the way Daphne could affect me, but something in me would not allow her to remain so defeated.

"Well," I said, around a last bite of my meat pie, "I can't imagine ya in a stuffy old classroom givin' lectures. I think yer right where ya belong, makin' new discoveries and helpin' people."

Her face lit up. It was like the sun coming out for a moment on the gloomiest of days. And something in my chest loosened at the sight. Pride bloomed in me and I sat up straighter. I wanted to do that again, and more than that. I wanted to make her laugh, to make her sigh. To find out what made her gasp and cry out. I wanted to know what made her cry so I could avoid it. All of it.

But I shouldn't. I can't risk it.

"Thank you for saying that," she said with a wide, bright smile. "I do love my job. The ability to make discoveries and touch things that have been lost or hidden for thousands of years…there's no feeling like it! I just wish I could talk about it to my family. They aren't really impressed by an assistant to the restorationist."

"Fuck 'em then."

The words were out of my mouth before I could stop it.

Daphne let out a shocked giggle and covered her mouth.

"I'm sorry, I shouldn't have said that."

"No, it's quite alright. Believe me, I've thought far worse the last few years."

"It's not right to insult yer family. I don't know why I'm stickin' my foot in my mouth."

"Don't be embarrassed, I stick my foot in my mouth at least six times a day. It's nice to see someone else do it for a change."

"I sound like an eejit."

"No, you sound nervous, and it actually helps that I'm not the only one."

"I'm not nervous," I said around a mouthful of pie. "I just want this over with."

Her smile faded and she looked down at her basket of fish and chips.

"Yes, of course," and then softer, "that should've been obvious."

"Damn it, lass, I'm sorry."

She set her shoulders, and looked me in the eye. A moment ago, her smile had been relaxed, genuine and flat out gorgeous. Now it was tight, forced, as if she were trying to keep it together. The sight made guilt slice into me and I wished I could take back what I'd callously said.

"Thank you, Mr. MacDonald. I'll be done here in a moment and then we can proceed. I assure you that I don't want to all of this to take any longer than it has to either. Now, if you'll give me a few minutes to finish my meal, we can do what you came here for."

She gave me a curt nod and took a deliberate bite of her fish.

I'd wanted to make a safe distance between us, to make sure that whatever was happening to my primal side wouldn't spill over into this mission. And, I'd succeeded. Daphne was now quite closed off, but she was also hurt by my actions, and the urge to sooth her was so strong that I had to clench my jaw to keep the words from coming out.

Instead, I said, "I can do that." I threw down some money for the meal and muttered something about needing some air before leaving her at the table.

CHAPTER SEVEN

DAPHNE

I tried not to be nervous as Fraser escorted me back to my apartment, but that was futile.

The fish and chips churned in my stomach as we climbed the stairs to my apartment in silence. It wasn't just the way dinner had ended that had my hands turning clammy. It was the knowledge that in a few minutes, Fraser would be showing me his true form and biting my neck. It was a terribly intimate thing to happen between two strangers and I wished that I'd insisted on knowing a little more about Fraser at dinner rather than get my knickers in a twist over his obvious dislike for the situation.

Now I was facing something that I had very little knowledge about, and didn't know what to expect or brace for. The database had shockingly little about the mating bite. What I did find only confirmed that it was kept a secret among the clans, rarely if ever shared with outsiders and often times the culmination of a hand binding ceremony.

Nothing about the effects or why it was even necessary, other than the obvious marking a mate with the scent of another.

It doesn't matter. With any luck I'll only have it for a few days before I find the artifact and Fraser can growl and glare at someone else.

"Do you need anything in particular before we get started?" I asked, unlocking the door and turning on a small lamp by the door.

"Naw," he said, his voice gruff and firm.

I nodded.

"Well, I don't especially want bite marks on one of my favorite shirts, so if you'll excuse me, I want to change."

Before he could answer I spun on my heel and went into my room, shutting the door firmly. I'd told him the truth, but I also needed a moment. Seeing Fraser standing in my apartment, his handsome glower firmly in place, his hulking frame taking up all the air in the room, well, it affected me more than I thought possible.

I took a shaky breath as I changed into a T-shirt and pair of soft pink sweat pants. Honestly, it was the least sexy thing I owned and usually the outfit I wore during my monthly cycle, which was known for its stomach splitting cramps. But it was also the T-shirt that would give Fraser room to bite me without getting a mouthful of cotton in the process since the neck was well stretched out, exposing some of my shoulder as well as my neck.

A glimpse in the mirror had me gasping in horror at the tangled mess of my hair, currently falling half out of the braid. I quickly took it out, brushed it and rebraided it to the side so Fraser wouldn't have to worry about it.

"Alright, then," I said to myself, "you are a professional. And this is part of the job. It's nothing. A small bite and then tomorrow off to Scotland for a few days. You can do this."

A deep breath.

A nod to myself.

And I opened the door before the nerves and eroticism of what lay ahead could make me more of a basket case.

My apartment was quite small, with a bathroom at the end of the hall, my bedroom across from the small galley kitchen, the dining room more of a nook and the living room to the right of the front door. But the view was wonderful on sunny London days, which wasn't very often.

I stepped out of my room, turned toward the living room and stopped short.

Fraser was standing with his back to me, the low light casting shadows across his face as he thumbed through one of my favorite books. I must've left it on the side table between my small couch and the door during one of my re-reads. I couldn't help it, I stopped and studied him. He'd been so tense from the first moment of our meeting that I didn't think the man knew how to relax. But he had almost peaceful curiosity about him now as he looked through the book, which appeared very small between his huge hands. He'd rolled up the sleeves of his shirt, exposing forearms covered in dark hair and corded with muscle that flexed as he turned the pages.

"You can borrow it if you'd like," I whispered, not wanting him to turn around and find me staring at him.

Fraser jumped and the book clattered to the floor. He scrambled to pick it up, giving me a rather good look at his ass in those jeans.

"I'm sorry, I didn't mean to pry," he said, plopping it back onto the table by the couch.

"Not at all. I'm the same way when it comes to books. I can't help it, when I see one I have to pick it up."

My voice faded on the last few words because Fraser was staring at me, his hands curled into fists at his side. The look in his dark eyes could only be described as feral, as if I were a rabbit caught in a trap and he was about to devour me.

I swallowed, willing my pulse to slow as I took a hesitant step in his direction. I realized too late that I'd forgotten to put socks on, so my feet slapped against the hardwood floors, my bright red toe nails peeking out from the hem of my sweats.

"I hope…I mean, I just wanted to be comfortable," I said.

His gaze intensified, darting down my body in a way that made my hands shake with nerves. Was it appraising or judgmental? I'd had my fair share of both, and I couldn't help hoping that Fraser was looking at me with former instead of the latter

"It's…it's fine," his brogue was rough, growly even.

I nodded, willing myself to think about this clinically. This was…this was…

An experiment! I am about to participate in something most people don't know anything about. So, it's like a research experiment. I'll take in all the sensations and then make notations of it in my book. Yes…this is an experiment.

It barely helped the drop of my stomach as Fraser's eyes snapped back up to mine.

"Have ya ever seen a Werewolf?" he asked.

I shook my head.

"Not in person."

He let out a long breath through his nose.

"I can't do the bite with my glamour on. But I didn't want to scare ya."

He said it with genuine fear, which made me wonder if others had made him feel monstrous in his true form. The thought gripped my heart with compassion. I, too, knew what it was like to be judged on appearance alone, and while I'd worked quite hard to be comfortable in my own skin, it still stung when others carelessly formed their opinions about me.

"It will be fine," I said.

"Ya don't ken that."

His voice was low, hesitant, and I couldn't help reaching out to him. The second my hand landed on his arm, Fraser's gaze turned hot and the words I was going to say died on my lips.

"I…I'm not afraid," I finally got out.

How had we gotten so close?

I craned my neck to look up at him. I could see the green flecks in his dark eyes, the sensual curve of his mouth, half hidden under his thick beard. His arm flexed under my hand and a second later, his large hands were on my hips, kneading the flesh there in a possessive way that stole my breath.

"What are ya doin' to me?" he demanded, his head lowered, breath hot and fast against my cheek.

"I…I don't know what you're talking about."

The air was suddenly thick, charged with a scent I couldn't quite place. It was heady, making my thoughts spin as if I were high on something. I came just to the middle of Fraser's wide chest, but his head was bent so that his mouth was dangerously close to mine, and his canines were elongating. Were those claws on his hands now, biting into my skin?

"If ya don't stop…"

"Stop…what? I don't…Fraser is this part of—"

"Naw, it's not…"

Now, instead of skin there was luxuriously soft fur, dark as midnight under my hands. I stared up into golden eyes, flared and filled with molten heat that sent shivers down my spine. His snout was shorter than I expected and I longed to run my finger there to discover if it was as velvet soft as it appeared.

I'd barely raised my arm when Fraser spun me around, my back to his suddenly bare front. One long, strong arm banded around my middle and pressed my hips back so that my ass was now flush with something very hard, and very long.

Oh my god, that can't be what I think it is.

I gasped at the low growl that erupted from his mouth as he pulled my head to the side, baring the left side of my neck and shoulder. My body braced for the sting of his teeth and I trembled, but not in fear. The way he took control of me, the sensation of such a large creature holding me tight and the feel of his nose brushing along my skin. I'd imagined such things hundreds of times, never expecting to experience it. And yet, here I was, trembling in anticipation of something that I should not have been wanting, but did.

"Don't be afraid," his impossibly deep burr rumbled through me like thunder. "I won't hurt ya."

"It's a bite," the words came out in puffs of air.

"I'll make it feel good. I can take the pain away. Please, let me?"

His teeth grazed the place my neck and shoulder met, hot breath skating across me like a physical touch.

"Yes," I moaned.

"Don't move. Trust me."

The request was sheer insanity. I'd only just met this Werewolf this afternoon, and now here he was, poised to sink his teeth into me while I was pinned against his very warm, very firm body. I should be terrified, whimpering and pleading for mercy. And I did feel a bitter pang of fear, but it only seasoned the more prominent feeling of lust and desire. Later, I would have a clear enough head to wonder at the sudden shift, at the way our bodies had reacted to a simple touch on the arm. But right now, I was on a wave that was pulling me further away from safety by the second.

And I didn't want to be saved.

I laid my head against his chest, he was too tall for me to reach his shoulder, and closed my eyes. The hand that had been holding my head traveled down to my shoulder and then my chest, the claws grazing my breast and circling my embarrassingly erect nipple.

"Fraser," the name floated out of my mouth, carried on a gasp.

It was involuntary, said by a different woman than the one I'd been when I walked into this apartment.

He groaned and ran his nose down the length of my neck, from my ear to my shoulder.

"I don't ken how yer doin' this,"

"I'm not—"

"And I don't care. I need…Oh, goddess above forgive me."

I had a moment to feel the sensation of his hot, wet mouth against the skin he'd been licking a moment earlier before the sharp pain of his teeth sank through my flesh. I cried out and he held me fast against him. I had expected something quick, but he kept his teeth deep into my skin for longer. I became afraid that perhaps something was indeed wrong, that he would kill me this way if his primal side was too far in control.

But then the pain began to fade, a comforting warmth taking its place, like the moment after taking a sedative, where the world was blissful and calm just before I fell asleep. The warmth spread and transformed into heat, blazing its way through my body and settling at my core. In seconds, I was utterly lost in a haze of arousal, my ass grinding against him, my hand reaching up to curl into the soft fur at his neck. I wasn't even aware of his teeth piercing me anymore, just the way he thrust against me, as if he too was powerless to do anything else.

When his teeth finally left my shoulder, I whimpered at the loss. But his mouth wasn't gone from me for long.

He turned my face to him and took my mouth in a brutal kiss. Distantly, I wondered how this wasn't far more awkward. His mouth was wider than mine but somehow his lips molded to mine perfectly.

I moaned at the strange sensation of his tongue plundering my mouth. It was so thick and rough, so foreign feeling, yet also, right in a way I could not name. Everything about him that had been alien before now felt like home. I wanted him to carry me to bed, curl around me and never let me go.

One huge, clawed hand captured my breast and squeezed, while the other tightened against my belly. I was too drunk on what he was doing to even care that he was gripping one of my most fleshy parts. I just wanted *more*.

His mouth left mine and he licked his way down my neck to the bite, his tongue laving it. Sensations burst like fireworks behind my eyes and I rubbed my thighs together. Whimpering moans left my mouth as he continued to work on my body.

"Mine," he growled, "my mate. Ya taste so good, feel so good."

"Fraser," I breathed, unable to say anything else.

There was only him, his heat, his soft fur against me, the claws grazing my skin as he roamed my flesh with a possessive touch that sent fire coursing through me. I writhed beneath his hands as his hips bucked into mine from behind. Everything that was proper, that was professional was a distant memory. The only thing I knew was the desperate, throbbing need between my legs.

"Please," I begged, "please touch me."

With a shuddering breath, his hand began to at last travel below my belly. But just as one long, clawed digit was about to slip beneath the top of my sweats, a different kind of sensation ripped through all the others and I gasped in genuine pain, as one of his claws tore through the shirt and drew a thin line of blood just below my belly button.

Whatever spell had been cast upon us shattered, breaking so completely that we were both brought back to ourselves, panting and gasping with the dregs of what had happened.

Fraser moved the hand resting on my belly and I hissed.

He jumped back, letting me go so suddenly that I stumbled and he had to catch me around the shoulders to keep me from falling. The moment his hands were back on my body, I knew without having to look that he'd put his glamour back up. The sense of something being very wrong hit me and I squirmed for him to let me go. He did, then lunged around to face me.

We both looked down at the place where one of his claws had scratched me.

"Oh my god," he breathed, pulling a fist full of hair. "Oh my god, I'm sorry. I'm so sorry, Daphne."

"It's—'

"Stay right there, let me get somethin' to…just stay right there."

He tore off down the short hallway to the bathroom at the end. I heard the water running as I stared down at the cut. It wasn't that long, maybe half an inch, and it wasn't bleeding all that much, but Fraser was acting as if he'd gutted me.

When he came back, his dark eyes were wild and there was a grim set to his lips under his beard. I reached for the wet cloth he had in a death grip but he ignored me. Instead, this beast of a man knelt in front of me and pulled my shirt up just enough to see the cut.

He pressed the cold cloth to the cut, more gently than I thought possible from a man of his size.

"I'm sorry," he whispered. "I never wanted to hurt ya."

"Fraser," I reached under his chin and made him look up at me. "It was an accident. I'm fine."

He let out a long sigh and nuzzled into my palm. A moment later, his eyes closed and I reached down with my other hand, brushing some of his hair back from his forehead. A sound, very much like a contented huff, came from him and I smiled.

"You don't have to wear the glamour," I said, hoping he'd drop it. "I'm not afraid of you."

"I…"

His hand on my belly moved, scraping the cloth across the cut and I hissed at the sudden, sharp pain.

Fraser's eyes flew open at my reaction and he jumped to his feet.

"I need to go," he shoved the washcloth into my hand before bolting out the door.

"Wait, I—"

But he was already closing the door.

I stood there, my mind stunned into stillness for the first time I could remember. It was beyond strange to feel bereft at Fraser's absence but that was precisely what it was like. I'd been warm, treasured for a few brief, wonderful moments. And then abandoned.

It was illogical, dramatic.

But also true, and I was having a terrible time shaking it off.

I need to do something…anything.

The cut had already stopped bleeding but it should have a bandage. Still, it took me a minute or two to convince my legs to move. When I got into the bathroom my reflection had me stopping cold.

I was flushed, my mouth swollen from his kisses, and the evidence of his teeth scraping against my jaw and neck was bright against my pale skin. But none of that really mattered.

No, what I couldn't stop staring at, what consumed everything until it was the only thing I could focus on, was the oval shaped mark on the top of my shoulder. I should've been bleeding, or at least have an open wound like the one on my stomach. But it looked more like an old scar, with its red and white raised impressions. I ran my finger along it and was shocked to realize just how hot it was, as if that part of my body had a fever.

This was where his mouth was only a few minutes ago. This marks me as his.

It was thrilling, and terrifying, and confusing.

I wanted him here with me, and yet I was also grateful that he wasn't as I tried to process all of this. I must've stared at the mark, touching and caressing it for another fifteen minutes before the brush of fabric against the cut made me remember that I hadn't taken care of that yet. It didn't take long to clean and bandage it but when I did, fatigue hit me like a truck and I stumbled to my bed. It was still relatively early, and I really did need to document my experiences.

But as I pulled my comforter up and around me, it was all I could do to reach over and turn off the bedside lamp. Before I could even run through my packing list for tomorrow, I was asleep.

CHAPTER EIGHT

FRASER

My entire body felt like a live wire, every nerve ending was firing, my muscles tense and shaky. I'd run out of Daphne's apartment and into the cool night air as if something truly terrifying was chasing me.

And in all honesty, it was terrifying. Just not in the way most would see it.

I needed something to take my mind completely away from the knowledge that was slowly dawning. I couldn't think of it without fighting every instinct in my body. If I wasn't careful, I would run back into that flat and finish what we'd started.

I needed something ugly, something difficult to channel these feelings into. And there was only one thing in this city that I knew of that would do.

I ran to the nearest underground entrance and down the stairs. It wasn't so late that it was deserted, but the crowds were light and either made up of tired people on their way home from work, or couples too caught up in one another to notice a large Scotsman charging around like a bull.

I found the door marked "No entry. Service only" and let my glamour slip just in my eyes. A red light came up and scanned my retinas; a second later the lock on the door popped and I stepped through. My glamour was completely stripped as soon as I crossed the threshold, which was fine by me.

When the door shut, the passage way was completely dark for a brief moment until the low lights that ran along ceiling came on. It wouldn't have mattered if they had stayed off, I could see very well in the dark. I made it down the bare, gray hall to the door at the end where a short Orc stood guard, his biceps as large as my head.

"Password?" he asked.

I cringed. This month's password was truly awful.

"Venus of the lovely buttocks."

As I stepped through the door, the stench of sweat and beer and too many different supernatural species all crammed into a tight space hit me and made my eyes water. Behind the smell, the air was thick with the excitement of illegal betting and the inherent tension of a fight in progress.

These kinds of supernatural fight clubs were in every major city in the world, and somewhat regulated to prevent too many causalities. Most of us knew, however, that when we crossed that threshold, we took our lives into our own hands. I'd never been afraid to wade into the fray, as it were. My family was big and liked to brawl to blow off steam. So when I finally took to the ring in these clubs, I knew how to take a punch more than most, and how to find the weakness in an opponent. It didn't take long for the other fighters to learn not to underestimate me.

There was a large crowd tonight, and I wove my way through the beings loitering near the door. The room was one big circle, with makeshift stands to my left and the simple canvas ring in the center. To my right was what passed for a bar in these places and that's where I headed. I needed a drink, and then a good and bloody fight to wipe Daphne from my senses.

I knew I wasn't thinking straight but that lass had turned my head. After tasting her skin and blood I knew that she didn't have a drop of supernatural in her. She wasn't even attuned to magic very much.

That left only one thing, one reason why she had affected me in such a way and it was something that I couldn't allow to progress. No, I had to smash these feelings, bury them under the pain of a brawl. And, if that didn't work, there was plenty of cheap Fae whiskey to be had.

I slapped some money down onto the sticky counter of the bar.

"Whiskey, and I don't wanna see the bottom of the glass."

The Fae behind the bar, a male with close cropped white hair and bright pink skin, nodded as he set the first drink down.

I stretched my neck and flagged down the fight coordinator to put my name in for a bout. Everything here was meant to make the outside world a distant thing so that people stayed far too long and spent far too much. And it usually worked for me. But no matter how many times I breathed deep of the stench, no matter how much I tried to watch the fight in front of me, or how fast I drank the whiskey, Daphne's smell, her face, the feel of her was sharply present.

She'd been so soft in my arms, pliable and responsive. I'd wanted to nibble on her breasts and find out if she liked her nipples suckled. Would she like my tongue through her soft folds as much as she seemed to like it in her mouth?

And dear god, the taste of her skin. It was sweet and rich, like wine on a Beltane night. I could be drunk just from running my tongue over every inch of her. Her ass grinding against my cock had driven me to the edge of self-control, I was seconds away from bending her over and rutting her hard and thorough.

Then I'd hurt her, just like monsters tend to do with fragile Mundanes.

I winced and tossed back the whiskey. I would get a hold of these feelings, I would.

They would not control me. They would not make me act the monster with her. If I had to drink the entire time, if I had to busy myself day and night to stay away from her, I would do it. And then the moment she found the item causing all this trouble with my clan, I'd bring in the witch to undo this.

The thought made something in my chest crack and I let out an involuntary whimper. The desire to keep her was deeply embedded in me already, another sign that she was…

Don't even think it, Fraser MacDonald! Don't acknowledge this insanity.

"I thought you didn't fight anymore," said a familiar voice behind me.

"And I thought ya were gonna to meet me at the pub," I shot back as I turned around and looked at the huge Gargoyle behind me.

James was seven feet tall and wide enough in his true form that fitting through doors was an issue half the time. His wing span was enormous, and rightly so in order to bear him up into the sky. In crowds like this, he glamoured them away so that no one touched them. His chest was bare, the tattoos of his clan in twin sleeves on his arms. His slacks were always fitted perfectly, a trick of his glamour I'd assume, especially since they always had a hole for his thick, long tail that was constantly twitching to alert him to enemies. And his clawed feet clicked on the floor as he closed the short distance between us. His dark hair was slicked down and pulled into a tight que at the back of his neck, his horns curling on either side of his head and giving off faint little glowing pulses as different supernatural creatures drew near to him.

Most Gargoyles had a sort of radar when it came to our kind; they could see through any glamour and determine different things about the creature. Some had this ability honed like a sixth sense, others barely registered anything. Given his profession, James was in the former category.

His dark eyes scanned the crowd behind me and his large mouth set into a thin line.

"It was unavoidable," he murmured, "my apologies."

"Well, now that yer back, can you take my case up or naw?"

"No, I'm afraid."

I swore and drained another whiskey.

"What's wrong?" James asked, frowning down at me.

"They've given me a green lass that's not right for the job."

James crossed his arms and his muscles bulged ridiculously.

"The director seems to know what she's doing, though I had my doubts at first. If she assigned this agent, then she must think it will work. So what's your issue?"

"My issue is that she's distractin'."

"Really? She must very pretty, beddable even."

I snarled at him.

"Don't talk about her like that!"

His eyes widened.

"No way, is she…are you—?"

"Annoyed? Frustrated? Not in the mood? Aye."

"I see."

James flagged down the fight coordinator.

"I'd like to ask to be placed opposite Fraser MacDonald for his first bout, please."

Now, that stopped me mid drink and I turned around to stare at my friend.

"Y-yes sir, um," the fight coordinator, a short Fae that I suspected was a Leprechaun, licked his lips nervously. "Do you want me using your real name, or shall I put down an alias?"

Agents of the Secret Archive weren't supposed to fight at these clubs. Hell, even being here was treading the line of what was and wasn't acceptable. And knowing James' love of following rules, I imagined that he had an ulterior motive for being here. Fighting me though? That was something else entirely.

"My name is just fine," he said and slipped the Leprechaun a Fae gold piece.

"Yes, sir! Right away!"

The whiskey was still clutched forgotten in my hand as I stared at James.

"What in the name of the Great Mother happened to ya?" I asked.

He chuckled, a deep sound like thunder.

"Relax, I'm not compromised. I have my reasons. I let you beat me up in the ring—"

"Let me?"

"— and then you help me with a suspect."

And there it was. James only ever appeared to break the rules when it was for a very good reason. Sometimes I wondered at the mental gymnastics he must have to perform to do his job and not infringe on his moral code.

"Besides," he continued, "I think you need someone you can truly unleash on. And that's not anyone else here."

"Ya have a point."

Just then the announcer called our names. I tossed back the whiskey and followed James onto the low canvas mat.

We both made a show of stretching, whipping the audience into a bit of a frenzy as they realized they were going to see two enormous beings beat the shit out of one another. I had to confess that their excitement was contagious. I hadn't been in a good brawl in too long.

"You both know the rules," the announcer, a short fella that looked half Goblin said. "No claws, no teeth, no supernatural powers. Grappling is fine unless the opponent taps out. We're not going for the kill so if you start to frenzy, we'll use the cattle prod, got it?"

We both nodded and squared off with one another. As my focus narrowed to James, I slipped past the memories of Daphne's skin, the sound of her breathy moans as I ground against her. All that was left was the giant gargoyle in front of me. Even the excited shouts of the crowd had dulled to the background.

When the bell rang, I struck first with a sharp jab to the face, followed by a body blow. James was ready for it and blocked my second punch. He followed it with an upper cut that sent me stumbling back. I tasted blood on my tongue and grinned at him.

Now this was what I came here for.

After that it was a wild flurry of blows, neither of us holding back. Since James couldn't put on his stone skin, I was saved from getting pummeled by fists made of granite, but he still hit harder than a truck. Soon, James grabbed onto me, grappling with me to try and throw me to the mat. If he'd been in earnest, I would've been done for, but he was holding back.

"The bookie is funneling artifacts through here," he whispered in my ear. "I placed bets on the previous fights, and I'll take him when I go to collect. Wanna be my back up? Blow off more steam?"

I grinned.

"Do ya even need to ask?"

"Let me throw you to the mat while you've still got some fight in you."

I snorted.

Usually, I would bite my own hand off rather than throw a fight. But James and I went way back, and if he needed my help, I couldn't say no.

"Fine," I growled, "but ya owe me a good pint."

"Deal."

He threw me down and pinned me to the canvas. I tapped out and the sounds of groans and triumphant yells mingled in the air.

James helped me up and we shook, both of us wiping blood off our faces.

"That was fun," James said as we made our way to the back. "You should come by the Archive gym some time. Show the younger agents how it's done."

"No thanks."

"Still a grumpy loner?"

I huffed out a breath and ignored the jibe. He knew I was, and I didn't have any reason to change it.

Except one. A bonny lass with dark hair and eyes that shine when she looks at me…Damn it.

"Where's this bookie?" I growled, doing my best to keep Daphne in the furthest cavern of my mind.

"C'mon."

I followed James to the bar and he flashed his Archive badge, indicating that the Fae bartender should be quiet. The man nodded, oddly unfazed and motioned at the door to the left of the bar.

James barely fit through it and I wondered how many times he had to use his glamour to shrink his size with most places too small for him. But I shoved the distraction away as we walked down the short hall to the doorway on the left. The room was in complete disarray as the young Orc began to shove clothes in a bag, his movements frightened. When the floorboards creaked under our weight, his head flew up, lavender eyes widening. But it wasn't James that he was staring at, it was me.

"I didn't have anything to do with that business with your clan," he said, holding out his hand as if to keep me back. "I swear it. That's not me!"

Anger rolled through me, and my fur stood on end. I stalked toward him, backing the Orc toward the far wall.

"What business with my clan?" I growled.

Something impossibly bright flashed through the room, momentarily blinding me. I cried out and clutched at my face, the sounds of scuffling in the room the only thing that told me what was happening.

"Damn it," James hissed. "Fraser, you alright?"

I blinked, bright spots dotting my vision as the room slowly came back to me. James appeared unaffected, likely because he'd raised his stone skin in enough time to avoid whatever that had been.

"He used an artifact, are you injured?"

"Naw," I snarled, "just very angry!"

When I could fully see the room, the Orc was face down on the floor, James holding him with one large foot. Around the Orc's wrists were a pair of glowing handcuffs.

"Elliot Ness' handcuffs," James explained. "Unbreakable and compels the wearer to tell the truth."

"Get the fuck off me!" the Orc snarled. "I don't know anything about the clan!"

I bent down, and bared my teeth at him. My blood was running hot from the fight with James and now this. I scraped one of my razor sharp claws along the wood floor by the Orc's face, carving deeply into the grain.

"Is that supposed to scare me?" he asked. "You two don't know what scary is."

"What is it then?" I growled. "Tell me, so I can prove that I'm the thing ya should fear."

He pressed his lips together, trying very hard not to say something. I glanced at the handcuffs that were glowing brighter.

"Trying to resist the cuffs isn't pleasant," James said with a sinister grin. "But by all means, keep trying if you wish to be in excruciating pain."

"Who are ya afraid of?" I demanded.

"The other agents!" he screeched.

"What other agents?" James asked.

He gasped, sweat breaking out on his forehead.

"I…I can't…tell you!"

He screamed like someone was carving him up.

"Just tell me and the pain will end!"

"I-I can't! They'll kill my mother…they'll hurt her bad!"

The Orc began to sob and James sighed.

"I know who it is," he said. "The rogue agents, the ones that stole the shipment in the first place. He's just one of several places where they've stashed the artifacts until they can move them. Isn't that right?"

The Orc sobbed out a "yes" and shuddered.

"Where are the artifacts? I swear, we will protect you and your mother but you have to tell us where they are."

"You can't even protect your own shipments," the Orc shot back.

I wanted to know about my clan, not the damn shipments but I also knew that James tended to be single minded when it came to his mission. I glanced up at him, and he must've seen the questions churning inside of me. He let out a long exhale and gave me a short nod.

"Fine, if you don't want to tell me about the shipments, then tell me about clan MacDonald."

He tried to hold the answer back and the cuffs now let out a hissing sound like cooking meat. He screeched and shook.

"They talked about your clan!" he screamed. "Said that you were a good experiment for what came next. "

James frowned at me and I could only stare back.

So the artifact was given to someone in my clan on purpose. But why?
James beat me to that question.

"It was an accident," the Orc said. "I heard them talking. Something went wrong. Your clan was shipping artifacts and someone stole one. But they were going to let it go, see what happened before getting it back. That's all I know, I swear it!"

My stomach dropped and I turned wide eyes to James.

"We would never ship artifacts," I said.

"I know that. Either the manifests were doctored to hide the fact, or someone in your company is dirty. But no matter the reason, your clan is now square in the cross hairs of this mess. I'm sorry, Fraser."

"Yer mission intersects with this. Now will ya talk to Director Dearborne about replacin' the agent she chose?"

"You may be right Fraser, but no, I won't do that."

I turned away from him, biting back a curse.

"I don't know what has your fur in a bunch," James said, putting a heavy hand on my shoulder, "but you need to let it go. We are stretched very thin and I can't just abandon my mission."

"She's too green for this!" I hissed out. "She'll get hurt if these other agents are involved."

"The director will see that she's outfitted properly to compensate for that."

It was the best I was going to get and it wasn't enough.

I'll just have to figure out a way to resist her.
It was a fool's hope, I knew that. But it was also the only thing I could do to refrain from crossing all the lines that an honorable Were

would never cross. No one but the lowest kind of being would ever force themselves on anyone just because they were…

Stop, don't even think it!

"I've got to wait for the team to get here and search the place," James said. "It's going to be a while. You can stick around if you'd like."

"Naw, thanks."

"Fraser," he stopped me with a hand on my chest as I was heading for the door. "I believe this will all turn out for the best."

I snorted.

"Well, that makes one of us," I clapped him on the shoulder and gave him a halfhearted smile. "Ya still owe me a pint."

James returned my smile with a hard one of his.

"And maybe a rematch?"

My grin widened.

"Deal."

CHAPTER NINE

DAPHNE

The next morning, I was awakened by the sound of someone banging on my door. After a moment of groggy confusion, I bolted out of bed with equal parts hope and horror that it was Fraser.

"Who is it?" I asked through the door.

"Marcus and Sprite from the Archive's Outfitters department."

I frowned. I knew of Marcus, he was one of the agents in charge of the Outfitters, the supply department that helped agents with gadgets and such. I had no idea who Sprite was, but I opened the door anyway.

The second the door was unlatched, it was shoved open the rest of the way by a person with thick soled knee high boots, ripped fish nets, short shorts and a magenta suit jacket without a shirt. Their light brown skin was dusted with glittery powder and a cascade of dreads in many bright colors fell down their back. They lugged a large case behind them, wearing a look of exasperation accented by dark makeup.

"You couldn't get a flat with a bloody lift?" they snarled.

"I'm… I'm sorry," I stuttered.

"Don't mind Sprite, they haven't had their coffee yet."

I turned to see a young Black man about my height with gorgeous brown eyes accented by Fox style eyeliner and mermaid eye shadow. His lips were a subtle pink shade and his faux hawk was silvery white. He was clad in dark blue skinny pants, white heels and a flowing white and blue top with huge puffed sleeves.

"I'm Marcus," he said, extending a hand with an impeccable manicure. "Pleasure to meet you, love. We're here to go over your approved supplies."

I eyed the two suitcases and duffel that Sprite was opening in my living room.

"Oh don't worry, that's not all for you. I just like to come prepared." He let out a low whistle and gestured to the bite on my neck. "Someone had an interesting night."

My hand clapped against the mark as heat rushed to my face.

"I, uh, it's for my cover. For the mission."

Marcus held up his hands.

"I'm not judging, love. I've had plenty of fucks on the wild side."

Sprite snorted.

"Is there any other kind with you?"

"Someone woke up with their knickers shoved up their arse."

Sprite flipped Marcus off and proceeded to lay out items on my couch.

"Might be best to put on a pot, love," he whispered, "or they'll just get worse."

"I heard that, you wanker,"

Marcus rolled his eyes and sighed heavily.

"Uh, sure," I said, stumbling over my own feet as I moved toward the kitchen.

Coffee actually sounded like an awesome idea since I'd had a terrible night of sleep. I'd drifted off just fine but then I found myself waking up all throughout the night in a panic.

I'm just worried about the mission. Once I get going today I should be better. I just need to see what I'm dealing with.

I stifled a yawn as I started the coffee maker and pretended that I couldn't hear Sprite and Marcus whisper fighting a few feet away.

"It should be ready soon," I hollered.

"Good, come over here," Sprite said.

I walked into my living room, which had suddenly become an Archive supply show room in the short time I'd been in the kitchen. There were devices laid out on my coffee table, half of which looked like they belonged in some kind of fantasy novel. Artifacts were laid out in transparent neutralizer boxes on my couch. And now Sprite was holding up a couple of different—

"A bustier?" I squeaked. "I-I don't need lingerie."

Sprite's dark eyes surveyed my body and I got the distinct impression that they knew my exact size just from that once over.

"It's bullet proof," Sprite said.

"I don't think I'll be getting shot at."

"You never know," they handed me a black one, as well as one in a Caucasian flesh tone. "These should fit but try them on anyway."

I clutched the beautiful and functional underwear and stared open mouthed at them.

"Go on, I haven't got all day."

"Geez Sprite, it's her first mission, go easy."

Sprite put their hands on their hips and glared at Marcus.

"You remember the last agent we went easy on?"

Marcus' expression softened and he put his hand on their shoulder.

"That wasn't your fault."

Sprite shrugged him off.

"I ignored my gut and they were killed."

Marcus sighed and glanced at me.

"It's been a rough week."

"A lot of that going around," I said and looked at Sprite. "I'm sorry about the other agent."

Sprite wiped a tear from their cheek and nodded.

"Trust me, when my gut says you need something, you need it," they said. "So come with me and we'll fit you for this."

"Um," my stomach dropped as I realized that they'd see me naked from the waist up.

Sprite sighed and headed toward my bedroom, with me following.

"I've seen every kind of body known to Mundane and supernatural. I once fitted a thong for a Basilisk woman, most beautiful tail I'd ever seen. But if you're uncomfortable, I can turn around while you put it on."

I desperately wanted to ask about the Basilisk but I refrained since this was business and Sprite did not strike me as someone who would be in to gossip. I took a deep breath and lifted my sleep shirt above my head, baring me in the chilly air of my bedroom. Sprite frowned and took a few measurements, then pressed on a few concealed buttons on the black bustier. I heard the fabric rustle as the lingerie began to change shape before my eyes.

"Oh my, that is fascinating!" I gasped.

"Yeah, it's spell cloth combined with some fancy nanotech. The new director is letting our design and research team finally get back to helping agents instead of…well, never mind. The only drawback is we can't sell any of this to the Mundane markets. Real shame if you ask me"

The lingerie fit as if it had been made for me. Not only did it tuck and smooth my torso, but it lifted my breasts perfectly. I looked like one of the plus sized underwear models I'd seen at a fashion show my cousin had dragged me to last year. Or at least, as close as I'd ever get to that.

"It's not as uncomfortable as I thought it would be," I marveled.

"They're only uncomfortable if they're aren't fitted correctly. The way the spell cloth and nanotech talk to one another means that it can take your measurements just by being close to you and then it alters its shape to fit."

"That explains the places you were pressing on?"

Sprite nodded, looking the lingerie over with a critical eye.

"I think this should do. I'll make the adjustment on the other one too. They'll be calibrated for you alone to not only fit you, but protect you as well."

"How? You mentioned bullet proof but what else?"

"There's a spell woven into each one of them. It will protect you against most artifacts. You'll still probably get hurt, but you won't die."

I nodded, mouth suddenly dry. It foolishly hadn't occurred to me to be worried about dying on this mission.

"Well, hello there," Marcus said from somewhere in my apartment.

A familiar growly burr answered him and I gasped.

"Oh no, that's Fraser. I'm not even packed or ready!"

"Relax, Marcus will explain everything."

I nodded, still not sure Fraser would be understanding.

"Should I wear this all the time or…?"

"I just give you the stuff. Not my job to tell you that," Sprite said abruptly, and walked out.

I stared at myself a little longer, wondering what I'd gotten myself into. I was no field agent; I was a researcher, a glorified librarian on most days. I belonged at a desk, pouring over old manuscripts, not being fitted for a bullet proof bustier!

It was getting hard to breath and tears fell in hot drops down my cheek. The mark on my shoulder began to throb and I ran my hand over it, clutching it for some reason, as if it were a life line.

A moment later there was a hard knock at my door.

"Lass, ya alright?" Fraser asked on the other side.

"Uh, yes! I'm–I'm fine! Just a little behind that's all."

"Well, don't worry. Our train isn't for another two hours."

"Okay…great."

I heard him walk away and closed my eyes.

I can do this. I can do this.

By the time I'd taken a quick shower, and packed my suitcase and largest tote with a week's worth of clothes, toiletries, and research supplies, Fraser had been alone with Marcus and Sprite for nearly forty-five minutes. I worried there might nothing left of the two agents by the time I got out there, considering how taciturn Fraser could be.

Imagine my surprise when I walked into my living room to see Marcus laughing loudly, Sprite smirking into their coffee cup and Fraser standing there with the biggest grin I'd ever seen on the Werewolf. Of course, he had his glamour on so he looked like a tall, bearded Scotsman with a body that would have made teenage me lost for words.

And, really, before I'd seen his true form last night, I would've thought that nothing could top Fraser's glamour. He was the fantasy of anyone remotely attracted to men.

But I found myself stifling a dual disappointment as I parked my suitcase in front of the front door. I wanted to see the real Fraser, the Werewolf with the strong arms and primal growl. And I wanted him to laugh as easily with me as he seemed to do with Marcus and Sprite.

When he saw me, his smile slipped a little, and it was like a knife to my chest. I reached up and absently rubbed the bite, as if that would sooth the ache his dislike of me caused. His gaze snagged on the movement, eyes flaring yellow for a moment and his jaw tightening before he turned away and focused on drinking his own cup of coffee.

"We understand you've got a train to catch," Marcus said, "so we'll make this quick."

I nodded, pushing my complicated feelings about Fraser aside. This was my job, not a hook up, for Christ's sake.

"These have been sanctioned by the director for your use," Marcus pulled on some protective gloves and picked up a pair of sparring gloves. "Amanda Nunes' training gloves. They'll give you speed, strength and agility in a hand to hand situation. The draw backs are minimal but you may experience some…well, rage issues."

I slipped the gloves into an artifact retrieval bag to keep them neutral until I needed them and put them in my tote bag.

Next, Marcus withdrew a small gun that looked more like something out of a science fiction novel. It was silver and sleek with a coil in the center inside a clear casing where bullets would go in a more traditional gun.

"This the Electric Coiled Stunner," Marcus said, "or the Stinger, as we've taken to calling it. It's non-lethal and stuns the target with an electrical charge. The previous director didn't use these much and so there aren't many that are field approved at the moment. You've got one of the few so bring it back in one piece. At full charge, you can expel two minimal bolts or one strong one. A strong one will stop the heart of most Mundanes so be careful. Also, it takes one minute to recharge between uses, so keep that in mind."

I nodded and took the gun with shaking hands.

"Do ya know how to fire a gun, lass?" Fraser asked.

I swallowed.

"Of course, it's…well, you point and pull the trigger."

His lips twisted in a wry expression and he came to stand behind me. His hands brought my arms up and he adjusted my hold on the gun. I was acutely aware of how similar this was to last night, the heat from his body radiating into mine. The bite mark pulsed and my heart began to pound.

"Now," he said, his growly voice in my ear, "ya hold it like this, firm but not too tense."

I nodded, not trusting my voice. Fraser adjusted my arms so that I was aiming at the wall and not at Marcus or Sprite. One of his hands tightened around mine, the length of his arm flush with mine. I longed to lean back into his body but I held still.

"Aim," he breathed against my cheek, "pull the trigger while holdin' the gun steady. And don't close yer eyes."

His lips skated against my cheek as he spoke and chills raced down my spine. The bite mark was now pulsing, a warm sensation starting to spread through my back. I turned to look at him and found Fraser's eyes intense on my mark, his nostrils flared and I swore he let out a whimper before letting me go so fast that I fell forward at the loss of his steadying arms.

"Wow," Sprite said, fanning themselves.

"Yeah," Marcus sighed, eyes wide as he looked between us.

Fraser was now in the kitchen, busing himself with something, his back resolutely to me. I'd obviously embarrassed him with my reaction and if I didn't lock this down, my mission was going to be ten times harder than it needed to be.

"Is there anything else?" I asked, slipping the gun into the holster that Marcus handed me. "Anything having to do with the supplies, that is."

I was sure by the way that Marcus' mouth snapped shut that he'd been about to make a comment about Fraser, and I could not bear it if I had to pretend that I wasn't at all affected by his presence.

"Uh, yeah," Marcus handed me a something that looked like a small artist's portfolio. It was black with a zipper around the edges. I opened it, and inside were gloves, neutralizing bags, a small collapsible box for more lethal artifacts, and a small black box with USB hook up for my phone.

"This is a standard field agent kit. That box-looking USB adapter is to secure the line to talk to the director, and I assume you know what the rest of it is."

I nodded.

"She wants you to check in when you arrive in Dublin and then every forty-eight hours after until you find the artifact. Also, if you need back up or run into any problems, she wants you to contact her immediately."

"Got it."

"Well, that's it for us," Marcus glanced at Fraser, who was still doing god knew what in my kitchen. "Have fun!"

I bit back on a retort and instead, gave him a short nod.

"Good luck," Sprite said with a subtle wink, wheeling their cases behind them.

In a few minutes, they had both dragged their cases out the door and Fraser and I were once again alone in my apartment. I put the agent kit and gun in my tote, making sure that the gun wouldn't be jostled and set off accidentally. I triple checked my toiletries, a day's change of clothes in the tote for emergencies and all my research materials and was tempted to do the same with my suitcase. It was awkward in the extreme to have Fraser puttering in my kitchen, especially considering that we were grinding against each other a mere twelve hours ago.

"Can I talk to ya for a moment?" Fraser asked, finally stepping out of my kitchen.

The thought of talking to him in an empty apartment with all the strange behavior lingering between us made me want to run. But I had to work with this male and if we couldn't find a way to act a little more naturally around one another fast, there was no way his clan was going to believe that we were mated and this investigation would end before it began. So I reminded myself that this was a professional relationship and nodded.

"Of course," I said.

He rubbed his hands on his thighs and took a deep breath, blowing it out through his lips. His eyes were flitting around my apartment, and I got the impression that he was trying to look anywhere but at me. Something about that turned my frustration into anger in a split second. What had I done that was so terrible he couldn't even look at me?

"Fraser," I said, my voice firm as I were reprimanding him, which in a way, I was about to. "If you want to talk, then do me the courtesy of looking at me when you speak to me, please."

He froze, his gaze snapping to mine. I expected him to be angry with me making demands, or frustrated. I did not expect him to look chagrined.

"My apologies," he said, "yer right."

"Thank you. Now, what did you want to say?"

"I wanted to apologize for my behavior last night. It wasn't right to take advantage of the situation. I'm also sorry that I hurt ya and if I scared ya at all. I'll never touch ya like that again, ya have my word. I'm not the kind of Werewolf that thinks I have any right to yer body just because of...of the mark."

He stumbled a bit on the last few words, his voice going hoarse and soft as if it were hard for him to get the sounds past his throat.

"Thank you for all of that but it is really unnecessary."

He tried to speak and I cut him off.

"I imagine that the bite is meant to arouse physical reactions in order to encourage procreation. Therefore, what we experienced was merely physiological and signifies nothing other than that. Am I correct?"

It took him a moment to speak, his lips working a little bit before the sound came out.

"Aye, that…that about sums it up."

"Now, may I say something?"

His lips quirked up into a grin behind his beard.

"By all means, lass."

"This is going to be a challenging week, and it would be easier if we could be friends. Not the braid our hair and talk about boys bestie kind, but friendly at the very least. And that can't happen if you're growling at me and obviously can't stand to be around me all the time."

He ran a hand through his hair.

"Aye, yer right but it's…I'm not a very social person. I prefer my own company."

"Well, I understand that and you don't have to change it, but when we're in the same room could you at least pretend to not hate me?"

"I don't hate ya," he said, his gaze sharpening. "I just…I have my reasons."

I sighed.

"I don't need to know them but we have to be able to convince your clan."

"Aye, we do. So…give me the train ride. I'll relax around ya but I just need a little time."

It was the best I was going to get so I nodded, even as my heart sank a little. I was sure now that it wasn't really me he didn't like, but instead, something in his past that was causing this tension. And, in that case, I would have to find a way to make this convincing while I searched for the artifact, in spite of Fraser's stand offish nature.

"And there's one more thing," he said. "Last night I ran into an old friend, one of your fellow agents. I helped him apprehend someone who mentioned that this rogue organization was usin' my clan as a test for an artifact."

My mind kicked into gear as I ran through all the things I'd both heard and been told about the group that had splintered from the Archive.

"Did he say why?" I asked.

"No. But he did say that whatever artifact is causin' all of this, it was an accident, that it wasn't supposed to end up in our hands."

"I need to tell Director Dearborne about this when I check in. Perhaps when I get to your clan tonight I can narrow down what it might be."

"Oh, we'll not be gettin' to them tonight. It's too long a ride. We'll be stoppin' for the night before reachin' the house in town."

My stomach flipped. A night in a hotel room with Fraser?

"I reserved two rooms," he rushed to say.

"Oh," I replied and managed a shaky smile. "That's good. Alright then, I'll tell her this when I report in."

"She might already know but aye, it would be good to tell her all the same."

We stood there, both us glancing at each other and then away. I fidgeted with the strap of my tote and Fraser rubbed his palm on his pants leg.

"Well," he said with a clearing of his throat, "we should get to the train station."

CHAPTER TEN

FRASER

After getting Daphne settled in the first class sleeper I'd booked, I had to call my brother and confirm that my hunch was correct and we were dealing with an artifact. But I held back what I'd learned at the fight club until I could be there to make sure he didn't blow a gasket. One of the few things he would lose it over was the thought that anyone even loosely connected with artifacts was having a go at us. I saved the fact that I was bringing home a mate that Angus and the rest of my brothers hadn't met for last.

A mate that was already starting to turn my head and soften my heart, two things I had to keep a firm hand on or risk letting this entire charade get way out of hand.

After the call, in which I'd uncharacteristically allowed Angus to pass the phone around to our brothers and our gran just to kill some time, I wandered around the entire train twice, checking on anything I could think of to make sure no one had followed us. I had no idea what I was looking for, but I needed something to do. And if this rogue group of agents was indeed keeping track of my clan, they could be here. Several times the hair on my neck stood on end, but when I turned around, there was nothing there. Even with that, I couldn't forget that just a few feet from me was my mate. It was torture fighting the instincts to feed her and then bed her and I cursed my infernal biology that made us like this.

After nearly two hours I found myself outside of our cabin, and I couldn't find the strength to stay away any longer. I slipped inside to find Daphne nibbling on the end of a pen. She had that wrinkle at the top of her nose that I already knew signaled that her curious mind was working on something. Her lips moved as she read and then scribbled it down in her notebook. I could watch her do this all day for some reason, and I'd never once had any interest in book stores and such. That was my younger brother, Liam. But to be able to watch her thoughts spinning behind her eyes like this, to see the moment when she realized something, that slow smile that she was getting right now…I'd brave the smell of dust and leather any day.

I shook myself, realizing that I'd been staring a bit too intensely and snapped the door shut. Daphne jumped up, eyes wide and looked around.

"Oh my, what time is it?"

"Past noon."

It was an effort to stop myself from asking if she was hungry, but as it turned out, I didn't have to.

Daphne pushed the button for the waiter and a few seconds later, someone knocked on the door.

"Can I help you?" said the woman.

"Yes, I'm starving," Daphne said. "Can I get a roast beef sandwich on rye please?"

"Certainly, fruit or chips?"

"Oh um…" she bit her lip.

I knew that look. Mundane women got it when they were sure they shouldn't eat the "unhealthy" food in front of a man. It was rubbish and annoying. If Daphne wanted chips, she'd get them.

"She'll take the chips," I cut in, "and I'll have the same."

"Very good. Water to drink?"

Daphne nodded and the woman slid our door shut.

"I…why did you do that?" she asked.

"Order for you?"

"Yes, it was…well, a little unexpected to say the least."

"In a bad way?"

She bit her lip again and I wished she'd stop. I wanted to be the one nipping at her pillow-soft lips, to feel them wrap around my…

I shifted and took a seat opposite her but next to the door so I could be as far from her as possible. I had to maintain control.

"Not in a bad way," she finally answered. "It felt like you were taking care of me."

That made my back straighten and I turned away.

"I liked it," she whispered.

My head swung back around and I stared at her.

"I know that sounds weird but I did."

"No, that's not…that's not strange," I said, trying very hard to keep my voice even. "The matin' bite causes certain instincts. I thought we'd be able to avoid most of them but it seems that it's gonna happen one way or another. I'm sorry."

"Don't be, I find this quite fascinating, actually."

It was a perfectly good response to a strange situation like this one. But it still made my stomach drop and my heart lurch. This was nothing more than an up close research project for her, a side benefit to the job of hunting down the artifact. And that fact should've been a good thing, should've made me relieved.

It didn't do anything of the sort.

"I'm glad ya can find somethin' good out of this situation. Perhaps ya can add yer experience to whatever information is in yer library. Make my species less of a mystery for Mundanes," my voice came out far harsher than I'd intended and she drew back, as if I'd struck her.

"I would never share this without your permission. It wouldn't be ethical."

"Well, I can tell ya right now ya don't have my permission. This is all supposed to be private, sacred. And here I've gone and done it with a lass I don't even know!"

"There's no reason to yell at me, I just said I wouldn't share it. And this was your idea in the first place. I was perfectly content just being a friend."

"It wouldn't have worked! Oh, what I wouldn't give to have James doing this."

"Well, that goes for two of us," she threw her books and notebook into her tote and flung the table back.

"Where are ya going?" I asked.

"Out of this cabin and away from you."

"Yer hungry."

"Yes I know! And your concern for me is nothing more than that physiological response. If not for this bite you wouldn't care whether I starved or not, so don't pretend you give a damn beyond that."

Her chest was heaving, cheeks flushed and eyes bright. It was the most inconvenient time to lose control, to let the primal side of mating come to the fore. But it happened so swiftly that I wasn't even aware of it until I'd grabbed Daphne by the waist and hauled her into my lap.

"What the hell do you think you're doing?" she asked, breathless.

"Makin' sure ya stay put and eat."

"Fraser MacDonald, you let me go right now!"

She hit my chest with small fist and all it managed to do was rile me up further, especially since she was moving around on my lap at the same time.

"Lass, stop that...stop wiggling!"

She opened her mouth to yell at me when the words stalled and her eyes widened. Between the way I'd pulled her into my lap and the way Daphne had been moving around, the bloody lass was now straddling me. And if her gasp was any indication, she could feel exactly how she'd affected me.

My arm wrapped around her from behind just in an attempt to keep her still but all it did was pull her closer to me until her breasts were brushing against my chest. Daphne's hands dug into my shoulders and I told myself it was anger that had her hanging onto me so tightly.

"Stay still," I ground out.

"I…I need to get off your lap."

"Naw, ya don't. Ya need to stay here."

Her face was level with mine in this position and though she wasn't close enough to kiss, I felt the whisper of her breath against my skin. I'd kissed her last night, something I'd never done with a Mundane when in my true form. I had been worried about scaring her, but Daphne had moaned as if kissing me was the best thing she'd ever done. I wanted to feel that again, to know that she wasn't afraid of who I really was. But I couldn't have that here, or anywhere. That wasn't going to be for us.

Even so, my body had a different opinion on the subject. I moved one hand up to the back of her head, her silken hair slipping through my fingers, and the moment my hand gripped the back of her neck, Daphne let out a breathy sigh that nearly undid me.

"Ya like that?" I asked.

"Yes. It makes me feel…"

"What?"

"Safe."

"Ya are with me. I swear it."

"I know that. But then you go and say things that are rude and I'm confused."

I cringed at that, knowing that aye, I had been a right arse to her since the moment we met. But how did I tell her that the instincts firing inside of me scared me more than anything ever had in my life? That if I ever saw that hate and fear in her eyes, it would kill me? None of that made sense to me and I knew the reason for it now. If I told her, Daphne would run from me and…

That would be for the best. And yet, I can't do it.

I pressed my forehead to hers and closed my eyes.

"I'm sorry. It's hard to explain why I'm actin' this way."

One of her hands glided up to my cheek, threading through the beard that was a part of my glamour. Her touch left sparks in its wake and I nuzzled into it in spite of myself.

"I would never betray you," she said. "You tell me that I don't have to be afraid of you. And you don't have to be afraid of me either."

Twenty-four hours. That's how long we'd known one another. And yet, I believed her.

I opened my eyes to find her closer than before. It would be such an easy thing to bridge the tiny space between our mouths and...

The knock on the door jolted us both out of this insanity. Daphne was off my lap so fast she almost stumbled and I had to reach out and steady her.

"I'm alright," she said with a shaky smile.

When she sat down, Daphne scooted all the way to the window on the opposite side of the cabin and I was glad of it. The further away she was, the more control I could regain. The waitress gave us both a shy grin, as if trying to hide her own embarrassment about walking in on us like that.

"Put them both over here," Daphne directed, not giving me a chance to eat anywhere but right across from her.

I stared at the lass, wondering why she would want me so close to her after I'd grabbed her like that. When the waitress had left, Daphne cleared her throat and motioned to the place across from her.

"Won't you join me for lunch, Fraser?"

Words failed me for a moment before I cleared my throat and simply nodded.

Her smile widened, the sunlight glinting off her wavy hair and bringing out unexpected red highlights in dark tresses. When I sat opposite her, she handed me a napkin and proceeded to cut her sandwich into quarters. I hadn't noticed before how long her fingers were, nor how deliberate she was about things.

"You had said earlier that you were alright with us being friends," she said, "and I think a good step toward that might be for us to talk about your family, since I'll be spending a few days with them."

"After the way I've behaved just now, you seem very calm."

Her cheeks flushed pink and she took a sip of water.

"We need to reset and this seemed a good way to do it. Wouldn't you agree?"

I would and yet, it also annoyed me that she seemed able to move past the way my body reacted to hers with such ease. Maybe it wasn't the same for her, maybe her skin didn't still tingle with the remembered pressure of my body against hers. And if that was case…

It's good and I must accept that.

"Aye, this would be good," I said.

Her smile returned and she took a bite of her sandwich. A second later she groaned and closed her eyes. Goddess help me, but the blood rushed to my cock at the sound and I was suddenly jealous of a stupid sandwich; it had the privilege of making that sound come out of her mouth.

"Oh my god," she said, and then her eyes flew open in shock and she blushed even deeper. "I'm sorry, it's just…I was very hungry and this is a really good sandwich."

To cover up the fact that I was about to growl at her, I shoved some of the sandwich into my mouth and had to agree. It was damn fine.

"What do ya want to know?" I asked around a mouthful.

"You said you had brothers, what are their names?"

"Angus is the first born and clan leader."

"The one getting married, or was? Is it still on?"

"The Campbells haven't officially taken back the offer, so technically, he is still engaged. Then me, Samuel, and then the twins Liam and Lowell."

"Five of you?"

"Aye. Weres have big families as a general rule. My dad had six brothers and they all had large families too. I think I have…well, close to forty cousins."

She coughed on a chip.

"First cousins?"

"Aye. But don't worry, no one will expect you to know everyone's names."

"I should at least know your brothers," she took a notebook and pen out, scribbling furiously.

I plucked the pen out of her hand and was oddly delighted to see the spark of indignation in her eyes.

"What do you—?"

"No notes, lass. I explained to Angus today that we had a kind of whirlwind matin'. He won't be expectin' ya to know everyone's names."

"Well, that was quick thinking. Now can I please have my pen back?"

There was something in her tone, as if I'd taken her favorite doll. And, childish as it was, I didn't want to give it back just yet. So I held the pen just out of her reach as she grabbed for it.

"Listen here wolf, that is one of my favorite pens, you give that back."

If she didn't have that spark of playfulness in her voice, I would have. But instead, I kept plucking it out of reach until she finally leaned over the table, seized my wrist and took it back.

I let out a long chuckle while she gave me the side eye and tried not to smile.

"Now, if you can refrain from playground antics," she said, giving me a school marm look.

Only the problem was, I had never, ever had a teacher whose look of disapproval made me want to clear the table and do unspeakable things to her on the surface. I'd never been one for much flirting, much less the kind that was cloaked in annoying the other person. But if Daphne's reactions kept being so damn adorable I might have to develop a talent for it.

"My apologies, Ms. Reynolds."

"Oh, that raises an interesting question. Should I have taken your name or kept my own?"

I halted mid chew as the thought of her having my name lanced through me in a possessive rush.

"It's so new," I replied slow so I could control my primal side, "I think we don't need to worry about it."

She nodded.

"So, then tell me about the clan, about your family. What are they like? What are some of the manners I should know? I don't want to make a severe misstep."

"My gran lives with us, runs the house and keeps us all fed. Her name is Oona, but she'll insist ya call her Gran. Angus will be…well, Angus. Samuel isn't there at the moment, he's in France for business. So that leaves Liam and Lowell."

"The twins."

I nod.

"Lowell is the baby, and he's a bit of a ladies' man, always datin' someone new every week. And Liam…well, Liam is the quiet one, bookish. He was injured a few years back with a spelled bullet. Didn't think he'd walk again but he did. Though sometimes his back hurts too bad and he has to be in the chair."

"I'm sorry. How did it happen?"

I wiped my mouth and tried to swallow down the rage that always accompanied the memory of Liam's injury.

"The previous director was angry at us because we refused to fall in line. She sent some men to our country seat. If it had been durin' the full moon time, it would have been a different story. But this was just a normal weekend. Liam was in the house alone, lost in his books. They attacked and he fought back. Took half of them down before the bullet pierced his spine. Our clan witch healed him but the spell made her unable to do it fully."

She reached across the table and squeezed my hand. It was such a normal, fearless thing to do. The kind of thing friends do and it weakened the defenses I was having a hard time shoring up around this woman. I wove my fingers through hers out of a need to not break the contact and she let me.

"I'm so sorry you went through that," she whispered. "I remember how frightening it was with her in charge."

Anger rushed through me, hot and sharp.

"Did she do anythin' to ya?"

"No. I never really saw her at all. But my department partner, Reggie, he'd been her prisoner since he was in an egg. He never knew his family. I know I'm fortunate, she never so much as glanced my way. I sometimes feel guilty that I escaped."

"Don't do that to yerself. I'm glad ya didn't have those scars on yer soul."

She smiled at me and withdrew her hand so she could finish her lunch. Stupidly, I had to stifle a whimper at the loss of contact.

"What is the full moon time?" she asked around a bite of sandwich. "I read a few things but I wasn't sure what was truth and fable."

"Well, it's connected with our creation."

"The Druids?"

"Aye. Do ya know much about it?"

"Only that you and Lycans are very different but that legends have sort of smashed you together."

I could not suppress a growl.

"We are *not* Lycans. They're created by a mix of lower demons and Mundanes. We were created by the Druids, the priests and priestesses that existed before the Romans came to conquer us. They needed guardians for the sacred groves, to protect their rituals. Our ancestors were the strongest warriors the villages had to offer and the Druids cast a mighty spell to merge us with the sacred wolves and bears of the grove. It took the power of the three nights of the full moon to accomplish this and ever after, we are tied to it. For those three nights every month we must go into the wild, the countryside and let our primitive urges out or risk losin' control altogether."

"So...do you eat animals or..."

Her eyes were wide, both from fear and excitement, and it thrilled me in a way I had not expected.

"It's more about…well, other fundamental urges. Fightin' and…and fuckin'."

"Oh," she said, and reached for her glass of water, taking a long drink.

It shouldn't have made me as happy as it did to see how my words affected her. A part of me, that was getting far too brazen, was having a good time bringing up all the things that I could never explore with Daphne.

"Wait," she said, "the full moon?"

"Aye. What's wrong?"

She opened her mouth to answer when screams echoed down the hall not too far from our compartment.

The hair along my back stood up and a low snarl escaped through my bared teeth. There was something out there, something that could threaten my mate.

"Do ya have that gun?" I asked.

"Yes," she took it out of her tote.

"Anyone comes in here, ya use it, understand?"

"Where are you going?"

"To see what it is and keep it away from ya."

"Be careful."

Just before I opened the door, I glanced back to see her sitting there, eyes wide with worry. For me.

"Stay put," my voice was rough, and I had to fight the urge to kiss her before I ran out of the compartment.

CHAPTER ELEVEN

FRASER

I started down the hallway when the lights went out and more screams erupted ahead of me. Someone was going through the first class cabins, looking for someone.

It's us, I just know it is.

I wanted to shed my glamour and let my true form out so I wouldn't be expelling even a little energy keeping it up. But I also didn't want to start a panic, so I kept it in place.

Just as I reached the third cabin from ours, someone in a balaclava ran out of the door and right into me. They took a swing with an electrified baton and I caught their wrist. On their pinky was a ring with the Campbell clan crest. The moment my mind recognized it, I nearly let go. What the hell was Campbell doing? The man was recovering from the shock of having a passenger fight back so I had to act fast. I punched him square in the face and he went down, a sign that he was a Mundane. If they were all Mundane this would be easy.

Another barged out of a different cabin and managed to get in a blow to my back with the baton. I winced at the electric shock and seized the person's throat. This one, however, wasn't so easily subdued. They batted my hand away and I managed to take the balaclava with me. I caught a glimpse of mottled gray-green skin and black lips, before his glamour slipped into place, and growled.

Goblin, the professional hit men of the supernatural world.

And the one supernatural species that Campbell wouldn't be caught dead working with. This didn't make any sense.

There was no time to unravel this mystery though. If there were more of them, this was going to get tricky. Goblins were tough little bastards and one of the only fights I ever lost was because of their extremely high tolerance for pain.

"We just want the girl," he said. "We have no beef with clan MacDonald."

If he thought that was going to calm me down, he badly miscalculated.

The glamour slipped enough for him to see my yellow eyes and the sharp teeth I bared at him just before I took him by the throat again. I lifted him up, squeezing tighter and tighter, before slamming him into the wall.

"That's my mate yer talkin' about!" my voice had gone unnaturally deep.

If this piece of shit laid one finger on my Daphne…

"Sorry," he gasped, clawing at my hands, "but we…have orders."

"From who? Who sent you?"

He shook his head, at least, what little he could with me holding his neck in a death grip.

"Tell me!" I roared in his face.

He tried to peel my fingers away but I tightened my grip. At this rate, I'd kill the poor bastard before he told me anything.

That's when I heard Daphne scream from our cabin. My heart leapt into my throat and fear sank its teeth into my brain. The glamour slipped completely and I couldn't care less. She was in danger. My mate needed me.

I tossed the Goblin to the side like a discarded toy, where he landed with a thud, as I tore off in the direction of Daphne's screams.

The door was open and there was my mate, eyes wide in terror as she discharged that weird gun at her masked attacker. He convulsed and fell at her feet. She whimpered, tears running down her face, as she stared at the assailant in obvious shock.

"Daphne," I growled.

She jumped and I thought for certain she'd start screaming when she saw me, but she didn't. Instead she whispered my name and reached out her arms for me. The look on her face, seeing me as a safe harbor, gave my heart a firm squeeze. I leapt toward her and wrapped her in my arms. She clung to me, and the rightness of having her so close, even under these circumstances, left a hollow ache deep inside of me.

"He had a knife," she said, breathing in huge gulps of air. "And…and he tore one of my books! Can you believe that? Just stabbed his knife right into it, of course I shouldn't have used to shield myself but who does that to a *book*?"

If the situation hadn't been so dire, I would have dissolved into laughter at the deep indignation in her voice. But all I could think about was how she'd been so close to being killed. Then, when she pulled away from me, I saw the cut on her head, right above her eyebrow.

I couldn't stifle the deep snarl and still the lass didn't flinch from me.

"Yer bleedin'," I said.

"I'm fine, it barely hurts. Fraser, we have to get off this train."

It was at that moment that the train screeched around us and began to shudder to a stop. The unexpected movement knocked us both off our feet and onto one of the benches. Daphne landed in my lap, but this time there was nothing remotely arousing about it.

"They would only stop the train," she breathed, "if they were getting off or more were getting on."

"Let's not wait to find out."

She nodded and scrambled for her enormous tote bag.

"Can ya run with that on?"

"I'll make it work."

I huffed out a breath but didn't see the point in wasting time arguing with her. I knew enough about Daphne at this point that she wasn't going to leave her books behind.

Before we stepped out of the cabin, I slipped the glamour back into place; best not to cause any more of a panic.

She followed me out to the emergency exit, which had a small crowd around it already. An attendant was trying to keep people calm but the fact that the lights were still out, and now the train was stopped, had everyone understandably afraid. The scent of it was pungent, so much so that I nearly missed the sharp tang of the damn Goblin. I turned just in time to see the knife in his raised hand take aim for Daphne's back. I pivoted and caught his wrist before he could drive blade into her soft flesh.

I turned my grip and felt his wrist pop. He stifled a cry and I was a hair's breadth from taking the knife and gutting the bastard.

"Fraser, let him go," Daphne urged. "We have to get out of here and killing someone isn't going to make that easy."

With one final twist to drive the pain home, I let him go.

"Run," I growled, "because if I see you again, I will shred you with my bare hands."

The Goblin spat out a curse and took off.

"Is there another way out?' she asked.

By now the crowd had thickened considerably around the exit and I swore.

"Maybe near the back, there aren't as many cabins down that way so people might not be there yet."

We tore down the hallway and I was relieved to see that the exit wasn't manned at all. It was a miscalculation that I realized too late. I reached it first and pushed the door open just as a large hand shoved me out onto the narrow platform. I just managed to hang onto the door so that I didn't go tumbling arse over tea kettle onto the tracks.

Daphne screamed in shock and brandished her gun. She leveled it at the huge man and fired, only to have him bat her hand away at the last minute. The electrical charge went into the ceiling and the man seized Daphne by the upper arms.

Panic gripped my heart, and I kicked him in the ribs, using all of my strength. He groaned and thrust a dagger at me, the blade embedding itself into my side above my hip. But I couldn't feel the pain. He was trying to drag Daphne away from the door when she delivered another swift kick, right to the man's cock.

The man yelped and let her go, curling over as he clutched himself.

She darted outside to me just as I pulled the dagger free and let it clatter to the platform.

"Oh my god, Fraser!"

I pulled her down the short set of stairs with me and into the open field on the right side of the train.

"Slow down, you're hurt!"

I was indeed, and the faster I walked, the more the wound burned, which meant that the blade had been spelled or coated with something that could make a small wound worse for a supernatural like me.

But I wasn't going to tell her that.

"I'm fine, lass. Weres can take a stabbin' better than Mundanes. We need to get to a town and call my brothers."

"Is there a town nearby?"

"Aye, but yer gonna have to pick up the pace."

"I'm doing my best!"

"If ya didn't insist on that damn bag…"

"My legs would *still* be shorter than yours no matter what size my bag was!"

Well, she had me there.

We tromped through the field until we came to a small house with an older man sitting outside, smoking his pipe. Under the tobacco, I could smell the fact this was a werewolf, though I had no idea from what clan. It didn't matter though because the second he saw the stripe on my tartan on my kilt that said I was second in charge of the clan, he would be beholden to help me.

I let my glamour fall for him, exposing not just my true form but my kilt as well and the man jumped up from his chair.

"Och, ya frightened the shite out of me!" his eyes locked onto my tartan and grew large. "Uh, what can I do for ya?"

"We need a car," I said.

"I have a truck. She ain't much but she's at yer disposal."

"Much thanks, I will ensure it is returned to ya."

"It's my duty, sir. My great gran was a MacDonald."

I nodded at him in thanks as he led us around back to the truck.

Honestly, "not much" was a very kind way of putting it but we couldn't be picky. I was more than a little surprised to find that the rusty thing purred like a kitten.

"I can drive," Daphne said.

"I'm fine," I snapped.

"You're bleeding, Fraser, and I'll not have you dying on me!"

I growled and wandered over to the passenger side.

The old man chuckled.

"Mates, they can be a real pain in the arse."

"Yes, they can."

I directed that at Daphne, who stuck her tongue out at me and adjusted the seat so she could reach the pedals.

"Much thanks," I said again.

"Don't mention it. Just take care of yourself, sir."

I directed Daphne out onto the road and sat back. The bleeding had slowed but it was still sore, a product of whatever had been on that knife, I'd guess.

"Where are we going?" she asked.

"Just keep drivin'. There's a town about half an hour down the way."

"And what then?"

"A hotel probably. We'll get a ride from Angus or Lowell in the morning."

She nodded.

"Who were they?" she asked after a few minutes.

I wish I had an answer for her. While the obvious answer was that Campbell had taken a hit out on us, I wasn't so sure.

"I don't know."

"I saw a ring on the finger of one of them."

I nodded.

"I did too but…"

"It's too easy, isn't it?"

I glanced at Daphne unable to stop the uptick of my lips at the sight of that wrinkle above her nose, which meant she was trying to unravel something. She was more than smart enough, of that I was sure.

Beauty and brains. A lethal combination.

"There was a Goblin," I answered. "The Campbells would never hire a Goblin for anythin'."

"So, someone wants us to *think* it was the Campbells."

"Aye, that's my guess."

"Then that means it's likely the rogue group. They don't want me to look too closely into what's happening with your clan."

My stomach clenched and I nodded. It was exactly what I was thinking as well. And the fact that they'd known so quickly that Daphne was assigned to my clan's case reeked of someone betraying the Archive from the inside.

Daphne let out a long breath through her nose, her frown deeper now. I could almost see the gears of her brain working on this mystery and it lifted a few of the nerves. I was so used to solving these kinds of things on my own since much of the time Angus was too busy with other clan business, and my brothers were…well, not suited to this sort of thing. But it struck me, watching Daphne try to figure this out, that for the first time, I wasn't alone.

CHAPTER TWELVE

DAPHNE

The town we found was larger than I would've thought, though still quaint. It looked like a tourist trap with its over-the-top Scottish decor and signs, almost as if it were trying to give a very specific kind of Highlander experience.

I'd seen a few kilts on the train, but they were everywhere here and from the way that Fraser glared at some of them, I got the impression that some of the people were playing dress up for the tourists that were milling around the streets and darting in and out of shops.

I pulled up to the hotel that Fraser directed me to, the whole time grumbling about something under his breath. He had put his glamour back on after we acquired the truck and had included his wound in the spell so when we walked up to the desk to get a room, Fraser looked like his normal handsome, grumpy self.

"Can I help you?' the woman asked, her voice bored until she looked up and saw Fraser standing there. "You need a room?"

I expected him to turn on the charm, use his obvious sex appeal to get us a good room or something. But he just growled out that we needed two rooms and slapped down his credit card.

"I'm sorry but we're quite booked at the moment," she said, her thousand-watt smile dimmed. "We have one room with a queen size bed available."

Fraser tensed and then clutched his side.

He was going to refuse it, I could see him about to say it, but he was wounded and I was exhausted from not sleeping last night and the excitement of running for my life.

"We'll take it," I said.

Fraser's gaze swung to me, eyes wide.

"It's one night, you can deal."

He huffed out a breath.

"Fine, we'll take the damn room."

The woman was now definitely not enamored of Fraser and checked us in so fast that she skipped the usual spiel about room charges and what not. The room number was on the key cards she slid to us and then she was gone.

"You're a real charmer," I said, slipping the key into my bag.

"I'm not in the mood."

"Are you ever?"

I'd said it under my breath but the damn Werewolf hearing meant that I might as well have been shouting it.

He didn't say anything though, just glared at me before stalking off toward the elevator. As I followed him, I noticed a small shop in the lobby that sold, among other things, some first aid items.

"You go on, I'm going to get a few things for that stab wound," I said.

"Ya shouldn't be alone."

"I've got the gun and I won't take too long."

"I don't think I need anythin'."

I crossed my arms and raised an eyebrow at him.

"Well, I also need something to sleep in unless you'd like me cuddling up next to you in my underwear."

I'm not sure exactly what I expected. Perhaps a blush, or a disgruntled murmur. Fraser leaning toward me with a hungry glint in his eyes wasn't even on my list of possibilities. I could almost feel the heat in his gaze as he glanced down my body, as if he were imagining the picture I'd just painted for him.

"Don't be long," he finally growled at me before turning away and stabbing his thumb at the elevator button. "And get somethin' for that cut on yer head."

My feet didn't want to move at first as my mind tried to shove aside Fraser's reaction. He was so damn confusing. Half the time, he acted like he didn't want to be around me, and the other half like he wanted to devour me. And, I hated to admit that my own body was having a similar whiplash.

It has to be the bite. I'm just going to have to be careful and self-controlled. Figuring out who attacked us and their connection to the artifact will be an excellent distraction.

My face was still flushed when I walked into the shop and began collecting some band aids for my cut and disinfectant. I was about to get the self-stick gauze pads but then I thought of his fur and wondered how in the world I was going to bandage him up.

Maybe some gauze that I can wrap round him and then tape?

That brought up images of his midnight fur soft under my hands, of touching his bare body in wolf form and my stomach flipped.

Calm down! Imagine that you're a nurse and you've got to help your patient…who just happens to be a hot Werewolf…and I'm going to be tending to his wound and…oh dear this isn't working.

I took a deep breath that did nothing to banish the now torrid images of bandaging up Fraser's wounds turning into something far more illicit. It was obvious I wouldn't be able to think about this rationally at the moment, so I just dumped some things into the basket I carried and acted as if it were nothing at all. The shop had some souvenirs in one section and I found a large sleep shirt with the name of the town across the chest. Not exactly what I was hoping for but far better than nothing.

As I made my way out of the shop, the back of my neck itched with the feeling of eyes on me. I turned around slowly, trying to discover the source of the discomfort. But there was no one there, just the same woman behind the desk and the same clerk in the shop.

Just leftover nerves I guess.

But the feeling stayed with me until the elevator doors closed. And even then, my adrenaline was spiked enough that I had to purposefully calm my breathing. I was safe…right?

One the elevator reached my floor, I ran to the door of our room and slammed it shut behind me when I got in. My heart was hammering against my ribs, and my breath was coming in short gasps. There was no reason to be so frightened, no one was going to barge in and—

The bathroom door opened hard enough to collide with the wall and I jumped.

"What's wrong?"

I turned around to answer Fraser and stopped cold.

He had his glamour up, standing in the bathroom doorway soaking wet, with a towel carelessly thrown around his waist. It was open enough to show a mouthwatering glimpse of a muscular thigh covered in a liberal dusting of dark hair. It was rude to stare, even more so to do it in such a lustful way, but I could not stop myself from taking him in.

That broad chest was accented with more thick dark hair that trailed in a line down to his navel. Droplets of water fell slowly down his six pack abs, and I was insanely jealous of the rivulets. His entire body was like one enormous, well sculpted masterpiece, but it was missing one thing that would've made it perfect.

Soft, midnight black fur and a temptingly long tail…

"Daphne," he began to advance on me.

"I'm fine!" the words flew out of my mouth.

He stopped, eyes narrowing.

"Are ya sure? Ya slammed the door and ya smell like yer afraid."

"I smell…? Well, that's just embarrassing."

His full lips quirked up into a crooked smile.

"It's just a normal thing for me to notice. Nothin' to get upset about," he reached out and slipped a strand of my hair behind my ear. His fingers lingered on my jaw before dropping. "Are ya sure yer alright?"

"Yes," I breathed, "just…just left over adrenaline I think."

He nodded.

"Well, I, uh, should get dressed."

I gave him a shaky smile and went to dump my purchases on the bed. The room wasn't large but it was spacious enough for one night. The bed was firm with a wonderfully soft blanket on top. A wide window was to the right of the bed, the curtains drawn, and a dresser was on the wall across from the foot of the bed. There were night stands with simple lamps on either side of the bed and I turned one on. I wasn't sure why most mid-priced hotel rooms all had the same benign wall color and forgettable water color paintings but this one was no exception. It was oddly reassuring.

"I need to look at your wound so don't put a shirt on," I said to the closed bathroom door.

"I'm fine."

"Do not argue with me, Fraser MacDonald! I'm scrappier than I look!"

The door opened and he chuckled.

"Of that, I have no doubt."

He had indeed left his shirt off but he still had his glamour up, which included hiding the wound in his side. And while I very much liked the sight of him in jeans and nothing else, it wouldn't do.

"I need to see what it really looks like so drop the glamour."

He hesitated.

"I've seen what you look like," I softened. "And I'm not afraid of you."

His jaw tightened and he looked away.

Something had happened in his past to make him so hesitant, I was sure. But I highly doubted he'd tell me what it was, so I could only guess and try to sooth him all the same. I went to him and took his huge hand in mine.

"I hurt you last time…" he murmured.

"Look at me, Fraser."

After a moment, he did, and there was so much sadness there that I couldn't help but press the palm of my other hand to his cheek.

"I trust you and I am not afraid of you. The question is, do you trust me?"

"Why would that matter? I'm the one that's…that's a monster right? Isn't that what Mundanes think of us?"

My chest squeezed at the words, spoken with such hardness yet laced with pain.

"I don't. I don't think I ever could."

"Ya don't know me, how can ya be sure?"

I gave him a little smile, trying to ignore the heat blooming in my body.

"Call it an instinct."

Somehow, I'd gotten closer to him, the tips of my breasts almost brushing against his bare chest as I breathed. It was so tempting to lean into him, to let my body do what instinct had me barely refraining from. The bite mark let out a little pulse of heat and Fraser's nostrils flared.

"Ya best step back," he said, pushing me away from him slightly.

It hurt in an unexpected way to have him treat me like this. It was stupid to feel the sting of rejection when this couldn't be a relationship. It was business, work, save the world kind of stakes. And here I was, gritting my teeth against an all too familiar pain that was only made worse by this damn bite.

"Very well," I said with a deep breath, "but the fact remains that I need to see your true form in order to tend your wound. Now, you don't have to keep the glamour down if you're not comfortable with that but for just a few minutes, I would appreciate your cooperation."

He let out a long breath and nodded.

"Fine," the word was full of defeat.

And when he let it drop, I didn't notice the way he squeezed his eyes shut, waiting for me to be repulsed. I was too overcome with wonder at the primal beauty in front of me. I'd caught a glimpse of him last night and this afternoon, but it was all a bit of blur between the mating bite and running for our lives.

But now I could take him in, see the hulking strength that I'd only felt before.

His glamour gave a very good estimation of his height and breadth, though like this, he was still a bit bigger than that. His muzzle was indeed short, and his intense yellow eyes stared at me, waiting. His chest was bare of both clothes and fur, but was exceptionally well defined and covered in a very short, fine layer of hair that continued down to his stomach where his skin was as dark as his fur. A tartan kilt was wrapped around his waist, hitting him at the knee joint. A long tail that curved up at the end swung at the back, the fur longer than on most of his body and I longed to run my hand over it. Under the fur of his arms and legs were clear definitions of muscle, that made my body heat with desire. Just when I was about to reach out and feel the bulge of his bicep, his foot started to tap, claws clicking on the bare floor.

"Had yer eyeful yet?" he growled.

I looked up to see that he'd folded his huge arms across his chest and had cocked his head to the side.

A nervous giggle broke free of my lips and I shook my head.

"I'm sorry, it's just…you're extraordinary. And the glamour is actually not that different from your true form, I mean in terms of size and shape and…well, I, uh…what I meant to say is…"

Fraser made a sound that was very much like a wolfy version of a chuckle and heat raced into my face.

"I suppose I should be happy that yer gawkin', not screamin' in terror."

"You're beautiful, Fraser, not terrifying."

Now it was his turn to be uncomfortable as he turned away and shifted from foot to foot.

"Thank ya, lass," he whispered. "Now, how about ya bandage me up?"

"Yes, of course, sorry."

Fraser raised his arm and I heard the barest hint of a hiss as I gently probed the knife wound. It wasn't all that deep or large, but it still seeped a bit of blood and there was probably some bruising around the site, though it was hard to tell with the dark fur.

"Look for anythin' unusual," he said through gritted teeth, "anythin' still in there, or that looks strange."

"What would be strange for you? It looks bruised but I can't really tell if there's anything in there. Move closer to the light."

He moved toward the bedside lamp and took the shade off to cast more light. I carefully spread open the wound so I could look inside, trying not to be affected by the way Fraser's breathing picked up.

"Nothing inside," I finally said.

"Okay," he breathed, his voice strained.

"Sit down, let me bandage this. It's bleeding more now."

He just nodded and plopped down onto the bed.

I poured some antiseptic liquid onto a patch of gauze and began to dab the wound with it. He jerked a little and then tensed, holding himself back from reacting to the discomfort that had to be present.

"Tell me something," I said, "does your clan have any other enemies that would hire goblins?"

"Maybe," he said, "but none that would dare to...to attack when we might be about to align with the Campbells."

I nodded and reached for a clean patch of gauze.

"So no one besides the rogue agents would have a reason to sabotage this and then come after me to try and keep me from stopping it?"

"Not that I can think of."

"That means the attack today isn't about your clan. It's about me."

I motioned for him to stand up and began winding some gauze around his middle.

"About stoppin' ya from gettin' the artifact," he said.

"Right. Which means this little experiment is now compromised and we will have to deal with the rogue agents trying to get their hands on it before I do."

"I'll not let anything happen to ya."

He growled it out, and I got the sense that his intensity was more than just a Werewolf's sense of honor. There was something else motivating him and I refused to think about it. This other group getting aggressive so quickly was a complication I hadn't counted on, and I would need all my faculties if I was going to succeed *and* survive to tell about it.

My hands shook a little as I cut the end of the gauze and began taping it.

"Do you think anyone in your clan might be aiding the other agents?" I asked.

"I don't like to think that anyone would but it is possible. The Campbell marriage wasn't popular."

He sat on the bed when I'd finished, huge hand clutching his side. I paced in front of him, mind working on the problem rather than focusing on the sexy Werewolf in front of me.

"Yer turn," he said.

I frowned, confused at first until I remembered the cut just above my left eye.

"It's really not—"

He held out his hand for the box of Band Aids and I sighed, handing it to him.

"Sit."

I plopped down on the bed while Fraser knelt in front of me and began to clean the cut with another piece of gauze. I winced as the disinfectant stung, and his eyes heated.

"It's not deep," he whispered.

"I know. You don't need to do anything."

"Ya took care of me. Now it's my turn."

His voice took on a husky quality that warmed me. It was almost comical to watch his huge hands open the small Band Aid wrapper and place it carefully on my forehead.

"There, all better."

But he didn't move. Neither did I.

We just stayed that way, his fingers trailing down my cheek and jaw as his hulking frame knelt between my legs. I wanted him to run those claws down my throat and between my breasts, to feel the clutch of his strong hands on my hips as he pulled me forward. I wanted to bury my face in his neck as he drove into me. This vision came on so suddenly and so clear, taking my breath away and making me wet. I knew that he smelled how he affected me because his nostrils flared and his eyes closed, as if he were savoring the scent.

"You shouldn't want me," he whispered. "Mundanes don't like monsters like me."

"That's rubbish."

His eyes flew open on a chuckle.

"Is it now?"

I flushed and bit my bottom lip. Fraser's gaze zeroed in on it and I knew, like I knew my own name, that he wanted to kiss me.

"Monsters like you," I breathed, "are the stuff of fantasies."

"Yers?"

His hands landed on each side of me on the bed, caging me in as he pitched forward. I leaned back on my own hands, my back arching so that my breasts were thrust forward. The tip of Fraser's nose grazed my throat and collarbone as I trembled beneath him. My breath came in short gasps and I was hot all over, but especially where he'd bitten me. It throbbed and ached, matching the sensation building between my legs.

I wanted say 'yes', to reveal to him how much I wanted his teeth and claws to mark me more. None of it made sense. I'd only just met him, and while it had been a while, I was never one to have casual sex. But since last night, nothing felt casual between us. The connection was raw and illogical, it defied every box my mind tried to place it in. And inexplicably, I found myself running head on for it.

One huge hand came to my waist as his tongue began to slip under the neck of my blouse. The hot, rough feel of him had me gasping. As his hand began a slow ascent up the side of my body, his chest rumbled with a growl that I felt everywhere. I was just about to beg him to take me when the phone on one of the nightstands gave a shrill ring.

Fraser leapt back as if I'd burned him, our eyes meeting with mutual shock and barely concealed arousal. For a second, neither of us moved, our bodies heaving as if we'd just finished a run. Finally, when it registered that the phone was still ringing, Fraser ripped the receiver off the cradle.

"Aye?" he snapped. "...Okay...I understand, Angus...No, I—...There's no reason to—...Fine."

He slammed it back down and stalked away from me.

It took me another moment to collect myself, to know that my voice would not betray the molten desire that had been over taking just a minute ago.

"Trouble?" I asked.

"Aye. Scuffle with some of our men and the Campbells. Angus is furious, still thinks that it was them on the train no matter what I've told him."

"This could be the artifact," I said, grateful for something to bring us back to the mission at hand. "You can't blame him."

"I know that, but if he's not thinkin' straight, it's gonna cause serious problems."

I nodded, my mind focused again problem solving. Even though the mission had become fraught with difficulties and dangers, it was still a hell of a lot safer than the territory Fraser and I had been in just a moment ago.

"Then let's see if we can figure out a few things before we arrive tomorrow. Who was the most vocal in their disapproval? Or might the most to gain by the marriage not happening?"

Fraser's shoulders slumped.

"Reuben, he's Lizzie's brother. He was furious at Angus for breakin' things off with her and enterin' an engagement with Imogen. But he was never a hot head, and I don't think Reuben would ever do anythin' to put the clan in danger."

"But sometimes emotions cloud judgment."

Fraser's eyes shot up to mine and I knew exactly what he was thinking.

Bring it back to the mission, Daphne.

"And when there's an artifact involved, things can go very sideways. It doesn't mean he's bad, just that an artifact took advantage of his emotions."

"Ya talk about them like they're…well, alive."

"In some ways they are. Some of them are relatively harmless. But the older ones? The ones that have been altered by strong emotions or significant historical events? Those can take on a life of their own. And if Reuben got a hold of one of those and it was a wish fulfillment artifact, one that might deal with passion or love? Then he might not even be able to control himself. The artifact could be the one driving him."

"But Reuben wouldn't have known about ya. I just told Angus on the train. Whoever sent them, knew before we left."

"That's true. So then we have to find that artifact before they do. And if they were willing to go to all this to stop me…"

My stomach dropped as a very obvious possibility occurred to me.

These people wouldn't have gone to all this trouble for just a run of the mill seduction artifact. Whatever this was, it likely had the potential to cause things much worse than simply breaking up an engagement. And if that was case, then this all just became much more dire. I had to be realistic and view this dispassionately. And consider the fact that I might not be the best person to stop this rogue group.

Failure began to claw its way up my throat. I hadn't been trained on field combat, and I couldn't ask Fraser to be my bodyguard on top of everything else. I also couldn't risk the safety of innocents just because my ego was hurting.

"I have to call this in," I said, the words hard to get out. "The director might want someone else on this now, someone with more experience or…"

He seized my wrist before I could get my phone out of my bag. His hand was warm, and the claws that had been there before were gone, replaced by very short nails. When I looked into his eyes, there was an openness and warmth that I had only glimpsed before. Not only was he not hiding his true form from me, he was letting his kindness show too.

"I don't want anyone else," he said. "So ya tell her that, understand? Yer the one I want."

My eyes widened as words failed me.

He's talking about the job…He's talking about the job…

I just kept saying it to myself over and over as the blush crept up my neck.

"Thank you, Fraser," I said, gently taking my wrist from his hand. "But you don't need to say that just to make me feel better. It might be for the best if— "

"I'm not. I'm sayin' it because I like the way yer thinkin' about this, and ya already started. It's too late now to bring someone else in without raisin' suspicion. Besides, I know ya can do this."

"How?"

He shrugged, which looked odd and adorable in his true form.

"The same way ya know I'm trustworthy, I guess."

I bit my bottom lip again and the flush took over my entire face.

"Thank you," I whispered, looking at my hands in my lap.

When he didn't answer, I glanced up and saw him staring at my mouth, his gaze now molten with hunger. He let out a long breath through his nose and met my gaze. Heat shot through me, and my body ached to feel him against me. The bite mark let out several of those pulses, all faster than I'd ever felt them before. For a second, it seemed like he was about to reach out for me and then his glamour went back up and he turned away.

"I think I should take a look around while ya make your call," he said, getting to his feet. "Make sure no one is lurkin'."

"Yes, that's…that's a good idea."

I turned away and focused on digging my phone out of my tote bag.

"I'll get dinner while I'm out," he offered at the door.

"That would be lovely," I said, not looking at him.

He didn't move at first, and I saw him rub his palm against the leg of his pants before jerking the door open and racing out.

It took me a full ten minutes to calm the racing of my heart. I didn't know what to think about Fraser's behavior. Half of the time, I thought he was annoyed at my very presence, and the other half, I could swear he wanted to bend me over a piece of furniture and fuck me into oblivion.

Stop thinking of that! I need to be calm, collected and professional when I call the director, and I am not going to be able to do that if I'm thinking of him doing that to me!

I took a few deep breaths, plugged in the USB adapter and called Director Dearborne. She answered on the second ring and I filled her in on the attack and Fraser's information.

"You're sure they weren't from the Campbell clan?" Director Dearborne asked.

"I trust that Fraser knows what he's taking about when it comes to them, yes."

Director Dearborne sighed.

"Then I think you're right, they were trying to stop you. Which means someone here told them about you. And it sounds like they won't hesitate to kill you, Daphne."

The words were heavy, laden with warning and I swallowed. This was much more than I had signed up for when I agreed to this mission, and yet I couldn't just abandon Fraser and his family. This artifact could do a lot of damage if it wasn't neutralized quickly. And if the rogue agents were this desperate to get their hands on it, then they probably wouldn't hesitate to hurt Fraser's clan in the process. I had to stop that, even if it meant putting my life at risk.

"Do you want to replace me?"

"Not unless you feel that you can't handle this."

"I'm not trained to fight and I hate the thought of putting the MacDonald clan in the position to defend me."

"I understand that, but I have a feeling this will need as much brains as it does brawn. I'd like to keep you in the field if you're not too afraid of what the Protectors might do."

"That's what the rogue group is calling themselves?"

"Yes, quite pretentious if you ask me."

I chuckled.

"So, where was the shipment from, what was the manifest?"

"It was a mix of things, collected from Germany, France and Italy. Half were things that used to be in Nazi warehouses and private collections."

Hitler was obsessed with the Secret Archive and its treasures. He'd waged a shadow war on the Archive and had destroyed several storage facilities. It was only the sacrifice of a dozen brave agents that prevented him from getting his hands on artifacts that would've handed him victory in the war.

"Good lord, those would be very dangerous. Any that would have belonged in my department?"

Director Dearborne paused, I could hear the clacking of keys on the other hand.

"Oh, holy hell," she answered.

"What?"

"Two things and…Daphne, these are class five artifacts."

I swear my heart stopped beating and my hands instantly became clammy. Class fives were the most dangerous, needing special containment that was often times at a secondary location.

"What are they?" I asked, my mouth dry.

"The Golden Apple of Discord and the hymn book of Enheduanna, she was—"

"The first named female author in history and a high priestess of Inanna, goddess of sex, warfare and vengeance."

"Either of these would be bad, but if both are in play…" her voice trailed off. "The last known person to have both of these was one of Hitler's generals. Some of that energy had to have tainted them, twisted their original purposes and even strengthened their darker aspects. I don't think I have to tell you to be careful."

"No, you don't. I'm actually quite familiar with the history of both. And now that I know what to look for, I can find it easier."

"Check in with me tomorrow night after you've had a chance to investigate. And I think it best if you check in every twelve hours after that."

"Understood."

Director Dearborne hung up and I stared at my phone for a few seconds after, my mind trying to process everything. As I put the USB device back into the field kit, I ran through all the possible ways to neutralize a class five artifact.

I glanced back at the kit, knowing full well that there was nothing in there that would bring a class five artifact to heel.

Unless…

It was possible for artifacts to cancel each other out, which was why shelving was so important. If I could find a strong enough artifact with the inverse properties, it would cancel the dangerous one long enough to allow me to get it back to the Archive. The tricky part was going to be getting just the right one.

I opened my email and sent out the idea to the Director, asking her if we had anything in the database that would do the trick since I couldn't access it remotely. It was the only plan I had at the moment, and it was thin at best, not nearly enough to take the edge off my worry. Without anything else to occupy it, my mind began to spiral into all the ways this could go wrong. The risk to Fraser's clan, hell, even to the entirety of Scotland. It sounded crazy and perhaps a little dramatic to anyone outside of the Archive. But for those of us who knew the power of artifacts, it was a very real possibility.

And I might not be able to stop it even if I do find the damn thing in time.

My self-confidence had been hard won in the face of so much derision from my family. But even so, in moments in like this, I was that sobbing teenager whose second place history medal wasn't good enough for her family.

But I am. I am smart, I am worthy.

I repeated the affirmation that a therapist had suggested years ago and tried to remind myself of all the things I'd achieved at the Secret Archive, the people that trusted me there. And now, the fact that the new Director had trusted me with a very important mission.

That has to mean something…it does.

I was just finishing up my notes when Fraser walked in with two bags of food. The scent of burgers and fries hit me and I groaned with hunger.

"Oh my god, please tell me there's a cheeseburger in there for me."

He chuckled and handed me one of the bags.

"There's a cheeseburger in there for ya."

It was pure instinct that had me jumping up onto my tip toes and planting a kiss on his cheek. He turned his head in surprise just as my heels hit the floor. Our eyes locked for just a second and the heat there shot straight through me. But before either of us could do anything that would make this more awkward, I took a step back and he cleared his throat.

There was a small table near the window and we sat down to eat while I told Fraser what the director had said.

"So, it might be one of those two items?" he asked.

I nodded.

"Has anyone seen Ruben with an old, strange book or a small apple?"

Fraser chuckled.

"Sorry, the picture that paints…"

"I know, it's odd but chances are that he won't leave them anywhere if they've attached themselves to him."

"I've not heard anythin' but we'll find out tomorrow."

I gave him a wobbly smile and finished my dinner. The burgers were delicious but I only half enjoyed mine. Worry gnawed at me, and I couldn't shake the feeling that I was in way over my head.

We cleaned up and decided on an early night since someone from his clan would be here bright and early to pick us up.

As I brushed my teeth and slipped into the sleep shirt from the gift shop, I thought about what had happened just before Fraser had left to get dinner. I could still feel the phantom press of his tongue on my skin and I worried that I was developing quite the crush on the Werewolf.

Which is the last thing I need.

I stepped out of the bathroom to find Fraser on the floor next to the bed. The bandage was hidden beneath his glamour, but he still winced when he laid on his side.

"Fraser, if you think I'm letting you sleep on the floor in your condition you've got another thing coming."

"There's only one bed, lass, and I'm enough of a gentleman that I won't have ya sleeping on the floor."

"Well, of course not. It's plenty big for the both of us."

His eyes widened.

"No, absolutely, no."

I crossed my arms.

"We are both adults and I'm sure we can control ourselves for one night."

He didn't budge, just glowered at me from the floor.

"I'll stick to my side of the bed," I said. "I won't even try to warm my feet on you."

That got a small uptick of his lips.

"I can't hold the glamour in my sleep," he said haltingly, "it would be…well, *me*."

I sighed and knelt down next to him so that we were at eye level.

"How many times do I have to tell you that I'm not afraid of the real you?"

He looked down at my abdomen and I knew exactly what he was thinking of.

"It doesn't even hurt anymore. And I know you never meant to do it. Now," I stood and held my hand out to him, "time for bed."

Fraser let out a long breath through his nose and ran a hand over his face.

"Alright," he finally said, ignoring my hand as he got up.

We climbed into bed without another word and switched out the lights. I turned my back to him, leaving only a few inches between me and the edge of the bed. It had seemed like a good idea to not let the injured Werewolf sleep on the floor, but as the mattress dipped under his weight and his breathing evened out, I wondered if I'd be able to get any sleep at all.

Imagine my surprise when it only took a few seconds for me drift off to the sound of Fraser snoring next to me.

CHAPTER THIRTEEN

FRASER

I couldn't remember the last time I'd slept so soundly that I actively resisted waking up. When I did, however, I found myself pressed up against the soft, tempting roundness of Daphne's body, the big spoon to her little one. Her breathing was even, her hand curled up under her cheek and her dark hair falling in waves around her face. My arm was around her middle, one of my legs over her hip, as if I were trying to make sure she was so secure in my embrace that nothing could ever take her from me.

Here, in this quiet early morning, with only the sound of her breathing, I let my guard down just enough to accept what had been revealed to me when I bit her.

This lass, with her mind that never quits, hair like sun kissed raven's feathers, and eyes that made me think of the highland grasses in spring, was my true mate.

It was something I had never thought really existed, something only old Weres spoke of in whispers soaked with wonder and awe. I have certainly never seen such a thing in my lifetime.

Oh, plenty of my family fell in love with their mates, it wasn't all like Angus and poor Imogen's mating. But a true mate? The one person in all the world who held a piece of your soul in theirs, the only one that could ever make you feel whole and be your perfect companion?

That was legend.

At least that's what I thought until the moment I sank my teeth into Daphne's beautiful, pale flesh.

The knowledge choked me, and I had to squeeze my eyes to keep tears from falling. Because as much as I was starting to realize that breaking this bond would likely kill a part of me, Daphne hadn't bargained for any of it. It wasn't fair to burden her with such knowledge. I wanted her to stay, that was true. I wanted it so bad that I ached with it. But I wouldn't accept it out of obligation. And that's what I was afraid to see in Daphne's eyes if she knew how deep this bond ran in me.

Usually, mates could sense one another's hunger or a hint of emotions. But with Daphne, it was so strong that I didn't just know that she was hungry, I knew what she wanted to eat even before she did. I could feel her fear, her worry, her pleasure, and I was driven to take away the bad and increase the good. It was getting hard to continue to act like Daphne annoyed me as much as the rest of the world, and I dreaded the moment when she realized that this was no longer some fake story for me. I needed her to solve the mystery of the artifact fast and leave before she found out, but the thought of losing her made me whimper.

Right now, in this moment, there is nothing but her. No artifact, no brothers or clan. Maybe I can give myself this one moment to hold her like I want to every time she's near.

I closed my eyes and inhaled her scent, knowing now why she smelled of heather and moonlight. I wanted to touch her everywhere, to make her moan my name again as she had when I bit her, but that was a breach of trust and I wouldn't cross that line. I meant what I'd said to her, I wasn't going to take advantage of her, not ever.

So I stayed still, careful not to let my body betray me.

And then she stirred.

Just a little roll of her round butt against me and I had to grit my teeth to keep my damn cock in check. It was no mean feat since I was already half-mast just from waking up next to her.

I was about to withdraw my arm when Daphne's arm came around and she wove her small fingers through mine. The breath caught in my chest and I stared down at her, a tiny smile now on her lips.

"Fraser," she whispered, her voice sleepy.

My mouth was dry and I wouldn't be surprised if she could hear my heart beating against my ribs. Then she wiggled back further against me and it was impossible to keep my body from responding.

"Lass," my whisper was harsh, "ya…ya might want to stop that."

The cheeky lass giggled, as if this were the funniest thing in the damn world, and turned around. My hand went to her hip, out of instinct, and Daphne put her hand over mine to hold it there. Sleepy green eyes looked up at me, her cheek red from its time against the pillow. I'd never seen anything more beautiful in all my life.

"Now I know why I was so warm all night," she said with a grin.

"I'm sorry, I didn't mean to take liberties."

She laughed again and shook her head.

"You know, if I wasn't alright with you possibly touching me in the middle of the night, I wouldn't have let you sleep next to me."

I swallowed at the confession, not sure what to do with it. She couldn't be saying what I hoped she was. And even if she was, it was a risk to let myself go with her. The usual mating rut was one thing, but I had no idea what a *true* mating rut might be like. Would I lock her in this room and fuck her until she was with child? Would I tear the heads off any other male who looked at her? Either possibility was something I could not risk.

"Are you alright?" she asked, putting her hand to my cheek.

Bloody high hell, her touch was intoxicating and I leaned into it when I should be letting her go. Instead, my hand tightened on her hip, bringing her closer to me. She gasped and I smelled her arousal, faint and just beginning.

She wanted me, and I wanted her so bad it was bordering on pain now.

My tongue flicked out and brushed against the inside of her wrist, once, twice. She shuddered and closed her eyes. The night shirt she'd worn to bed was bunched up around her waist, exposing a pair of pale pink panties, so delicate that all I'd have to do is drag one claw down the middle and they'd split, exposing her sex to me.

"I'm never like this," she breathed. "I don't…I don't just rub up against men like this."

A sudden picture of another man's hands on her, kissing her, fucking her, invaded my mind and before I could stop it, my lips curled back on a growl. She jerked back a little, shock and wariness in her eyes where there had been desire before. It was enough to jolt me back to reality.

Daphne may be my true mate, but she was also a Mundane. And if there was one thing I knew about Mundanes, it was that once they saw a glimpse of the monster that lived in Werewolves like me, they never looked at us the same way again. That was one thing I didn't think I could bear from her.

Even if she'd said that I was her fantasy, I doubted it included the truly primal side of me, the one that had scared every Mundane that had ever seen it.

Including Silvia.

I pulled back from her and got out of the bed.

"Did I do something wrong?" she asked, just before I made it to the bathroom.

"No, lass, it wasn't you."

"But you growled at me."

"Not at ya, no. It was…the bite makes my instincts a tad primal, that's all."

"Oh," she said, her voice small. "So…the mention of other men then?"

This time I managed to bite back the growl, though my head whipped around to look at her over my shoulder. I'm not sure what my expression was, but she swallowed and nodded.

"I'll be more careful."

"That's a good idea."

I took my time in the bathroom, calming my emotions and the instincts that were becoming frighteningly strong. When I could no longer reasonably monopolize the bathroom, I walked out with my glamour firmly in place. It was strange, but the damn thing felt a little like armor, reminding me that I had to hold my true self in check. And I needed that constant barrier now more than ever. Because the second Daphne's scent reached me, I wanted to rip off the shirt and pants she now wore and bend her over the bed, spending the rest of the day rutting her until neither of us could walk.

I tightened my jaw and walked to the other side of the room to open the curtains. The morning was cloudy, a drizzle fell and draped the town in a haze. I stared outside, willing myself to not speak to her, or even look at her. If I did and there was even a hint of desire, or worse, hurt in those eyes, I'd relent and then we'd really be in a situation.

I heard the door to the bathroom close, heard the water run and tried to tell myself to just let this whole thing go. But it had its hooks in me now and the only thing I could manage was a sullen distance when Daphne came out of the bathroom.

"Are ya hungry?" I asked, even though I knew the answer.

"A bit."

Her answer was curt, careful, and it was like a punch in the chest. I'd hurt her, confused her, and I hated myself for it.

"What time is your brother getting here?" she asked.

As if on cue, there was a playful knock at the door and I groaned. There was only one of my brothers that knocked like that and he was the last person that I wanted around Daphne right now.

"Oy, ya peely-wally arse, open up," Lowell said from behind the door. "Yer chariot awaits!"

Before I could stop her, Daphne opened the door and smiled up at my brother. His glamour was so fucking pretty it was nauseating, and he knew it. His ice blue eyes twinkled at Daphne and a shock of black hair fell across his forehead as he gave her crooked grin and leaned on the door jamb toward her.

"Well, aren't ya the bonniest lass this side of Edinburgh," he drawled. "I can see why my brother was in a hurry to mark ya."

Daphne flushed and giggled.

"I'm Daphne," she said and held out her hand.

Lowell took it and kissed her knuckles. She would smell like him for the rest of the day if I didn't do something about it. I marched over and took her hand out of his, placing myself between them.

"That's enough."

But Lowell, ever the eejit, just leaned around me and said, "If ya ever get tired of the grumpiest Werewolf in Scotland, ya can always trade up."

A long, loud growl rolled through the room. My fists curled as my instincts primed for a fight. He dared to flirt with her, to ask her to his bed!

"Och, calm down, ya bawbag. I was just jokin'," Lowell said, and gave Daphne a wink.

"You should know better than to flirt with a mate so soon after the markin'!" I roared, my entire body going hot.

"Oh, I do," Lowell squared his shoulders and raised himself up to his full height, which was only a few inches shy of me. When he spoke next, his voice was pitched low, meant only for me. "And I also know that sometimes beatin' the shite out of a virile Werewolf can take the edge off a frenzy. Why else do you think Angus sent me?"

That took some of the bite out of his behavior and I uncurled my fists.

It made sense that Angus might think that I'd mated Daphne in a frenzy of some kind. After all, I wasn't known for being impulsive. That would be the eejit standing in front of me. So Angus sent Lowell, the one brother who could get a quick rise out of me and who I'd have no problem beating the shit out of, in case I needed to blow off some steam before coming back to a tense situation.

"No, I'm fine," I said.

Lowell's eyes narrowed as he took me in, his nostrils flaring on a sniff. Most people discounted my baby brother because he was the pretty, arrogant one. But all of that hid a keen intellect and a Werewolf that saw far more than anyone gave him credit for.

"Good," Lowell said after a moment, and slipped back into his playboy persona. "I'm starved, let's get a bite before we go home."

Lowell turned and offered Daphne his arm. She glanced at me, obviously unsure what she should do after witnessing the confrontation.

"Och, will ya tell yer mate it's fine to walk with me?" Lowell whined.

"No," I growled before I could stop myself.

"Then offer me *your* arm," she said, raising an eyebrow.
Lowell chuckled.

"Oh lass, yer going to fit right in."

CHAPTER FOURTEEN

DAPHNE

Lowell packed away more food than I'd ever seen anyone consume, and in record time too. But while his brother regaled me with tales of Fraser in his youth, my "mate" was silent through most of the meal. The only time he spoke was when he ordered exactly what I wanted to eat though I hadn't told him. He even flagged down the waitress for more coffee before I'd even known my cup was low. It was spooky, to say the least, especially since I didn't think the instinct was supposed to border on precognition.

But while we sat side by side in the booth, Fraser, having taken the outside so he could stretch his long legs out in the aisle a bit, was very careful not to touch me. It was so painfully obvious that I caught Lowell frowning at his brother a few times through the course of the meal, as if he were genuinely confused.

While Fraser had said that his growl in bed was due to my mention of other men, and while I also knew that many of these reactions were likely beyond his control to some extent, a nagging doubt had me wondering if there was more to it. The way he'd looked at me this morning…

I swear he was going to kiss me or…or something else.

The memory of his black fur-covered body wrapped around mine brought a flush rising from my chest all the way to my face. I was grateful for the crisp morning air as we stepped out of the little restaurant; perhaps it would hide the flush as something the cold had produced. Fraser stood close enough to put his arm around me, but he still didn't touch me, and it was starting to make me grouchy. To say that I longed to have his hands on me was an understatement. I wondered if I'd have any residual feelings left once the mark was removed. I hoped not.

The thought of being deprived of a reason to be near Fraser left me even more confused and tied in knots. Our future had a clear expiration date and the knowledge was like a spike of anxiety in the back of my mind, growing ever more painful as the hours past.

"Alright you two love birds," Lowell said with a grin, "time to meet the rest of the clan."

I blew out a breath and nodded.

"Och, don't worry, they will love ya. Though, they may not understand why ya fell for this one, but they won't judge ya for it."

Lowell smirked at Fraser, who just crossed his arms and glared at his younger brother. The car that Lowell led us to was an old military Jeep that had been restored and upgraded to a certain kind of modern comfort. I was about to climb into the front when Lowell stopped me.

"That's not a good idea."

He glanced at Fraser, who was already sitting in the back, his jaw clenched as he stared straight ahead.

"It'll pass," Lowell whispered, "but the first month or so is tricky for mated males. And with the full moon so close…well, he's bound to get a little possessive. Don't worry though. If yer uncomfortable, just let us know, we'll take care of it."

I swallowed and nodded, remembering what Fraser had said about the full moon frenzy.

"How soon is the full moon?" I asked, my voice trembling.

"Tomorrow is the first night. You'll get to spend some of yer honeymoon at the clan country house. It's beautiful there."

"Wait," Fraser, opened his door and jumped out, "that's not right. The full moon isn't for another week."

Lowell frowned and shook his head.

"Boy, ya fell hard if ya lost track of all that time. It's tomorrow! Remember, we were timin' the handfastin' to it?"

Fraser stared at the ground and then back up at me, eyes wide. I could almost read his mind. He was worried about the frenzy's effect on our mating mark. And, to be honest, I didn't know if I was excited to know what would happen, or scared.

"What's the matter with ya two? It's not like he's going to tie you to the garden wall and have his way with you. Although, I've done that once, it's fun with the right hen."

Fraser growled at him and I wanted nothing more than to have the earth open up and swallow me.

"Just drive the damn car," Fraser finally said and pulled me inside after him.

The back of the Jeep would've been spacious with someone smaller, but with Fraser, it was tighter than the booth at breakfast. Our legs touched and I found myself leaning toward him, hungry for any contact.

"I'm sure it will all be just fine," I said to Fraser, "you don't need to worry."

He held my gaze for a moment and I swear he was fighting a smile when he turned away from me. Lowell shook his head and said something under his breath as he pulled out onto the main road. After a few minutes, my fingers brushed against Frasers and something loosened in my chest at the simple contact. An involuntary sigh slipped out and Fraser wound his fingers through mine. The tension he'd been carrying since this morning started to slip from his shoulders, and even though he still didn't look at me, I could tell that he was calming down.

Perhaps this was the solution; simple, small touches that would take the edge off the physiological and primal needs of the mating mark. The thought brought with it more peace and laid my head back, relishing a little bit of quiet to prepare myself for the next part of this mission.

But we'd barely pulled out of the small town when tires screeched behind us and the sounds of gunfire pierced the morning.

I screamed as they hit the back of the Jeep and Fraser pulled me down onto the seat, shielding me with his body.

"The Jeep is bulletproof! Just hang on!" Lowell yelled.

We veered to the right and careened over a bumpy road. My body caught air several times as Lowell attempted to lose our pursuers. But the ping of bullets on the Jeep and the sounds of shouting outside told me that these people weren't giving up so easily.

"Lowell, where are you goin'?" Fraser yelled.

"You'll see."

We turned to the left and then the right and I had no idea where we were because Fraser was forcing me to stay down. His eyes had turned yellow by this point and his hands and forearms were in his true form, razor sharp claws extending from his long fingers.

"I'll not let them hurt ya," he promised.

"I know but what about you two?"

"Don't worry about us," Lowell said, dialing a number on his cell. "Yeah, we need assistance! Comin' right at ya!"

He hung up and we continued along at a break neck pace. When the gunfire started up again, it was followed by the sound of a car screeching to a stop and crashing. People were yelling, and Lowell chuckled.

Fraser looked behind us and laughed as well.

"Angus called in a favor with the Brawlers," Lowell said. "He knew somethin' might happen."

"Angus sounds like a smart leader," I said, peeking my head up now that Fraser wasn't hunched over me.

"He can be a paranoid arse. But sometimes it pays off," Lowell responded.

Behind us, a group of supernaturals, mostly Werewolves but also a few Orcs, one or two Mothmen and what looked like a Leprechaun, were pointing guns at a large SUV. Smoke rose from the hood and six men were being hauled out at gun point. They were wearing the same black gear that those on the train had worn. It looked like we had driven out onto a country road and had gone through a tiny village. The SUV was off the road at the end of the short row of houses. No one said anything until we'd gotten back on the main road, far away from the scene. While it was unlikely that another team was waiting around the bend, I still couldn't relax.

"Was that Jeffrey?" Fraser asked. "I thought he was in jail again?"

"He was, but got out for good behavior."

Fraser snorted.

"In other words, he was more trouble than he was worth."

"Exactly."

"Who?" I asked.

"The Leprechaun."

"Oh."

There really wasn't anything else to say.

"So, who did ya piss off, Fraser?" Lowell asked.

I glanced up at him, guilt eating at me. I'd just placed Fraser and his brother in danger.

"It's complicated," he replied, his arm tightening around me.

"Is it anythin' to do with the Campbells and whatever craziness is happenin' to our men?"

My stomach flipped.

"Maybe."

Lowell nodded.

"Angus thought so. He's decided to move everyone out of town and to the country seat early. So that's where we're goin'."

"Why did ya not say anythin' sooner?" Fraser demanded.

"Because if we got out of there and nothin' happened, I was going to take ya to the house in town, let ya two love birds have a day to yerselves to fuck as loud and long as ya wanted."

My blush was horribly deep and I forced myself not to look at Fraser.

"But," Lowell continued, "this proves that ya two are in danger and the country seat is more defensible than the city house. No one should suspect that we've gone out there this early, so for today at least, ya two should be safe."

Fraser let out a long breath next to me.

"It's alright," I said, forcing a smile. "I'm sure it will be a lovely place to spend a few nights."

He nodded but refused to look at me. Thinking that he probably wanted his space, now that the danger had passed, I tried to scoot to the other end of the bench seat. But Fraser wasn't having it. His arm tightened possessively around me and a tiny snarl escaped his lips.

"I'd like to hold ya if…if that's alright," he whispered.

I looked up into his eyes, still yellow and intense. I swore I could almost see his true form under the glamour and feel the fear rolling off him in waves.

"It is, I just thought you might want space."

In answer, he brought me flush to his side, both arms encircling me and I let out a contended sigh. He was warm and safe, his muscles firm under my hand as I let myself curl into him and close my eyes. I should be far more panicked after the chase, after knowing for certain that the Protectors had no problems killing all of us to get what they wanted. But here in Fraser's arms, his steady heartbeat in my ear, his strong arms around me, I was calm with the knowledge that, with him, I was completely safe.

I awakened to the warmth of Fraser's body against mine. His arms still encircled me and I nuzzled into the middle of his hard chest. My ear was pressed so close that I could hear his heartbeat pick up. I should've opened my eyes, but it was just so nice to be held by him that I stayed as still as possible to eke out a few more seconds. One massive hand on my back rubbed little circles as if to sooth me and I relaxed.

My hand was splayed against his stomach and I mimicked his motion, loving the way he felt under my palm, even through the glamour of his shirt.

"Wake up, lass," he whispered against my hair, "we're home."

It was so gentle, so soft. The attention was like a balm to the disquiet I had before, and I greedily lapped it up.

When I raised my head and looked up at him, Fraser was leaning down, his arms still securely around my body. Our faces were close and I smiled up at him. Without hesitation, he placed a tiny kiss to the end of my nose. It was the kind of thing two people who adored one another would do, and it made my belly do a flip.

I glanced back and noticed that Lowell wasn't in the Jeep anymore. We were in a large garage that would easily fit three cars, the walls covered in neatly arranged tools and boxes. I wondered how large the house was if the garage was this big.

"My brother went in first while I woke you up," Fraser explained. "I thought you'd want a few minutes of quiet before everyone came at you. But this evenin', we could go into the village. They have a very nice book shop. It'll be safe since no one knows we're here."

It was sweet and exactly what I needed. Once again, Fraser was anticipating things that I had yet to think of.

A girl could get used to this. But I can't. I have to remember why I'm here.

"I would love to see the village, though I do need to find that artifact before anyone else gets hurt."

His gentle smile faded and he gave me a short nod before releasing me. It was foolish, but I fought back a stab of disappointment when he leaned away from me. He was obviously asking for distance, so I sat back into my part of the seat, though our thighs still touched.

"Aye, that ya do," he said after a moment." I…I wasn't thinkin'. We should go inside."

He started to open the door and I stopped him with my hand on his arm.

"What's wrong?" I asked. "I know we haven't known each other long but I would never hurt you or your clan. And if there's something I'm doing wrong, that's affecting you, I want to know about it."

His gaze swung to me, the heat brushing against me like a physical touch. In the span of a breath, his glamour fell away and I saw my Were-wolf gazing back at me. His massive arm dwarfed my hand, muscles tense under his soft dark fur.

"Yer not doin' anythin' wrong," he said, his voice now that deliciously low tone with just the hint of a growl behind his burr. "It's me, lass. It's…it's the bite, what it's doin' to me…I'm afraid of hurtin' ya, of crossin' a line I could never take back."

My heart lurched at those words and I wanted so badly to believe that he was saying he felt something for me. That this was now more than just a cover story, because as much as I didn't want it to, I was definitely starting to want more than that.

But I tried to stay calm, to breathe. He needed me to be level headed, reassuring, not to let my imagination run roughshod.

"Ask me then. If you want to do something, if your instincts are making it hard to resist, ask me and I'll tell you if it's okay."

His long hand, now without the claws I'd seen before, reached out and hesitated. His golden eyes met mine, swimming with questions.

"Can I touch yer leg?" he asked.

"Yes."

Slowly, he lowered his hand onto my thigh, the fingers so long that he could grip it all the way around. But he didn't do that. He just sat it there, light at first and then he flexed his fingers and I giggled.

"I'm very ticklish there," I said.

"I'm sorry."

He began to withdraw his hand and I slapped mine on top of his to stop him.

"No, it's alright, really."

He studied me for a moment and then looked down at where my hand sat on top of his, only half the size.

"Yer so tiny," he whispered.

"You're one of the first to ever call me that."

My voice was a little too light, too glib to cover up the lingering pain of every man that had ever judged my curves, the softness of my belly, the stretch marks on my breasts and thighs.

"They're wrong, Daphne. There's not a thing wrong with the way ya look. Yer perfect," his fingers drew circles on my leg and shivers ran up my spine. "So very perfect."

"Oy, you two can rut later! I'm starvin'!" Lowell shouted.

I jumped at the sudden interruption and Fraser growled. Then my mind caught up with what Lowell had said and I suddenly felt as red as a tomato.

"Oh my god, is that what they think we're doing?" I groaned, covering my face with my hands.

"It's not unusual for newly mated Weres to be…well, very focused on that part of things."

I peeked at him through my fingers, heart pounding in my chest. Was that what was wrong? Was his libido starting to get annoyed with not being indulged?

"Are you…um, focused on it?"

His hand tightened on my thigh and he breathed deeply through his nose.

"I promised I'd never cross that line with ya, and I intend to keep it. You have nothing to fear from me."

Should I tell him that I'm not afraid but entirely up for it?

I wanted to. The words were on the tip of my tongue, an odd sort of courage, making all of my shyness with other men a distant memory.

Perhaps that's because no one has ever looked at me like I'm on the menu and he can't wait to sample me.

I flushed deeper, which I had not thought possible and looked away.

"You two come the fuck on!" Lowell shouted again.

Fraser growled again and looked back at where his brother must've been standing.

"It's alright," I said, forcing a shaky smile on my face, "we can talk more later. But in the meantime, just know that it's fine if you want to hold my hand or put your arm around me, alright? I think that would not only sell the cover story, but it would help us both."

The openness he'd had this whole time shuttered and I kicked myself for whatever misstep I'd made.

"Right…yes the…cover story. Now, would ya give me a moment to calm down? Go on and I'll be along in a minute."

"Of course."

He gave my leg one last squeeze and then withdrew his hand. I didn't look back as I got out of the Jeep and walked through the garage on unsteady legs. When I reached the door at the back, I looked up to see Lowell in his true form. His glamour was beautiful but it was nothing compared to this. His eyes were a brighter blue, bordering on white. He was slighter than Fraser, lanky for a Werewolf I suspected, with short silvery fur that had a slight bluish tint to it. He was standing in the doorway with his arms crossed, a smirk on his snout, bare chested and wearing a kilt like Fraser's.

"Get a little mussed?"

"Do you always stick your snout where it doesn't belong?" I asked.

"Of course, it's more fun that way."

In spite of myself, I laughed at his "devil may care" attitude.

Lowell's gaze settled over my shoulder, a mischievous twinkle in his eyes, and I knew he was looking at Fraser.

"Need a cold shower there?" he called.

"Fuck off, Lowell."

My eyes widened. I'd never heard Fraser use such language, more proof that he was indeed on the edge.

I turned to follow Lowell into the house, when Fraser's hand stopped me and he scooped me up into his arms. I squeaked in surprise and grabbed onto his shoulders.

"What are you doing?" I asked.

"It's tradition for a newly mated female," he said.

"Oh, just like humans."

He smirked at me, which, in his true form, was somehow twice as enticing as when he was in his glamour.

"Where do you think they got it from?"

"Fascinating," I marveled, as he carried me through the door. "How long does that go back, I mean was it something that originated with the Druids or did it evolve after? And did the tradition become passed down from integrating your clans into Mundane settlements or was it from mating? Or perhaps both, which might explain why…"

My voice trailed off as Fraser stopped inside a large living room and I felt eyes latch onto me. I turned in his arms to look out at the room and saw three male Werewolves in nothing but kilts, and two very tall women, all focused intently on me. The oldest woman, who had short cropped gray hair and deep wrinkles on her face and hands, was smiling at me with tears in her eyes, while the other was glaring at me with crossed arms.

The older woman was standing next to the largest Werewolf I'd ever seen. He was taller than even Fraser and his muscles were rippling under his dark brown fur. He eyed me with curiosity bordering on suspicion and it made me want to shrink back. But then, there was a Werewolf that looked very much like Lowell, with the same silvery fur and bright eyes. Except he was standing with a very tall cane, a welcoming grin on his muzzle.

The last Werewolf in the group stood in the very back; his build was like Lowell's and Liam's, and he had a reddish fur that actually seemed to bristle as I met his dark brown eyes. There was something unsettled about the way his gaze darted between Fraser and me. When he and the young woman glanced at one another, I suspected that this was Reuben and his sister Lizzie.

The room was expansive to accommodate the Weres, with oversized chairs and a couch that took up half the space. A large flat screen TV was mounted to a wall to my right, and a wall of photographs was in front of me, some of them very old black and whites. There were books scattered on one of the end tables, and magazines in a rack on the floor by one of the chairs. Lamps were placed liberally around the room, off for now. The whole room was cozy; it was meant to be a place to gather and connect, which I assumed was why it was chosen for my inspection.

"Are ya gonna to put her down?" Lowell asked.

Fraser growled, the fur on his tail puffed out, and the one that I assumed was Angus shot his little brother a scowl.

"Och, Lowell, ya should know better," the older woman smacked the young Were on the arm and he rubbed it. "I'm Oona MacDonald but I insist that ya call me Gran."

I smiled down at her and tried to reach out my hand to shake hers, but I was still being held by Fraser.

"You can put me down, it's okay."

He didn't move, but eyed the others in the room as if he were expecting trouble.

Gran just laughed and shook her head.

"Don't worry dear, it will pass. Why, when I mated my Gerald, he wouldn't set me on my feet all day! Carried me around like I was a child, but it was better than him fightin' with the others."

I gave her a shaky grin and tried to be at peace with it but it felt so odd to be carried around like this.

"Now, this is Angus," Gran pointed to the very large Were next to her, "Liam," to the one that looked nearly identical to Lowell, "Ruben," to the one scowling in the back, "and dear Lizzie," she pointed to the woman.

It was disconcerting to be the focus of so many pairs of eyes that all held such different feelings within them. I wasn't sure if Ruben wanted to toss me out or slice me up. And Lizzie looked like she was ready to snarl at me. Liam was the only one, besides Gran, who was smiling.

"It's nice to meet you all."

"Isn't that nice?" Lowell said. "Can we eat now?"

Gran smacked him again, more playful this time, and walked past us to what I assumed was the kitchen. Fraser stood there, hands tight on my body as the rest of his family walked past us. I half expected him to snarl at Angus when he came near. And while Fraser did tense, he didn't make a sound.

"Welcome to our family," Angus said, his voice impossibly deep. "I had someone pick up yer bag from the train station. It's in yer room upstairs. I look forward to getting' to know ya better."

"Thank you," I said weakly.

Next came Lowell, who winked at me, oblivious to Fraser's thin restraint being taxed, and then Liam, leaning heavily on his cane.

"I hear yer an academic," he said.

I swallowed, nerves ricocheting through me. What had Fraser said to them? And what did "academic" mean to them? Would I be expected to have a certain level of knowledge about a range of subjects? To act a certain way?

All I could think of was how I constantly didn't measure up in my family, and how devastated I would be if that were the case here. Which didn't make any sense considering I'd only just met them, and this relationship wasn't real.

Still, the feelings were, and that's what was winning at the moment.

"I-I am," I finally said.

Liam's smile widened and I could almost picture the Werewolf with a pair of glasses on his snout, pouring over books in a library.

"I am somethin' of an amateur scholar, mostly antiquities and such. If ya have the time, perhaps we could talk about our areas of interest? I have a small library here, if ya ever want to peruse it?"

Something loosened in my chest at his simple, gentle words and I smiled.

"That would be lovely, thank you."

Ruben was next and the moment he was near me, a dread settled in my stomach. He radiated fear and something else that I couldn't quite pin down. He swallowed, eyes darting around, before giving Fraser a quick nod and making for the kitchen. The last one was Lizzie. She was quite pretty, with dark brown hair and gray eyes, a smattering of freckles on her face. I had assumed that since she was part of the clan that she'd be in her true form but perhaps the women didn't do that.

"So," she said, crossing her arms and giving Fraser a hard look, "you can mate whoever the hell ya please, but Angus and I have to suffer? Must be nice being the second son. No one needs ya to do anythin' other than rut and be obedient."

"No one wanted to hurt ya," Fraser whispered. "It was an unfortunate circumstance."

"Yes, unfortunate. But for who? You were the one that negotiated the terms. You were the one that told Angus he had to put me aside. Do ya have any idea how much it hurt? How much we both…" she swallowed, and closed her eyes, collecting herself. When she looked back at us, the hard glint in her gaze was breathtaking in its cruelty.

"I just hope ya both have better luck than we did."

The threat was thinly veiled at best, and Fraser bared his teeth at her, his arms holding me very tight.

"Ya touch her and—"

"What, Fraser? What could ya possibly do to me that is worse than what has passed?"

"Why are ya even here?" he asked.

"I keep askin' myself that very question. Ruben seems to think it's important, and Angus. said that it would show that there's unity in the clan, that there's no hard feelins from us."

"Ya better not make any trouble at the handfastin'. For all our sakes, Lizzie."

"Don't worry, Fraser, I'll be a perfect little bitch."

And with that, Lizzie walked into the kitchen.

Fraser was breathing heavily, his grip on me firm. I ran my fingers through the fur on his shoulder and around to the back of his head.

"Look at me," I said.

His eyes met mine and I massaged the back of his head with one of my hands. Little as I was by comparison, just the act of touching him seemed to help, and he relaxed.

"It's going to be alright," I insisted. "We'll find it, and the handfasting will go forward as planned."

"I never meant to hurt Lizzie or Ruben. But a marriage was the only way…" he trailed off.

I finally saw the guilt attached to all of this for him and it broke my heart. Under the grumpy, hard exterior was a soft hearted Were whose loyalty to his clan ran deep.

"Sometimes, we aren't faced with a good choice," I whispered, "but we do the best we can. That sounds like what you did. Lizzie's heart will mend with time. She'll be happy again."

"I hope yer right."

"Oy, you two get your arses in here!" Lowell yelled.

"Don't be rude," Gran said.

"I'm hungry!"

I chuckled at Lowell's whining and Fraser shook his head.

"I hope yer ready for this," he said.

"As ready as I'll ever be."

We turned for the kitchen and Fraser stopped.

"Oh, uh…this is embarrassing but…I may need ya on my lap. If yer too close to any of my brothers, it could set me off."

My stomach dropped and I stared at him.

All through the meal *on his lap?*

Right on top of the anaconda he's got under that kilt?

My pale skin was going to become permanently pink with how often I was blushing, but I just couldn't seem to control it.

"I, um," I straightened my shoulders. "Alright. That's unexpected but…sure," I wagged a finger at him. "As long as you don't try and feed me."

It was his turn to chuckle.

"I make no promises."

CHAPTER FIFTEEN

FRASER

Lunch couldn't have been worse with the tension thick in the air. If Daphne noticed, however, she didn't show it.

She laughed at Lowell's stupid jokes, and inquired about Liam's studies. She complimented Gran's cooking and even drew out a bit of conversation from Angus, though it made me nervous when she did. He was acting more withdrawn than usual, but it was his own fault.

Ruben and Lizzie were mostly quiet throughout the meal, and I had no idea why Angus would want either of them here. It was bad enough he'd cheated on Imogen with Lizzie, only to throw her over again, but Ruben looked like he wanted to throttle Angus every time he laid eyes on him. And Angus took great pains to not look at Lizzie. He'd sat at the opposite end of the table from her, and hadn't said one word to her the whole meal. As for Ruben, when he wasn't glaring at Angus, his leg bounced under the table and his gaze skittered all over the place.

And then there's the way he looked at Daphne. If I hadn't been holding her, I would've dragged him outside and pummeled his arse.

If Ruben had the artifact, it was obvious that what Daphne had said about it taking over someone, had probably happened to Ruben. It made me simultaneously glad he was here, so she could find the damn thing, and nervous. He had already caused serious problems, and the handfasting had to go off without a hitch if we were to make a path forward for both clans.

Why had my brothers allowed Ruben and Lizzie here this full moon of all times? Why didn't Angus…

But I knew why.

Lizzie had been his mate in everything but name. Even though Angus had agreed to the arranged marriage, and that it was the only way to make peace, it didn't change how he felt about her. And the artifact had taken advantage of that, for both of them. The way she looked at him, with longing and sorrow that made my chest ache. It was like looking into my future. Except after the clan witch removed my mark from Daphne, I knew it would be far worse.

My grip tightened on Daphne's hip at that thought. She was mine now, mine and here with me, and I would take every second I could with her before it was over.

She smiled up at me, sensing the tension in my body. Of course she did. Whether she knew it or not, the instincts of the mating bite went both ways. And while Mundanes took a bit longer to for their senses to catch up, it was possible that Daphne was already developing a feel for my moods and needs.

Especially since she's my true mate.

The more I thought it, and accepted it, the harder this was going to be, but I couldn't seem to help myself.

On the one hand, I was relieved my family had bought the cover story. If they hadn't, then Angus would have put his foot down and I would've had to send Daphne away. But on the other, having her so close, holding her in such a familiar way was chipping away at my resolve. I saw the way Gran looked at us, with barely concealed joy shining in her eyes. She'd wanted us males settled and happy for years. And while Angus might be getting settled, he wouldn't be happy. It had pained her to know that he was giving that up, especially since she'd grown quite attached to Lizzie and Ruben. They'd spent more time with our family than their own over the years, so it wasn't exactly surprising that they were here now. They always spent moon time with us.

Though I would've insisted that things be different this time.

"That was delicious," Daphne said, wiping her mouth with a napkin.

"Are ya sure ya ate enough?" Gran asked. "Yer portions were so small."

Daphne's eyes widened and her body stiffened against mine. She was afraid of offending Gran, but I also knew that Daphne wasn't shy in any way when it came to food. Gran had made her famous meat pies with roasted potatoes, greens and rum cake for dessert. It was a feast indeed, but she was used to feeding Weres, and we had enormous appetites.

"She's Mundane, Gran," I reminded her.

"Oh well, yes, that's true," Gran patted Daphne's cheek. "When you're swollen with his cub you'll have to remember to eat more. Were cubs take a lot out of Mundane mothers."

Daphne's mouth worked and her face did that adorable flush that was becoming a daily occurrence.

"I will remember that," she said, with a nervous chuckle.

The thought of her belly filled with my cub, a Were that would have her eyes maybe and her strength of mind…it made my body stir and I pulled her closer against me out of instinct.

"Way to go, Gran," Lowell said around a bite of his third slice of cake, "as if Fraser needs any more reason to think of ruttin'."

"Lowell!" Gran chided. "That's not proper table talk. Yer on dish duty. Come on, you too Ruben. Take yer sulkiness and do something productive with it. Oh, and Fraser, I have a healin' tonic at the ready for ya. Don't like the thought of ya havin' a wound from anything spelled."

Liam's mouth tightened, almost imperceptibly, but I pretended not to notice. When he'd first been injured, Gran poured every kind of concoction down his throat. None of it helped. I knew she was just worried, but it still felt awkward hearing her say that in front of Liam.

When Gran plopped down a steaming cup that smelled like boiled grass, Daphne hopped down from my lap and I clenched my hands to keep from grabbing her again. She seemed to know that it wasn't easy to let go because she turned sparkling eyes up at me, a smirk on her face.

"I'll be right back," she said and started to help clear the dishes.

"Oh no, not this time," Gran said to her. "You and Fraser should go into the village, take some time for yerselves before the busyness of the handfastin'. It doesn't have as many fine shops as town does but the village is still quite nice for a walk and a pint. But first, Fraser, drink your medicine!"

I began to down the healing brew when Lizzie bolted from the room and Angus turned away, his jaw clenched tight.

Gran sighed and patted Angus' arm, and I was grateful she didn't see me grimace at the sour taste of her brew.

"I know this is hard, and I'm sorry. But it's reality now, no turnin' back. She'll accept that."

"Before she does somethin' stupid?" he growled.

"She's got a better head on her shoulders than ya give her credit for. It was you that reopened that old wound," Gran said with a disapproving frown. "Ya want someone to blame—"

"I know," Angus snapped and immediately sighed. "I'm sorry. Yer right. It was my fault."

"No, I shouldn't have poked. This should be a happy time but instead…Well, nothin' to be done but go through it."

Angus nodded, his usually straight posture bowed as if under a great weight.

"Brother," I said to him, "is there anything I can help with?"

"Yes," he said, glancing back at Daphne, "tell me how, when ya were supposed to bring back answers to why these disturbances have happened, ya walk in with a mate instead?"

Guilt gnawed at me. He was right, and I hadn't thought of how it would look when I agreed to the cover story.

"It…it's a long story. But I do think I have an answer. I got some direction, things to look for."

"Then do it, before the Campbells get here tomorrow. Nothin' can go wrong Fraser, you understand? I just barely got the old man to agree to go through with this. If somethin' happens to Imogen, or if the handfastin' is disturbed…"

"War."

He nodded, his frown deep.

"War."

I glanced at Daphne where she stood behind me and she gave me a slight nod.

"I understand. I'll get to work on it."

Angus snorted.

"Between ruttin' your new mate?"

"Why is everyone so damn obsessed with me beddin' her?" I growled.

"Because we need everyone focused, brother," Angus answered, rising from his chair. "And a newly mated Were male is only focused on one thing. Get it out of your system before the handfastin' and find the artifact. That's all ya have to do. Think ya can handle it?"

I was taken aback. Angus could be curt and distant, but I'd never known him to be mean.

It must be the stress. Or the artifact.

"Don't worry about me," I said, barely able to control the snarl in my voice.

Angus turned and walked toward his study. A moment later, I heard the door slam.

"Don't be mad at him," Liam said from where he still sat at the table. "He's been carryin' a lot the last couple of weeks."

"I know, and I was supposed to help."

"Ya have," Liam grinned at Daphne, who was chewing on her bottom lip, staring out the window. "Gran was so happy to hear about yer matin', and while Angus might be irritated right now, it was a good sign to the Campbells that ya were bringing a mate. They figured ya wouldn't be doing that if things were dire."

"That's good to hear. How have ya been?" I couldn't resist asking.

His smile became tight.

"Hurts more lately. The witch said that the healin' might be unravelin'. But I'm hopeful. I have a spot on the dig at Hala Sultan Tekke this summer and I intend to make it."

"On Cyprus?" Daphne asked, whirling around from the window.

Liam's eyes lit up and he nodded.

"Yes, the very same! Do you know it?"

"I've always wanted to go there! How did you secure a spot on the team? I've applied every single year and never gotten very far."

"Oh, it took quite a lot of convincin' but I have a connection with someone at the Cairo University in the cultural preservation department."

"Oh, that *is* lucky."

I couldn't help grinning as the two of them chattered on about the dig site and the artifacts that had already been found.

I need to get her out of this house before I drag her into my room and do every base thing I've been thinking of since the moment I sank my teeth into her.

"Ya ready to go?" I asked. "I believe I promised ya a book store."

"Yes, though you may regret it," she chuckled.

Standing here in the home that I grew up in, the smell of Gran's cooking hanging in the air, my brothers playfully arguing in the next room, I could almost see a future for us. Daphne had fit in surprisingly well with my brothers, in spite of the tension of having Ruben and Lizzie here. It was the most natural thing in the world to slip my arm around her and pull her close. She threaded her fingers through the fur on my shoulder and laid her head on my chest. I closed my eyes, tail wagging happily, and just for a moment, I let myself sink into how complete I felt.

Daphne showed no fear of my size, though I was so much bigger than her, nor did she seem to mind how much different I was physically from her. In fact, it seemed as if she preferred my true form to my glamour, though I had no proof of that and it was probably just wishful thinking.

"This is nice," she whispered against me.

"Aye, it is."

Lowell chose that moment to come back into the dining room, half a piece of bread shoved into his mouth.

"Och, get a room."

Daphne turned her face into my chest and laughed.

"Well, I guess we should go then," I growled.

"Yes, I have books to buy."

We walked out to the garage, the large doors still open to the outside. I could hear voices from the gravel driveway to my left and it made the fur on my neck stand on end.

"Oh, shoot," Daphne said. "I left my tote inside, I'll be right back."

I nodded.

"When ya get back, wait for me in the car. I've got to talk to Ruben."

"Fraser, be careful, he might have the artifact."

I glanced down at her and gave the tip of Daphne's nose a quick nip, which brought that adorable flush to her cheeks that I was starting to love so much.

"Don't worry, I just wanna talk."

"Alright."

When Daphne had gone inside, I walked to the edge of the garage doorway where I was just able to see Ruben and his sister talking.

"I'm goin' back to Edinburgh," Lizzie said. "Comin' here was a mistake."

"It will all work out, I promise," said Ruben.

"That's what ya said before, and the only thing that's changed is that everythin's worse!"

"I have this under control."

"Have you? That bitch is still comin' here to mate Angus, and ya look worse today than yesterday."

"I'm fine," Ruben ground out.

"No, yer not. I don't ken where you got that damn thing, but ya need to get rid of it."

Ruben snarled.

"I'll no take orders from *you* or anyone here for that matter!"

"Keep yer voice down, I don't want Angus hearing ya."

"That weak excuse for a clan leader? He's no better than—."

I could endure a lot of things, but hearing him disparage my brother wasn't one of them.

I stalked over the gravel toward Ruben and Lizzie, next to Ruben's car. Lizzie saw me first and put her hand on Ruben's arm to stop him.

"No better than what?" I asked.

"Nothin', he's just upset for me, that's all," Lizzie said.

"Is that true?"

Ruben clenched his jaw and shrugged his sister's hand off his arm.

"We were just leavin'," he said.

I stepped a little closer until I was within striking distance of Ruben. I was bigger than him, always had been. And there had never been a time when Ruben could take me in a fight. But all the same, there was a gleam in Ruben's eyes that had me treading a bit more carefully than I usually did.

"Maybe it would be better if ya stuck to the land around yer cottage for the full moon," I said to him, "or go back to Edinburgh, just in case."

He gave me a derisive laugh.

"Why? You afraid I'll disrupt yer precious handfastin'?"

"Something like that. But also, it might be good not to force your sister to attend somethin' that will be hard for her."

"She's tougher than ya give her credit for."

"Standing right here, ya bawbags! And I had decided to go back before ya marched over here, Fraser, so you can stuff it!"

"That's quite a bonny lass ya've got," Ruben said.

I bared my teeth at him and closed the distance until we were almost snout to snout. Ruben didn't flinch. If anything he seemed to welcome the intrusion into his space.

"Ya keep yer words and yer eyes off my mate."

Ruben also bared his teeth and laughed at me.

"We both know she's not the sweet little bookworm she appears to be, Fraser. Yer not the type to have a whirlwind romance, not since Silvia rejected ya."

He was trying to provoke me, though I didn't ken why. It wasn't important though because I couldn't lose control and cause a scene. I needed Ruben to reveal something, to make a mistake. And short of that, I couldn't afford for him to not be around. If he disappeared, and he did have the artifact with him, chances were that it would disappear with him.

So I took a step back, though every instinct told me to throttle the bastard.

"If ya two are done actin' like eejits, can we go?" Lizzie demanded. "I have a long drive."

Ruben smirked at me

"I'll be seein' ya, Fraser."

The words had the fur down my back standing up. There was a weight to them, a promise of something dark and I didn't ken what it was.

CHAPTER SIXTEEN

DAPHNE

Fraser had reverted to his usual taciturn self as we pulled out of the garage. I was relieved that Ruben hadn't tried anything but also intensely curious about what had happened. But if the way he gripped the steering wheel and huffed out a growl was any indication, it hadn't been a good encounter.

Best to wait and ask when he's not so upset, I think.

I got my first real look at the house as we cleared the garage and it took my breath away. I knew that the size was to accommodate the Weres, but I had no idea I was staying in something that looked like a small mansion. It had three stories that I could see, and it stretched very wide on either side, and deep into the back yard where I glimpsed a beautifully manicured lawn with several seating areas and a forest beyond. The house looked newly painted in white with green trim. Roses grew in oversized granite pots around the front. We passed a large walled in garden a few feet beyond the front gravel drive, with ivy almost completely obscuring the stone walls. Just beyond the garden was an exceptionally large open space where two delivery trucks were off loading what looked like giant tents. I assumed that was where the handfasting would take place and wondered what that would be like, to have a formal ceremony to bind oneself to this clan.

The entire estate was so big, it made me wonder why I hadn't seen any staff, housekeepers or cooks. Maybe the clan was too private for that?

"Do you have people to help run this place?" I asked.

"Usually yes, but at moon time we send most of them away. Most are not Weres and those that are generally like to be with their own families around that time, though we'll have to ask some of them back to help with the handfastin'."

When we left the gravel drive of the house, Fraser put his glamour up and I bit back my disappointment. The drive was lovely. There were rolling green hills on either side of us, sometimes broken up by homes or people just hanging out in the open. I spied what I thought maybe some of Scotland's famous Celtic ruins in the distance, but I couldn't be sure.

"It's really beautiful," I murmured.

"Aye. No other place more so," Fraser agreed.

"You really love it, don't you?"

"It's said that, when the Druids made us, their love for this land seeped into the spell. Over the hundreds of years, some Weres have lost that love for Scotland, but it's always replaced by passion for another place, and that's where they choose to become guardians. We are hard wired to love a land to our very bones. I'm just happy that it's Scotland for me."

"You make me quite jealous." I leaned my cheek on my hand and gazed out the window. "I've never felt that way about a place before."

"What about where ya grew up?"

"No, it's…well, it's hard to feel love for a place when one feels like they don't fit in with their family."

"So it was like that, was it?"

"Yeah."

I usually tried not to think of how lonely it had been to grow up with such a deep sense of abnormality among my family, but every now and then it snuck up on me. And, like now, it usually produced a few tears.

A calloused finger brushed against my cheek, scooping up a tear.

"Don't cry, lass," he whispered.

"Sorry, it's quite unprofessional."

"No, it's understandable. After what happened on the train and then this mornin', runnin' for our lives, I'm surprised you haven't done it before now."

"Oh, I think it will catch up with me, just hopefully not until this is settled."

His fingers wove through mine on the seat between us.

"Is this alright?"

I gave him a sniffling smile.

"Fraser, you don't have to keep asking that. You have my permission to touch me."

He didn't say anything and I was worried I'd been harsh with him. I was going to ask and stopped as we turned a corner and found ourselves on the outskirts of a quaint village. Stone and brick buildings were nestled on either side of us, people walking around with bags or toting children in carriers or strollers. Several of the buildings were taverns, of course. But there were also shops with clothing, food and the single most charming bookstore I'd ever seen.

He pulled into a parking spot and before I could even reach for the door, Fraser pulled me half into his lap. People were walking around, a few of them glanced our way but I didn't care. All I could see was Fraser and the way he was devouring me with his eyes. His whisper was rough as he clutched my hip with his hand.

"Sometimes I just can't keep my hands off ya and it frightens me."

"Why?"

"Because the more I touch ya, the more I…"

My mouth went dry imagining what the end of that sentence might be. In that moment, all of the good sense I should've had disappeared and I decided to do either a very daring thing or a very stupid thing.

I pressed my lips to his.

Even knowing that this wasn't the real Fraser, that his glamour kept me from truly feeling him, my body melted against his. He opened his mouth to me and I brushed my tongue against his. His groan sent shivers down my spine. It was the sound of a hungry animal, and I wanted him to feast on me.

Fraser's long fingers threaded through my hair, tugging it out of the ponytail and he angled my head to take the kiss deeper. I wasn't aware of the little mewling sounds I was making until he broke the kiss and gently moved me off his lap.

"I'm sorry lass, I shouldn't have started that," he said, his eyes glowing yellow.

"I believe I started that, actually."

He stared ahead, hands tensing on the steering wheel.

"It's not that I don't want to."

"Then what is it?"

"It's not right," he growled. "This isn't real, it's a lie so ya can find what's hurtin' my clan, nothin' more. And I won't use it as an excuse to take advantage of ya."

"Even if I say it's what I want?"

He closed his eyes and took some breaths. His one-word answer was a dagger to my chest.

"Yes."

I took in a sharp breath and tried to steady myself. We had said at the beginning that these feelings were just the result of the bite, it changed things physically for us. It had been what we'd agreed upon. Yet instead of remembering that, I had let myself think that Fraser might actually want me for me, not for the bite.

I let my libido run away with itself. Isn't that embarrassing?

"I'm sorry," I said, shoving down the way my voice wanted to crack. "I thought...I'm sorry."

"No, don't apologize," Fraser said, "this is more difficult than I thought it would be and I...Daphne, I'm the one who's sorry. You are beautiful and intelligent and ya deserve better than this."

My hand cut through the air to stop him. I couldn't bear to hear him say anything else that reminded me of all the times someone had dumped me, but tried to do it nicely.

"Stop Fraser, please."

We both let out a long sigh and if lunch had been awkward this was ten times so. I had to think of a way to bring us back to some kind of normal. But the only way I saw was to meet this head on, to not pretend it hadn't happened.

"This was just physiological," I said, echoing what we'd both agreed on yesterday. "And okay, it's harder than we thought, but we're both adults, and I hope we've started to become friends?"

His gaze slid to mine, a confusing soup of emotions swirling in those dark depths. I refused to figure them out, however. I needed my logic, my brain right now, not my heart.

"Aye, we have," his voice was rough.

"Alright then, this was a slip up. We've talked about it, and now we'll go shopping like friends."

My voice was too light, too sure to be true.

Fraser must see right through me. How could he not? I'm a mess inside whether I want to acknowledge it or not.

"Aye," he said at last, "that sounds like a good plan."

I couldn't get out of the Jeep fast enough. And before he was even at the sidewalk, my hand was on the door knob of the bookstore. I waited until he was behind me to open the squeaky door and go inside.

The shop was old, as evidenced by the way the floor slanted, and the sheen on the well-worn wood of the counter tops and book shelves, which rose almost to the low ceiling. A smiling young woman and an older man stood behind the counter ringing up a shopper and chatting about the book they just bought. I was relieved when they only nodded and smiled at us, not seeking to guide me in any way. I wasn't here to speak to people, I was here to discover a new friend, a new world, a new obsession. My fingertips grazed the spines of a nearby collection, all books on gardening. I had a decidedly black thumb, but my heart was still pulled by the beautiful lettering and the few covers I could see. If it was a book, no matter the subject matter, I seemed to be in danger of enchantment.

It was like magic the way books could steady me, the instantaneous way they had of making my fears and sadness go away. At least for a little while.

"What do you want to look for?" Fraser asked.

"Everything," I said.

I wandered to the back of the shop, drawn by the way the sunlight streamed in and illuminated the dust in the air. Our feet caused the floor to creak, and the slope was worse now, but I didn't care. There was no one else back here and the tall shelves hid us from those in the front.

After a quick perusal of the shelves I realized that I'd wandered into the history section and let out a sigh of pleasure.

"What is it?" Fraser asked.

"One of my favorite places of any book store is the history section."

I plucked down a book on the women who had ruled the Egyptian empire and thumbed through it until I found the pictures that inevitably were included in books like this. I stared at them, studying and longing to get my hands on the statues and bowls, the funeral masks and such that they showed.

"I love ancient Egypt, I've always wanted to go," I professed. "Actually, I want to go *everywhere*. Egypt, Cyprus, Greece. I want to touch the pillars of Aphrodite's temple, and stand at the foot of the Colossi of Memnon. To climb the great pyramids and walk through the valley of the kings. I want to dig in the earth and find something that no one has touched in a thousand years and unlock its secrets. Maybe finally find Nefertiti's tomb or the resting place of Alexander the Great. I want to…"

I looked up at Fraser, whose gaze had gone soft as he leaned on a shelf and listened to me. A relaxed smile graced his lips under his beard. Normally, when I ramble, people tend to tune me out, or try to show interest that they don't really feel. But not Fraser. I could tell that he'd been not just listening, but invested in what I was saying. These dreams of mine, so precious that I'd hardly told anyone about them, had come tumbling from my mouth as if Fraser's kiss from before had been laced with truth serum.

I blushed and looked down at the book.

"I talk too much."

"No, lass. I could listen to ya talk all day like that. Yer face…ya get all glowy when ya talk about the things ya love."

"I think that's my penchant for blushing at the drop of a hat."

He chuckled and I had to force myself not to let the sound rumble through me.

"Aye, but it's glowy nonetheless."

I longed to bask in this moment, the way he was gazing at me, the warmth of being found interesting not boring. But I couldn't. Not when we'd just had a conversation about our feelings and how we couldn't let them get the better of us.

So I turned away and began to replace the book on the shelf when Fraser took it from my hands.

"Ya want this one?"

"Yes but—"

"My treat. As many as ya want."

I choked out a laugh.

"Do *not* make a promise like that to someone like me."

"Why not? Ya think I can't afford it?"

"I think you won't be able to carry them all."

Now his eyes sparked with amusement and his grin widened to show straight white teeth.

"Let's see, shall we?"

I crossed my arms and pretended to think.

"You sure? I know how fragile your Highlander egos can be. I wouldn't want to bruise it."

"Och lass, I think you'll find my stamina is up to the task."

I knew he was talking about books. And yet, I still had to remind myself that he was talking about books.

"Alright then, I did try to warn you," I said, and placed another choice in his arms in an effort to bring my mind out of the gutter it so longed to be in.

We traveled along the history shelves and I added a book on goddess worship and another on the history of the sex toy, which I couldn't help but squeal over when I found it. When Fraser's eyes landed on the title his grin turned a tad lascivious and I had to lock down my body's reaction.

"I *am* a sex historian," I reminded him.

"Hmm," it came out half yummy sound and half growl. "And is that all it is? Purely research?"

I turned away from him, trying to maintain some control, some distance. This was playful, friendly. Nothing more.

"Maybe," I said, as I walked toward a different section. "Though sometimes I find myself in need of… experimentation let's say."

Fraser made a muffled sound between a cough and another growl and my face heated. It was thrilling to flirt like this, to trade verbal banter without the fear that usually accompanied it. I didn't know why I felt so comfortable with him, but one thing was for sure. This was starting to cross the line we'd both agreed upon in the Jeep. And I didn't want it to stop. I wanted to find out how far I could go before he pushed me up against one of these shelves and shoved his hands down my pants.

Stop, stop, stop! You can't think like that Daphne!

To distract us both from this line of thinking, I chose a couple on Celtic legends that made Fraser snort.

"Something wrong?"

"If you wanna know about these legends, ya won't find the truth in these books."

"Really? Where will I find it then?" I asked with a smirk.

Fraser stepped closer, eyes glittering. God he was beautiful. Even if I did prefer his true form, Frasers glamour was a cross between a gladiator and a highland lord, all powerful and virile with a hint of the feral energy. It was an intoxicating mix, especially when he gave me that wry smile he was currently wearing.

"Right here, Daphne," he whispered.

My breath caught and I remembered the kiss in the Jeep.

And his rebuff.

I stepped back and shook my head, the playfulness souring in my gut.

"What's wrong?" Fraser asked.

"Nothing I just…I want to get some fiction before your arms get tired."

Though the last part was spoken with a trace of a smirk, it was muted now. I was starting to feel like Fraser truly didn't realize how he was affecting me, how this flirting was barbed, wounding me because it would never be anything more, never mean more to him than just friendly banter.

I was so focused on getting away from him and just finishing this shopping trip that I wasn't watching where I was going and I ended up bumping into a woman in the romance section.

"Oh, I'm sorry," I said, and then my eyes widened in shock.

The woman I'd bumped into, who was now grinning at me with lipstick smeared on her teeth, was none other than my Uncle George's wife, Prudence.

"Why, is that you Daphne dear?"

"Aunt Prudence," I said, giving her a halfhearted kiss on the cheek and trying not to gag on her perfume. "What are you doing here?"

"Why, is that anyway to say hello?" My aunt's overly made up face turned to Fraser and she thrust her chest out a little more. "Who is this now, someone you're working for?"

"I'm her boyfriend," Fraser replied, slipping into the lie easily.

Aunt Prudence stared with wide eyes and then dissolved into a fit of snorting giggles.

"Oh, what? No! Come now, what is this? Be serious now, you're joking!"

Fraser's look turned cold and he looked his nose down at my aunt.

"No, I'm not. In fact, I'm quite serious about your niece."

"Oh, well, *quite serious*, eh?" she winked at me. "That sounds…well, unexpected. Well done, dear. You *finally* caught a good looking one."

I wanted the floor to open up and swallow Aunt Prudence whole.

Or maybe just a shelf to fall over and conk her on the head so she'll shut up.

"Is Uncle George with you?" I asked, desperate to get the attention off of me.

"Yes, he's here on some business for the University. We were supposed to be vacationing in Italy this week but no, he had to cancel it. Now we're running around here. You know, we were in Paris first and he wouldn't even let me shop, just a quick pop in, and then he got a phone call that we had to come to this place. Not even a proper city. What the university could have him doing in this tiny village is really beyond me."

I cringed at her loud voice and wondered how in the world I was going to get her to leave us alone. Once a family member was cornered by aunt Prudence, it was best to just pour a big glass of wine and wait until she tires herself out. But that wasn't a strategy I was keen to experience at the moment.

"If you'll excuse us," Fraser cut in, "we should be going."

He tried to guide me away toward the front but then Uncle George appeared in front of us and I wondered what the hell I'd ever done to deserve this level of torture.

"Oh, George," Aunt Prudence said with a chortle, "this is Daphne's 'boyfriend'."

She actually put air quotes around it. Fraser looked like he was reaching his limit and while that could be entertaining, I was in no mood to deal with any fall out from it. I just wanted to get away from them and continue my conversation with Fraser.

"We really do need to go," I said.

"He looks like he can take care of your purchases," Uncle George said, looking at Fraser like he was an unwashed troll. "I want a word with you."

Fraser looked at me, clearly asking if it was alright and I nodded.

"Oh, I'll go with you," Aunt Prudence gushed. "I saw some postcards up front that I simply must have."

When they were both out of ear shot, Uncle George's tight smile faded and he glared at me.

"You didn't get your way at the University and so you decided to whore yourself out on assignment."

I thought perhaps I hadn't heard him right, and blinked.

"What?"

"Letting the Director send you out like this with that…that *Werewolf*. It's disgusting. I thought you had more self-respect, but it looks like I was wrong."

Blood rushed to face and I heard ringing in my ears. Fury wasn't an emotion I was overly familiar with, so when it erupted in me, I was always too swept up in it to notice until it was too late.

Normally, there was regret at the end. However, I highly doubted that would be the case today.

"His name is Fraser MacDonald, and he's been nothing but wonderful to me since I was assigned to his case."

He snorted.

"Oh 'assigned' is what they're calling it now?"

"You can't stand it can you?"

"What?"

"That I'm better at this than you are, that I fit in there more than you ever did. That I was sent out on assignment, on a real case and you're still barely trusted to be their errand boy. You and I both know that the University didn't send you here, but I also know that Director Dearborne wouldn't trust an arrogant, cruel, short sighted man like you with anything other than something a trained dog could do."

Uncle George stepped into my space and I took a step back from him. He was so furious that the corners of his tightly pressed mouth were white and his eyes were bulging.

"You have no idea what's coming," he spat at me. "But I won't be inviting you to come on board this time. No, we don't need you *Daft-ne*. You and your idiotic belief that you are anything but a joke with your obsessive study of such base subject matter. You are nothing but what we all have thought for years. A joke, a silly girl with nothing to offer."

"And you are nothing but a sad old man grasping at glory that will continue to elude him."

He laughed in my face.

"Go back to your Werewolf and don't be surprised he tosses you away when he's gotten what he's wanted from you, *Daft-ne*."

A huge hand shot out and grasped my uncle at the back of the neck. I stared up in shock at Fraser's enormous body, eyes aflame and face contorted with rage.

"Her name is *Daphne*, and she's worth more to me than you will ever know. She's one of the smartest, most extraordinary women I've ever met. And stronger than I ever gave her credit for, to have survived ya for as long as she has without shatterin'. Do not speak of her again in such a way if ya value yer life, do I make myself clear?"

Uncle George stared up at Fraser and whimpered, his mouth moving as if to form words but none came out.

"You are a disgraceful man," Fraser continued, "to treat a lass in such a way. And not just any lass, but one as bonny and fine as Daphne. Apologize."

He gaped and Fraser shook him a little.

"Do it."

"I–I'm sorry," Uncle George breathed.

"Daphne."

"I–I'm sorry, D–Daphne."

"Now go, get out of this village. And if ya ever come back here, I'll have the other Weres around here run ya out. And trust me, ya peely-wally bawbag, they will not be as gentle as I've been."

He let my uncle go and the old man didn't even look at me as he scampered and stumbled out of the shop. I stared at Fraser, disbelief and embarrassment quickly mixing with the anger that still burned so hot inside me.

"Are ya alright?" he asked, his hand cupping my cheek.

"You didn't have to do that. He…I'm used to it, Fraser, you didn't have to—"

"So that makes it alright? That they've done it to ya so long that yer 'used to it' now?"

"No, of course not, but I can defend myself."

"Of that I have no doubt. But yer my mate. And when someone talks like that to ya, it's not just you they insult. They insult me, my family. You are my family as long as ya have that mark on ya, and I will not let anyone treat ya so."

My mouth went dry at his words, at how *right* it felt to be called his family, how much I wanted to believe that I was everything he said I was, even if this was all fake.

And that right there. The doubt that maybe this was all just part of that bite, that he couldn't stop himself from defending me because of that and nothing else, had my control shattering and I started to cry.

"What is it? Why are ya cryin'?" he asked, wiping the tears away.

"Is this just part of…of the damn bite?" I asked, my voice breaking. "Is that the only reason you did that?"

He stared at me shock and confusion.

"Naw, of course not!"

"But your instincts, you have to defend me, right? It's not real."

"Daphne," he captured my face between his large hands and brushed my tears away with his thumb. I couldn't help but look him in eye like this and I saw there the sincerity I desperately needed to believe in. "I wouldn't lie about any of that. It's not the bite, it's *you*. With or without it, I meant every word."

"But you called me extraordinary," I whispered. "I know how important family is to you and…Fraser, I'm not all of those things you said. I'm annoying and I talk too much and I lose track of time because I get lost in a book and…."

"You are all those things I said and more. And for the record, I find your talkativeness rather adorable, especially when yer flushed with embarrassment."

A laugh escaped through my tears and I shook my head.

"You don't understand what's it's like to always feel like you're a stranger in your own family. Always too opinionated, too weird, too stubborn, too sensitive. Always just *too much* and also not enough. Not smart enough, or accomplished enough…"

"Och, Daphne," he wound his arms around me and let me cry on his chest. "I'm so sorry. I wish I could make ya see that yer not too much, it's all them. They're too small."

Something inside of my cracked at that simple statement, and I sobbed against Fraser's broad chest. Even if it was exactly what I'd always wanted someone to say, that I'd yearned for someone to see me the way Fraser said he did, his words *hurt*. Because sincere or not, I wouldn't be able to keep him. I'd have to give up this man who saw me and thought I was everything I'd always wanted to be.

My chest throbbed with the pain of it and all I could do was cling to him and hope that it went away soon, so he wouldn't know how much was I was falling for him.

CHAPTER SEVENTEEN

FRASER

I was still seething with anger when we pulled into the garage at home. How could anyone treat a lass as wonderful as Daphne in such a way? And someone from her own family to boot!

I'd held her in the book shop until her tears had abated and it took everything in me not to insist that she sit next to me on the way home. I settled for simply holding her hand but even that wasn't the same as it had been. There was a wall up around Daphne, and I suspected that it was my own fault.

When she'd kissed me in the Jeep, I had wanted to run into the hills and take her in every way I'd dreamed of since the biting. My mating urges were becoming untenable, and with tomorrow being the first night of the full moon, I worried deeply about how I would control myself around her. Distancing myself from her had been necessary, even if it did turn my insides to know that I'd hurt so.

Daphne trusted me, and that meant I had to remain in control. While she may have liked my true form, it wasn't the same as being willing to let me rut her like I longed to do. Even if I kept my glamour up there was no guarantee that I'd be able to control the more primal mating urges that were beginning to awaken in me.

No, the distance is good. Even if kills me to do it. Now to see about protecting her through the next three nights.

"I need to talk to Liam," I said as we got out of the car. "I'll carry up your books after if that's alright?"

She gave me a weak smile and nodded.

"Thank you for the shopping trip," she said. "It was very kind of you."

Kind of me? When the only real reason I did it was so that I'd have you all to myself just once more? So that I could see that gleam of delight in your eyes and know that I was the one giving it to you, just once?

"It was my pleasure, Daphne," I whispered.

She nodded again and walked through the door into the house, leaving me with the distinct feeling being punched in the gut. I'd wanted to make her happy, to please my mate and while I had, I had also hurt her.

My mate…no, I can't think of her like that. I have to try.

I stomped from the garage and through the house, grateful that I didn't run into anyone until I found Liam's study at the end of east wing of the house. It was our Grand-dad's old study and Liam hadn't changed it much if anything from when it was his. Floor to ceiling shelves were crammed with books, and the precious finds Grand-dad had dug up all over Scotland. Large bay windows were at the far end, with the huge mahogany desk that had been gifted by Robert the Bruce to one of our ancestors in front of it. A large comfy chair with a foot stool was nestled between two book cases, a table next to it with a forgotten tea service. It was here that Liam sat, a heating pad on his back and his face contorted with pain.

My stomach lurched at the sight of my little brother like this. He'd been in near constant pain since it happened, though he refused to tell anyone but me.

If it had to happen to anyone, why not me? I have no desire to leave Scotland. But Liam? He was meant to travel, to explore the world. Just like Daphne.

I cringed. As if I needed one more reason I wasn't right for her.

"Are you going to lurk there and watch me like a creeper or come inside?" Liam demanded.

I walked in and closed the door, needing a little privacy for this conversation. If anyone else knew that I didn't want to be with Daphne during the full moon, they'd know our mating wasn't real.

"What's wrong?" Liam asked when he saw my face.

"I…I need to tell ya somethin' and I need you to keep it between us."

"Is it that yer matin' to Daphne isn't what it seems to be?"

I stopped short and gaped at him.

"Am I being that obvious?"

"I doubt anyone else picked up on it. So tell me, is she really here to investigate and ya just didn't want Angus finding out?"

I nodded.

"And with the full moon comin' up tomorrow…" I began.

Liam sighed.

"I see. Well, what can I do to help?"

I swallowed and paced in front of him.

"You remember that old shed, the one that the groundskeeper used for all his tools and such?"

Liam gave me a warry look.

"Yeah."

"Well, I was thinking that ya could maybe lock me in there at night."

"What? Are ya out of your bloody mind? You'll go into a frenzy and rip anyone apart who comes near ya!"

"Not if I take some of those sedatives I know ya get from the witch in town."

Liam's mouth snapped shut and he glared at me.

"That's my business."

"And mine, little brother."

Liam had become pretty dependent on the pain medication that our clan witch gave him in the early days of his recovery. We'd had an intervention with him and he'd gotten off the drugs. But I knew that sometimes he couldn't sleep, whether from nightmares or pain, and that he had a stash of sedatives to help with that. He didn't abuse them like he did the others, but I kept a close watch on him all the same.

"I haven't been overdoing it," Liam said, his voice quiet. "It's just...sometimes..."

"I know. I'm not judging ya, I'm sorry if it felt like it."

Liam looked down at his hands, just as long and strong as any of ours and shook his head.

"Sometimes everyone still treats me like I'm so bloody fragile. I hate it, Fraser."

"I know. It's just...almost losing ya like that? It's not something any of us can ever forget."

He gave a mirthless chuckle.

"Believe me I, understand," he took a sip of cold tea and grimaced. "But back to what ya want. Fraser, are ya sure the lass isn't...ya know, into ya, even a little?"

I huffed out a sigh.

"She is, but Daphne has no idea what she'd be gettin' into."

"Brother, ya know not every Mundane woman is like Silvia, right? What if Daphne is different? What if you two could be happy?"

"It's just a cover story," I snapped, mostly to remind myself. What Liam was saying was far too tempting. "I promised her I wouldn't take advantage, but the bite is making things more difficult than I'd anticipated. I need your help. Please, brother?"

Liam exhaled long through his nose and nodded.

"I understand, I really do. But the answer is no."

"Liam—!"

"Ya can't hide from love for the rest of yer life."

I raised my head, looking my nose down at him to hide the way his words had rocked me.

"Who said it was love?"

Liam snorted.

"Don't insult my intelligence. Ya look at her like the moon rises in her soul, brother. I would be nauseated if I wasn't so happy for ya."

I looked away, arms crossed and tried to stem the tide of rising panic inside of me. Liam wouldn't help me, but that didn't mean that I couldn't just lock myself up anyway.

"I forgot, I wanted to show you something."

Liam got up slowly, wincing as he did so, and I tried not to notice. Instead, I glanced at the papers on his desk while he searched his desk drawer. Liam handled most of the financials for the family business and he often preferred to work out here than in Edinburgh, which had been how he was injured in the first place.

Odd that he has no aversion to this place. I wouldn't want to be in the same place where I'd almost been shot to death.

I was just about to ask him about it when a file caught my eye.

"What's this about?" I asked, picking it up.

"Oh, that's…damn! I thought I put that away. Angus will have my head for letting ya see that."

"Why?"

As I flipped through it, the answer appeared very quickly. My eyes flew up to Liam's and he pressed his lips together as if he were truly annoyed with me now.

"These are a list of thefts."

"Aye."

I looked quickly through the dates and my hands tightened on the delicate paper.

"Please don't rip that," Liam said, snatching it from me.

"Those go back at least a year. And the most recent one was only a few weeks before all this trouble started."

"Aye and? What's yer point, Fraser?"

I ran my hand through the fur on the top of my head. If this were Angus, I'd have to come up with a clever lie, but Liam had guessed the truth; he was already looking into thefts. Did he know if it was Ruben or not? Did he know there had been an artifact smuggled in with the general goods we usually transported?

"From what Daphne and the director know about this artifact and how it might've gotten to our clan, I think our company might have been used to smuggle artifacts into Scotland."

"Whoa now, we never agreed to anythin' like that!" Liam said, hands out.

"Naw, I know, and I said as much to Daphne. But I think what's happened is that whoever has stolen all this stuff over the past year also got their hands on one of the artifacts that was being smuggled. And that's what's responsible for all of this. We have to find them, Liam."

I didn't see a reason to name Ruben quite yet without any proof. It may not even be him, his odd behavior notwithstanding.

Liam's lips pressed into a thin line and he exhaled long through his nose.

"Angus would kill me for tellin' ya this."

"Why? I'm family."

"Yeah well, he didn't even want me to know."

I stepped closer and lowered my voice.

"Know what?"

"As you can see, we've had small discrepancies for months now," Liam said. "Shipments that were light or shippin' manifests that were altered. Samuel has been trying to figure out what's going on, that's why he's in France because all the shipments came from there. And from what I can piece together...I think it might be Ruben who's been doin' it."

My heart kicked up and I stepped forward, pitching my voice low.

"Why? What's he done?"

"Every time somethin' went missin', Ruben would show up a week or so later with some expensive trinket or new suit, somethin' for his sister. He would say it was from a good night at the tables, but...I don't think we ever really believed him."

"And Angus never confronted him on it?" I asked, heart hammering.

"He would have a talk with Ruben and he'd seem to straighten up but then it would happen all over again. I think, if anyone might've stolen the artifact, it's Ruben. And if the most recent events are any indication, someone has noticed."

My stomach dropped.

"Tell me what happened."

"The customs' police have been all over us, stoppin' our shipments, harassin' our employees. Our offices were rifled through twice and someone tried to hack into our book keepin'," Liam said, taping his cane on the rug in frustration. "Whoever that artifact was going to, they're looking for it and I have a feeling they're not going to stop until they get it."

"Naw," I said with sharp exhale, "they aren't."

"What's wrong? What do you know?"

I told him about this rogue group, about what the Orc at the fight club had said about us being an experiment. By the time I was done, Liam had gone completely still, like a beast who was about to leap upon their prey. When he looked at me, his blue eyes glowed and his canines dripped with saliva.

"I'm gonna to kill Ruben," he threatened, his voice much lower.

"Hold on, I don't think Ruben is their agent."

Liam snarled at me.

"He's got the artifact! He's doin' all of this! Our family is being threatened again, Fraser. I will not allow it!"

He took step toward me and gave a yelp of pain as his leg went out of from under him.

I caught him under his arms and helped him back into his chair, even though he snapped me the whole time.

"I'm no invalid!" he screamed.

"I know, Liam," I said, keeping the way the sight of him tore at my insides to myself. "Yer just havin' a bad day, that's all."

He huffed and snarled at me but didn't deny it.

"I need yer brain right now," I continued, "yer body will come in later."

"No, it won't," his voice was broken, filled with anger and pain. "The witch, she said…I'm going to end up in the chair, Fraser. It's inevitable.

Not 'if' anymore but 'when'. And I'm tryin' to make my peace with it, I am. I can still study, do most of the things I love. I can still travel though it'll be difficult. I just…I'm gonna miss runnin' under the full moon with all of ya, teachin' my nieces and nephews how to wrestle in the grass, climbin' the hill of our ancestors on the remembrance days. I…I wanted all of that too."

I caught him around the neck and pulled him to me, letting Liam cry into the fur on my shoulder. He'd been so brave through the years, never letting Gran see how all of this affected him, putting on a brave face so Angus wouldn't feel like a failure as a clan leader, never letting his twin know that everything had changed for him in the blink of an eye. I had been the only one that Liam allowed to see how often it hurt, how much of his life he'd had to change or give up because of this.

Liam pulled away and wiped his eyes.

"Don't tell the others," he whispered. "Let the handfastin' and all that work out first, and then I'll tell Angus."

"Alright, I'll keep it."

"Thank ya."

He wiped his snout and straightened his shoulders, once again gripping his cane and thumping it on the floor.

"Now, Ruben stole this artifact, what does that mean?" his voice hitched just a little when he asked. "Will the archive come here?"

I wanted to tell him no, that he'd never have to see anyone from there ever again, but I wouldn't lie to Liam.

"I don't ken. If we could tell them where Ruben stashed the bloody thing, maybe not."

Liam frowned.

"I assume artifacts are addictive."

"From what Daphne tells me, aye."

"He's been spendin' a lot of time at his family's cottage. I think that's where he'd likely hide it."

I nodded.

"Aye, he hates that place so he wouldn't be there just for the sentimentality of it."

"So what's next? If he's got this thing, then we need to take it back right? Prove that we're not involved?"

"Naw, at least I didn't think so. If this other group is keeping an eye on us, then bringin' the artifact here just puts a target on us."

"But if the Archive knew about it, maybe they'd raid the cottage, save us the trouble."

And keep Daphne safe.

"Aye, that's a good idea. I'll tell Daphne everythin' and see if she can get a team here. Thank ya, Liam."

I was at the door when Liam stopped me.

"I see the way she looks at ya," he said. "She cares for ya."

My heart lurched against my ribs. I wanted to believe that it was enough, that she would accept me as I am. But fear was a terrible mistress, and I couldn't let it go.

"It's just the bite, ya know what it does to Mundanes."

"Naw, Fraser, I don't think it is. Give yerself a chance to be happy. Ask her what she wants, trust her answers."

"Ya only just met her, how can ya tell me to trust her?"

Liam shrugged.

"Instinct."

I snorted and walked out before Liam could chip away at my resolve any further.

CHAPTER EIGHTEEN

DAPHNE

The words Fraser had said to me in the book shop echoed in my mind, and as much as I tried, I couldn't escape them. Not as I made my way down the long hallway to the staircase, not as I climbed the stairs, or when I made it to the room that Fraser had told me we'd be sharing.

I couldn't help wanting him. It was now a constant ache, an incurable illness that had me in its grip. Maybe when the bite was removed I would be able to move past it, but something told me that was unlikely. With one moment, Fraser had moved past all the reasons I should keep my distance, and worked his way into my heart. No one had ever *seen* me before, not like he did, and I found myself loathe to just walk away from that as if it were nothing.

I need to tell him how I'm feeling, to be honest with him. And if he rejects me…

A jagged pain erupted from the bite mark and I clutched it.

I've got to do something. I can't just pretend everything is fine while I spend three nights sharing a bedroom with him.

And that's when it hit me.

"Oh my god," I looked around the spacious room, my palms sweaty, "this is *his* room. We're going to share that bed."

I stared at the four poster bed that was much larger than a standard King size, with its fluffy pillows and heavenly soft homemade quilt, and couldn't help picturing Fraser naked on top of it.

I was so wet so fast that it took my breath away.

That's it. Time to break out the vibrator. If he's not going to do anything about this, then I will.

I quickly unzipped my suitcase and found the two small cases I'd stuffed at the bottom. I'd brought two of my favorite vibrators with me partly out of habit, but also because I knew I'd need some kind of stress reliever.

I eyed the small pouch with my travel bullet in it, then spied my eggplant shaped one. It had been a gag gift, but then turned into one of my absolute favorites. I had no idea how long Fraser would be, and I didn't care. I needed this.

I grabbed the eggplant and crawled onto the bed.

On Fraser's bed.

The thought had me halfway there before I'd even found my favorite setting.

I slipped my hand into the cup of the bustier and pinched my nipple as I pressed the toy to my clit. The vision of Fraser in my mind came back, only now instead of just lying on his bed, he was jacking himself off, his huge hand around what I knew would be a beautifully long and thick cock.

I gasped as my stomach tightened and my toes began to curl. But I wanted this to last, I wanted to stay here, in my mind, with him.

Now, Fraser turned to me, and growled my name as he reached for me and speared me with his dick, using me like a toy and dragging me up and down until…

I bit down on my lip to keep from crying out as my body spasmed.

It may have taken the edge off for a moment, but when the elation faded, I was left feeling empty, alone. I reached out to the other side of the bed, and ran my hand along the empty space, longing for it to be filled.

In that moment, I hated that I wanted him so much, that he seemed to want me too and yet denied us both. And indeed, the want was fast becoming a need, one that I knew my vibrators would be useless against.

As tempting as it was to go another round, to expel as many fantasies as I could before Fraser came upstairs, I knew it wouldn't really do the job. I didn't need just a physical release. I needed Fraser.

I went to the bathroom to freshen up, and was just coming out when a sharp knock at the door froze me in place.

"Daphne?" Fraser's voice was rough, impatient. "Are you…are you decent?"

"Uh…almost! Gimme a moment!"

I ran to the side table by the bed and tossed the eggplant into it, then buttoned up my shirt and tucked it into my jeans. It was only as I approached the door I realized that Fraser would be able to smell exactly what I'd been doing in here.

I tensed, waiting for the stab of shame but instead, there was a spike of anger. What did I care if he *did* know? If he wasn't willing to do the job, what was I supposed to do? Suffer through it the way he was doing?

If he is. I bet he's getting some relief with his own hand.

The thought just made me angrier and I ended up ripping the door open, my lips pursed into a scowl.

"Yes?"

Fraser was standing there, hands braced on either side of the door frame. He looked like he'd run a mile, the way his chest heaved. He speared me with an intense stare, oblivious to my feelings.

"What were you doing in there?" he growled.

I saw no reason to lie to him, especially when he could smell it.

"Getting off, why?"

I'm not sure what I expected. Maybe anger that I'd thrown that in his face. Or maybe jealousy?

But I got neither of those. Instead, he leaned close, the short fur on the side of his face tickling my cheek. Fraser took a deep, slow inhale of my skin, his nose just barely brushing against me.

"Getting…off," he repeated, breath hot against my ear.

"Yes."

"And did it work?"

You arse.

"Yes," I lied, pushing defiance into my voice.

"Oh my god, you two!" Lowell said from down the hallway. "That's what bedrooms are for, ya know."

I was going to kill Lowell.

Fraser spun around and snarled at his brother before pushing past me into the room and slamming the door closed.

Then he started to pace, quick, frantic movements and I wondered if my scent and the fact that his brother had interrupted us had gotten to him.

I swallowed down any trepidation, determined to stand my ground but also wondering if he was about to confront me about how I'd acted. I should've thought of how the scent would linger in his room for a species as sensitive to smell as he was. It was actually quite thoughtless of me.

I started to mentally prepare an apology when Fraser turned around and his words cut into my thoughts like a hot knife.

"I spoke with Liam about Ruben. He confirmed that the arse stole something."

It took me a second to absorb that and form the right words.

The mission. He wants to talk about the mission when I just told him…Fine. Fine, that's just…fine.

I cleared my throat and schooled my features, doing my best to mentally shift from anger and lust to business professional.

"Oh? You seem pretty upset though. Anything else happen?"

"He's been stealin' from us for a while and Angus didn't do anythin' about it. If he had, maybe this wouldn't have happened," he growled out the last few words.

Instinct had me putting a hand on his shoulder.

"I'm here now, and it's not ideal but we can stop this. Do you know where he might've stashed it?"

"Aye, his cottage, about an hour from here."

"Okay, we should go out there tonight or tomorrow. Catch him by surprise."

"Naw."

His tone was firm and full of command. It was the kind of voice that brooked absolutely no arguments.

"Excuse me?" I raised my eyebrows. "This is my job."

"Yer my mate."

And just like that, I was furious again. My entire body went hot as I absorbed what he'd just said.

He was just fine pulling out that card when it suited him, when *he* wanted to touch me, or keep me from doing my job. But when it meant following what we both wanted, he told me it was fake, that it was just part of the mission.

Tears filled my eyes but it was less about being hurt this time and more about being so angry that I almost couldn't breathe.

"I can't believe you," I hissed.

"Daphne—"

"As you keep reminding me, we are mates in name only."

"That doesn't matter!"

"Yes, it does!"

"I'm tryin' to protect ya."

"Why?"

He huffed at me.

"Why do you think?"

"Because you care about me?" I asked.

"Aye."

"But not as your mate."

"I don't understand—"

"No, you don't, Fraser," I said, my voice breaking, no matter how much I tried to keep it steady. "You want to be my mate when it's convenient for you, but when it's something that I want, that *we* want, we aren't mates, are we? It's fake, it's a cover, it's…it's not anything more than a burden."

"Daphne, naw, that's not how I see it!"

"Yes, it is."

"Ya *are* my mate but it's complicated."

"No, it's really not," I swallowed down the fear trying to keep me from the truth, and forced the words out. "I want you. And I think you want me too, but you keep saying it's not alright. But if we were *really* mates, if that's who I was to you, then we'd be locked in here fucking our brains out right now!"

"Aye, we would and you'd be terrified of me!"

His eyes blazed, chest heaving as the words roared out of his mouth.

I stared at him, shocked that he'd actually done more than tell me that I wouldn't understand.

"Why would I be afraid of something I want?" I demanded.

"Oh aye, ya want me. But I'm just a fantasy, right?"

The way he said it made me flinch. It was full of pain and fear.

"I didn't mean—" I began.

"You have no idea how much I want ya," he stepped closer to me, his deep voice broken with longing. "Every moment since I bit ya, I've been in hell. No one has ever done this to me, Daphne, no one. Ya occupy my every thought, my every breath. There's not a moment when the sight of ya doesn't set me on fire. I'm complete when yer in my arms, at peace for the first time in my life. And yet, I also wanna to shred the clothes from yer body and bury myself inside of ya. I wanna to fill ya with my seed until yer belly rounds with my pup. I wanna to take every base instinct out on ya until neither of us can stand anymore."

His words heated my blood and sent shivers through my body. Was this real, was he serious? I hadn't been imagining any of it? But if he really did want me...

"Then why?" I begged, tears falling down my face. "Why are you pushing me away?"

He cringed and the next thing I knew, he had his glamour on.

"I'm afraid," he answered.

This big Werewolf, with his strength and intimidating glare, was afraid.

No, not afraid. Terrified.

I was about to reach out to him when he stepped back and leaned against the wall as if he needed its support.

"Her name was Silvia," he whispered. "She was a Mundane, like you. I loved her but she didn't ken who I really was."

"You never showed her your true form."

He shook his head.

"The night I was going to show her, we were attacked by a rival clan. They were trying to stop us from coming to peace with the Campbells. I flew into a rage, and my glamour slipped. By the time I realized it..." he hesitated and I could see him censoring himself. "Silvia was terrified, rightly so. She...she broke everything off with me, told me she never wanted to see me again."

My heart shattered for him, for the pain that was written so plainly on his face. I knew what it was like to be rejected when someone saw that the reality didn't match up to their fantasy. It was a scar on my mind, reopened more times than I cared to think about. I, too, worried about it more than a little with Fraser. To find out, though, that he had a similar fear, soothed something in me even as his pain tore me open in a different way.

More tears burned my eyes and I clenched my hands into fists to keep from reaching out to him. I had a feeling Fraser wasn't done yet, that he needed space before I could reassure him that I didn't care about his primal side, that I was actually falling in love with all of him.

So I stood there, shaking with the need to comfort him and waited as he gathered the courage to continue.

When he finally looked up at me, there were tears in his eyes, which had become yellow at some point during all this.

"She looked at me like I was a monster. A disgustin' beast. If I ever saw that look in your eyes," he rasped, "I think it would kill me."

Unable to wait any longer, I went to him and captured his face between my hands. It was his glamour, the mask he wore out of fear and heartbreak. But I would take it right now because I understood.

And maybe I also know what might help. Maybe I'm the one that needs to be brave for him, to show him that I see all of him, and I'm not afraid.

I pressed a gentle kiss to his lips, his beard tickling my mouth. His long, muscular arms went around me in a fast press, clutching at my body as if he were afraid I might run away. My cheek lay on his chest, his heart thumping under my ear. It was a sound I'd never tire of.

"I already know your true form," I said, running my hand up and down his back. "I'm not afraid of you, Fraser."

"Ya haven't seen me. Really seen me. There's a whole part of me that I've kept locked up from ya that's screamin' to get out since the moment I bit ya."

"And you're afraid that I'll not accept it."

A shudder went through him and that was my answer.

With one last squeeze I stepped out of his arms. His gaze was questioning, fearful. And I'd be lying if I said I wasn't also afraid of what I was about to do. It was everything that I'd been taught by past partners to avoid. The room was bright, late afternoon sunlight streaming in through the sheer curtains. Even if I closed the shades and turned out the lights, there would be no place to hide from him.

I wanted him to trust me when I said I wanted all of him. So, maybe exposing my own scars, my own fears, and showing him that I was choosing to trust him, would be enough for him to start doing the same.

I took a deep, shaky breath and stepped away a little more.

"I've only had sex with the lights one twice. With my first college boyfriend. I'd been in therapy for body image issues for just a few months at that point, but I felt…well, I felt like I'd conquered quite a bit. And here was a man who said he loved me, so I thought I could trust that," I began to undo the buttons of my blouse. "I thought that he had liked my body, soft parts and all. But he started suggesting that I might want to hit the gym to tighten a few things up. That it would help him to not stray."

Fraser's eyes sharpened, lips tightened into a thin line.

I placed the blouse on a nearby chair and began to undo my jeans with trembling fingers.

"We didn't last long, as you can imagine. It took me a long time to trust anyone again. Years, actually. Years of therapy and learning to love myself as I am."

I slid the jeans down, unable to look Fraser in the eye. My stomach was knotted so tight that I felt sick and my voice had started to tremble. I'd never told anyone this. Never bared these scars to my partners in this way. I was stripping more than my clothes. I was stripping my soul for him, and hoping that what he saw, inside and out, was someone that he wanted.

"And still, I would usually find a reason to turn the lights off, to be under the covers as much as possible. I got really good at slipping a robe while I was covered up, or while partners were in the bathroom or asleep."

I dropped the bustier to the chair with my blouse, my eyes glued to the floor as I stood there in nothing but my red lace thong.

"Daphne—"

"I'm afraid too, Fraser," my whisper was broken. "I'm afraid to see disappointment in your eyes because I'm not the way you imagined. And even though I know I'm worth more than your opinion, it will still hurt deeply. But here I am…trusting you. And you don't have to do the same. I won't force you to shed your glamour or be with me but…I just needed you to know that I'm afraid too but I'm willing to try."

I took a deep, shaky breath and wanted to look at him but anxiety held me in place. While I'd come a long way, there was still that kernel of fear that I could never seem to get rid of. And it was for that reason that I just couldn't meet his gaze right now. I'd done this out of a need for him to know that I understood, that he wasn't alone with these feelings. But I also realized, in this moment, that I needed to know if Fraser would be one more person that couldn't accept me, or if he would be different. And I wanted him to be different. Oh god, how I wanted it.

The floor creaked and I knew he was moving toward me but still, I couldn't make myself look up. The two feet that came into my view were human, and my inhale felt jagged, like glass was pressing on my heart. I'd meant it, he didn't have to shed his glamour, but I had hoped he would. One very thick, human finger tipped my chin up, tears dripping down my neck as he did. I closed my eyes on instinct, wanting one more moment before I saw the answer in his eyes.

"Look at me," his voice growled.

I forced myself to open my eyes and gasped out a sob. It was *him*, the real him. My gaze caressed his beautiful soft fur, the short ears that were twitching, his snout where his lips were pressed into a thin line. I looked lastly at his eyes, the place where I would have my answer. And my breath hitched at what I saw.

There was no thinly veiled disgust, no disappointment, nothing unsure. No, what I saw was hunger, naked and raw. Not only had he trusted me enough to give me his real self, but he also wanted what he saw in front of him. My body and my soul.

He wanted *me*.

His clawed fingertips went around my throat at the base of my jaw, a grip of possession, desire. His hand was big enough that his thumb rubbed on the hollow of my throat, my body relaxing into his touch.

With his other hand, Fraser skimmed the side of my torso and I held my breath. This was the one place that I was most self-conscious of, the place that often drew the most criticism.

"Yer so beautiful. Anyone who couldn't see that, they're all fools, unworthy of ya. And I…I'll try to be worthy of ya, Daphne, if you'll let me?"

I couldn't help it. I laughed through the tears falling down my face. A huge, burst of sound halfway between a giggle and a sob.

"Yes, Fraser. Yes, I will…"

He swallowed, his eyes on mine.

"If at any time ya don't like what I'm doing, if I scare ya, tell me to stop. Understand? Promise me."

I skated the back of my fingers across his soft cheek and ran my thumb along the top of his velvety snout. I relished the sight of his eyes rolling back as he nuzzled into my touch.

"I promise. Just give me you, Fraser. That's all I ask."

"Daphne," he moaned, "beautiful, impossible Daphne."

The rough callouses of his fingertips skimmed under one of my breasts and down my stomach, then he brushed the back of his hand up the path, his fur luxuriously soft against my skin. Back and forth, he took his time mapping the skin of my torso with his hand. Every inch of me precious, adored under his attention. It was the most intimate thing anyone had ever done to me, and Fraser hadn't even come close to my mons or my very, very wet cunt.

By the time his claws skimmed the top of my thong and low growl rolled up from his throat, I was tingling all over, breathless. He went to his knees and looked up at me like a worshiper at the altar, and I was his goddess.

He ran his nose along my skin and followed it with the heat of his tongue along the underside of my belly, the tip dipping under the top of my thong. It was erotic in a way that was bestial, dangerous. His arms were so long that he could kneel and still hold onto my throat. I wasn't usually into being controlled during sex, but this was different. This was my Werewolf taking control, claiming me. The thought sent heat to my core and I made a tiny whimpering sound as his tongue ran along my hip.

"Mine," he whispered against the curve of my torso.

I knew I was still hurting from what had been said to me in the past, the harsh judgment of those that I had wanted to love may have scabbed over but it still affected me. And here was this beautiful, powerful Werewolf mending those wounds with the scrape of his claw and the caress of his tongue. The cracks inside of me ached a little less as he loved my body in slow strokes. Tears fell down my face and I let my hands roam over his head and shoulders, wanting to give back the bliss he was gifting to me.

He stopped at the Band Aid on my stomach and planted a gentle lick there.

"I'll be more careful this time," he promised.

"I know. I trust you."

"Ya have no idea what that means to me."

"Yes, I do."

He stared up at me, and I dared to believe that what was shining back at me was love, true and unabashed. This all may go away in a few days, it may just be the needs of our mating bite, and I may be left hollowed out by the loss of him. But right now I was going to grab a hold of what he was giving me and not look back. Future pain be damned.

I was shaking by the time his tongue grazed the underside of my breast.

"Mine," he repeated and took my stiff nipple into his mouth.

My fingers threaded through the fur on his head, holding him there as he bit and sucked.

"Yes, Fraser," I breathed, "I am yours."

My words ended on a cry as his biting edged on the most exquisite pain, winding my pleasure into tight spirals under my skin. When his mouth left my breast, the imprint of his teeth stayed on my body. Another mark, another sign that I was his.

"So responsive, so perfect," he ran the claw of his index finger over the marks of his teeth.

"Do the other one."

His gaze snapped to mine.

"Leave your mark all over my body," I whispered.

Just like you've left it all over my heart.

I'd always laughed at the word "smolder" to describe someone's gaze, but that was just because I had never seen it in real life. The instant the words left my mouth, a spark lit in Fraser's eyes and I saw it, his gaze smoldering so hot that I was shocked I didn't catch fire right there.

But then his mouth latched onto my other breast while his hand tightened ever so slightly on my throat and I couldn't think of anything other than the pinch of his claws as they bit into my neck, the pressure of his teeth as he worked my nipple between them. He was owning me, and I couldn't find a reason to care that it was against everything I was taught was proper to desire. I meant what I said, I wanted his teeth marks all over me, the red of his claws, the smell of his cum and fur. I wanted him to make a mess of me, to ruin me for anyone else and leave me panting for more.

I wasn't aware of his hand traveling down my body until the cool scrape of his claw grazed my hip. I gasped and looked down. The sight of this huge Werewolf, tail undulating, fur rippling as his teeth drew a line of heat from my breast down to the top of my delicate thong. It was then I saw that his claw was hooked into the lace of it at my hip. His other hand left my throat and soon he had two claws at either hip. Gone was the careful, cautious Fraser MacDonald I'd known. In his place was indeed a beast; a hungry, savage one that had me at his mercy.

Holding my gaze, his claws cut the lace of my thong and his teeth went to the top and slowly, inch by torturous inch, Fraser drew it down until he looked up at me with it in his mouth.

He grinned at me, triumphant and dropped it at my feet.

"Such beautiful skin," his tongue flicked out, rough and playful just above my mons. "I want to taste all of ya. Here," he licked my stomach, "here," the outside of my hip, "here," the inside of my thigh now with a delicious scrape of his sharp teeth.

Tremors licked through my body, hot and overwhelming, as his hands followed the trail of his teeth and tongue. I was lost on a sea of sensation. Soft and rough, claws and teeth but never where I desperately needed him. Time and again, he teased me with the hot breath of his mouth and I ground my hips toward him, only to have him chuckle and bite my thigh instead.

"Please, Fraser," I begged, my voice a sob as he once again denied me the contact I needed.

"Mmmm, aye. Ya want me to lick you there, don't ya?" he ran one knuckle between my folds, dragging an obscene groan from me.

"Yes."

A trickle of moisture slowly dripped down my thigh and I blushed. I'd never been so wet in my life, especially not from one brush of someone's finger through me.

He captured the wetness on his tongue, working my flesh where it had dripped, sucking the very last bit of it from my skin as if it were ambrosia.

"So good. I'm going to lap up every drop of you, and then make you give me more."

With one swift motion, Fraser scooped me up and dropped me on the bed. I braced for his body to stretch out over me but he didn't. He stalked around the bed, snarling and staring at me. I was his prey, caught in the trap he'd woven with his hands and teeth, invisible bonds of need that held me to the bed as he walked around it.

"Open your legs," he commanded.

My breath stuttered out of my parted lips as I did what he asked.

"Put yer hands over yer head and hold onto the headboard. Do not let go."

I was hypnotized by the growling power of his voice. He was a predator that changed my life irreparably, and instead of trembling with fear, I was breathless with anticipation.

He stopped at the foot of the bed. His gaze had gone from smoldering to outright fiery, leaving licks of heat on my skin as he took me in.

I'd never been so exposed, so at someone else's mercy, as I was in this moment. Balanced on the edge of ecstasy and fear, I was desperate for release. But I couldn't ask for it. I knew, somehow, that to speak would break whatever spell Fraser had woven, and I didn't want to escape it for anything in the world.

With deliberate movements, Fraser took his kilt off and tossed it aside. He stood there for a beat, letting my eyes take him in. I knew from the times I'd brushed against him when he'd been hard that Fraser had an above average cock. But nothing had prepared me for the sight of it.

It jutted proudly out from his body, impossibly thick and long, a pink head peeking out from a dark gray foreskin that matched the skin on his chest and hands. Veins ran the length of him and at the root, just above what had to be his short sheath where his cock resided within his body, was a pair of bulbous protrusions; his knot. The sight of it had me licking my lips. I wanted to take his hot length into my mouth, to taste him and make him growl as I massaged his knot. I wanted him as undone as I was right now, to ride his dick until he was a snarling mess under me.

As if knowing exactly what I was thinking, Fraser took his cock in his hand and gave himself two rough strokes.

"Not yet, Daphne."

A whine curled up from my lips in protest and he laughed at me, the sound full of dark promises that I longed to experience.

Slowly, as if he were afraid to startle his prey, Fraser crawled up onto the bed and toward me. A bead of moisture fell from the tip of his cock and onto my calf, warm and thick. His hands seized my thighs and pushed me wider, spreading my pussy's lips in the process.

"Stay," he said with smirk.

I let out a shaky laugh. He was so close to where I needed him.

"Fraser…"

His hand on my belly stilled me. He was staring at my mons and cunt, and I hoped he wouldn't mind the hair I had…and then thought that would be funny considering the fact he was covered in fur.

But then his fingers were spreading me more and I couldn't think of anything at all as anticipation blinded me.

A growl of hunger rolled up from him. His rough hands held my thighs apart, the claws digging into my skin and he stared up at me from between my legs.

"Oh, Daphne," his growling burr rumbled. "Do ya know what happens to beautiful women who play with big bad wolves?"

"No," I breathed.

The grin he gave me was feral, hungry.

"They get devoured."

CHAPTER NINETEEN

FRASER

Moonlight and heather filled my senses the moment she'd bared herself to me body and soul.

I had never been so overcome by the sight of a female as I had been when Daphne slowly disrobed in front of me. And then to show me her deepest fears, her secret scars. It had disarmed me utterly and I was powerless against it. She was my weakness, my greatest strength. She was the desire that could ruin me and yet I ran toward her, unable to help myself.

She deserved all that I had to give, broken and frightened as I was. She deserved more than me really. She deserved a male who wouldn't have to restrain himself, wouldn't live in fear of who he really was. But I shoved all that aside. I'd longed for this woman all my life, even if I hadn't known it until now. She was the missing piece of my soul, the true north I'd been searching for. And if it took every scrap of strength I had, I would hold onto her.

And now, here I was, between her thighs at last, her body stretched out at my mercy. I indulged in a long inhale of her cunny, her scent rich and all woman. I couldn't hold back any longer, and with one long, slow drag of my tongue through her folds, I nearly unloaded my cock against the mattress. She tasted better than anything I'd ever had. I meant it when I told her I was going to devour her. I would, slow and savoring, until she was spilling herself over and over against my mouth.

My fingers parted her pussy lips more, until the swollen bud at the top was revealed, waiting for me to torture it. I chuckled against her mons, letting her know that something was coming, winding up her anticipation and getting a mewling whimper as a reward.

"You want me right here," I withdrew my claws and brushed the tip of my finger against it.

She hissed and bowed her back off the bed.

"Tell me how you like it," I demanded as I began to play with her.

"U-up…yes…circles…harder…nnnh!"

I took her direction greedily, a supplicant desperate to please his goddess. For that was what she was to me in this moment; my world, my religion. I worked until I found the right rhythm, until her hips bucked and her cries became nonsensical, unhinged. She needed more, needed to be filled and I was just barely holding myself back from plunging my aching cock into her. She would hold me so tight, I just knew it.

But I also didn't want to hurt her. She had to be properly pleasured first.

Slowly, so I could drink my fill of the sight of her writhing with need, I slipped one finger into her dripping cunny. A high pitched keen left her throat and I watched, making sure she was enjoying it.

"More…more."

With a grin, I slipped in another, her tight walls gripping me as I pumped in and out of her. My tongue continued to work her clit, dragging little mewls and cries from her.

There was one thing I'd always wanted to try though, one thing I couldn't do with Silvia, and I knew that my Daphne would love it. So in spite of her sobbing protests, I withdrew my tongue and fingers.

"Patience," I crooned. "I'll make you feel good."

My thumb found the rhythm she liked against her pearl and I grinned up at her, craving her reaction of what I was about to do. Her whispered purrs of appreciation were cut off when I delved my long, thick tongue into her cunny. I groaned against her. The taste was intense now, and I was parched for it. Within moments of my tongue curling and twisting inside of her, Daphne cried out with each exhale and began to fuck my face with wild abandon. I had done this to her, I had released this wild, wanton female. And she was *mine*.

It all snapped the tenuous leash I had on my ferocious needs. With every savage thrust, I was begging to taste her release, to know that I had given her pleasure in my true form. No masks, no hiding.

When at last she came apart on my tongue, I feasted on every drop until she was begged me to stop.

"Too much…too much."

Carefully, I withdrew, lapping up the last bit of her cum with gentle lashes.

"Fraser," she whispered and reached for me.

It didn't matter that she'd let go of the headboard before I told her to. I was helpless not to respond to her silent plea for me to come to her. In that moment I realized that I would give her the beating heart from my chest if she asked for it.

My true mate, my Daphne.

The words were on the tip of my tongue, but I held them back. I wasn't ready to admit that yet, to risk scaring her off.

I stretched out over her luscious body, so much smaller than mine. The slide of her soft skin against my bare chest was sheer heaven. When her fingers ran through the fur on my sides and hips I rolled my head back, utterly lost in the touch of her hands. She was my master, the only one I wanted to please. When her hand grazed my tail I let out a low howl and bucked my hips forward, my weeping crown just slightly entering her wet cunny and I thought I'd die. She was so hot, so tight. What would it feel like to have my knot in her, to fill her with my seed over and over again? Would she want that? Would she want to be locked with me?

"Your tail?" she asked.

All I could do was nod because she was gripping it tightly. Not all of us had sensitive tails when it came to sex, but I did and, much like pleasuring her with my tongue, I had never been able to explore tail play with Silvia or know what it was like to have her take my knot. So many parts of myself that I'd locked away as if they weren't important, weren't a vital part of me.

She never really knew me at all. But my Daphne, she does.

Suddenly I longed to expose everything to her. My love for tail play, my desire to breed her, to feel my knot slip into her and stay locked in her wet heat while I spilled myself into her.

She watched me as she slowly ran her hand down my tail. Her arms were too short to reach the root of it, and that was something we'd have to explore later because I was not ready to change positions. I was still just inside of her and the amount of self-control it was taking to not plunge in the rest of the way had me shaking.

Then Daphne rolled her hips up and took me in a little more. I let out a longer howling growl and gave my hips a small shove forward. Her hand stilled on my tail and her eyes fluttered.

"Oh my god," the last word came out guttural and it almost undid me. "More…please, Fraser."

I was panting, my tongue lolling out to the side a little, my control slipping as she kept moving under me, the head of my cock slipping in and out of her.

"D-Daphne…if you…I want…"

She grabbed my face between her hands and made me look at her.

"Fuck me, Fraser. Please."

And that's when I realized I wasn't wearing a rubber.

"Wait," I began to pull out.

"I take the shot," her face flushed as she looked me in the eyes and said, "I want to feel your cum inside of me."

My self-control snapped like a dry twig.

That part of myself that wanted to breed her, rut her until she passed out, lunged to the fore. My mouth latched onto the matting mark on her should and I bit down, not hard enough to break the skin but enough to release the latent mating hormones stored there. It wasn't something I thought I'd ever do to her, but the second I did, she screamed out a moan and her cunny released a rush of wetness, making her ready to take me.

My mouth released her and I sat up and hooked my arms under her thighs, raising them up as I spread them wide. She was panting now, mewling out little cries as I rubbed my cock against her. The instinct to protect my mate overpowered the desire to just bury myself in one stroke. I had to make this good for her; it was even more of a drive than to see her belly fill with my seed.

So I held her eyes with my own, keeping her hips elevated as I slowly sank into her. I wasn't halfway when her head rolled back and she cried out again.

"Touch yourself," I commanded, "I want you to come on my cock."

With a shaking hand, Daphne reached down and began to touch that perfect little pearl at the top of her pussy lips. With shallow thrusts of my hips I sank deeper into her with each pass. She was so tight, so hot and perfect that it was only by the sheerest luck that I didn't shoot my load before I'd even made it all the way inside of her.

"More," she whimpered when I was half way there. "I want…I want all of you."

So I gave her more, grunting and growling as I went deeper. When my knot was right at her entrance she bowed back and gave a long, obscene grunt. I was butting up against her clit and swirled my hips to press more even as I thrust. She came with cry that sent me into a frenzy.

Before I could stop myself, I withdrew and pulled her to me as I thrust forward. Over and over, I dragged her along my cock, faster and deeper until my knot contracted and fire exploded low in my belly. Through the fog of my rutting frenzy, I knew that Daphne wasn't ready for that, so I stopped with it just outside of her, but the sensation of her wetness dripping from her, soaking me, the way she groaned and begged me for more was enough to make up for it. With one final, snarling thrust, I buried myself deep inside of her and spilled myself. Wave after wave hit me, my hips thrusting in tiny movements to keep it going.

When I could finally open my eyes, my seed was flowing out of her cunny. I'd filled her and then some, a true mating response if there ever was one.

Even though it was against most of my instincts, I pulled out of her, slowly and carefully. When I did, more of me leaked out of her, down her thighs. I ran my hands up her legs and hips as I stretched out beside her.

"My beautiful mate," I whispered, gathering her in my arms.

Daphne was sweaty and flushed, her eyes heavy lidded and her hair a tangled mess on the pillow. She'd never looked more gorgeous, more alluring than she was in this moment, covered in my teeth marks, my seed running down her legs.

She nuzzled against me, fingers tangling in the fur on my neck.

"Are ya alright? Was I too rough?" I asked.

"No," she purred, "it was perfect."

I cradled one cheek of her luscious arse in my hand, a little sad that it was one of the few places I hadn't left my mark.

Next time, I'll lave her peach of an arse with my tongue.

I could have stayed curled up with Daphne in my arms for hours, coaxing her tight cunny to life again when my cock demanded another rut. But I knew she'd be sore, and I also knew that there were bath salts and creams in stock for her nethers thanks to my Gran's foresight. Daphne would need those tonight, before taking me again.

But just the thought had me rousing and Daphne giggled.

"So soon?" she grinned wickedly up at me as her fingers grazed my half-mast.

"Not exactly. I'm not the young Were I used to be."

"That's alright," she wound her arms around my neck and kissed the tip of my snout, "I need a little break anyway."

"Aye, and speakin' of which."

I scooped her up and stood in a swift motion that had her squealing. Having her naked body pressed to mine had me stirring again but I ignored it. There would be time for more later, I would make sure of it. But right now my mate needed to be cared for. I could sense the achiness that was coming to her, and also the hunger that was about to overtake her.

First, a bath and then some food.

I sat her on the soft edge of the sunken Were-sized bath tub. It had jets and several different height of benches, as well as multiple large bath pillows, which I set up for her. She watched me with sparkling eyes and a surprised grin, as if she'd never been cared for like this before. The thought had me both angry, at the others who'd been with her and didn't cherish her, and proud that I was proving my worth as a mate to her. I began to warm the water and found the bottle of bath salts marked "For after".

"What's that?" Daphne asked.

"Back in our history," I said pouring a generous amount of salt into the warm water, "Mundane women concocted many things to help their cunny recover after sex. Bath salts, salves, they're all to help take out the ache and speed healing. Gran thought you might need some of them."

Her eyes widened and I recognized that look. It was the expression she wore when her brain was latching on to a new mystery to be solved, a new topic to delve into. She was adorable and arousing all at once when she looked like that.

Daphne snatched the jar from my hands and turned it around, searching for an ingredients label.

"What's in it?" she asked. "And how far back does this go? I mean, did you all mate with Mundane women at the start? Or just Weres who were female?"

"There weren't any female Weres at first."

Her smile fell.

"How very misogynistic of the Druids."

I began to light candles around the tub.

"Naw, lass, the female warriors stayed behind to defend the villages. It was the agreement the elders settled upon. They had no knowledge that we would someday be without our sacred groves and cast into the wilds."

"So there's no female Werewolves? I thought Lizzie and Gran were Weres."

"Aye, but the spell doesn't stick to females the same way it does to males. Females only have a Were form during the full moon."

Daphne's eyes lit up.

"Fascinating. So then, are the salves and such only for Mundanes or also for Were females? Or is their physiology such that they can take male Weres without much pain?"

I chuckled as I lifted her into the tub and settled a bath pillow behind her.

"That you'll have to ask Gran about. I confess, I am not too curious to ask my female family members such things."

Daphne flushed.

"Oh yes, of course. I'm sorry."

I tipped her chin up and ran my thumb across her full bottom lip.

"Ya never have to apologize to me for yer astonishing mind. It is a part of ya that I…that I like very much."

If Daphne noticed that I almost used a very different 'L' word she didn't show it, for which I was grateful. I began to step back and give her some time in the bath when she grabbed a hold of my arm, a seductive little smile blooming on her face.

"Would you like to join me?" she purred.

The answer was 'yes'. Yes, I wanted to join her, and knot her and rut her for hours. But her body needed time to recover. She must've seen my hesitation because she shifted just a little, giving me a tantalizing view of her wet breasts.

"We don't have to do anything," she said, "I just…it sounds strange, but I want you to stay. Please?"

I sighed. The little vixen had me wrapped around her beautiful finger.

"Alright, but this is not to seduce ya."

Her expression became serious, though in a completely playful way.

"Of course not. That would be terrible."

"Oh, you are going to be so much trouble," I said with a head shake. And I didn't care a bit.

CHAPTER TWENTY

DAPHNE

After Fraser had washed me clean and massaged my shoulders, I insisted that it was his turn. I hadn't touched him nearly enough in intimate ways yet.

Fraser shifted so I could sit on a bench behind him. I started hesitantly, unsure of how hard to go, but soon I was digging my little fingers and thumbs into the hard muscles of his shoulders. His fur wasn't as thick when it was wet, and I could see and feel the body underneath so much better. Fraser was indeed as built as his glamour was, probably more so. In the back of my mind was a soft voice warning me that a man or Werewolf this beautiful wouldn't be satisfied with someone like me for very long. That eventually he'd tire of my round belly and hips.

But I remembered how he'd looked at me, how he'd made me feel. No one had ever gazed at me like that. And even though the bite mark may be giving Fraser rose colored glasses, did that make it any less real?

I didn't have the answers and maybe I wouldn't ever if Fraser decided to stick to what we'd agreed on. All I had was now, and I could either trust in what was in front of me and enjoy it, or I could waste it in worry.

To hell with that, I'm going to take every second of this. Even if it breaks my heart.

My fingers had stilled on his body and Fraser reached back, eclipsing my small hand with his.

"Ya alright, lass?"

"Yes, just lost in thought."

"Hmm…bad thoughts?"

I wound my arms around his neck and laid my head on his back, my chest pressed into him.

"Worries," I finally said.

He didn't say anything, just ran on hand up my leg, which was pressed against his hip and thigh. And with the other her lazily drew circles on my arm with one of his claws.

Unspoken questions seemed to hang on the air, like specters intent on infecting our happiness. How could I rebuke them and safeguard this bubble we'd just recently created for ourselves?

"I can't speak to the future," Fraser finally said, "but for right now, with you, I am the happiest I've been in a very long time."

I let out a long breath and leaned harder into him. He was so solid, so warm and comforting. It was like coming home, being this close to him, and the last thing I wanted was to examine it too closely right now.

"Me too."

Soon, Fraser's hands became a little more insistent and I found myself being pulled around him until I straddled his lap, his cock nudging me as it grew by the second. His gaze raked over me, landing on my breasts, which were just barely submerged. He cupped one and brought it to his mouth, taking my nipple hard into his mouth. Coiled tension unspooled from where he was biting and sucking, luring me far away. Tighter and tighter he wound me until I couldn't help but touch him too.

I reached between us and grasped him in my fist. He was fully erect now and my hand didn't close over him. The fact that this had been inside of me, making me feel so deliciously full, rubbing and pressing on parts of me that I had thought were a myth, made my core clench and heat pulse through me.

Fraser let out a hiss as I slowly stroked him.

"Tell me what you like," I urged.

"Ah…ya…you're doing pretty good so far, lass."

I tightened my grip a bit and when I reached the top where his foreskin was, I gave it a little twist. He nearly came out of the water, a tiny howl escaping his mouth.

"Just like that."

I kept at it, alternating my grip until his head was thrown back and his tongue was hanging out of his mouth. It was a powerful feeling, to make this big, wild Werewolf whimper and plead with me to keep going. I could make him come like this, I could make him beg for more.

"Tell me what you want now," I whispered.

I didn't recognize the sultry, wanton voice that slipped out of me, nor the confidence to ask, no *demand*, to know what Fraser wanted. It was like being drunk, uninhibited and free. Only instead of a monster headache in the morning, I had a feeling other parts of me would be aching. And I welcomed it.

Fraser whimpered and I began to slow my movements.

"No…No, lass…"

"What do you want, Fraser?"

"I can't…you would no…"

"Please? Tell me…"

"I wanna fuck your breasts," he yelped as my hand slipped. "I want to paint you with my seed."

I pulled back and stared at him, a thrill shooting up my spine.

"I've never done that before."

He frowned and cupped both of my breasts. I filled his hands and it felt so decadent to have him squeeze them, run the claw of his thumb over the stiff nipples.

"No one has ever asked to slip their cock between these perfect mounds?"

I shook my head, a grin lighting up my face.

"Let's do it," I breathed.

"Really?"

"Yes, I…ah!"

In one smooth, fast motion, Fraser had somehow managed to scoop me up and stand up. Water cascaded off his fur but he didn't care. He stepped majestically out of the tub, leaving streams of water in his wake.

"We'll get the bed wet," I protested.

"Do ya really care about that?"

It took less than five seconds for me to shake my head.

"Good, because my cock is ready to explode right now. You'll be the death of me, lass, with this body."

He laid me on the bed, and gave himself a mighty shake to get some of the water off him.

"Fraser!" I squealed as droplets hit me at full force.

He grinned down at me.

"I like the sight of you all wet."

And he dragged his tongue up the outside of my thigh to my hip before laving my belly with nips and sucks.

"You know what I want," he rasped against my skin. "What do you want?"

I bit my lip as an idea struck.

"I like toys. Are…are you okay with a vibrator?"

"Of course."

"Some men aren't, they feel replaced."

He snorted.

"Only an insecure bawbag would be intimidated by a vibrator."

My eyes went to his cock, so big and thick, a bead of moisture at its tip. Without thinking, I bent forward and licked it off.

He hissed and slapped his hand on the bed.

"Bad?" I asked.

"Och, lass…so good!"

I dove back to it, and though I could only fit the tip in my mouth, I gave it all the attention I could. I swirled my tongue along the foreskin and the pink head peeking out, I used my hand as he liked it in the tub. And as more of the salty moisture began to fill my mouth I groaned in delight. Fraser's hand was in my hair and he was panting, his hips giving tiny thrusts. He couldn't really fuck my mouth, he was too big, but I knew that he wanted to and that made me feel like a bona fide sex goddess.

Just as he was about to lose himself, my lips came off his cock with a pop and Fraser threw me onto my back.

"Vibrator," he growled, "now."

I dove for the bedside table where I'd stowed my one from before, not thinking that it was a rather unconventional choice. When I handed it to him, however, the look on his face was a like a record scratching.

"An…an *eggplant*? It's shaped like an *eggplant*?" he asked.

"Yes?" I said with a little wince.

Fraser's cock looked like it was aching to spend itself, and he was still panting from my blow job. And yet, he began to laugh. A full throated, open mouthed chortle that had me snort-laughing right back.

"It's my favorite one," I almost couldn't get the words out I was giggling so hard. "Don't knock it until you've tried it."

"Fucked many vegetables, have ya?"

I fell back with a full belly laugh.

"Not…not recently," I wheezed.

"Oh, lass," he said, after we'd both gotten some control. "You are full of surprises."

A sharp crack of worry pierced me and my smile wobbled.

"Is that a good thing?"

Fraser's heated gaze softened and he gave my lips a tiny lick of his tongue.

"It's the best thing."

My throat tightened and all I could do in response is press a kiss to his lips, which somehow shaped themselves to fit onto mine.

"Now," I said with a sigh, "are you going to fuck my tits or what?"

He chuckled, though the predatory fire came back to his yellow eyes, sending a rush of heat through me. I loved it when he looked at me like that, possessive and hungry. I was his prey, his mate, the one he wanted to devour and rut. Laying there with my hair drying into a frizz and all the lights on, I'd never felt more sensual, more *wanted*. I realized with a start that this was perhaps the first time in ages that I didn't want to hide myself from the eyes of my lover. Instead, I wanted to spread my body out before him and let him look his fill. I was free, truly free of the jagged spikes of fear that had kept me unsure in bed, even after all the years I spent working on my self-acceptance. Fraser's worship of my body had been the thing to finally start breaking all of that.

I reached out for him, running my fingers over his snout, his cheek, planting little kisses in the wake of my touch.

"Lass?"

"You make me feel beautiful."

"I'm just a mirror showing ya the truth. Somethin' someone should've done for ya a long time ago."

He nipped at my throat and set me back down on the bed with extreme gentleness before he opened the drawer of the other bed side table and withdrew a large bottle of lubricant. He pumped a generous amount into my hand, it smelled faintly of lavender and my academic mind found that rather funny.

Without a word, I gripped him and spread the lube up and down his hot, hard shaft. I even dared to rub a little onto his knot. And the second my hand closed around it Fraser's mouth opened, a whimpering howl escaping him.

"No…don't…lass, this'll be over…too fast."

I let go and was now more determined than ever to know, just once, what it was like to have his knot inside of me.

But not now, later.

He straddled my body, careful not to put his weight on me, and slid that gorgeous cock into the valley between my breasts.

While holding my gaze, he handed me the vibrator.

"Find the settin' ya like."

I fumbled a bit, my hands shaking with excitement and just a touch of fear. Fraser was getting *that* look in his eyes. It was a wild, unhinged glow, reminding me that he had an animal side, feral and ancient. But instead of scaring me, like it should have, my body began to tremble with anticipation. I wanted to be at his mercy, knowing he would satisfy those darker desires I'd never told anyone about while also never doing me any real harm.

He watched me carefully as he began to position the vibrator, taking my guidance without anger or embarrassment. It was a revelation to be with someone who was not threatened by direction, or by my desires. How many times had I heard that I was hard to please, or that I expected too much?

I'd started to believe that maybe I just wasn't able to orgasm with a partner. But Fraser was showing me that it wasn't me, it was them. And the power, the relief I felt set me free to be carried away to wherever Fraser wanted to take me.

When he finally found the right place, a shocked cry came from my lips and my hips thrust up.

"Right there…oh god…yes…yes!"

He used the vibrator in the circular motion I loved and my eyes rolled back. Over and over he coaxed my body to new heights with the toy until I was sure I was going come completely apart from the pleasure. My toes curled and my throat let loose a low moan as the orgasm shattered me.

"Yer breasts, now," his voice was raw as the dregs of my orgasm receded.

I pushed them together, aftershocks still rolling through my body, when Fraser slid himself back and forth between them. It was the most erotic thing I'd ever done, watching his cock peek out from them and then recede, to see his tongue loll out the side of his mouth, his head thrown back as he pleasured himself slowly and thoroughly on my body.

"You're so soft…so perfect, Daphne…oh goddess above. I wanna rut ya so hard."

"Do it," I pleaded, longing to see him as unhinged as I felt. "Please."

It was all he needed. His hands came down on either side of my head and I felt his breath on each pass, hot and snarling as hips snapped hard and fast between my breasts.

"You like it…" he demanded.

"Yes, I love it."

"I'm going to…mark ya…cover ya in me!"

His last words came out on a downright chilling howl and I saw the moment when the animal slipped its leash. His eyes closed, head thrown back and he was thrusting so hard that we were moving up the bed. When his knot slipped between my breasts, I groaned at the feeling. It was obscene how he was using me and I'd never been more turned on in my life. In spite of the orgasm that I'd just had, my hips began to arch up, seeking sensation that was not there.

I whimpered and moaned his name until I thought I'd die if he didn't touch me.

Then, just as my head hit the end of the bed, Fraser gave a growling howl and pulled free of my breasts seconds before warm ropes of cum shot from him, painting my breasts and torso in a thick, white layer.

He carefully moved off of me but still at my side and braced himself on his hands and knees. We were both panting, sweaty and breathless.

My hand traveled down to my cunt, which was still aching for sensation. His hand shot out and stopped me before I could.

"Ya need more?" he breathed, eyes still a little wild. "Yer cunny not satisfied?"

"No."

Fraser grabbed the vibrator.

"Can this go inside of ya?" he asked.

My eyes widened. It was half the size of a real eggplant and therefore, a bit wider than other dildos I'd used, but after taking Fraser, I could probably handle it just fine.

"Yes."

As I watched with shocked anticipation, Fraser trailed his fingers in the cum on my breasts and began to coat the eggplant shaped vibrator with it.

"Oh my god," I breathed, half wondering if I was dreaming.

No one had ever been willing to be so filthy with me, to use me in this way and I found myself downright ravenous for every moment of it.

"Yes or no?"

"Yes! God, yes!"

When he was satisfied that it was slick enough, Fraser smirked at me, showing teeth.

"I will always give my mate everythin' she needs. Now open yer legs and show me that pretty cunny, Daphne."

The deep burr skittered over my body, causing tremors to course through me in anticipation of what he was about to do. I've never spread my thighs so fast as I did just then.

Fraser knelt between my thighs, eyes never leaving mine, and began fucking me with the vibrator. Slow and careful at first, obviously worried about how sore I was from before.

"Touch your breasts."

My breasts were currently covered in his cum, but I didn't care.

I ran my fingers through the thick, still warm layer, and circled my nipple, dragging it over me. I pinched my nipples and his pupils dilated.

"Cup them, both hands."

I was like a puppet, moving where and how he told me and I didn't care. Not when he was igniting my body in ways I'd never known before. As I cupped and rubbed my breasts, Fraser picked up his pace and added his other hand. He worked my clit like he was an expert at it already. It was still sensitive from before and soon I was writhing around like a wild, unhinged woman as I chased the release I so badly needed.

"That's it. Come apart for me," he urged.

"I…it's…so good. You're…going to make me…!"

"That's right I am, because Daphne, you are *mine*."

He pinched my clit on that last word and I screamed as sensation incinerated me. Wave after wave until I was babbling and sobbing with it.

I was barely aware of him removing the toy and going to the bathroom. My mind was foggy, my body boneless. He'd just reduced me to the most carnal part of myself and I could not bring myself to care or regret any of it.

In fact, as I watched him come out of the bathroom, two washcloths in hand, I still wanted him. I wanted his hands on me, his mouth, his teeth and claws. I wanted him to wrap me up and never let me go.

I love him. I love him…oh god, I do.

It was terrifying and wonderful and insane. Yet, it was there, bright and true in my heart.

He began to clean me up, his touch so gentle. And when he was finished, Fraser gave my nose a little kiss and threw the soiled washcloths into a hamper.

"Will you hold me?" I asked.

"Always," he whispered, sliding into the bed with me and pulling up the covers.

His fur was still a little damp, but I didn't care. His arms pulled me tight to him, my back to his front, and I'd never felt more cherished or safer than I did in that moment.

No matter what happens, I'm not letting you go Fraser MacDonald. I'm keeping you.

CHAPTER TWENTY-ONE

FRASER

*T*here was blood everywhere.

On my fur.

On the grass.

On Daphne's legs and chest.

And most certainly, there was blood coming from the enormous Orc at my feet.

I heard her screaming as a distant thing. Like it wasn't real.

My ears rang with the adrenaline and animal instincts that had bathed my muscles in fire. A terrible baptism that I had only ever experienced during the full moon. And even then, I had never spilled blood like this before.

Finally, I didn't know how long, Daphne's keening screech pulled me from below the surface of the rage I'd been submerged in. In the back of my mind, I knew this wasn't accurate. It had been Silvia on that day, not Daphne. But in the dream, it was all real. Only this time, I knew what was coming and it sliced at my heart like a hot knife.

"Daphne," I said, lunging for her in desperation to make this time different.

She became a wild, unhinged thing. Scrambling back, kicking at me, clawing at the ground in an effort to get away from me. It was then that I saw my hand, claws shining with blood, fur matted with gore.

"Daphne," I panted, "it's alright. It's me, Fraser. This is…this is just me. The real me. He was going to kill us. I had to save you. Please…"

"Stay away from me!"

She threw the bottle of champagne at me. Then the glasses, the food, the basket. When she ran out of things from the picnic, she resorted to rocks.

"Stay away!"

"Okay," I stopped, tears flowing down my snout and cheeks. "I won't hurt you. I swear. I love you, please, Daphne!"

"You're a monster. Y-you murdered him with your bare hands! You touched me, fucked me with that…with those…! Oh my god."

She promptly vomited on the ground.

I snagged the picnic blanket, which had somehow remained mostly blood free, and ran back to her with it.

"No…no!" she crawled from the sick on the ground. "You stay the fuck away from me, you freak!"

My heart froze and I came to halt. The fear and hate in her beautiful blue eyes, the way she clutched at another rock, ready to strike me with it if I moved a muscle.

This was the woman I was about to ask to be my mate, the one who said she loved me, wanted bairns with me. And she was looking at me with such raw revulsion. If she had skinned me alive, Daphne wouldn't have been able to wound me more.

I fell to my knees on the blood soaked ground, the stain reaching out far more than it had in real life on that day. Daphne's words echoed in my head, over and over. Until I raised my head and howled out my pain.

I woke with a start, the pain of Daphne's rejection still burning inside my body. It took me more than a few minutes to recognize that she was sleeping in my arms, her hand tangled in the fur on my arm. She was breathtaking with the pale light of the sunrise casting her skin in gold.

The scent of her soul uncoiled, calling me to sink back into the bed, to wind myself around her and forget the nightmare. But I couldn't do it.

The memory of it was a sick taste on my brain, one I couldn't stand one moment longer. I got up slowly, careful not wake her, and threw my kilt on. The house was quiet, but I could still hear her cries, her vicious words from the dream. I could still feel the blood cooling on my body, the sting of the rocks on my skin. Everything about it was real, driving away the perfect peace and love I'd known in Daphne's arms tonight. She'd welcomed me as I was, trusted me with her body. The animal in me had come out more tonight than it ever had with another person. It had frightened me, until I saw the intense pleasure in Daphne's cries, the way she looked at me with such pure affection.

I'd almost called it 'love'. I'd wanted to, but didn't dare, fearing the agony of getting my hopes up only to have them dashed again.

And now tonight, I'd seen my fears made manifest in my dreams. It was so real that I had a hard time believing it wasn't true, that Daphne wasn't going to wake up and run screaming from me.

I slumped against a wall near the kitchen and buried my face in my hands. Everything ached to go back and hold her. To wake her up with licks and nips to her beautiful body, to wring cries of pleasure from her slender throat and forget all about what I'd seen. But I couldn't move, couldn't think past the replay of those horrific images, over, and over in my mind.

The full moon affected all of us in different ways. Lowell's usually high libido went into overdrive, but that was fine because there was always some female Weres that were more than happy to scratch that mutual itch with him.

Liam and Samuel seemed to be able to control their urges with long runs over the moonlit hillsides, the full moon giving Liam enough strength to temporarily overcome his injury.

Angus and I were the ones with the temper at this time, and that worked out fine. We'd usually beat the shite out of each another for three nights, and forget about it after. But this time was different, I could feel it in the way it burned through my veins and made rational thought impossible. Alongside the instinct to fight was the fire of lust coursing through me like a runaway train. What if my mating instincts were not strong enough to prevent me from hurting her? What if I took her too roughly, what if her request to stop didn't get through soon enough and I did something unforgiveable?

No, I need to stay away from her today and tonight. That's the only safe option.

"Fraser?" Liam asked, limping out of the kitchen. "What's wrong?"

I shook my head.

"I shouldn't have given in. She…she didn't ken what I am, Liam. And with the full moon comin'…she'll see. She'll see *me* and she'll hate me, just like Silvia did."

Liam's hand landed heavy on my shoulder.

"No, brother. She is different, I can tell. She works around monsters, she's used to all of this."

"She doesn't work with Weres. And even if she did, she would have never seen 'em during moon time."

"Are ya still wanting me to drug ya, because my answer is still a very emphatic 'no.' I think it's a shite idea personally. Ya need to be honest with her."

"I've tried! She won't listen! She thinks that I won't hurt her."

"She trusts ya."

"Aye. The more fool her."

Liam let out a long breath and crossed his arms.

"Ya have let what happened with Silvia rule ya for far too long. She was one Mundane lass. Does Daphne strike ya as like her at all?"

"Ya mean besides her terrible taste in Weres?"

Liam's hand snapped out and he smacked me on my head.

"Ow!"

"That's for being an eejit. You are one of the best Weres I've ever known. And I'm not just sayin' that because yer my older brother. You are honorable, brave and true. Ya stood by me after I was injured and pushed me to try when no one else did. You were brave enough to forge a peace agreement with the Campbells and to go to the Archive, after everythin' they'd done to us, to try and get help when it was all goin' to shite. You are worth it all, Fraser. Daphne sees it. It's time ya did, too."

I wanted to let his words in, by the goddess I did.

It was everything I wanted to believe about myself and had been denying since Silvia. And for a few precious hours last night, I'd opened that door to those beliefs again, to the possibility of happiness, of a real life with Daphne.

But I can't be foolish. I have to put her first and protect her from me. Starting with today.

"Could ya do me a favor, Liam?" I asked.

"Depends. If it's helpin' you push her away, then naw."

"It's not that. Daphne believes that Ruben will be at the cottage and needs to investigate. I promised her I'd go with her, but you know how I am at the full moon."

"Aye, ya wanna fight anythin' that looks at ya sideways."

"And I shouldn't be alone with Daphne like that. Could ya go with us, please? Pull me back if I start to frenzy or…or anythin' close to it?"

Liam's eyebrows raised and his arms dropped to his side.

"Ya want me to go?"

"Aye, why not?"

Liam opened his mouth and then closed it.

"Are ya sure?"

I knew why he was asking. It was day time, and the strength he received from the full moon wouldn't be present. He wasn't as fast as he once was, pain kept him in check far more than he used to be. And he'd be walking with his cane. But there wasn't a thing wrong with his mind. And Liam tended to hide weapons in his canes these days so if anything, Daphne would be very well protected, even if Liam wasn't as quick as before.

"There's no one I would trust more," I said.

Liam's throat worked, trying to swallow back his rising emotions.

"Thank ya, brother."

"Aye. Now, what are you doin' up so early?"

"It's the only time of the day I can do my therapy exercises. Lowell is always poking around the sparrin' yard like a bloody mother hen. And today, there's gonna be so many people about, I wanted some privacy."

I nodded.

"It's gonna be a mad house."

"Ya sure ya don't just want to come clean about her so Lowell and Angus can come too? If Ruben is under the control of an artifact, he could be more dangerous than he would normally around the full moon."

The thought sent my blood pressure racing and I snarled. In seconds, I was ready to rip someone's head off just at the mere thought that Ruben could be a danger to her.

I closed my eyes and breathed through the rage, and the instinct to find someone to pummel. When it was over, Liam was frowning at me.

"It's coming on early for ya this time," he said.

"Aye. Why do ya think I'm so worried? I don't ken what to expect."

Liam nodded thoughtfully.

"I can understand that. Though I'm still not sure avoidin' her tonight is the best plan. But let's table that until after we've investigated the cottage."

"I need to clear my head before she wakes up," I said, starting to walk past him before he could say anything more. "I'm goin' for a long walk. I'll be back by breakfast."

I could feel Liam's eyes on me as I stalked from the house. The summer morning was bright and cool, birds singing in the trees nearby, and the dew shining on the fresh cut grass. It was peaceful, simple out here. I longed to run over the hills and keep going. Outpace the terror chasing me.

But I couldn't be too far away from her. If today didn't go as planned, if Ruben still had the artifact as of tomorrow, my clan, my mate would need me here to make sure she was safe.

So I settled for a run around my home, sinking into the sensation of the cool earth under my feet, the scent of prey still thick in the air from their slumber in the woods. Yes, the animal in me was waking up. I just hoped I could keep it leashed enough to not lose my true mate.

CHAPTER TWENTY-TWO

DAPHNE

I woke up alone the next morning, the bed still warm from where Fraser had spent the night wrapped around me. It was a little disappointing to not find him at my back, his giant cock pressing into my ass. But if the small twinge in my nethers was any indication, I would be needing some of that salve he'd talked about before I could take him again.

I went to the bathroom to shower and spotted a beautiful, blood red rose on a fresh towel. A thrill shot through me at the romantic gesture. For such a grumpy Werewolf when we first met, Fraser was turning out to be quite the sweetheart.

The hot water from the three shower heads hit me and I groaned at how good it felt. It turned out more than just my cunt was sore this morning but I wouldn't have traded it for anything.

As I dried off though, the afterglow of last night wore off and I was forced to confront the fact that, if today was successful, my mission would essentially be over. And that's when I realized that I'd failed to check in last night.

"Damn, damn, damn!"

Hurriedly, I wrapped a large fluffy robe around me and scrambled to get the USB adapter on my phone.

"Agent Reynolds, I was starting to worry," Director Dearborne said. "Report?"

"Apologies ma'am, a lot has happened."

Like being stuffed full of Werewolf cock.

My face heated, my grin wide. I would never tell her that, but I was also not in the least bit ashamed of how much I'd enjoyed Fraser's special endowments.

I pushed those thoughts to the back of my mind and filled her in on what Fraser had learned about Ruben.

"I was thinking of taking Fraser out to the cottage today in an attempt to secure the artifact before anything else happens."

"Make sure that you do. We just got word from the team in Edinburgh that the Protectors are planning on trying to secure the Apple within the next few days. I don't think I need to tell you how important it is for us to get it before they do."

"No, ma'am, you do not."

"I can dispatch the agents out to you tomorrow," Director Dearborne said. "You'll need to find a way to bring the artifact to a neutral state temporarily until we can reach you with the proper containment unit."

"There were no artifacts that you could bring to disable the Apple?"

"Unfortunately, the only ones I could find would need their own containment protocols, we don't have that kind of time or manpower. I'm relying on you to get creative and make it work, Agent Reynolds."

"Yes, ma'am. I'll do what I can."

"I'm leaving for Edinburgh within the hour so you won't be able to get a hold of me. Be careful and I'll see you tomorrow."

It wasn't until I'd hung up that I realized that Director Dearborne hadn't reacted the way everyone else in my professional career did when I suggested something. She'd deferred to me, listened to me, treated me as an equal, as someone who knew what I was talking about. My mouth hung open for a few seconds as the sense of pride, of confidence burst inside of me.

"So…this is what it's like to be treated like I'm a competent professional. It's…it's pretty wonderful!"

I shook my butt in an impromptu victory dance and gave myself a high five.

"Okay," I squared my shoulders, "time to pick out the perfect artifact-getting outfit and then go kick some ass."

I surveyed the clothes in my suitcase, trying to find a balance between function and something that would make me feel like the in-control agent I was. My flesh toned bustier was a must have considering it would protect me if the artifact went haywire. After several minutes of debating, I settled on a pair of vintage suspender trousers with a cinched waist and a simple white button down. My boots would go well with it, not mention the fact that shoulder holster for the Stinger looked quite amazing paired with the vintage style.

"I look like a forties FBI agent," I said with a giggle before remembering that I couldn't go out there brandishing the gun without raising a lot of serious questions. "Oh well, it's still a banging look, stun gun or no stun gun."

I stowed the gun in my tan sling purse with as many bags and bottles of solution that I could fit. Then I pulled my hair back into a high, tight ponytail and finished it off with some light lip gloss.

"There," I said with a nod, "strong, put together and competent."

"Ya forgot beautiful," Fraser said from the doorway.

I jumped but recovered quickly, rushing to him and launching myself into his arms. There was a wariness in his gaze, in the way he held me, like a breakable thing he was sure he was going to ruin. After last night I had hoped he'd realize that I am made of tougher stuff than that.

But maybe he just needs to see it a little more. Maybe tonight's full moon will show him that we really are a good fit.

"Morning," I smiled.

"Good morning," his rough burr rumbled, sending delicious vibrations through me. "Hungry?"

"Yes, very."

His eyes roamed my body, taking in my outfit and I flushed under the obvious approval shining in his eyes.

"What's the occasion?"

"Clothes are my way to overcome nerves. A good outfit can make all the difference in how one sees themselves. So, since I need to go out to the cottage today and snag the artifact, I thought I'd dress the part."

His gaze shuttered and he set me on my feet.

"Fraser? What's wrong?"

"Liam will be goin' with us to the cottage as additional muscle. He knows who ya really are and he's scrappier than he looks."

An embarrassing stab of disappointment hit me that I wouldn't have time alone with Fraser. The day would be packed full of things to do whether or not I retrieved the artifact. But, even so, I tried to keep a smile on my face. Though, from the way Fraser cringed, I knew that my emotions were clear as day across my face.

"Oh…well," I cleared my throat and straightened my shoulders. "I would love to spend more time with Liam. He and I didn't have a chance to talk about his scholarly interests. And I never doubted his capabilities. He looks like he uses that cane for more than just walking."

Fraser huffed out a half nervous, half relieved chuckle.

"Aye, that he does," his tongue flicked out onto my forehead and his hand came around my throat with a light touch. "Thank ya for being alright with it."

"Of course."

The whole exchange had set me off balance and I was suddenly desperate for reassurance that Fraser didn't regret last night, that he hadn't changed his mind about me in the light of day. I jumped up and pressed my lips to his, his firm mouth fitting mine in a way that seemed to defy their natural shape.

"Do you change the shape of your mouth when I kiss you?" I asked.

"Maybe. Do ya like it?"

"I'm not sure. I prefer the real you, but I do quite enjoy kissing you as well."

"It's not a big thing for Weres, kissing that is. At least, not like Mundanes do it."

"How do Weres do it?"

His tongue darted out and grazed my mouth. I opened my lips out of instinct and with a touch of curiosity, sucked on it just a little.

The low growl that rolled up from Fraser was unlike any of the ones I'd heard previously. It was deeper, longer, more animal like. It thrilled and frightened me all at once and I found myself pressing into his body.

Instead of pushing me away, as I half expected him to do, Fraser's strong arms crushed me to him. He picked me up and plopped me onto the bed, as his tongue and teeth worked a path down my throat. When he came to the mating mark he sucked it into his mouth and I came off the bed with a yelp. Wetness flooded my core and I ground myself up into the hand that Fraser had possessively placed on the crotch of my pants.

His mouth didn't let up, and neither did his hand. I'd never gone from zero to one hundred on the arousal scale so fast before. But there was something about the mating mark that made me half-crazy with need. I whimpered and cried out as the heel of his hand worked me through my pants. A mere moment later I clung to him like a life preserver in a stormy sea as he wrung an exquisitely brutal orgasm out of me.

I wanted to stay here, floating on the sensation of being so wanted, so adored and cherished by my Werewolf, but a voice from the doorway tore right through all of that.

"We have doors for a reason, ya know."

Fraser growled and swung his head around to look at Lowell, who was leaning against the doorjamb with a shit eating grin on his face, devouring an apple.

"Don't stop on my account, lass. That was quite a good show."

Fraser snarled at him to go away and stalked to the door.

"Ya can't expect me to just walk past that," Lowell protested just before Fraser slammed the door in his face.

Meanwhile, I was trying not to die of embarrassment.

"I'm sorry about that," Fraser said, "I should've closed the door."

I bit my lip and failed to suppress a giggle.

"I've never had anyone get me off so damn fast," I said, hopping off the bed and darting into the bathroom to change into a dry pair of panties.

When I came out of the bathroom a few moments later, I'd thought he'd maybe come up behind me and hold me. But Fraser stood at the closed door and pulled on a shock of fur at the back of his neck, staring off into the distance.

"What's wrong?" I asked, hating how small my voice sounded.

I couldn't help bracing for rejection, for him to tell me that this had all been a mistake, that we should've kept it professional.

"I'm worried," he confessed after a moment.

"About?"

He closed his eyes on a long exhale.

"The full moon. It's…it's never been this strong in my blood. I'm not in control as much as I'd like."

"Oh," I said, my shoulders relaxing. "Well, that's okay. If we need to spend more time in the bedroom, I don't really see a problem with that."

I let a giggle into my voice, liking the thought of that. But any merriment died a swift death with Fraser's next words.

"This isn't joke Daphne! I could hurt ya! Why can ya not see that? Do ya have no sense of self-preservation at all? I am a beast, and for the next three days, those instincts will be at the fore. Do you really want to bear the brunt of that?"

"I trust you. I know you'd never— ."

"Och, Daphne! Stop being so naive!"

If he'd slapped me I couldn't have been more hurt. And he saw it, written in large letters across my face.

"I'm sorry," he said. "But this is what I mean! My baser instincts. Fighting and fucking, it's all tangled up together and I'm afraid. *You* may trust me but I don't trust me!"

I approached him slowly, my heart in my throat as I tried very hard to put aside my hurt feelings and focus on Fraser. It was foolish to think that one night of mind blowing sex was going to wash away all his fears about his primal side, but that was exactly what I'd done. Now, I had to pivot. If Fraser needed me to say it, to show it every hour of every day until he believed that he could be trusted with me, then I would do just that.

His fur was rippling, tail swishing back and forth in agitated motion that told me exactly how distressed he was. Still, I didn't fear him. Maybe that *was* naive, maybe it was just that I was blinded my new love. I didn't know, and didn't care. I took his hand in mine as he watched with a wary look that was very much like a frightened animal. I turned it over, palm up and pressed kisses to the calloused hand until every inch had been touched by my lips. At the same time, I ran one hand through the fur on his shoulder, soothing and slow.

When I looked up at him, his gaze was less wild but he was still afraid.

I repeated the process with his other hand until his chest was rising and falling at normal rate and he took me in his arms.

"I'm sorry," he whispered against my hair.

"I know."

I wasn't sure what else to say. He still thought I was being blind to his true nature. Words were ineffective. So I'd have to use actions. The only question was, what action?

I have all day to think of it. At least I got him calmed down. That's a start.

"Come, Gran made a feast this mornin', and I don't want ya to go hungry."

"Yes, please! I'm starved."

I shouldn't have been surprised at all that Fraser scooped me up in his arms and carried me, bridal style, from the room.

"You know I can walk," I said with a smirk.

His smile was back, the one just for me and no one else.

"Aye. But I like havin' ya in my arms."

I snuggled against him.

"I like it too."

He carried me downstairs, where the most delicious smells were coming from the dining room. But as we passed the front room, I spied a Werewolf I didn't recognize at first, kneeling on the floor in front of a large trunk. Her fur was a beautiful steel gray and she had glasses perched on the end of her long snout. I gasped as I realized that it was Gran. I had expected the women to change tonight but I supposed that today was technically the first of a three-day full moon cycle.

"Oh, Daphne, would ya stop a minute and talk with me?"

I planted a small kiss on the top of Fraser's snout and he set me softly on my feet.

"Don't be too long. I'm not sure I can keep Lowell from eatin' all the food."

"Oh, I can make more," Gran said, waving her fur covered hand at Fraser.

I shrugged and stepped into the living room. I wasn't there more than a few seconds when the most beautiful sensation hit me. It was the kind of soul touch an artifact would do, reaching out to interact with someone. Only this didn't have the slick feeling of malevolence that some did. My curiosity piqued, I walked further into the room. As soon as my eyes fell on the trunk in front of Gran, I knew that I'd found the source.

It radiated a sense of warmth and family. This was an heirloom, as were the things inside most likely. Heirlooms were the first stage of creating an artifact. Generally, when they remained with the family of origin, they were stable, benefiting the family as they were meant to do. It was only when the chain was broken or the item was corrupted by misuse that an heirloom became a danger to its owners, and therefore, in need of being with the Archive.

This trunk and its contents weren't in danger of any of that, but still, I felt very much like an interloper as Gran began to take some items out to show me. When I sat down beside her and laid a hand on the oak trunk, even more emotions came over me, like a gentle wave of warmth. Love. Gratitude. Sacrifice. Devotion. It was emanating from the trunk in such a gentle way that I doubted anyone who hadn't spent much time around artifacts would even notice the delicate power contained here.

"This is beautiful," I whispered.

Gran gave me a gentle smile.

"This is the trunk that contains our weddin' heirlooms."

"You have a whole trunk of wedding heirlooms?"

"Och, aye!"

She lifted a delicate crown of dried flowers out, the veil attached to it yellow with age.

"This is the crown I wore when I wedded my beloved Gerald. It was my mother's, and her mother's before her."

Next she lifted a beautifully carved box of onyx.

"Every bride that marries a clan leader writes down a hope for her future as a clan leader's mate, and then puts it into this box. It was a gift to our clan from one of the last true Druids. It's said that if the bride's heart is true, her hope will come to pass, even if it is not in her lifetime."

I ran my fingers over the Druidic symbols, a zing of power running up my arm.

Gran gave me a knowing look when I gasped and pulled my hand away.

"I knew ya were sensitive to the power. I could sense that about ya."

I fought back a grimace. She had no idea *why* I was sensitive, and with each passing moment I felt like a horrible liar keeping this from her. She was welcoming me into the family, revealing secrets and special heirlooms to me because she trusted me.

And I will honor that trust by helping to protect her clan. I have to remember that.

"Now," Gran said with a smile, "this is what I really wanted to show ya. If you and Fraser agree, I would like ya both to have a proper handfasting and use *this* to bind yerselves."

Just the thought that Gran would even *want* us to remain mated thrilled me, but my worry about what Fraser might want put a bit of a damper on it.

I took the long box she gave me. It was made of a reddish-brown wood, carved with roses and moons. The sense of love and devotion from the box alone was enough to make my heart skip. Whatever was in here, was possibly one of the most powerful things in the trunk.

Gran opened it and withdrew a long, red strip of cloth. The ends were embroidered with more roses and a full moon, while at the center was the Celtic word for love.

"This," Gran said, holding it out, "has tied the hands of every one of our family's marriages for the past three hundred years. It's what Angus and Imogen will use tomorrow."

I was held breathless by the gentle thrum of power coming from the ribbon. It was warm, kind, without a single malevolent thread.

"It's incredible," I finally whispered.

"It's brought happiness to every couple, even ones like Angus and Imogen who might not exactly like each other at first."

"So, Angus and Imogen aren't an anomaly then?"

"Sadly, naw. There have been many a time when marriages had to bridge the divide between clans. But each of those couples found happiness, even if they didn't find true love. It's why I'm insisting they use it tomorrow."

I ran my finger over the soft fabric and smiled at the peace that rippled through me.

"Daphne?" Fraser asked from the doorway. "Breakfast, lass."

"Go on and eat," Gran said. "I'll rope you into helping me later."

Before I could stop myself, I threw my arm around Gran and pulled her into a hug.

"Thank you for showing me these things."

"Of course, dear. It's all yer history now too."

Tears burned my eyes. I wanted that to be true, more than I realized before this moment. I had barely been here two days and already they were treating me with more respect and acceptance than my own family had in my entire lifetime. The thought of giving that up made me want to beg Fraser on my knees to keep me as his mate.

When I looked up at him, there was a flash of longing on his face but it was gone again so fast that I couldn't latch onto it. I wanted to ask him about it as he escorted me into the dining room, but this wasn't the time or place. After the artifact, after the handfasting, then we'd have time to explore this.

I just have to be patient and hold onto my hope.

CHAPTER TWENTY-THREE

DAPHNE

The drive to the cottage was tense. Fraser was either snappish or sullenly quiet, and I assumed it had to do with the full moon tonight. I knew he was scared for me, but I also felt like I still didn't have all the information about what had happened with his ex. There was something in the story that was the real crux of his fear. I wanted to know it so I could reassure him that I wasn't her. But given the mood he was in, I knew it wasn't a good idea to push him.

So I chatted with Liam as Fraser drove us. By the time we parked at the foot of the hill where the cottage sat, the tension in the car was so thick that Liam and I hadn't spoken for the final twenty minutes of the drive. Fraser stalked from the car, grumbling to himself as he led us toward a thick outcropping of trees on one side of the property.

I slipped my hand into his only to have him jerk back and stop.

"I'm sorry," he whispered. "I'm…"

"Angry? In a bad mood?'

"Aye."

"I know, and if you don't want me touching you, I won't. I just want you to know that I'm here, and I'm not going anywhere."

His gaze heated in an instant and he gathered me up in his arms, flicking his tongue along my lips and jaw. I wound my arms around his thick neck and smoothed his fur as he liked. His tail began to swish in smooth movements, instead of the agitated, jerky ones it had been.

"It's all going to be okay," I whispered.

His ears drooped a little and he set me back on his feet.

"I hope yer right, lass."

"I don't mean to break up this tender moment…" Liam began.

Fraser spun around and bared his teeth at his brother. My breath caught in my throat because for a second it looked like he was going to lunge for him. Liam didn't flinch, just stood his ground and stared Fraser down until my mate finally shook his head and backed up.

"We need to get that artifact," Liam continued as if nothing had happened. "Let's get going."

We crested the hill without further incident, even though Fraser seemed to be one big ball of barely contained frustration.

When we reached the edge of the trees at last, I saw a tiny, dilapidated cottage half covered in climbing roses that I was sure were holding up the sides of the house in some way. The roof slanted oddly, as if it weren't exactly sure it wanted to remain on the house. Paint peeled off the sides and the small porch in great clumps that hung like shredded clothing. The yard was severely overgrown, dotted with wild flowers in places, and odd bare patches in others. The windows were all dark, and no smoke came out of the chimney. The whole place was looked sad, lonely and it made my heart hurt that this was where Ruben had retreated to.

"What does it look like?" Liam asked.

"It's about the size of a small apple, but golden," I explained, handing out a containment bag to Liam and Fraser both. "If it begins to glow, do not look at it."

I double checked my Stinger, slipping it into the shoulder holster. Then I dug Amanda Nunes' sparring gloves from my purse and slipped them on. The second I connected the Velcro ties, a tingle zipped up my arms and through my body. I felt strong, lithe and sure in my skin, in a way I supposed only pro athletes feel.

"What are those?" Liam asked.

"Amanda Nunes' sparring gloves. They give me extra speed, strength and agility."

"I didn't think you were supposed to use artifacts."

"Sometimes agents are given permission. But it's only the artifacts that aren't going to cause chaos out in the wild."

"And only agents they trust, I'd imagine," Liam surmised.

My stood up taller at that and smiled.

"Yeah, I suppose so. Okay, so tell me the layout of this place."

"There's the front door and then one in the back that leads to a small mud room just outside the kitchen. I haven't been here in ten years or more. Damn shame what's happened to the place."

"I don't see Ruben, but that doesn't mean they aren't here. Any hidden rooms or anything I should know about?" I asked.

"Naw. Though who knows since the last time was I was here. Ruben could've built a bloody Tardis in there for all I know," Liam said.

My head whipped around to look at him as a smile bloomed on my face.

"Are you a Doctor Who fan?" I gushed, unable to keep the fan girl part of me harnessed.

"Absolutely. Twelve all the way."

"Hmmm, I'm a number ten gal. Tenant was…"

"Yeah, yeah, hot. If I had a nickel…"

I nudged him with my shoulder and Liam gave me a grin.

"If you two are done flirtin'," Fraser snarled, "let's get this over with."

Liam maneuvered himself between Fraser and me, much to my confusion. I would've thought that letting me close to Fraser could help with his mood, but when I began to move around to do just that, Liam gave me a slight shake of his head and I didn't ask. Obviously, the two of them had worked something out and I just needed to go with it.

My heart was pounding with fear and excitement as we approached the back door of the house. I never dreamed I'd get the chance to do this kind of field work. And while I didn't want to switch to a field agent full time, there was something about being trusted like this that had me believing that I belonged here, that I could do this job, even if I hadn't before.

Fraser insisted on going first, and I was a little surprised that he opened the door instead of breaking it down. Liam nodded at me to go ahead of him this time so that I was sandwiched between the two Werewolves.

The mud room was dark but neat, as was the kitchen. Apparently the outside of the house didn't reflect the inside, which was spotless. The smell of bacon lingered in the air and a coffee pot sat on its warming plate on the counter. I went over and touched the pot, which was still hot.

"If he's gone, it hasn't been long," I whispered.

Both Weres nodded and we proceeded through the kitchen and into the small dining room. Once that was cleared, we moved into the living room. But this too was empty, save for some very old furniture and thick window coverings.

I went to the fireplace, which was swept clean and looked for any signs of a loose brick or hiding place. I was just about to give up when my foot landed on a board with a hollow sound.

"Under here," I said quietly.

Liam was closest, but Fraser bared his teeth and pushed forward instead.

"You know I'm yours right?" I asked when Fraser bent down to try and pry it up. "You don't need to snap at your brother."

"Aye, I do. That's why I'm this way. You've dug yerself deep inside of me and now I'm threatenin' my own brother!"

I stood back and crossed my arms.

"That's not my fault."

"Oh really? You and yer Doctor Who and that damn outfit that shows off yer waist," He ripped the board up. "Yer smilin' eyes and laughin' at his jokes," another board, "the two of ya chatterin' nonstop about that bloody expedition!"

And then a third came up, broken in half in his hands.

"Um, that was a little loud," Liam said, glancing at the doorway.

"I understand that you're having a hard time right now, and I offered to help, but you won't let me," I said, heat rushing to my face. "Besides, you asked him to come."

"To keep ya safe from me," Fraser ripped up another board.

"I think you can stop with the boards now," I said, looking into the empty hole.

"Both of ya are gettin' very loud," Liam tried again.

"I didn't ken it would be this hard to watch him with ya!"

"And I'm sorry about that, but there are bigger issues than your jealousy!"

"I'm no jealous!"

"Oh really?" I stood up and clenched my fists. "You don't even want him next to me."

"Fraser, get a hold of yerself," Liam said.

Fraser leapt to his feet with a loud snarl and got in my face. I should've been afraid; he was twice my size and his tail had gone still, his fur rippling over his back. But I was too angry by now. How dare he tell me I can't be near him, can't help him through this, demand to take Liam and then be *angry* at me because I followed his rules.

"You," I poked him in the chest, "need to make up your damn mind about me, Fraser MacDonald. Do you want me in this with you or not? Because this back and forth shit is really starting to piss me off!"

"Yer gonna do this right now?" Liam asked.

"I thought we had an understanding last night," I continued. "And this morning, you are *once again* putting up walls. It's not fair to jerk me around like this."

"I'm doing it to keep ya safe!"

"I think that ship has sailed," Liam said, raising his hands.

I glanced around Fraser to see six or so men and women in dark suits with guns pointed at us. Though I didn't know every field agent at the Archive, I knew from the kind of guns they were currently wielding that these agents weren't on our side.

I let Fraser step in front of me, a low growl rumbling from his chest. The Stinger was at full charge. I could do a small jolt twice or a large one once. Considering a large one could put a man into cardiac arrest, I chose two small ones and adjusted the settings.

"How nice of the two of you to come here so we can get you out of the way before tomorrow," said one of the men.

"Ya have no right to be on these lands," Liam said, his voice deeper than I'd ever heard it.

"Easy," Fraser whispered to him.

Oh god, this must remind Liam about how he got shot.

"Who's your friend behind you, Werewolf?" asked the male agent. "Come out and play."

My insides churned and spun with nerves, but on the outside, my hands were steady, my mind clear. I didn't know if it was a side effect of the gloves or just the fact that I'd already faced attacks. But whatever the reason I wasn't so much scared as angry at their words, their arrogance, their selfishness when it came to this artifact. They didn't care what it did to Fraser's clan, or the rest of the world.

"Come on, don't be shy," said the woman, "or we'll have to start shooting."

"If you insist," I said, and darted out from behind Fraser.

Without even stopping to think, I shot the Stinger at the woman in the front. Her body convulsed and she went down. I swung the Stinger to the next man and shot him as well. He shook, but only went down on his knees, having been much bigger than the woman.

Then all hell broke loose.

Liam drew a sword, of all things, from his cane and lunged forward with a howling snarl I'd never heard from him before. Fraser roared to life and sprang at a woman who was now aiming her gun at me.

He couldn't reach her before she got a shot off. It wasn't a bullet that launched from the gun, but electricity, very similar to what the Stinger expelled. The force of the bolt threw Fraser back and he collapsed.

Everything slowed; sound, sight. Everything but the small rise and fall of Fraser's chest, reassuring me that he was still alive. The anger I'd felt before was a trickle, a mere drop compared to the torrent that was pounding through my veins in that moment. I'd never experienced the sensation of 'seeing red' before, but I did now. The rage that embraced me like a lover was an oddly clear space, every decision simple.

They had dared to hurt Fraser, *my mate*, and they would pay for it.

I lunged forward with a yell and punched the woman in the stomach. She doubled over, eyes bugging out of her face. Then I back handed her, followed by a swift kick to her knee. I heard the pop and her scream of pain, but somehow it didn't register through the fury coursing through me.

Strong arms encircled me from behind but were gone just as quick. There was a crash of furniture behind me, and a chorus of snarls and shrieks. I pivoted to the left and jumped onto the back of a man who had just fired a shot at Liam. Without even stopping to think, I scrapped my fingernails down his cheek and then wound my forearm around to his throat and squeezed. He batted at my arm, desperate to get air. But I held on until he fell onto the floor.

When I climbed off him I spun around, looking for the next attacker only to find the room in complete disarray. The few pieces of furniture in the room were completely destroyed. Men and women were lying on the floor groaning in pain or not moving at all. In the back of my mind, I hoped they were still alive but it was hard to think of such things when my fists ached to punch something.

"Daphne," Liam said.

I turned to him and bared my teeth. He jerked back, wary of me. When I finally took in the fear and apprehension in his eyes, the way he held himself at the ready as if he might need to subdue me, that's when I remembered the drawback of the gloves.

I tore them off my hands and stuffed them in my pockets.

"Fraser?" I asked, worry and fear quickly taking the place of my previous rage.

"Here," he groaned from the floor, clutching his chest.

I ran to him and fell on my knees.

"Can you move? We have to get out of here," I said.

He nodded and got to his feet.

"You were fierce," he said as Liam and I helped him up.

I practically preened under the praise.

"Yes, well, it was the artifact."

"No, lass, there was some of you in there."

"Ya almost looked like you'd gone into a frenzy over Fraser getting hurt," Liam agreed as we bolted out the door.

"But I'm Mundane."

"Don't matter, not when it's real," Liam said.

I glanced up at Fraser and caught a confusing cocktail of emotions in his yellow eyes. Pride, affection, desire, worry, fear.

We made it back to the Jeep and Liam tore out of there like the devil himself was after us. Fraser and I were in the backseat, our hands clutching at one another. I couldn't stop touching him just to reassure myself that he was alright, and Fraser seemed to be doing the same.

If the Protectors were at the cottage that meant they knew Ruben specifically had the artifact and they were now done with their little 'experiment'. But where was he? Had he fled the cottage knowing they were coming or was it luck? Or did he not know and when he went back would the artifact be taken?

There were too many variables. I could scour the country side looking for Ruben but if he didn't want to be found, he wouldn't be. I tried to focus on what I did know, the things I could possibly predict.

Ruben is missing now. He's full of anger and hate…most of that about the Campbells…the Campbells… the handfasting…wait…wait!

"That's it!" I sat up quickly, startling both Liam and Fraser.

"What's it?" Fraser asked.

"The Apple, it takes people's desires and twists them, creating discord that it then feeds off of, that then creates more discord in an endless cycle until the artifact is neutralized."

"Okay, and…?"

"Some of the most potent reports of the Apple are when it's in proximity to situations that there is already a seed of strife. So, if Ruben wanted to completely destroy the peace agreement, to make sure that the clans don't unite—"

"He'd bring it to the handfastin' tomorrow," Liam said.

"Exactly. He won't be able to resist it. The Apple will make sure of it because it's in the artifact's nature."

"It's the only place we know he'll be," Fraser said slowly.

"Yes."

The brothers exchanged a worried look and I knew they weren't happy about the situation.

"I'll neutralize the Apple when he comes out into the open with it," I reassured them both. "I swear to both of you that I will not let this hurt your clan."

Liam glanced at us in the rear view mirror and Fraser let out a long exhale through his nose.

"Trust me," I begged him. "Please? This is the only way."

"We trust ya, lass," Fraser said.

But did he really? Because while he might be willing to believe in my abilities as an agent of the Archive, when it came to being his mate, Fraser was still holding back from me. And I had no idea how to change that.

CHAPTER TWENTY-FOUR

DAPHNE

I didn't see Fraser for the rest of the day. Even though Gran had me busy helping her get the house ready for the Campbells in the morning, my mind was never far from how Fraser had distanced himself from me.

When I finally saw him at dinner, his entire body tensed as I came near.

"Fraser," I said, my voice thick with unshed tears, "please, don't push me away. Let me help you through this, whatever it is."

His jaw tensed, hands clenching into tight fists over and over again.

"Dinner time ya two!" Gran called from the kitchen.

"We'll talk about this later," Fraser said.

The words caused frustration to bloom in my chest and now it was my turn to make fists with my hands.

"Will we? Or is that just your way of avoiding the conversation?"

Fraser didn't answer. Instead he picked me up and nuzzled my throat, taking a big inhale.

"You smell like moonlight," he purred, "and heather."

The sudden change in his demeanor gave me emotional whiplash and I could only stare at him as he walked toward the dining room with me in his arms.

"Don't toy with me," I whispered to him.

Fraser stopped cold and I thought maybe I'd made him angry. But then his arms brought me closer, his tongue darted out against the mating mark and I gasped as my nipples tightened.

"Naw, lass. I'm not toying with ya. I'm having a hard time with the moon."

"Tell me what you need."

His long, hard exhale ruffled my hair.

"You, lass," he admitted after a moment. "I need you."

"You have me," I pressed a palm to his cheek, smiling as he rubbed his face against my hand.

His rough tongue gave my inner wrist a hot lick that made my core clench, and goose pimples pop up on my arms. He made no promises, no response to what I'd said other than that. But as we sat down at the table, Fraser was much more relaxed. Though he did still insist on perching me on his lap and loading up my plate for me, growling at his brothers if they tried to do something for me.

"I sure hope ya calm down after moon time is done," Lowell grumbled. "I'm not gonna take your mate away."

Fraser bared his teeth at Lowell, who growled back.

"Enough you two," Gran's hard voice cut through the growing tension. "Save it for the sparring area after dinner. I'll not have ya breaking another table."

"How many have they broken?" I asked.

"Seven," Liam said.

I choked on a sip of water and Fraser rubbed my back.

"You've broken seven tables?" I asked him.

"It was Lowell's fault," he said, taking a savage bite of his roast.

Lowell opened his mouth to retort and Angus interrupted.

"Enough!"

After that, dinner was rather subdued, with everyone finishing their plates in record time before leaving the house as if their tails were on fire.

"Is it always like this during the full moon?" I asked Gran as we washed the dishes.

"Aye. Don't worry, you'll get used to it."

I gave her a wobbly smile and started her dishwasher. I wouldn't mind learning to get used to it honestly. Getting the chance to? That's another story.

"Oh, has Fraser told ya what to expect tonight?" she asked.

"Um…no?"

She shook her head and muttered under her breath.

"For newly mated Were males, full moon time is a little more difficult. While most Were males could take or leave the chase as part of their ruttin', durin' the full moon it's one sure way to help them get some of the wildness out of their systems."

My heart beat out a harsh rhythm in my chest and my palms became sweaty. The thought of running through the night, Fraser behind me, catching me and then…

Rutting me under the moon…with his primal side unleashed…

It was everything I'd been secretly longing for since college. Everything that I'd tucked away, too afraid to let anyone see. No one would have understood, my partner and friends at the time made that perfectly clear. But now here I was, about to experience something I'd only ever hoped for in the dark of my room by myself.

Fraser, my Werewolf, my monster, is really the only one I could ever be so vulnerable with, the only one that would see this side of me and not be disgusted.

I licked my lips, hoping that my sudden arousal was not noticeable.

"Is there…I mean, any place in particular I should…. run?" I asked, my voice breathy.

"Well, most of his brothers will be in the hills and trees around the property, or at the sparrin' area. The walled in garden and the land around there should be mostly empty," Gran said with a knowing grin.

"Oh. Thank you."

She patted my shoulder.

"I left two jars in yer bathroom. One is a special lubricant for ruttin' that will help your walls to stretch a bit more easily, even Were females need that help sometimes. And the other is a salve for after."

I would've been mortified except I was too grateful to care. This was exactly what I needed, both the information and what was in the jars.

"Thank you, Gran," I said, giving her a quick hug.

"Ah, to be young again. Now, go on and get yerself ready. When the sun goes down, that's when he'll need ya."

After pacing the room, waiting impatiently for the sun to set, I applied a generous amount of the lube and tried to calm my racing pulse. I wasn't afraid, not really. It was more excitement and nerves at the unknown. What exactly could I expect from this? Would Fraser want me out there? After all, he'd told me more than once that he was scared to experience the full moon with me.

Or would this be the thing that at last proved that I was in this for the long haul? That he could trust himself with me?

I ran my hands over my loose hair, hoping the waves were smooth and not frizzy. The nightgown I'd chosen for this was a knee length white one that was just the teensiest bit see through. The only thing I regretted wearing were the white sneakers on my feet, but there really wasn't an option if I didn't want my feet getting cut up on the gravel outside the house.

I took a deep breath and stepped outside. In spite of it being June, the night was cool, making my nipples pebble. The hair on my arms stood up when I heard a distant howl and I wondered if Fraser would know I was out here, or would I be wandering around for hours without luck?

Still, I wanted to try. I walked over the gravel and toward the walled-in garden. My feet had just touched the grass when he appeared from around the far wall. The moon shone in a cloudless sky, illuminating him from behind. Like this, he looked so much bigger than usual, a hulking, massive figure with gleaming claws and my heart kicked up a notch.

Fraser always moved with a hint of something wild about him. But this time, he moved toward me as if he were stalking me. Slow, purposeful.

"What are ya doin' out here?"

The low thunder of his voice floated on the summer air, stealing my breath.

"I…I…"

He laughed, a deep, growling sound full of danger as he stopped close enough for me to see his face. Yellow eyes glowed under his dark fur, canines shining in the moon light.

"You've come to tempt me?"

I licked my lips, trying to find the right words. What does one say to a sexy beast when all I want is for him to rip my clothes off, shove me against the wall and knot me for hours?

"Yes," I managed to breathe out.

The Werewolf that began to circle me, his hot gaze a lick of fire over my whole body, was a different Fraser than the one I knew. This Fraser radiated a predator energy that sent stabs of terror to my brain. He was rippling with a primal power, wild and uncontained. His chest rumbled, breath hot on my back. One claw ran down my arm, not breaking the skin, but leaving a red scratch in its wake.

"So fragile," he murmured. "So beautiful."

I began to quake, my brain unsure whether to turn and embrace him or run for my life.

His nose brushed my ear and cheek, and Fraser took a sharp inhale.

"Yer cunny is soaked for me, Daphne."

A low moan escaped from my lips before I could stop myself.

"Ya want me to rut you like a beast in the grass, fill ya with my cum until it's dripping onto the ground from between yer thighs?"

It wasn't a question. As surely as the moon hung full and bright in a midnight sky, Fraser knew that I wanted all of that.

My breath was coming fast, chest heaving under the low décolletage of my night gown. Fraser's eyes zeroed in on my nipples, achingly hard under the thin fabric. He reached out with one claw and circled the areola with it. Jagged bolts of sensation bloomed from that single point of contact and my eyes rolled back for a moment as I let him tease me.

"Mmm…. Ya know what I want?"

My nod was erratic, punctuated by a whimper.

His eyes snapped to mine and he grinned.

"Run, Daphne. Run, and don't let me catch ya unless ya want me to use ya in every base, filthy way I can imagine until yer beggin' me to stop."

I wouldn't have thought my legs could move that fast, but I sprinted forward, scrambling on the damp grass as I careened around the garden and through the clearing. A few minutes later, I heard rough panting behind me, and the scratch of claws on the ground. A cry launched itself out of my mouth, carried on my quick breathing.

I darted to the right and the sounds of pursuit got louder. My legs were shaking, but not from exhaustion. A sensation, like bees under the skin, was coursing through my body, and I screamed as a dark shape closed in on me, its breathing punctuated by growls.

I lost my footing and one of my shoes on a slippery patch of grass, almost falling face first. But I managed to stay on my feet and careened forward.

I hadn't realized that I was heading back toward the garden until the walls were in front of me. With a last burst of speed, I tried to make for the out cropping of trees to my left.

That's when Fraser pounced.

The moment his hands seized me, I let loose a screech of terror. He didn't even acknowledge it, or the way my hands began to hit him of their own accord. He just threw me over his shoulder and ran into the walled in garden. I beat his back, pulled his fur, kicking at him with my feet and losing the other shoe in the process. My mind seemed to have forgotten that I was safe, and that was the point really. I wanted it to feel like I was being hunted by a beast, I wanted to be overcome by fear before the monster fucked me senseless.

With one long, vicious swipe, his claws, Fraser tore the nightgown to shreds and then pulled the remnants from my body in snarling swipes. My brain was quickly short circuiting at the savage way he was handling me when he dropped me, completely naked, onto a soft patch of grass.

I didn't have time to process any of this before Fraser leapt onto me, seized my wrists with one hand and pinned them above my head.

"Ya want the beast?"

His breath was hot against my face and I stared at him, my mind unable to come up with a response.

"Answer me," he growled.

"Y-yes...yes, I want the beast."

His jaws snapped onto my matting mark, harder than the last time and a shock wave of heat coursed through me just before he plunged three fingers into me. This was no gentle exploration, no attempt at finesse. He pumped hard and fast, as his jaws stayed locked on my flesh. Somewhere, someone was screaming in fearsome pleasure, the cries echoing off the walls.

It took me a while to realize that it was me. And when I did, I let go of every inhibition that had ever told me it was wrong to want this. I was utterly exposed and laid out under the night sky like an ancient sacrifice, given to the beast to sate his hunger. It was base and profane, darkly sexual, and I embraced it all.

Fraser's thumb worked my clit with a brutal expertise as his fingers kept up their divine pace. But each time he brought me to the pinnacle of ecstasy, he backed off, never letting me go over the edge.

He did that over and over. Winding me up, only to leave me tight and aching with unfulfilled need.

"Please," I sobbed as he began again. "Please, let me come."

Fraser at last released my mating mark and instead sank his teeth into my inner thigh and I jumped with the sudden sharp sensation. He bit my thighs and hips as if he would devour me. Just when I reached the place where he had left me in agony before, Fraser kept going, pushing me over that cliff. Sparks went off behind my eyes, toes curling on the cold ground as he wrung every last bit out of me.

When I was weeping, trembling with the aftershocks of what he'd done, Fraser sat up and tore his kilt off, tossing it to the side. A white line of precum trickled from his pink head down one side of his cock, the crown itself covered in a glistening white coating. Still holding my hands, he began to pump himself as I watched. I don't know how, but he seemed larger tonight, the veins on his cock more prominent, his knot bigger than before. There was no fear of not being able to take him; all I knew was a soul deep hunger to feel him stretching my walls to the point of pain, to feel him ravish me as he took his pleasure from my body. The dregs of my orgasm were still warming my insides, but I was craving more. I wanted him to claim me with every wild instinct he possessed, to taste fear on the edge of the pleasure he was pounding into me. Just the thought of it had me bringing my thighs together to get any kind of sensation on my aching cunt, until he separated my legs with his knees.

"I'll have yer next release on my cock, nowhere else. Yer mine."

"I'm yours," I agreed.

He brought the head of his cock to my slick folds and ran it up and down, toying with me just because he could.

"Again," he demanded.

"I'm yours."

The head breached my opening and I gasped in anticipation.

"Again," his burr so rough, so deep that it sent a tremble through me.

"I'm yours."

He slid half way in and my back bowed off the ground. Yes, he was definitely bigger tonight, a pinch of discomfort blooming alongside the most erotic moment of my life.

"I'm yours," I whimpered.

One more brutal thrust and he was seated completely inside of me. I was so impossibly full, my walls stretched and tight around him. His entire body was shaking as he held himself still above me, his fur rippled like a stormy sea and his tail was sticking straight out. Fraser's chest heaved as he stared at me, his pupils wide as his breath huffed out of his open mouth, hot and damp on my face.

He was trying to be careful, to check in, but it was a terrible effort to fight what his nature wanted from him right now.

"Please, Fraser," I swirled my hips slightly, his knot rubbing against me.

I was so over-sensitized that I groaned and rolled my head back. I'd only intended to let him know it was okay, but he'd tormented me into a frenzy that nothing seemed to satisfy and my body was crying out for more. I writhed against him, my pleas echoing in the chilled air.

The hand that wasn't holding my wrists, slammed down on my hip, pinning me in place. I whimpered and cried, begging him once again.

Fraser withdrew so slow that I felt every thick, hot inch of him as he rubbed against my inner walls. He was nearly all the way out when he thrust hard back into me, his knot barely breaching me. I stared down in shock and back up at him. That's when I realized just how gentle he'd been with me last night. That had been a restrained coupling, a mere sample of what he'd kept caged within him. And I wanted him to unleash that monster. I wanted his darkness, his wild lust. I wanted everything he had to give because I'd hungered for this all my life and Fraser was the only one who could give it to me.

I nodded at him, hoping he could see the longing in my eyes.

He bared his teeth at me, and a raspy growl rolled up from his throat, eyes smoldering and feral. Before I knew what was happening, Fraser had pulled out of me, flipped me onto my stomach and hiked my ass up into the air. With one hand tangled in my hair, he pressed my cheek against the soft grass and jerked my legs wide with his other. Cold air washed over my most vulnerable places and it was all the more exciting to know that anyone could walk into this garden and catch us performing scenes from my most illicit fantasies. I moaned at the thought, my ass wiggling in a silent plea to fill me, to fuck me, to fulfill my obscene desires at last.

Fraser's husky laugh filled my ears, his tongue lashed out around the shell of it and I gasped.

"Ya want the beast, don't ya?"

"Yes, please."

"Well, be careful what ya wish for."

And with one violent pull of my hips, Fraser speared me sharply onto his cock. I screamed at the sudden painful stretch of him and he didn't give me a chance to adjust to the new angle. I had begged for this, had made sure I would be irresistible to him, and now here I was, being mounted without mercy, his hips snapping forward at the same time he pulled me to him.

How many times alone in my room had I imagined this very thing? Had made myself come over and over to just this exact image?

But the fantasy was nothing compared to the reality of being rutted on the cold ground, of feeling the rasp of fur on my thighs, the bite of his claws on my skin, the grit of the earth under me as he pounded so hard that I moved against the grass and moss. I was fast becoming lost between reality and the fantasies I'd kept so deeply hidden. Pleasure wound around every tinge of pain, every bitter taste of fear and made it beautiful. But still, I was just beyond the release of it all and I began to cry, thinking I'd always be teetering on the edge.

Fraser reached between us, as if he knew how much I needed a release. His finger circled my clit, pressing hard and working it like he'd been doing it for years. Everything went bright, my body tight and hot, and Fraser began to piston his hips harder, spittle flew from his mouth and onto my back. With each brutal thrust, his knot crept more and more inside of me.

My groans grew louder and, mixed with the growls and snarls of the monster he'd kept leashed, and I was blessedly lost in it all. Just as his knot slipped into my channel, the delicious sensation of it expanding tore through me and broke me apart. I was distantly aware of my cries, so fractured and loud but I couldn't care. I was coming apart around him as his knot pulsed and Fraser painted my cunt with his hot cum.

My orgasm was still going when Fraser pulled me back and onto his lap. I was facing out, his cock locked into me, and as he made little thrusts with his hips, the fingers of one hand were at my clit while the others pinched my nipples. It was all too much and I began to sob at the sheer volume of sensation. I had no idea if I was coming again or if I'd never finished, when Fraser raised his snout to the sky and let out a long howl. His knot was still inside of me, and he continued to fill me with his seed, though tiny trickles were running down my thighs and onto his lap. We panted as if we'd run a marathon, sweat dripped down my back and torso, cooling in the night air.

Slowly, Frasers fingers skated up to my stomach, his other hand to my throat where he held me like he had on the train. It was a possessive move, but it steadied me while I was still being tossed around by the aftershocks of my orgasm. I leaned into his touch, knowing I was safe but it wasn't enough to overcome the fact that I felt everything to a degree that was halfway between exquisite and excruciating.

The soft skin of his chest and stomach.

The fur on his hands and thighs.

The flick of his tongue as he lapped up my tears.

The huff of his breath against my cheek.

The air on my bare breasts and stomach.

"Fraser," I breathed, "Fraser."

"I'm here," he whispered. "I'm here, my beautiful mate. My one and only."

His arms encircled me and we laid down on the same mound of grass we'd been fucking on just a moment before. He couldn't withdraw from me yet, and the movement brought a fresh wave of friction to my clit. I whimpered and began to shake.

He wrapped his legs around me and dipped his head to rest on top of mine. I was completely engulfed in the warmth and softness of his body.

"Shhh…deep breaths. I've got ya."

I focused on him, his chest rising and falling. My own breath coming in through my nose and out of my mouth. Slowly, by aching degrees, I came back down to earth. I could enjoy the feel of Fraser's body against mine, the tight fit of his knot no longer overwhelming me.

"I took your knot," I whispered.

"Ya did so good, my love."

Pride bloomed in my chest at the praise. It was odd to want to please him so much, as if it were an imperative.

Perhaps that's the mating bite. The need to please one another and…wait, did he just say…?

"Love?" I turned my head to look at him.

His mouth pressed little licks to my shoulder as he avoided my gaze.

"You don't have to…"

"I love you too, Fraser."

His eyes snapped to mine.

"Daphne, are ya sure?"

"I know it's fast but…I don't want to be without you. I just didn't know if you would want that."

Tears fell down my face as I realized that I wouldn't have to give him up at the end of all this. Fraser was mine and I was his.

"I love you," I said again, clinging to his arms. "I love you, Fraser."

"My mate, my love. You'll stay with me?"

"As long as you'll have me."

"Forever," he said, and I thought his voice hitched on the word.

I nodded.

"Forever."

CHAPTER TWENTY-FIVE

FRASER

I never wanted to leave the garden, this blessed pocket of time. Daphne and I could rut and hold each other without the world threatening the happiness we were finding. I had never hoped she'd love me, especially not after taking her with the moon time frenzy searing through my blood.

I hadn't been gentle, that's for sure. But she had not only taken it, Daphne had been wet and ready for me, begging me to take her. She'd *enjoyed* it. I'd never thought to find a Mundane mate that would embrace my true form and nature so completely.

She'd understood that I needed her to give me the thrill of a chase. And Daphne had *liked* it, I could smell it on her as she ran from me. Her fear and arousal were mouthwatering as it trailed after her. I could've chased her for hours, but my cock was aching to fill her. And when I had, she'd been so ready for me, it had broken any restraint I might've been able to keep.

"Are ya alright?" I asked, as my knot finally slipped free.

She wiggled a little, as if testing something and her luscious ass rubbed against me. I groaned and gripped her hips as desire spiked through me.

"You cannot be ready to go again," she said turning around and eyeing my cock.

"It's the moon time. It can give us more stamina and quicker recovery. But, yer probably too sore for—"

"I used some special lube before I came out here and I'm a little sore, but not much at all."

Her bright eyes turned up to mine and she bit her lip. Could she possibly be as aroused so soon after? Would she able to handle taking me again, even with the 'magic' lube she'd found?

"I won't hurt you," I said.

"I know, but…"

She bent down so that my half-mast cock was at her mouth and licked the cooling cum from root to tip. On instinct I bucked up as her mouth closed over my crown.

"I wanna fuck yer mouth," I hissed, threading my fingers through her hair. "I wanna own every part of yer body, mark it with my seed."

She hummed in approval and I stared down as she attempted to take more of me into her little mouth. Her skin was glowing silver in the moon light, dark hair tangled like an ancient crown around her pale face. The curling hair on her mons was wet with our combined juices, and my seed coated the inside of her thighs. My mate was wanton with lust as she used her hands and mouth together. In a few short minutes, I was rock hard again, as if I hadn't just been as deep as possible in my mate's tight cunny for the last fifteen minutes.

I wanted, *needed* to give her pleasure, it wasn't something I could resist. So I slipped three fingers into her. The squishing sound it made as I pumped her was carnal, more of my seed seeping out. I'd indeed filled her to overflowing, and pride swelled in my chest. I wanted more in her, I wanted to plant it so deep that her belly would round with our pup.

"I wanna breed you."

It slipped out before I could stop it, and her mouth popped off my cock, eyes meeting mine in surprise.

"I've always wanted children but…not yet. Can you wait, just a little while?"

I was so relieved that she wasn't panicking that I nodded without hesitation.

"Aye. I'll wait as long as ya want."

Daphne grinned at me and moved off my fingers before pushing me onto my back and climbing on top of me. Her hand fisted my cock and stroked me hard before bringing me to her wet entrance.

"Are ya sure?" I asked.

Her smile was wild and beautiful.

"I want to ride you under the moon, Fraser. Would you like that?" She slipped my crown through her pussy lips. "Would you like to use me again, like a toy on your cock? Dragging me up and down your length and making me come before you knot me again?"

My groan ended with a low growl as I bared my teeth at her. The animal in me was awake once more and I hadn't the strength to cage him. Not when my mate was begging the savage part of me to come out a play.

She shivered, cheeks flushing as she stared down at me, and I knew my mate desperately wanted my beastly side. It made me howl in triumph as I gripped her hips and brought her down onto my cock. She was so tight that every slide through her made me hungry for more. And when at last she was seated, with my knot pressing against her pearl, the little vixen began to swirl her hips, pleasuring herself against me.

With her head thrown back, dark hair trailing down her moon-baptized flesh as she played with her breasts, Daphne's sensual beauty took my breath away. She may have believed that I was in control, but really, the creature in me bowed to her whims, her wants. If she had told me to stop, I knew that I would, without hesitation because I couldn't hurt her, couldn't do anything but what she wanted. It was part of the makeup of my beast now, a realization that had me letting go of my fears and being swept away with Daphne. I reached up and circled her throat with my hand, needing to possess her completely.

"Yes," she groaned, "own me. Use me."

Her movements sped up, little mewls accenting her breaths. I matched her rhythm and bucked up at the same time. Soon she was trembling, her breathing erratic as her release began to coil like a spring within her. I saw the moment it snapped. Her fingernails dug into my chest and her tight cunny milked my cock so hard that I nearly knotted her instantly.

She was so beautiful when she came, free and unfiltered, incomprehensible words flowing from her lips. Only I could do this to her. Only I could make her cry and beg for more even as she was overcome with the power of her release.

The beast in me howled once again and I flipped her onto her back. I was snarling now, my only thought to rut her hard and deep.

"Mine, mine," I breathed as I thrust over and over into her.

When my knot finally breached her pussy, she gripped it so tight that I saw stars and I roared into the night as I expended inside of her. This time, it wasn't just the sensation of her cunny. It was everything.

My soul sang to hers in this moment, a Mundane woman with not a drop of supernatural in her. Yet, she was my true mate, the answering call of my deepest loves and wants. Daphne was the missing piece of my soul, calming the beast in me with her gentleness, her bravery and love.

"My mate," I licked her stomach, her breasts, her throat. "My mate."

It was all I could say as my orgasm ebbed, leaving me raw inside.

"Yours, Fraser," she whispered, winding her arms around me.

I rolled us onto my side so I could hold her while we waited for my knot to release her. She wasn't so over sensitized this time, but I could see her fatigue. My little mate had been used thoroughly, and there wasn't a hint of regret from her. In fact, she grinned up at me, her eyes glassy with the afterglow.

"So," she said nuzzling against me, "it's going to be pretty hard to top this tomorrow night."

I chuckled, running a hand over her peach of an arse.

"I'm sure I'll think of somethin'," and I spread her cheeks just a little to run a finger through them.

Her eyes widened in surprise.

"Have you ever been taken here?" I asked, a sudden spike of jealousy at the thought that anyone had the privilege before me.

"No," she breathed. "I…I never really trusted anyone enough."

"But ya trust me enough?"

"Yes," she pressed a kiss to my chest. "Though I think we'll have to start slow. I'm not ready for you back there just yet."

"Mmmm…" I ran my finger once again between her luscious cheeks. "Then that's what we'll do. But someday, dear Daphne, I'm going to take this virgin arse while ya use one of those toys on yer pretty little cunny. Would ya like that?"

She took in a sharp inhale, licking her parted lips.

"Yes. Very much."

"But for right now," I stood up, my arm banded around her to keep Daphne flush with me, "we're gonna get ya into the bath."

"Someone will see!" she looked around as she clung to me.

"Naw, they're all on the outskirts of the property. I think Gran might've given them a talkin' to."

My knot was starting to soften already, and I was a bit disappointed by it as I took her swiftly toward the house. I had never thought I'd love being knotted. I knew it would feel better than anything I'd ever experienced, but I wasn't prepared for the emotional part. The sense of mutual belonging that passed between us when I was knotted inside of Daphne. She was mine and I was hers in that moment in a way far more intimate than the purely physical. Now that I'd experienced it, I knew I'd crave it like a drug. But I also knew I'd have to be careful with my mate. She might have lube to help take me twice in one night, and salve for after, but she was still Mundane, and I could still hurt her.

So I carried her into the house, laving her mating mark with my tongue, savoring every sigh I conjured from her lips. I couldn't seem to stop running my hand up and down her spine, over the curve of her arse, the swell of her breasts. She pressed little kisses to my chest and I jumped when she bit my nipple.

She arched an eyebrow, smirking at me.

"Turnabout is fair play, my mate," she said.

The thrill that shot through me to hear her call me 'mate', the heated way she looked at me, and the sting of her little teeth against my flesh, all made it very difficult to keep myself from finding a way to stay knotted inside of her. But by the time we made it to the bedroom, my knot had slipped free and a rush of my seed came from between her legs.

"Oh my goodness!" she clamped her knees shut as a set her down

"It's alright," I said with a chuckle. "I'll draw you bath and you can get cleaned up."

She stared down at the puddle she was making on the bathroom tile and then back up at me.

"Was it that much before? It couldn't have been."

"Och, no."

"Moon time is going to take some getting used to," she said, cleaning off her legs as I drew a bath.

Daphne had said she loved me, she'd called me her mate, and every little thing she said about the future with me made my heart soar. After the bawbag I'd been all day, Daphne still wanted a life with me.

How did I get so lucky? And how do I hold onto it?

There was one thing she had not seen, and I prayed she never would. It was the one thing that I didn't know if she could ever accept. But if it meant having a chance to make a family together, weathering the happy and the sad beside one another for the rest of our lives, then I'd find a way to control the violent side of my nature. Daphne was worth every bit of sacrifice I had to give.

CHAPTER TWENTY-SIX

DAPHNE

I would've done anything to stay wrapped up in Fraser's arms the next morning. But we were barely given enough time to wake up fully before Lowell was knocking on our door telling us that we had over slept. I wasn't exactly sure what to wear to this handfasting until Gran came in with a beautiful dress made of MacDonald tartan.

"I guessed at the size so I hope it fits," she said, decked out in a Were version of the same dress.

"It's beautiful, thank you," I said through tears.

"Och, it's nothin'. Yer a MacDonald now, you have to look the part. Now, get dressed, breakfast is a grab and go. Campbells will be here in two hours. So much to do!"

The rest of the morning rushed by at a shocking pace. Breakfast and final preparations happening mere moments before the entourage of black SUV's pulled onto the property. Many of the Were's from clan MacDonald were already here and waiting at the clearing for the ceremony to begin. So most of the Werewolves that poured from the vehicles wore Campbell tartan and looked around as if they were here under protest.

I glanced up at Fraser, who'd been stern faced all morning. He was looking straight ahead, but he gave my hand a squeeze of encouragement so I straightened my shoulders. I'd not give the Campbells any reason to think ill of Fraser's mate, even if I was one of the only Mundanes here.

My gaze scanned the Were's present, searching for Ruben as I had been all morning. So far, he hadn't shown up and I started to worry that I'd miscalculated. Perhaps there was another play at work that I hadn't thought of.

Or maybe the Protectors got the the Apple after all.

I banished the thought quickly because a very old Were leaning on a cane and the arm of a devastatingly beautiful female Werewolf were approaching us. I assumed this was Calum, the very old leader of clan Campbell, and his grand daughter Imogen.

While he was hunched and frail looking, Imogen stood proud and tall beside him in a dress of Campbell tartan. Her fur was a coppery red that shimmered in the sunlight and her blue eyes missed absolutely nothing as it took in the scene before her.

Calum nodded to all of us and waited for Angus to step forward. Fraser had run through what to expect today and I had to admit that behind the fear and worry, was an excitement at what I was about to witness. Not one book that I'd come across had been able to detail a traditional Werewolf handfasting ceremony. Yet here I was, seeing it all.

I'll have to ask Fraser about writing this down later. He was so upset when he thought I'd write a tell all about their traditions he may not want me reporting any of this.

The traditional handfasting that Calum had insisted upon began the moment the bride and groom spied one another and would find it's culmination at the trellis. I held my breath as Angus broke off from us and stepped up to Calum and Imogen.

"I request the hand of this female to be my mate," he said, loud and clear.

"Will ya provide food for her belly, shelter for her head, and fire for her warmth?"

"Aye."

"Will ya give her pups to cherish, joy in the darkness and comfort for her tears?"

"Aye."

Calum turned to Imogen, whose expression hadn't changed the entire time.

"Dearest Imogen, do ya accept him?"

Her glittering gaze hadn't left Angus, and there was a tension between them made up of many shades of emotions.

"Aye grandfather," she said at last.

From what Fraser had told me, if Angus was going to back out, he'd have done it at that point. There was no turning back now, at least none that would result in anything but extreme shame to our clan and the highest kind of insult to the Campbells.

Calum took his grand daughters hand, brought it to his forehead for a brief moment and then handed her to Angus. He took her hand with a stern expression on his face and tucked it into the crook of his arm. With that, the two of them led the procession of close family members first, followed by the rest of the clan toward the clearing and the trellis, where a priestess was waiting to bind their hands.

My eyes darted around, missing nothing as we made our way near the front of the procession. I felt like I was being watched, and not by the curious stares of the Were's from both clans. Someone else was watching me, and my skin crawled with the knowledge.

Something was going to happen, but when and from where?

"What's wrong?" Fraser leaned down to ask.

"Something isn't right," I whispered back. "I can feel it."

My hand went inside the small purse where I'd stowed my Stinger, Amanda Nunes' gloves and a few artifact bags. I found the Stinger, and my hand clasped the butt of it. I doubted I could be a very quick draw, but it was better than scrambling when the time came.

Imogen and Angus reached the trellis and the rest of us were spread out on either side of the aisle that had been strewn with rose petals. There were no chairs except for Calum, so we were all standing, with Angus' family at the front to the left. That same feeling of eyes watching me intensified and I looked around. But there was no one but the two clans and those supernaturals that had been hired for the event standing at a respectable distance.

The trellis was made of oak, and decorated with a riot of summer flowers and bright ribbons. If not for the grim expressions of everyone present, one would think from the decor that this was a happy event. To the right of Angus and Imogen was a table covered in a green cloth, wine, bread and the beautiful ribbon for the handfasting laid out on top.

The moment my eyes landed on the ribbon, the power contained with the heirloom reached out and brushed up against my consciousness.

Devotion, kindness, love…oh my god! That's it!

The priestess began to speak and a chill went down my spine. My gaze snapped to Fraser, his eyes wide. He'd felt it too.

The crowd behind us began to murmur, anger rippling from them. Then, from one of the tents came a very self satisfied Ruben, holding a small, beautiful Golden Apple in one of his clawed hands.

"Well, well, well, what a happy day!" he sneered.

Angus angled himself between Imogen and Ruben, the move protective in a way that was odd considering how much Angus had seemed to hate this arrangement.

"You are not welcome here," Angus snapped, a furious growl in his chest.

"Yet here I am. And with a gift for the bride and groom."

"No!" I shouted, launching myself at him as I realized what he was about to do.

But it was too late. Ruben was too fast and the Apple was already in motion.

He'd lobbed it right in the middle of the two clans. A high whining sound built as the Apple grew in brightness until it was glowing like a wicked siren. When the sound reached a crescendo a wave spun out from the Apple and then there was a moment of utter silence before all hell broke loose.

Campbells and MacDonalds began to brawl, clawing and biting one another in a writhing mass of fur, claws and teeth. The only ones unaffected were myself, and Fraser's family, along with Imogen and Calum.

"I want ya to see the destruction you've wrought before ya tear one another apart!" Ruben shouted.

Angus went to grab him when Lowell restrained him. Imogen dove for her grandfather and pulled up out of the fray and with the rest of us in front of the trellis.

"Fraser, get me that Apple," I ordered and turned to the others. "I know how to stop this but I need that."

I pointed to the ribbon and Angus stared at me in shock.

"Yer an agent," he whispered. '

"Yes."

His eyes narrowed and he opened his mouth, probably to tell me off when Imogen put her hand on his arm.

"We don't have time for yer anger," she said, then looked at me. "Go on then."

"That belongs to my family," Angus snapped.

"And mine now too, or it will be if we survive this."

"Let her have it if she can stop this!" Gran yelled.

"Here's the Apple," Fraser leapt forward, his forehead bleeding.

"Are you—?"

"Fine lass, now end this."

I snatched the ribbon and couldn't help smiling at the peace it radiated. The Apple, on the other hand, made me grimace to touch. My bustier was protecting me from the damn thing, but still, I felt unclean handling it, as if all the discord and strife it had collected over the years was spilling out onto my skin.

Swallowing back a sudden rush of bile, I wrapped the ribbon around the Apple until it was covered completely and held my breath.

But nothing happened.

Not a spark.

Not a waver.

"Well?' Angus demanded.

"Wait," Liam said, "this is about the Campbells and MacDonalds right? About strife and hate between those two clans."

I gasped.

"Oh right! How could I have missed that!"

I unwound the Apple fast and went to hand the ribbon to the priestess when I realized she had disappeared.

"What am I missing?" Fraser demanded.

I opened my mouth to speak when Imogen beat me to it.

"We have to heal the breach by joinin' our hands with the ribbon. Then ya can use it on that thing."

'Yes, exactly. Your act of devotion not just to each other, but for your clans is the exact opposite of what the Apple is using to cause all of this."

Angus locked eyes with Imogen and I saw it then, the thing I'd almost found when Angus had jumped in front of her.

He's falling in love with her. That should make this even stronger.

"We don't have a priestess," Angus said.

"I'll do it," Liam said, stepping into place and taking the ribbon from me.

"Is this what ya want" Angus asked Imogen.

"Ya ask me now?"

"Aye."

She stopped, considering his words and I wanted to tell them to hurry it up as the sounds of fighting were now becoming unhinged. More than one Were was lying on the ground not moving and I worried that if we didn't do this fast, there'd be even more blood shed.

"Aye, Angus MacDonald, this is what I want."

They clasped hands and Liam began what I hoped was a very short version of the binding. As he wound the ribbon around their joined hands a pressure began to build, two forces pushing against one another.

The Apple.

And the Ribbon.

Hate and strife against love and devotion.

It pressed on my chest as I held the Apple, angry voices whispered in my head and I winced. The Apple was stronger than whatever spell was woven into my bustier if it was able to affect me like this.

"Daphne!" Fraser grabbed for me and I put my hand up.

"Don't touch me," I gasped as the pressure built. "Just…get it done!"

When the ribbon had at last been completely bound to Angus and Imogen's hands it was so intricately wound that it would take too long to undo. My hands shook as I raised the Apple to the ribbon. The artifact had become impossibly heavy and I began to sweat from the effort. The moment I touched it to the heirloom, another pulsing wave sprang out from it, knocking me off my feet and onto the hard ground.

My ears rang and zings of power rushed over my skin like electricity. Distantly, I realized that it was from the spell breaking on the bustier and I wondered just how much Sprite was going to kill me when I got back to London.

Fraser picked me up and cradled me against him.

"My love, are ya alright?'

"Yes…did it…?"

"Aye," Fraser's eyes roamed over me, looking for injuries. "The fightin' stopped."

"I have to get to the Apple."

He sprang to his family, who were still at the trellis. Liam had just managed to unwind Angus and Imogen's hands and the Apple lay on the ground, everyone giving it a wide berth.

"Put me down," I pushed on Fraser's chest.

He growled, his protective side kicking up to eleven.

"Fraser, I have to get that contained and then you can carry me around all day if you want."

I thought he was going to fight me but instead he huffed out a sigh and set me on my feet. My legs wobbled and I swear if I hadn't been so focused on finishing this, I would have bent over and vomited right then and there. But I managed to walk to the Apple and held my hand out for the ribbon. This time, when I wound it around the golden surface, the artifact gave a final glimmer and became a dull yellow color.

"Oh thank god," I sighed, and slipped it into an empty artifact bag.

I knelt on the grass, trying to catch my breath and still my heart, which was doing its best to beat its way out of my chest.

"No! No!" a voice screeched.

Ruben ran toward us, spittle flying from his mouth, his eyes glowing a harsh yellow that reminded me of the apple a little. The power of the artifact over him had been broken, but the fury, the hurt and selfishness that had let the Apple attach itself to him remained.

Lowell and Liam both bared their teeth, their claws extending to an alarming length.

"I'll rip ya apart ya traitor!" Lowell howled.

"Stop," Imogen ordered and turned to her new mate. "I ask, as a matin' gift to me, that ya spare him. He should face justice from both clans."

Angus, who had pulled Imogen tight against him when Ruben had shown up, nodded.

"So be it. Lock him up in the cell and use the spelled manacles."

Lowell and another Were I didn't recognize managed to subdue Ruben, who howled and foamed at the mouth as he was dragged away.

"You have a cell?" I asked Fraser.

"Oh aye, we can't have mundanes lockin' us up. That would be a disaster," he sniffed at my hair, tail swinging low and somehow I knew that meant he was worried. "Are ya alright?"

"I think so. The way it reacted was very unexpected."

"Ya should sit down, rest."

"No, I have to call this in and get the artifact in one of the containment boxes. The agents should be here sometime soon but I still need to tell the Director that we were successful."

Fraser frowned at me, obviously unhappy that I wasn't doing as he wanted.

I smiled up at him and pulled him down so I could plant a little kiss on his snout.

"I'll be back in a few minutes, I promise."

"And in the mean time brother," Angus said, glaring at me, "ya can tell me why ya thought it would be alright to lie to me about yer mate, if that's really what she is."

Fraser bared his teeth at his older brother and snarled at him.

"Play nice," I whispered.

"Not a chance if he's goin' to make me give ya up."

Those words sent warmth blooming in my chest and I gave him a swift hug before making my way to the house. The Werewolves I passed were talking about what happened, about Ruben and the Golden Apple and what it meant. More than a few stared at me, and the looks weren't all that friendly. I realized then that clan MacDonald wasn't the only one to have faced harsh treatment at Francesca's hands. I hoped that what I'd done here today would show them that the new Secret Archive could be trusted.

The house was empty when I got to it, everyone outside and likely already starting in on the cases of whiskey that had been delivered yesterday. I hurried through the entry way and toward the stair case when rough hand seized me from behind, clamping a hand over my mouth. I struggled against the arms that held me in place but it was no use.

A familiar laugh reached my ears and my stomach plumetted to my toes.

The director had said that we had a mole, I just never thought my uncle would be that stupid.

"I did warn you Daft-ne dear, did I not?" my uncle said, flanked by a man in a balaclava and black tactical gear. "A new order is coming, and you will not be needed. But I do thank you for doing all the hard work for me, once again."

He plucked the bag from my hands and I struggled to get free. I had the gloves in my purse but my hands were pinned. If I could just get a little bit of room to move…

I bit the fingers over my mouth, hard enough to draw blood. The man holding me screamed in pain and I was able to move my arm just enough to dig into my purse and grab one glove. Hoping it would work just by holding it, I swung up at his face. The satisfying crunch of his nose made me smile and I slipped the glove the rest of the way onto my hand.

"You are such a bother!" Uncle George screamed, and leveled a gun at me.

I didn't have time to react when he fired. The bullet hit me center mast and the impact forced all the air from my chest but it didn't make it through the bustier. I coughed and gasped, desperate to draw in some air and immensely grateful that the bullet proof part of the bustier hadn't been attached to spell work. When I looked up, uncle George was staring at me in shock.

"How…? It doesn't matter. The Archive is finished."

"You're a traitor," I hissed at him as I got to my feet and slid the other glove onto my hand.

"Maybe, but I'm not like you."

"Sane?"

"Gullible. If that Werewolf doesn't spit you out, the Archive will. Angelica will be just as corruptible as Francesca, wait and see."

"Uncle? Shut up."

I drew back and punched him hard across the face. Blood flew from his mouth and my uncle staggered back before falling to the floor. I was just about to pick up the artifact bag when someone else tackled me to the floor and pinned me down just before pressing a blade to my throat.

A trickle of warm blood seeped from where the blade had broken the skin. Out of the corner of my eye, I glimpsed dark green skin under his balaclava and razor sharp teeth.

Oh god, a goblin.

There wasn't a chance I'd be able to beat a Goblin. They were too strong even with my gloves and vicious when they had a bounty to collect.

"It's nothing personal," he rasped in my ear, "but you gotta go."

"Please don't," I begged, tears filling my eyes.

I'd never see Fraser again, never find out what it would be like to have children with him, to build a life together. And I wanted all of that, as complicated and strange as it might be. The wonderful would outweigh it all, and this man was just going to tear it away from me.

"Please!"

His grip on the blade tensed and I knew he was about to draw it across my throat when a blur of fur and rage tore him from my back. I snatched the bag with the Apple, which had fallen in front of me and rolled on my back in time to see Fraser rip through a goblin's chest with slashes so fast my eye couldn't track all of them. Blood flew from his claws like red leaves from a tree.

"How dare ya lay hands on her!" he roared.

The goblin's only response as Fraser tore his throat out was to gasp and gurgle. Spit flew from Fraser's mouth as he screamed, eyes wide and glowing with pure animal rage.

It was a horrifying, unbelievable display of power. It should have terrified me, should have had me running from the house. But it didn't. Because this was Fraser, my mate. He may have been a gruff, nearly seven foot tall Werewolf, but I knew that beneath all of that beat the heart of a sensitive male that just wanted to be seen and loved.

And I did, both see and love him.

His gruffness.

His brutality.

His gentleness.

His passion.

All of it and so much more.

So when what was left of the goblin's body slid in a wet puddle onto the floor, I didn't hesitate to walk toward him. He may be a beast, but he was *mine* and I didn't want another.

"Fraser," I put my hand on his arm.

The fur was matted with gore and blood but I ignored it. He needed to see that I didn't care. When he whipped around, splatters of blood shook off him and onto me. I ignored it, even though it made a little nauseous. Fraser was covered head to toe in more blood and bits of flesh, it was as if he'd taken a bath in it, which I supposed in a way, he had. His eyes were glassy, unfocused at first. But when he did finally see me, all of that protective fury drained from him and he gaped at me.

"No," he breathed, staring down at his hands, then at what was left of the goblin. "No…I…"

"It's alright. I'm alright."

"No, no, no…" he shook his head and backed away from me, refusing to look at me.

I stepped toward him when another pair of hands grabbed a hold of me.

"Ya need to let him be," Liam whispered in my ear.

"No, I need him to know it's alright!"

But Lowell was leading Fraser away from me while Liam held me fast. And that's when the rage set in. I was being kept from my mate, who the hell did they think they were?

"Let me go you son of a bitch!"

I snagged Liam's hand and squeezed. He gasped with pain.

"Agent Reynolds, stand down!" said Director Dearborne's voice from down the hall.

I didn't want to. It would be so easy to simply break Liam's wrist and go after Fraser, damn all the consequences. But then I heard Liams grunt of pain, saw the Director come toward me with her Stinger out, ready to use it on me if I didn't cease. Fighting in this way was pointless, and my logical brain knew it.

So I released Liam and I tore the gloves off, throwing them away from me. I gulped in air, my legs shaking and I fell to the wood floor.

"Fraser," I whispered, praying the room would stop spinning.

The smell of blood and bile, the adrenaline of the gloves, the fear that Fraser might never come back to me, it all combined into one oily mix. I somehow managed to run to a bathroom before I promptly threw up.

CHAPTER TWENTY-SEVEN

FRASER

It took an hour to clean me up, and I was grateful that the whole time, Lowell didn't say a word.

I was dazed as the soap and water were worked into my fur, my brain replaying the look on Daphne's face over and over again. Her wide green eyes, the blood splatter on her face from my fur, the way her soft lips gaped at the sight of me. She'd been shaking, and her hand had come away from my arm soaked in the sin of my actions.

How could I think that I could hide this from her? That I could hope to be anything but what I was?

A monster.

"Are ya going to talk to her?" Lowell asked after I'd dressed in a fresh kilt.

"Why? So she can cower in fear?"

He stared at me for a moment and then snorted.

"You can be the dumbest bloody bawbag, ya know that?"

"I don't need ya to give me a fucking pep talk."

"How about a slap on the head then? That lass *loves* ya. I can't fathom why, but she does. And yer just going to hide out in the back room of the house like a coward?"

I should've been angry at his words but all I felt was numb from loss.

"Tell me when she's gone and I'll come back out for the rest of the handfastin'," I said.

I knew as the brother of the clan leader that I couldn't just hide in here all day, no matter how much I wanted to. But I couldn't stand the thought of seeing the woman I loved run from me. Or worse, look at me with revulsion.

I closed my eyes and let the crushing weight of it all settle on my soul. Lowell looked like he wanted to say more but blessedly decided against it.

I'd woken this morning with so much joy because I believed Daphne and I stood a chance. But just because I could live up to any fantasies she may have about rutting a beast, didn't mean she bargained for the flesh-ripping side of it.

The stench of blood still hung in the air around me, and I longed to simply run away. But that would never do. I had to go back out there, make sure there wasn't any fall out with clan Campbell over this whole mess and give at least the appearance of solidarity with my brother. But only after she'd gone. I wouldn't put her through the fear of seeing me.

Unbidden, visceral memories flooded my senses. The soft perfection of her body, the sound of her moans when she was about to come. The smile that felt like it was just for me. I'd been whole in her arms for the first time in my life, and now my chest cracked at the thought of losing her. A whine curled up through my parted lips and I hurt all over. Nothing had really happened yet, she still wore my mark. But just thinking of losing my true mate was enough to debilitate me. What would actually happen when the mark was gone and I never saw her again?

The pain was probably all in my head, a product of my morose thoughts, and yet it made me curl in on myself as my muscles cramped.

Hours passed.

I heard the Archive agents leave.

The sun made its slow progress across the sky, and the party for the handfasting eventually began. And the entire time, no one came to my door.

Had Daphne left with her colleagues? Had she begged them to take her as far away as possible from me?

I didn't know and part of me didn't want to find out.

She accepted me last night, welcomed me even. But this…this is different.

That's what I told myself over and over again, but each time I believed it a little less. Was that the case? Was it possible that she could love me after seeing what I had become?

I winced at the hard knock on the door. Lowell had come back like I'd asked him, which meant she was gone. I would be needed outside; it was time to leave this room. But I couldn't make my legs work no matter how much I tried. So I stayed on the floor, my back to the door as it creaked open.

"So she's gone then?" I croaked.

"No," said a soft, beautiful voice.

I couldn't believe it. Had I become drunk and was hallucinating? Was I already so far gone that I was hearing things?

"I'm not going anywhere," she said again, closer this time.

I turned slowly and looked up into her tear streaked face. Were those tears of fear, or something else? Why was she this close to me after what I'd done?

I shied away and Daphne was having none of it. She knelt beside me, lightly brushing against my fur but not touching me completely. She wiped the streaks off her face and shook her head.

"Why did you run from me?" she asked. "I could've helped you get cleaned up. I could've been here for you."

I stared at her, unsure if I was hearing her right. Was she serious? Was this real? My mind spun on a blank space and I couldn't find any words to answer her with. I must've sat there like an eejit for longer than I thought because she sighed and turned her wet eyes up at me.

"Say something," she pleaded.

"How can ya stand me?"

The question was out before I could stop myself or think better of it. I didn't want the answer, and yet I needed to hear what she'd say. I trembled as the fear hit me but I couldn't look away from her. Now that she was before me, so close, I drank in the sight of her in case it was the last time I'd have it.

"What are you talking about?" she asked. "Stand you...are you serious? You saved my life! He was going to kill me."

"I tore him to shreds," the words were dragged out of my mouth and I cringed. "I was covered in...in blood. Ya saw me."

Her hands suddenly on either side of my face made me gasp and I let her bring me near.

"I saw my mate after he'd protected me from a murderer. I saw how far you're willing to go to protect me. I'm not afraid of you, Fraser. You've never made me feel unsafe. Quite the opposite really."

The words were everything that I never let myself hope for. They were forgiveness, absolution. I lapped them up and still couldn't quite quench my fear.

"This is who I am," I said, my heart in my throat. "I try to control it, and I succeed most of the time but...when the people I love are threatened, I become this monster. It happened when Liam was hurt. It happened with ...with ..."

"Silvia?"

I closed my eyes as shame swept through me.

"I'm not her," Daphne said, running her thumb across my cheek. "I know who you are, Fraser. I...I love who you are. Every piece of you."

"Ya love me? Even after that?" I whispered.

"Of course I do! Fraser, do you really think that would be enough to make me run? I meant what I said last night in the garden. I love you."

Everything snapped into focus at those words. The fog in my mind cleared and it was as if sunlight broke through the clouds.

"I love ya too. You're…Daphne, you're my true mate, the other half of my soul. I never want to be parted from ya, ever. I'll follow ya wherever ya go, I'll stand by yer side and be yer mate if you'll let me."

The words tumbled out, fast and rough. Even just last night the thought of speaking such things had unsettled me, mostly because I hadn't wanted to frighten her. But now, with her one small confession, I found myself unable to hold it all back. I needed to stay with her, and I would do anything for that.

Even make a fool of myself by spewing all of my feelings.

But instead of laughing or being frightened. Daphne sighed, a wide grin gracing her beautiful face.

"Yes, yes I want that. All of it!"

She launched herself at me and I caught her awkwardly. We went sprawling onto the floor, her body on top of mine, and I held her tight.

"My mate," she whispered as she planted little kisses on my snout.

"Damn right ya are."

I licked along her jaw and throat, down to the mark I'd left on her skin. The mark that was supposed to be a lie, a means to an end. But it was never that. Not from the first moment I laid eyes on this impossible female. This mark was one of the truest things I'd ever done.

"Mine," I breathed against her.

She moaned and arched against me, fingers pulling on the fur at my shoulder. I could smell how wet she was already and I growled low in my throat. I needed to feel her around me, to seal this promise between us in the most carnal way.

I reached under her dress and used one claw to rip her delicate panties down the middle, my knuckle grazing her cunny. Daphne's eyes widened and her lips parted. Without a word, she simply nodded in answer to my unspoken desire.

We shoved clothing out of the way, a desperate tangle of limbs and fabric, before I grabbed her around the waist and hauled her onto my lap. I was hard and waiting for her, shaking as I tried to hold onto some self-control.

But Daphne, my lusty mate, was having none of it.

She fisted me and brought my head to her wet heat, dragging me back and forth through her before notching me at her entrance. I panted as she worked herself slowly onto me. Our moans and growls rose thick on the air, and the smell of our bodies merging flooded my senses. Her hips rolled and sank onto me, deeper with each pass and I knew that this was what dying from bliss felt like. It wasn't only the tight perfection of her body wrapping around me; it was the way she offered herself up to me, the way she'd embraced all of me. This was what I was like to be truly loved.

When my knot slipped past the lips of her cunny, both of our heads rolled back with a loud groan, and I could no longer let her take the lead. I was locked into her but still I thrusted, desperate to see her fall apart even as my own release was mere moments away. As her cries became mewls of intense pleasure and her cunny milked me tight, lightning coursed through my body and I spent deep inside of her on a roar.

Daphne slumped against me, my cock pulsing with the dregs of my orgasm. I held her close, a weight lifting off me at the knowledge that this thing between us didn't have an expiration date. I could keep her, cherish her, protect her, be her partner in all the adventures she wanted out of life. A thrill shot through me and I smiled.

"I love ya," I breathed against her hair. "I love ya, Daphne."

Her fingers curled in my fur and she looked up at me, eyes shining and face glowing with joy. I resolved then and there to do everything I could to make sure she wore that expression as often as possible.

"I love you too, Fraser. *My* Werewolf."

I licked her lips and she giggled, then formed my lips to match hers and kissed her deep and long, just as she liked. When I was done plundering her mouth, Daphne curled against me with a sigh. I would've been content to remain here the rest of the day and night, but the sounds of the celebration were starting to pick up and I knew that we would have to leave soon.

"What now?" she asked.

"What do ya want? I'll give ya anything ya ask."

"Oh, that's a dangerous promise!"

I chuckled.

"Naw, it's not. Ask and it's yers, my mate."

She looked up at me, biting her bottom lip and flushed.

"I want a handfasting," she said at last.

"A handfastin'?"

It wasn't what I'd expected.

"Yes. I want the arch and flowers, and your family and I want to use the ribbon to bind us together for always. Is that alright?"

"When I said ya could have anythin', I meant it. Of course we should have a ceremony, it's only right. We did do things somewhat backwards though. The bite usually comes after the handfastin' these days."

She squealed and threw her arms around me.

"Thank you!"

"In the meantime, we should look for a new flat in London. Yers isn't exactly Werewolf sized."

She pulled back, eyes wide.

"But I thought…I mean, Scotland is so important to you."

I cupped her cheek with my hand, the fingers curling far onto the nape of her neck.

"Lass, Scotland is my home, but you are my heart. I can always come back home, but I will not live without my heart. And I won't ask ya to give up a career you love and all the things that could come out of it for ya. I just ask that ya let me be with ya, wherever ya may go."

"Fraser…" fresh tears slid down her cheeks and she shook her head. "You're…I don't…"

"Ya do and I am."

She laughed and wiped her cheeks.

"You don't even know what I was going to say."

"Aye, but I could guess."

A sharp knock on the door dragged us out of the conversation.

"Och, ya two! Enough with the fuckin', I can smell it all over the house!" Lowell shouted.

"Then go outside!" Daphne shouted back.

I let out a long, low laugh and gave her cheek a lick.

"Oh boy," Lowell said through the door, "I hope yer up for this one, Fraser. She's gonna be a handful."

I looked into her eyes and inhaled deep of her scent of moonlight and heather. Warmth spread through my chest, lightness in my limbs.

"Aye," I whispered, "she is, and I am."

CHAPTER TWENTY-EIGHT

DAPHNE-ONE MONTH LATER

The day was already sweltering, but I barely noticed it. This was the day I'd dreamed of for the past month, the day that Fraser had promised me in that room when I'd feared that I had lost him. This was a promise to one another in front of our friends and family.

"Ready?" Liam asked me with a grin.

"Yes," I breathed.

He offered me his arm and I slipped my hand onto it just before the doors opened that led out to the gardens of the MacDonald's country estate. It was four weeks ago that Fraser had told me I was his true mate. Four weeks since I'd completed my first artifact recovery mission. And in all that time, Fraser and I had hardly been separated.

He'd traveled with me to London to secure the Apple and debrief with Director Dearborne, who had been relieved to hear that I wasn't leaving the Archive. My department had received a shiny new security system, as well as a floor to ceiling magical sprucing that made it feel far less dingy. I'd even gotten an actual office that could accommodate my ever growing book collection.

Fraser and I had just put a down payment on a much larger flat in London that included a lift, and he'd already begun to work with a decorator to make it feel like home for both of us while I put in long hours at the Archive.

But perhaps most surprising of all was that Liam had decided to join the Archive as a field agent in training. The director assured him that, even with his limited mobility, he would be a valued member of the team. Angus wasn't happy to hear about it, of course, and he still didn't quite trust me, despite the fact that I'd saved his clan and was marrying his brother. But I would wear him down, I was sure of it.

Now, here I was, walking down a flower strewn path toward an enormous trellis overflowing with the most beautiful array of summer roses I'd ever seen. Gran's wedding crown had been outfitted with more fresh flowers and was perched on my head, the veil trailing behind me. I wore a white sundress with eyelet lace that skimmed the tops of my bare feet. Simple and perfect for the summer heat.

As I looked to either side, there was a small twinge of disappointment when I saw that my family had indeed refused to attend. They hadn't seemed all that shocked to discover supernaturals were real in this world. Their problem was that I was marrying one and refusing their generous offer of an internship with a university in the states.

It had hurt and angered me that they'd rejected Fraser, but the fact that his family had embraced me so fully took much of the sting out of the situation. And it was Gran's cheerful face, Lowell's eyebrow waggling grin and the faces of the MacDonald clan that I'd started to get to know that all made me feel as if I were home.

Liam handed me off to Fraser, who was beaming in his dress kilt. His eyes raked down my body and I knew what he was thinking from the purring sound he made as I stood closer to him. The heady scent of roses mixed with the lilacs in the garden, and birds sang in the trees, which provided some much needed shade.

The priestess began the ceremony, but I hardly listened. All I could see was Fraser. His dark fur was gleaming in the sunlight, tail swishing side to side in a lazy arc that I'd come to recognize as contentment. When Gran handed the hand fasting ribbon to the priestess, the look she gave me made tears burn my eyes.

As the priestess bound us, the power of the heirloom suffused our joined hands with warmth and I knew we were adding our love and devotion to the legacy it already carried.

"I pledge my love, my life and fealty to ya," Fraser vowed. "You are my mate, my heart and soul, and I'll have no other but you."

Tears flowed unashamed down my cheeks as I repeated the vows.

Fraser bent down and licked the tears from my cheeks, eliciting a chuckle from our assembled friends and family.

The priestess shook her head with a grin and handed Fraser the wine. He took it with his unbound hand and put the cup to my lips. After I'd drank, I did the same to him. Next came the bread, and finally, a dab of salt on our tongues.

"Bound by love and the vows you have exchanged," the priestess intoned, "I present you as mates from this day forward."

The crowd cheered as Fraser licked my lips first and then kissed me.

"Now to the Ace and Gryphon for the handfastin' feast!" announced Lowell.

I hadn't been thrilled at first when I heard that our celebration would be followed up with a party at the local supernatural pub. But then I learned how significant the place was to the community I would become a part of, and I couldn't say no.

Of course, everyone who was supernatural had to put their glamors up on the way to avoid discovery, but that was alright. Now that Fraser wasn't using his glamor as a way to hide from me, I didn't mind it as much. In fact, I quite liked some aspects of it.

We made quite the loud, raucous group as we walked down the sidewalks. Or rather, everyone but me walked. Fraser had scooped me up the moment our hands were unbound and he refused to put me down. I'd gotten used to his need to carry me and hold me on his lap these past weeks, so I didn't care that we got many an odd look as we lead the procession to the pub.

The moment we stepped through the door, we were met with cheers from those who had gone ahead of us. Although everyone had been without their glamours at the ceremony, I realized as I took in the packed pub, that I hadn't really noticed how many different supernaturals there were. As Fraser sat down on a chair with me on his lap, a very large Gargoyle sauntered up to us.

"James," Fraser said, extending his hand, "it was good of ya to come."

"I wouldn't have missed it," he said, also shaking my hand. "It's a pleasure to at last meet the female that swept my friend off his feet."

I flushed with pleasure and ran my fingers absently through Frasers fur, giving it a little tug just how he liked it.

"I've heard a lot about you," I said.

James quirked an eyebrow.

"Oh, really?"

"Most of it good. Although, please try to keep my mate out of trouble in the fight clubs in the future, if you don't mind."

"Well, I can promise that at least for the next few months. I'm headed to the states for a case."

"That's a far distance to send you," Fraser said, frowning. "Is everything alright?"

James' smile slipped.

"There's an artifact. A very dangerous one."

I sat forward.

"Do you know what it might be?"

He sighed as he slumped into a chair, the piece of furniture groaning under his weight.

"Jack the Ripper's knife set."

I drew in a sharp breath. That was one of the most elusive and dangerous artifacts in the history of the Archive. And considering how long we'd been around, that was saying something.

"Ya know it then?" Fraser asked me.

"Only by reputation. Half the agents that went looking for that artifact either never came back or wished they hadn't. No one knows the extent of its powers. Or even if Jack made the knives or the knives made Jack. I hope the director is sending you with a partner on this one."

James' eyebrow quirked up and he gave me a crooked grin.

"Don't think I can handle it, huh?"

The tone may have been playful but I saw what was underneath it. I had heard about James from Fraser and knew that he'd been with the Archive for a very long time. He was well aware of the dangers, and very good at masking his worry.

I put a hand on his arm and squeezed.

"From what Fraser tells me, I know you can. Just be careful."

For just a moment I saw the weariness in James' eyes, and a hint of fear. But then it was gone, replaced by a wider grin and a pat on my hand.

"This is far too somber a conversation for a wedding," James said, getting to his feet. "Let me be the first to get the two of you a drink."

As he walked up to the bar, Fraser shifted uneasily under me.

"I hope he comes back alright," he said. "James hasn't been back in the states for over a decade. Something to do with his last partner."

"He seems to know what he's doing. But I'll keep tabs on him if I can."

Fraser licked my lips and then kissed me deep, stealing all thoughts of work for several minutes.

Just as his lips popped off mine the opening strains of a very familiar song began to play. My eyes widened and I leaned back, taking in Fraser's wide grin.

"I thought you said this was the whipped man's national anthem," I teased.

"Och, lass, that's was before I understood it."

He stood and set me on my feet before extending a hand to me.

"Will ya dance with me, Mrs. MacDonald?"

A thrill shot through me at the name and I placed my hand in his furry one.

"I'd be happy to, Mr. MacDonald."

Thank you for reading! Don't forget to check out James' story, Bound: An MMF Gargoyle Monster Romance. Click here to read the steamy story or copy and past this into your browser: https://www.amazon.com/dp/B0B52QMYPQ And read on for a chance at some NSFW artwork.

One of the things I loved about writing this book was commissioning original art work of Daphne and Fraser. One piece though is too spicy for me to release on Instagram so I've decided to make it a special treat for anyone who signs up to my newsletter. If you'd like to see the NSFW art of Daphne and Fraser in the garden, sign up and join the Naughty Readers by clicking here. Or copying and pasting this into your browser: https://landing.mailerlite.com/webforms/landing/r2c5j0

Acknowledgments

This book has been a wild ride!

While writing it we had a series of unexpected…well, let's call them minor disasters. Our car needed several thousand dollars worth of unexpected repairs. There were tree roots in our sewer system. A simple replacement of a part of our porch turned into a major one due to rotted beams. All of this hit us within the span of a few weeks, with kids coming down sick on top of it all (thankfully it wasn't Covid). It was a scary, stressful few weeks in which it was exceptionally hard to write. We got through all of that, though some things are still up in the air. And I finished this book with a sense of keen accomplishment.

This list of 'thank yous' is going to look a bit different than other books, but it's no less true and all of these people have my undying gratitude.

Thank you to the contractor that was willing to take payments when a half day project turned into four full days. Thank you to the guy online who suggested rock salt to dissolve the roots in the sewer line (it works super well). Thank you to the mechanic that helped us find out that we were being price gouged at the Toyota dealership for repairs. Thank you to my kids who were so patient while mommy and daddy lost our minds and zoned out with us watching Doctor Who to escape the stress. Thank you to my best friends who listened to me cry. Thank you to my work husband and across the country bestie Jeremy Flagg who helped me find a solution for additional income. Thank you to that big beautiful Goddexx who watches over us and helped me get through the panic and come out the other side a bit braver.

And for helping whip this book into shape:

Thank you to my book doula Raechelle Downing. It's because of her that Fraser's Scottish accent is at all legible and not driving you absolutely nuts to decipher. Rae, you always encourage me, always tell me the truth, and always, every time, make me a better author. I don't want to do this without you.

Thank you to my cover designer Jeremy Flagg, who, in addition to helping me through some really tough stuff this time around, went above and beyond to design an amazing cover. I don't know what I did to deserve a friend like you, but I'm glad for whatever it was.

Thank you to the Coven, you ladies continuously challenge me, encourage me and teach me. I'm the luckiest author in the world to found a group like this one to be a part of.

Thank you feels too small of a thing to say to Dan, my husband, my partner, my best friend. I'm speechless with how much you believe in me, how much you want all of this for me. You never give up, even when it seems impossible, you believe for me and with me. I love you baby.

And lastly to you dear reader, thank you for reading. If this is the first of my books that you've read, thank you for taking a chance on me. If you're a fan already, thank you for continuing to enjoy my stories. I wouldn't be able to do this without all of you!

Also By

Craving more books by me? You can find all of my books on Amazon and read free with your Kindle Unlimited subscription! Check out my backlist below!

The Silver City Celestials
Devil's Temptation
Devil's Desire
Angel's Awakening
Angel's Agony

Monsters & Artifacts
Feral: A Werewolf Monster Romance
Bound: An MMF Gargoyle Romance
Abandon: An Orc Monster Romance

About Author

Trish Heinrich's dark and dirty romance is fueled by caffeine and panic. When not daydreaming about the latest book boyfriend she's creating, Trish is geeking out with her two kids about the latest superhero movie, cuddling with her husband or binge watching Lucifer...again. You can find her books on Amazon and Kindle Unlimited. Her next steamy romance offering will be a mix of Warehouse 13 and monster romance with Monsters & Artifacts, coming to Amazon and Kindle Unlimited Summer/Fall of 2022.

9 781733 188098